Thread for Pearls

A Story of Resilient Hope

———

Lauren Speeth

Thread for Pearls

Copyright © 2018 by Elfenworks Productions, LLC

ISBN 978-0-9997071-0-4

Printed in USA

Second Edition

Disclaimer

Thread for Pearls is a work of fiction. All names, characters, places, events and occurrences are fictitious. Any resemblance or likeness to actual persons, places, events, or occurrences is not intended and wholly coincidental.

Note to Readers from Publisher

In this digital age, word-of-mouth matters more than ever before, and this is especially true for small publishers, such as ourselves. If you enjoy this book, please consider giving it a rating on Amazon Goodreads, or wherever you share your love of books. Thank you!

Acknowledgement

Grateful thanks to my editors Lisa Crawford Watson and Marian Brown Sprague, to previous editors and helpers, and to graphic artist extraordinaire Mike Dalling for helping bring this book into the final shape we now present here to you. Thanks to all my readers over the many revisions, and for those who have provided so much moral support and so many great suggestions for how the story could sing out more clearly. I am forever grateful!

Introduction & Dedication

As we work to make sense of life, gathering experiences like pearls for a necklace, it becomes clear that the thread on which we choose to hang our pearls of experience is as essential as the pearls themselves. Through the ups and downs of Fiona Sprechelbach's story, set during the "benign neglect" parenting movement of the '60s, we see how the choice of a shiny thread I call "resilient hope" can make all the difference in a young girl's life. Thank you for joining me as we embark upon this journey with Fiona toward a deeper truth we all share. This book is dedicated to you, my readers, for I do believe there is a bit of Fiona in every one of us.

TABLE OF CONTENTS

1. START WITH A BANG!

What a strange and sudden stillness. Full stop in midtown Manhattan, one lovely fall day in 1963. Over the car radio, Skeeter Davis was still singing, asking why the sun kept shining, why the sea rushed to the shore. Wondering, "Don't they know it's the end of the world?"

It all happened so fast. Eighteen-month-old Fiona had shaken her special pearl rattle a little too playfully, and it had fallen at her mother's feet near the accelerator. Peggy had reached for it, looking down for a moment to see where it was. What happened next? Hard to tell. The next thing she knew…BAM!…her front bumper crumpled as it met the car in front of her. BANG!…the truck behind them had plowed into them. Hard. Between the jolts, Fiona had gone flying into the dashboard. And then came that eerie stillness.

Peggy snapped back into the moment and started scrambling at the floor for the pearls from the rattle. Maybe she could put it back together again. Fix things. But every time she grabbed at them, they'd roll away from her. One had been crushed into powder. This wasn't working.

Slowly, she began to hear the honking of the cars, from behind. "Move it, lady!"

Still shaking, Peggy put the car in gear, and it limped to the side of the road. She looked over at Fiona, strangely quiet where she lay in the seat, and noticed the purplish walnut emerging on her baby's head. "Wake up, honey." Peggy didn't yet know it, but when Fiona had flown into the dashboard, she'd fractured her tiny skull; one small fragment was lodged dangerously close to the part of her brain that controlled her coordination.

"What do I do? What do I do?" she whispered, her heart pounding and her own head beginning to hurt. "I've got to get out of here, got to get her home and to a phone. I need to call someone. What will I even say?" Completely undone, Peggy started to think back on what had just happened. Her mind raced. How would she explain what had happened? Yes, it was she who had looked down at the floor, who had reached for the wayward rattle, who had turned her attention from oncoming traffic—never seeing the truck heading her way. But it was Fiona who had thrown the rattle. And she was the one who got hurt. Desperately.

She blamed the accident on Fiona

Peggy lurched the car forward. She headed back home, faster than the law allowed. She pulled up to the front door, threw her purse over her shoulder, and flung open the car door. Dashing around the front of the car to get Fiona, she hardly noticed the smashed headlight and chrome bumper hanging on by a thread. She felt that she, too, was barely hanging on.

Peggy opened the passenger door, lifted Fiona into her arms, and ran toward the house, without closing the car door behind her. At the front door, she cradled the toddler in one arm and fished around in her purse for her keys. "Ah, c'mon!" They were still in the ignition.

She pounded on the door. Minnie, her housekeeper and baby-sitter, opened the door, dropped her mop, and reached for the child.

"Put her in the crib," Peggy called out, as she disappeared into the kitchen to dial Celia, her older, calmer sister, who had four kids of her own. Nine-year-old Karen, Peggy's other daughter, ran out of the TV room to see about the fuss. "Aww, poor baby! Can I hold her?" Minnie shook her head no, and settled her softly into her crib.

"Ce, you've got to come; something's happened," Peggy said.

"What? What's happened?"

"Fiona dropped her rattle, and it caused a car accident."

"What do you mean?"   *She blames Fiona again*

"We were in the car, and she dropped her rattle. Just come. Please."

"Oh, God, Peggy. I'll be right over."   *She is vague so no one places blame on her*

~oOo0O0o~

Celia was always ready to help, and this time her little sister needed her. Her own four kids would have to content themselves at a neighbor's house. She quickly made the arrangements and took off. Ten long minutes after Peggy's call for help, Celia's Buick Special pulled up to the curb. Celia got out of the car and ran inside.

Celia looked at Fiona, asleep in her crib, and gasped. She studied the purple plum on the side of her little head, the area of discoloration that had traveled to her eye, and Ce instinctively rested her hand on Fiona's torso, feeling fear for her beloved baby niece, and wanting to be sure she was breathing. She pushed past her sister into the kitchen, picked up the phone and called Dr. Rusoff, the family pediatrician.   *ce wants to help*

"He says to get her to Mt. Sinai for an X-ray, as fast as humanly possible," Celia said to her sister.

"We're not doing that," said Peggy. "It's just a bump on the head; she'll be fine."

"Are you kidding me? You have no idea how bad this might be! Your baby clearly slammed into something. Her whole face is turning bloodshot. She's in there, sleeping, with an eggplant on her head. You don't let anybody sleep with a head injury. We need to take her in, Peggy; we need an ambulance."

"We're not getting an ambulance. Imagine what the neighbors would think."

"You could lose her, Peggy. What would the neighbors think, then? Either we call an ambulance, or I'm taking you both to the hospital, myself. You decide. And make it fast."

Peggy looked up at her older sister, then over to her daughter, then back again. Finally, she gave in to her authority, something she'd always resisted doing. "Okay, we'll both take her. You drive."

Peggy has no maternal instincts

Celia got back behind the wheel, while her sister settled into the passenger seat with Fiona. Now very much awake and clearly uncomfortable, Fiona began to cry. Her mother rolled down her window and let Fiona stick out her head for a little fresh air and distraction.

"Peggy! What are you doing?" said Celia.

"I can't stand it when she cries," said Peggy. "She likes this."

"She has a head injury, for Pete's sake. Close the window and hold her."

"Just drive. We don't need another accident."

Celia tried to drive as gently as possible. But the streets were old and punctuated with potholes. With every turn or touch of the brakes, she winced, worried about Fiona. All she could do was drive steadily on.

~oO0O0Oo~

Celia had instructed Minnie to call Fiona's father, Wolf, who rushed to the hospital. Distraught by his limited understanding of the day's events, his pre-judgment of Fiona's mother, and in a rush to reach his child as quickly as possible, he drove like a madman. He was secretly hoping a policeman would notice him and escort him, with lights and sirens, parting the traffic like Moses. No such luck. Wolf swung into the hospital parking lot, parked illegally, and ran into the building, bringing along his own brand of chaos. A New York City hospital sees all kinds, and they weren't impressed with his yelling, pacing, or demands for information.

Wolf was shown the door before he ever saw his child.

~oO0O0Oo~

At that same moment, wide-eyed and wondering from the table on which she'd been laid, Fiona saw foreign faces, all peering down at her. Too frightened to move, she lay there as if frozen...the cold metal surface beneath her, the cold hands touching her, and the cold, harsh, blue light in her eyes. Where was Mother? Pop? Blankie?

"Hello, Fiona," said a strange man with a mask over his mouth. "You're okay. See this red balloon? Can you blow it up?" As he said these words, a mask was brought over her mouth, attached to what, indeed, looked like a red balloon. She tried to push away the mask, but the nurse held it firmly in place. The doctor and nurses all had smiling eyes, so she stopped struggling. On her first try, Fiona didn't make the red balloon move at all. On the second try, she breathed in instead of out. But it worked. Within moments, the lights went out.

The delicate neurosurgery lasted eight long hours, as the surgeon, Dr. Watkins, carefully lifted the fragment of bone from where it had lodged in Fiona's brain and, with practiced precision, set it back into its proper place. He ran a thin line of glue along the edges, and then lifted Fiona's skin over the site and began sewing the baby doll back together. If the operation was a success, the hospital would be this child's home for the next six weeks.

But a lifetime outside the hospital was what he was hoping for.

It was a miracle, thought Dr. Watkins, that she hadn't died at the scene of the accident. Or during the delays before she was brought to him. Such a little wisp of a thing. An older, larger child would have required a metal plate in her head, replacing the fractured bone shard. A less-experienced neurosurgeon would not have been able to pull off the operation at all. But an experienced one, such as himself, also understood that anything was possible. Anything could still happen.

For now, though, all they could do was wait.

Peggy is a bad
Mother

~oOoOoOoo~

Peggy came to the hospital often, but watching her sleeping child just made her anxious, so she usually made her visits brief. Despite the needs of her own four children, Ce was there every day, for hours at a time, wanting to make sure someone familiar was there when Fiona woke up.

When Fiona finally opened her big blue eyes a few days after her surgery, she looked around without moving her head. As it happened, Peggy was there, and so was Aunt Ce.

"Hi, Baby," said Peggy, as she regarded her child's face. She was, indeed, awake, but something had changed. The light in her eyes was different, a little darker, maybe.

Aunt Ce slipped her index finger into Fiona's hand. Slowly, her dimpled fingers curled around her aunt's finger, and held on. Ce breathed a sigh of relief. "Well, she still has fine-motor skills in her hand," she said. "Maybe she's going to be all right."

Turns out it was too soon to tell.

Before the car accident, Fiona had been toddling around quite well. But now, she wouldn't walk or crawl. Wouldn't or couldn't? Her family began to worry that the damage to her head might leave lasting limitations to her mind, her memory, her larger motor skills… Would she never walk again?

"I had a perfect baby," Peggy said to her sister. "A beautiful baby, so smart and special. It's hard enough, raising two kids who are basically okay. I can't handle a special-needs child, Ce. I just can't. I'm not a caregiver like you."

"Calm down, Peggy; you're getting ahead of yourself," said Ce. "Let's focus on Fiona and see what Dr. Watkins has to say."

Dr. Watkins agreed that Fiona needed more time to heal, and suggested that she might be upset or thrown off balance by the football-style helmet she had to wear, making her top-heavy on her little legs. Or maybe she was more head-strong than they realized, staging a bit of a sit-down protest because she didn't like the hospital, the helmet, or the way her head felt.

During Fiona's six-week stay at Mt. Sinai, Dr. Watkins adopted her as a pint-sized mascot, carrying her around the ward, pointing out pretty pictures, frothy fountains, and rainbow-colored birds flitting by in the garden. When, at long last, she started to walk again, her Pop was visiting.

"Thank God," he said, as more of a pronouncement than a prayer. After all, Pop didn't really believe in God. An atheist by tendency and training, he held firmly to his tenets, particularly that the expectation of miracles was mere "magical thinking." Everyone in his scientific circles, even his own psychiatrist father, agreed with him wholeheartedly. So, why this reflexive thanking of God? If his own father could hear him, he'd remind Pop that Sigmund Freud had said religion was "patently infantile" and "foreign to reality." Freud cast a long shadow across Fiona's family's path, blinding Pop from seeing what was so obvious to others. He hated all talk of miracles, because it made him feel uncomfortable, the way snakes and spiders did. If a miracle had been a snake, it could have slithered right up and bit him in the butt. And he never would have seen it coming.

~oO0O0Oo~

A few months earlier, Wolf Sprechelbach had experienced his own near-fatal accident. He'd been driving home from work early one evening, when a pickup truck plowed into him. He remembered little of the accident or who had caused it, except that the truck had come, seemingly out of nowhere, to hit him, head on. His car was totaled, and he was unconscious. He later found himself in the hospital with a whopper of a headache and blurred vision. His doctor explained he had sustained a monstrous blow to the head. That's all Wolf ever understood about the event. Nobody around Wolf was all that very surprised he'd been broadsided. And nobody was at all surprised when Peggy called it quits and moved out, their brief marriage having suffered its own irreparable injuries.

You never knew what was going to happen around Wolf because he didn't pay close attention to the routine. Everyday life didn't interest him very much. He kept his head firmly planted in the clouds, nearly all the time. He'd already broken his leg falling into an open manhole on a New York street, having been too busy thinking to look where he was going, and had been hit by a car when crossing a busy street, having forgotten to look both ways. Wolf knew he was perpetuating the mad scientist stereotype, but there was little he could do but embrace it. Peggy, however, had had quite enough.

The month and a half that Fiona spent out of the custody of either parent gave them a much-needed cooling off period. As expected, the court had awarded Peggy full custody. Wolf couldn't bear this thought. He decided to pay Peggy a visit in the brownstone she had found to rent for herself and her daughters. It would be good to see how Fiona was doing. He would sit down with Peggy, maybe over a cup of Earl Grey, just like old times. He would reason with her and explain why he should be the one to raise Fiona, the child they had named for her fiery red hair and light blue eyes. The daughter he'd keep safer than Peggy had.

But when Peggy opened the door to the home she was making without him, when Wolf saw Fiona sleeping peacefully in her play-pen and heard Karen, singing, as she played in her room, he began to fill with a strange sort of sadness his heart couldn't stand. So, he wrapped it in the peculiar comfort of rage. As he surveyed the scene, he found himself losing control, threatening Peggy in ways that even she found uncustomary and frightening.

As Peggy reached for the phone to call for help, Wolf grabbed it and threw it against the wall. Possibly before even he understood what he was doing, he yanked the telephone cord from the jack, wrapped it around Peggy's neck, and began choking her. Hearing the commotion, Karen walked in on the scene, wide-eyed and won-dering. Her mother whispered, "Get…the…baby…" Karen grabbed Fiona and ran out of the room to hide.

Both Karen and Peggy were sure he was going to kill them all. And Karen, shaking uncontrollably in the back of her closet where she hid, desperately trying to hush Fiona, felt certain her mother was already dead. But the sight of Karen's frightened eyes as she fled with Fiona, seemed to bring Wolf to his senses.

He let go of the cord, which caused Peggy to fall to the floor. As she scuttled away from him, he looked at the raw ring around her neck, turning a deep purplish red. He looked down at his hands, at the red lines, marking what he had done. A silent gasping sob attempted to escape his mouth. With thoughts of apology, he ran out of the house. Mortified, he was sure he had apologized. He hadn't said a word.

Peggy huddled against the wall, still trying to catch her breath. She wanted to cry, to release all the trauma she carried inside, but the tears wouldn't come. Her life with Wolf ran through her mind like a slideshow, until Fiona's crying snapped her back into awareness. She needed to see to her kids. She wasn't sure she had it in her.

Peggy eased herself off the floor and up the wall until she could stand securely on her own. She buttoned her blouse up around her bruised neck, ran a hand through her hair, and walked down the hall to collect her children and head over to her parents' home.

Peggy considered calling the police to report Wolf's attack, but she imagined the call would only bring on more trouble for herself. The last thing she wanted to hear was, "What did you do to deserve this?" Fortunately, her parents hadn't gone there.

~oOOoOOo~

None of Wolf's efforts at apology were enough, and Peggy felt they never would be. She wasn't sure she would ever be able to forgive him. She wasn't sure she even wanted to try. Maybe it's true what they say, she thought, that harboring unforgiveness is like drinking poison and expecting someone else to die. Then again, she wondered whether a dose of "healthy enmity" could keep her out of harm's way. That man was out of control.

Wolf kept saying he couldn't imagine what came over him; it must have been the concussion. Peggy wasn't so easily reassured. All his adult life, he'd never reached this level of violence, had never lost control quite like this, he argued. Peggy, though, thought otherwise. She had seen him lose his cool long before he hit his head. Whatever it was that threw Wolf into such a violent rage, Peggy didn't want to see it come over him or experience such terror again, or subject her children to it. Whatever trauma it had engraved on her children, she, too, was still badly shaken and had no intention of ever talking to him, either in person or on the phone, again.

Concerned first and foremost for Karen and Fiona, the grand-mothers got involved, talking for hours by phone, as they tried to figure out a way to move forward. Wolf was adamant about wanting custody of Fiona. Peggy couldn't see herself handing a child over to such a violent and volatile man, despite his status as her father. While the courts would likely side with Peggy in any custody battle, her grandmothers weren't sure it was in Fiona's best interest to live with a single woman who had a career as a writer, another child, and who was, in their eyes at least, more suited to the board room than the nursery.

But there was another option. Wolf's first wife, Hanna, was still in love with him. They imagined she'd take him back, even after the way he'd broken her heart when he'd left her for Peggy. If she did, would she agree to raise Peggy's daughter, as well? If so, she might be the key that could unlock a workable future for them all.

Wolf was enthusiastic about the plan, and Hanna, who'd wanted a family, was delighted. Peggy had her misgivings, but because Hanna was involved, she set them aside and agreed to the arrangement. Wolf's dearest wish was granted. Wolf needed her cooperation, because she'd retain legal custody as far as the courts were concerned. Mothers generally did. Still, if he had Fiona in his care, and Peggy agreed, what did it matter what the document said?

Peggy decided never to share any of the story with Fiona. She had begun to study Buddhism, and the concept of "right speech" made sense to her. If I can't say anything positive, she thought, I won't say anything at all. Unless Fiona asks. If asked, she would not lie. But Fiona was unaware there was anything to ask about. Peggy fretted that, in a few years, Fiona would probably forget she'd ever lived with her mother, or that she even loved her mother at all. She hoped she was wrong.

~o0O0O0o~

Wolf was delighted by the turn his life had taken, albeit a bit dazed, and thrilled to have Hanna back. He loved being a family man once again, and he had big plans for an even bigger family. They'd have eight children. Why not? He had loved Hanna, so quietly intelligent, since he'd met her as an undergrad. He loved her even more now—this woman who looked more like a girl than a grown-up—with her long, wavy black hair and slight frame. She was raising another woman's daughter, being a real "Mum" to her. Soon, she was pregnant with their first child together: a daughter they named Holly. Another girl quickly followed, whom they called Violet. To do all this, she'd turned her back on her work—work for which she'd spent a lifetime in training—and was now walking a sort of balance beam of scholar and servant.

Whenever he thought back to the route he'd taken to get back to her, to his threatening words and how close he'd come to killing Peggy with his own hands, he brushed it aside. Wolf wanted to be the kind of man who uplifted women, not someone who terrorized them. Yes, he had been filled with a murderous rage, but it wouldn't have gone further, he reassured himself. And surely, it was an aberrance caused by the concussion; he'd left the family legacy of violence behind, long ago. He was determined to deny any violent aspect of his nature; it didn't fit his self-image as a peace activist for social justice, and a forward-thinking feminist. He married only brilliant, headstrong women, so there were bound to be arguments, he told himself.

Now, he planned to raise Fiona to realize her true potential. He'd raise her, an any others that might come along, so differently from the way he'd been raised. All his life he'd been reminded that he was a genius, creating a pressure-cooker of expectations. He wouldn't place the same burdens on his children, or even talk to them about their intelligence. He'd simply cultivate their gifts. That was the plan. Sometimes, he feared he'd fail. Sometimes, he feared he wouldn't get the chance.

Below the calm surface of Wolf's smiling countenance, currents of fear still ran deep. Fears of nuclear war and the bedlam that might follow. Fear of disease. Of death. Below those, a deeper dread, of being searched and found wanting. What if his best scientific years were behind him, and he'd never patent an invention, or win a Nobel Prize to appease his own demanding parents? What if Peggy came to her senses, decided he was unfit, realized she had the power to demand Fiona back, and dared to exercise it? Sometimes, he felt himself drowning. He'd managed his asthma since childhood, but when caught up in the undertow of his fears, he could hardly breathe. His thoughts, held at bay by all the fascinating projects that occupied his working hours, stalked him by night, damning his dreams into nightmares, and ransoming any hope of a sound sleep.

Sleep did not come any easier when, with the passage of time and a dawning practicality, Peggy slowly began to engage in conversation with Wolf again—only by phone and only when necessary. Fueled by the fear that Fiona would be reclaimed, Wolf procrastinated the planning and refused to set the dates of delivery for Fiona's summer vacations and holidays with her mother. Fiona often had no idea she was going to see her mother and big sister until her stepmother or father had dropped her off and driven away. The visits—so unplanned and disruptive—strained everyone involved.

Wolf never considered how hard it already was for Peggy, making her way as a career woman and single mom, or the extra risks that the chaotic last-minute visits presented. Bosses are understanding until they aren't, Peggy knew, and doors once closed are hard to reopen. Peggy was reluctant to take the time off from her job as a book editor or her sideline as a reporter, despite seemingly understanding bosses. Even so, she often found herself having to make last-minute excuses for leaving early or bringing Fiona into work with her.

No matter how hard she tried to be good, interesting, appealing, smart, Fiona felt her visits with her mother were too short. Always too soon, she found herself being sent back to Mum and Pop. Because she didn't understand why Mother always sent her back, she decided it must be her own fault. That made sense. After all, wasn't she the reason for all those heated telephone calls? Her name surely peppered her parents' conversations, like a swear word.

Although young Fiona wasn't misunderstanding that most of their arguments were centered around her, Wolf and Peggy found all sorts of other reasons for bickering, as well. Their arguments became a tradition: the only way they knew how to communicate. Lately, the Vietnam War was the topic of choice for their own little war. Peggy had three brothers in the service. Joe was in Vietnam in an elite group of Marines special forces akin to Navy SEALS, Jim was in California, in the Air Force band, and Bob was a communications and navigations tech in Thailand, who focused on Electronic Countermeasures Inertial Navigation Techniques. Peggy had lost her dear nephew, Ted, in Vietnam. This shaped her perspective as a supporter. Wolf called Peggy a hawk, an apologist for the war, and Peggy called Wolf a peacenik with a security clearance, and made sure to point out that his working on the Cold War effort was both incongruous and absurd. And yet he begrudgingly allowed Fiona to vacation with Peggy and Karen in Colorado Springs, to visit Peggy's first ex-husband, Scott, an Air Force man.

Wolf had never much liked Scott. He didn't appreciate that he was a dashing man in uniform with a fancy car. Nor did he like that Scott had been recommended for a job teaching at the Air Force Academy by both a congressman and a senator. He wondered why he should be jealous of anything in Peggy's world anymore. But when Fiona returned home, gushing about Scott-the-pilot, and Scott's car, and all the beautiful Corvettes in the parking lot, Wolf fretted for days. "I'm not jealous about Scott," Wolf lied to himself. I just don't like the whole war machine.

Wolf was keen to get a fresh start and put some distance between himself and Peggy, so he found a good research and teaching job in in Providence, Rhode Island, where he did his best to create happy memories for his growing family. He took his family to the drive-in theater, and tobogganing, skating, and horseback riding. Any good memories of his own youth were hazy at best. He mostly remembered the hard times and his father's fierce temper. Most vivid were the recollections of the nights his mother had sent him, accompanied by his brothers, to retrieve their father from the pub. The boys would sing the song "Come Home Father," just as their mother had taught them, hoping it would soften his reaction to being called away. It had the opposite effect, causing Wolf's father to storm back home, eager to berate their mother for embarrassing him. "Who do you think you are, the Virgin Mary?" he'd thunder at his wife, as he crashed through the door, drunk and angry. Generally, she said nothing, quietly receiving her sons and helping them remove their coats. Wolf would scuttle to the dining room, away from the fray, often finding his younger brothers huddled under the table. While their parents were at it, he'd soothe his siblings by mapping their escape route for that beautiful "someday" when they'd all run away together. But someday never came. Instead, they just grew up, and drifted apart.

It was the bad parts of his childhood that seemed to come rushing back when Wolf's mind wandered back in time to try to retrieve some model of how to parent his daughters. The parts he wanted to remember—all the music and success at school, and the fun times the boys had, watching their uncle work backstage at a local station during the dawn of the television era—all this seemed to fade into a buried backstory in the graveyard of his spirit.

And, yet, Wolf dutifully brought his own girls to visit his family in Philadelphia at the holidays. Having roots, no matter how twisted, was somehow a good thing for children, who loved his mother, their Gram, dearly. Now that his father had passed on, these visits were a little easier. Gone were the awkward silences and argumentative conversations. Still, the ghost of his father remained, forever inhabiting the small, airless rooms of his childhood memories.

Wolf and Fiona began enjoying different conversations than those he remembered, growing up, and he looked forward to the day when his younger daughters, Holly and Violet, would be able to join in. There was no dredging through the muck of feelings. This was about ideas, not family dynamics. Wolf preferred the realm of the mind. All his daughters had fine young minds, and he intended to develop them, in every spare moment after work and on weekends. The rest was left to Hanna, who embraced her job as a stay-at-home mom.

~o0O0O0o~

Growing up with half-sisters is a math problem Fiona was tempted to solve. Longing to have or be a whole sister to someone, she told herself that three half-sisters equaled one whole plus one half-sister. Or, maybe, since she lived with only two of them, two halves made a whole. It certainly would have been easier to abandon the math and simply see them as sisters. But Fiona had such an analytical mind, and she couldn't shake the sense that things didn't entirely add up right. Mostly, she just wished she were part of something whole.

For a very short while, she had been a part of something whole, even if she had been too young to understand it. Even then, though, Mother already had a daughter from an earlier fractured marriage. Pop now had two more, a multiplication problem that created division.

Sensing Fiona's confusion, Hanna drew Fiona a chart, to help her understand her world. She drew a circle with Fiona's name, and circles for her mother, stepmother, and father. Then, Hanna added two more circles, to show her own children, Holly and Violet. She added in a dotted line between Fiona's mother and a fellow named Scott, and another circle for Fiona's older sister, Karen. Fiona said, "Wait, you forgot someone!" and added Heart, the dog. Heart was Pop's big German Shepherd, whom Fiona had known all her life, and he was really easy for her to understand. Heart mattered a lot, to Fiona.

The chart made one thing clear: her family was complicated. For Fiona—Pop's headstrong gift from a marriage that lasted a minute—that was enough information.

~oOOoOOo~

Fiona loved having baby sisters to care for, though she left the hard parts (diapers, mostly) to Mum, and focused on the fun. She loved helping—after all, she was so much older (at least two whole years!)—and Mum could surely use the help. Especially with Heart, Pop's German Shepherd, whom Fiona had learned to love as much as her little sisters.

Fiona's favorite jobs were feeding Heart and brushing him. She also tried to teach him manners and tricks, like learning how to shake. So, when Heart began terrorizing Fiona's little sister Holly, who was just learning to walk, Fiona scolded him. "No, Heart!" It did no good. Heart seemed to think it was great fun to knock Holly down like a bowling pin each time she got up. "Mummmmmm…" Fiona called out for help.

This can't continue, thought Mum, taking Heart by the collar and locking him in Pop's study. Unhappy in his new, restricted home, Heart began gnawing at the furniture and howling. Feeling sorry for Heart, and believing he was only trying to help Holly, Fiona snuck into the study to console the family dog. "Mum, look at the mess in here," Fiona called, "Hey look, there's poop!" Heart had knocked Pop's papers off the desk and trampled them beneath his less-than-clean paws. Mum shook her head, surveying the damage. Just then, the front door opened. Pop was home. Little Holly toddled over to Pop and flashed him the biggest smile he'd ever seen.

"Pop! Heart study! Heart study!" It was her first sentence, ever.

Pop caught Mum's eye, looked over to his study, and then down to Holly. Then he snatched her up in his arms and said, "Yes, he is, Holly. He sure as hell is." And he started to laugh. It was a resounding laugh, the kind that can wake the dead. "Ha haaaaaaaa!" Mum, grateful for his sense of humor, changed the subject, "Okay, everyone, let's go eat."

Nothing more was said over dinner, but Mum and Pop exchanged a look and a nod. After they were sure the kids were fast asleep, they'd discuss it. Something had to change. Heart wasn't being malicious; he was just playing or, as Fiona had said, helping. And he hadn't damaged Pop's study purposefully. Still, Mum laid down the law: Heart had to go; this was supposed to be a safe home. By the weekend, Heart had disappeared from the house. Fiona wasn't told what happened to him, and she didn't ask. But she most certainly didn't understand.

~o0O0O0o~

The house might not have had a dog anymore, but it still had animals. Whenever Holly and Violet with their stuffed animals, the house was alive with the beasts of the forest—and that included Fiona, the mouse. An enormous, four-year-old freckle-backed Sprechelbach mouse, to be exact. In Fiona's favorite game, she was a miniature red mouse, nestled safe and sound in the cupboards, munching on cereal, and ready to pounce. She especially loved playing this game while Pop ate his breakfast. So long as Wolf could keep from getting too deeply lost in his reading or his own thoughts, he'd be able to remember to act surprised when Fiona popped out of the cupboard and into his arms for a hug before work. Today, that was his plan. It was a sunny Sunday morning, and Wolf sat at the kitchen counter drinking his coffee, absentmindedly waiting for the inevitable "BOO!"

Yes, it was a Sunday, but Pop had a big project brewing. An earthshaking one, he hoped. As the thought crossed his mind, he laughed. Providence was not earthquake country, and yet the cupboards were shaking. Something much bigger than a mouse was rustling, and making a mess of things, from the sound of it. He had such a joyful place in his heart for his eldest daughter, Fiona.

Pop never seemed to tire of her countless questions. Just the other day, she'd asked, "Pop, why is the sky blue?"

"It isn't actually blue, Fiona; it just looks blue," he'd said. "The light coming from the sun is white. When it hits the atmosphere, like a prism it breaks apart, and the light scatters." He usually stopped, after a short but sophisticated response for her age, and waited for her next question, "Why, Pop?" accompanied by the search of her earnest blue eyes that seemed to be questioning his soul.

"We see the blue, Fiona, because blue has a shorter wavelength than other colors."

"Why, Pop?"

"Let me tell you about waves again. Remember when I was telling you about frequency?" He realized she wasn't understanding everything he said to her, but he knew she was absorbing enough in that quick little mind of hers, to make it worthwhile. He knew because she'd come back to the conversations, later, for more.

"Tell me again about my paper dolls, Pop." Pop had shifted to paper dolls after trying to make a point about dimensions with a dot, a circle and a sphere, and failing to be understood. He had invited Fiona to think how a flat paper doll character on a page might feel, trying to experience what it's like to be a nice, thick rag doll. It can't. The best we can do for her, he said, is explain thickness using math. Fiona might as well have been that paper doll, straining at the impossibility of grasping everything Pop wanted her to understand, willing but unable to pop off her page, become fully human, and to experience fully all he was talking about.

With his white shirt and pocket protector filled with pens, a dark suit, and a narrow black tie, Wolf certainly looked the part of the young intellectual. His short, black hair was groomed back with a gel. His thick, black glasses, framing a young, yet already seasoned eye, had been broken by a quick grab when Fiona was a baby, and were still being held together on one side by make-do masking tape and a rubber band. Little Fiona could see clearly without glasses, which had been a worry in the months following the car accident and her brain injury. But, her eyes were bright and curious, and full of sparkle, always inquiring into the reasons behind everything. Wolf talked quickly and walked fast, but Fiona was happy to run and skip beside him, as she tried to keep up with all he was saying and doing.

Sometimes, Wolf just had to laugh, thinking about how ridiculous it was to engage a young child in a conversation about Einstein's theories or the shadows of Plato's cave. On some level, it registered with Wolf that he was expecting too much of his young daughter, to hold up her end of these conversations. Sometimes he wished he could simply link his mind to hers so it could flow freely into hers. He could not. Still, she was showing progress.

Just last weekend, working on a project, he'd asked Fiona to bring him a Phillips-head screwdriver. She'd gone to the toolbox and had brought every screwdriver in the box. Knowing the word for screwdriver, she'd found a way to be successful in her venture to the toolbox. He loved that! Which was why, whenever the thought crossed his mind to dumb it down a little, he batted the thought away. He kept up the conversations in the conviction that it wasn't about the words, but the relationship. The point was to pass the torch. He was promoting a life of ongoing inquiry. His plan was to keep explaining for as long as she kept asking. For every one of her questions, "Why?" he would continue to give her the "Because."

This Sunday morning, as he waited for Fiona to pop like a Jack-in-the-box out of the cupboard, he didn't mind, at first, waiting for the game to play out. But Wolf wasn't a patient man, and he was now running later than he'd hoped. He wanted to spend time with Fiona, but he also had a lot of important work to do. Wolf was a specialist in deep-water sonar clutter, working on classified military problems—fully aware of how incongruous it was to be a peacenik with a security clearance. Hanna liked to call him her "clutter bug." He preferred to think he was using his musical, accomplished-pianist ear to invent new ways to defend the nation.

Wolf played with echoes for a living: specifically, counteracting the effect of echoes from objects that "cluttered the field of view." He was helping to enhance the sonar system performance at the height of the Cold War. The importance of that work meant a lot to him—he and his team had done well. While he waited for Fiona, with mounting anxiety about the prolonged delay, he let his mind wander to the computer program he'd recently created that he hoped would take his work one step further.

Now his mind snapped back to his growing impatience; he couldn't wait for Fiona any longer.

Wolf shuffled his papers into his briefcase, gulped down the last of his coffee, and set his cup in the sink. Fiona took that as her cue: "BOOOOOOO!" There it was, at long last. The signal he'd been waiting for. Time to act surprised and scared. Time to snag his little daughter and laugh, give her a tickle and a hug, and call her his snuggly-wuggly bug. Time to snap into "Pop" mode.

As Fiona jumped into his arms, Wolf decided on an impromptu Take-Your-Daughter-to-Work day. After all, he was just stopping in to check on his latest computer program. He had managed to wrangle precious time on the computer to run his program. If it ran into trouble, the computer would simply stop dead in its tracks.

Wolf needed this program to run its course, and this meant he was required to do some shepherding. He told Fiona he'd bring her along, if she wanted. She did. Skipping around the room, she asked him if he could carry her there in a grocery bag as he sometimes did, calling her his "sack of potatoes."

Fiona loved going with Pop to his work. She ran over to her very own little blackboard, which sat right beside Pop's. She stood admiring Pop's equations. She knew not to erase or change a thing. If she wanted to get creative, that was what her own blackboard was for. "Pop, what does your blackboard say?" Fiona asked. Pop tried to explain the numbers and symbols on his bigger board. When it proved futile, he gave up, saying, "That's okay, Fiona. Even my boss doesn't quite understand, sometimes. Why don't you tell me what you've got planned for your own blackboard?" That was Fiona's signal to take center stage. Today, she'd be working on how a cow could take a rocket ship to a moon and jump over it. Pop was beaming. "What a very important project, Fee. NASA would surely approve. Now, you might need some calculus for that." Fiona didn't know what calculus was, but she drew a rocket and some numbers, and did her best to draw a cow and some grass, and then, modeling the numbers and symbols from Pop, added a few "equations," after a fashion.

Wolf noticed that Fiona was running out of space on her blackboard, but he knew he needed another half hour or so. His next trick to keep her happy involved the secretary's typewriter. Fiona loved it. He scrolled some paper in and, after typing, "Fiona's Secret Paper" on top, he let her type up whatever she wanted. "I can't write Top Secret," he explained, "because I have only a Security clearance, not Top Secret. If we type Top Secret on your paper, I am not authorized to read it back to you." He raised one eyebrow very high, and winked.

With that, Fiona laughed, and started typing. She couldn't wait for him to read it back to her: "324jerdf;lfkjs s;o34958uer;flgkmd e;lrkjf; oeirjd." A few minutes later, Fiona appeared with her paper, filled with letters. Pop was nearly done with what he needed to do, but not quite. Wolf turned to Fiona, who was excited for him to read it back as well as he could.

"So, Fiona, does this say 'three, two, four jerd fliff keejees, so 34, 95, eight-hour flag command'?" he asked. She nodded. He kept going until they both broke out laughing. He gave her a tickle and a hug, saying, "My little secret coder. I'm almost done here, Fee, just a few more minutes." Slipping a second sheet of paper into the typewriter, he said, "Why don't you type me another one of your secret coded documents?" And so, she did.

~oO0O0Oo~

Wolf was ready to head back to the house. In his haste to lock up and get back home, he entered the alarm code too quickly, mistyped the numbers, and tripped the alarm. While he and Fiona were waiting for his boss, who had to make an obligatory site check following the alarm breach, Wolf took her across the way to a small shop and bought her a YooHoo, her favorite chocolate-flavored drink. He liked to think it might reinforce the idea that science tasted sweet. Science still tastes sweet, he thought, even when the scientist gets the codes wrong.

As Wolf watched his child happily slurping down her drink, he felt he could already see Fiona's future. Yes, she'd grow into a fine young scientist. His intellectual heir. She'd been born on April 21, 1962, the opening day of the great World Fair in Seattle, the Century 21 Exposition forecasting the dawning of the new millennium. Of course, she'd be a scientist. How could she be anything else? Wolf didn't quite realize the weight he was setting on such little shoulders with these great expectations of his. He didn't realize it because the same weight had been set on his own shoulders as a very young child. He thought back to how Gramps had wanted Wolf to follow in his own footsteps, as a pianist, quashing his hopes for guitar. Once Gramps had made a decision, there could be no arguing. He'd been raised in an old-school home, ruled with an iron hand. Wolf quietly participated in his piano lessons, and eventually grew to love the instrument, or so he told himself. He used his musical talents to help pay for his tuition when he entered M.I.T. and, later, at Princeton.

Wolf could still hear his father's voice chiding him, telling him he hadn't achieved enough. Would nothing satisfy him? Going to college at 13 as a Ford Scholar hadn't. Perhaps only the Nobel Peace Prize would be enough. To win one, though, the judges need to be aware of the work he was doing. That's difficult when his work was classified. So, for now, all his angst for earth-shattering world achievement, all his steam, fell on his eldest daughter, Fiona. They say parents are harder on their firstborn, and Wolf was no exception.

~o0O0O0o~

The following Sunday was overcast, and the weight of the air threatened a thunderstorm by late afternoon. Still, Hanna was in such a good mood, she felt like cooking a homemade, hearty breakfast for her family. Better yet, she decided the children should help her make the meal. Hanna's parents had passed down the Jewish tradition of baking cookies in the shape of letters or a Torah scroll, dipped in honey. The message: learning is sweet. Words are like honey. She loved the cookies, she loved the baking sessions in the warmth, surrounded by elders, as they cooked and chatted, and sang in Yiddish. She had these memories in mind this morning, as she began pulling ingredients out of the cupboards. Instead of cookies, she was going to show her three girls how to cook delicious sweet matzo brei, a dish of Ashkenazi Jewish origin made from matzo fried with eggs.

Fiona was excited when Mum brought the little play table into the kitchen, so the girls could work together. Mum helped each take a piece of matzo, run it under water, and set it in a bowl on their table, where it would become soft and pliable while they busied themselves with the rest of the recipe.

"Who wants to crack an egg?" asked Mum.

"Not me!" Fiona said, in her most exuberant voice. Uncomfortable with the sensation of anything gooey, she didn't want to get her hands sticky with egg. And she knew she couldn't crack it as cleanly as Mum could. Fiona didn't even like finger paint. No, Fiona liked her life and herself clean and neat and utterly organized.

Holly was game to get her hands right into the goop. Mum held her hands over Holly's and helped her crack the egg into the matzo mix. Fiona felt a stab of regret that she hadn't put herself in the position to have Mum gather Fiona into her arms hold her hands. Maybe a little egg slime would have been worth it. Mum helped Violet add a little milk into the mixture, while Fiona stirred carefully, taking care not to splash anything onto her dress, or anyone else. While they were working together, Mum taught the girls their first Yiddish word: "umgeschlagene matzo" or "mixed-up matzo." Mum settled herself, cross-legged on the floor, where the children could watch as she gave the mix a good scramble. Then she stood up and set it aside.

While they waited for the matzo to set up, Mum let the girls try their hands at a "blended pie," picking out whatever ingredients they wanted from the kitchen, as an experiment. They chose olives, ketchup, maple syrup, salt, pepper, nutmeg, flour, yogurt, milk, peas, and carrots. Mum helped them whip it all together before she poured the concoction into a greased pie tin, and then popped it into the oven to bake. Then, she turned her attention back to the matzo brei, which she fried in a skillet, like scrambled eggs.

Mum served the girls their breakfast, steaming hot, with confectioner's sugar sprinkled on top. Then, she joined them at the kitchen table.

"Hmmm, yummy!" said the girls in a chorus.

Yes, thought Mum, learning is quite yummy.

After breakfast, the girls cleared their dishes to the sink, and helped their mum wash and dry them. A peek into the oven told them their blended pie was almost ready. A few minutes later, they each grabbed a spoon to take a little taste.

"Yuck! Why does it taste so terrible when everything we put in it was good?"

"Great question, Holly. What do you think?"

"Because not everything goes together?"

"Right you are." Exactly, Mum thought. "Okay," she said, "Learning is such a fun adventure. Even when what you make tastes weird, the learning itself is just delicious, isn't it?"

The girls all nodded in agreement. With tummies full and the experiment at an end, Mum gave the girls a hug and told them to go play in the living room while she cleaned up the rest of the considerable mess they had made during their cooking lessons. She placed crayons, pens and paper on the coffee table for the girls, and then went back into the kitchen to address the mess.

Fiona wrote a note to her grandmother and created a drawing to accompany it. Just as she had the week before. She was determined to send her grandmother a message every single week, forever.

Mum helped Fiona slip her messages into an envelope, and then addressed it to her mother-in-law before giving Fiona a stamp to lick and affix on the top right corner. Fiona skipped outside to the mailbox by the gate, and waited impatiently for the mailman, who accepted her letter and tucked it into his worn leather bag. "Thank you, Ma'am," he said, and tipped his hat. Fiona felt very special as she skipped back inside, wondering how long it would take before she heard from her Gram.

Fiona still had the first letter Gram had sent her, tucked in a shoebox she had decorated for keepsakes. She needed help deciphering Gram's beautiful cursive script, so sometimes, when Mum wasn't available, she just sat with it, hearing Gram's voice in her head, as she remembered what Mum had read. More important than what it said was the fact that it was from Gram. It *was* Gram. She was looking forward to getting Gram's next letter, which she planned to tuck carefully into her box to keep company with the first.

My dear Fiona,

How are you and your sisters doing? Thank you for that interesting picture of Tigs having three brains. I agree, Tigs was a very smart dog. Did Pop tell you that Tigs has gone to the Happy Hunting Ground? We miss him and know you do, too. But think of how happy he is, romping through the meadow, chasing after squirrels. He never did catch one in this life. The only one I ever knew that was smart enough to have three brains was your Pop. Remind him there is a great big brain on display at the Franklin Institute. Perhaps he can take you to see it. I hope to see you soon, darling Fiona.

I love you,

Gram

Fiona loved her pen-pal relationship with Gram. She had spent an entire hour writing a response to Gram's letter, trying to cheer her up. Maybe Tigs was with Heart. That made sense! Maybe she and Gram could go find the Happy Hunting Ground and bring back the dogs, and teach them not to run away like that, ever again. She traced Gram's elegant writing with her finger, hoping to teach herself to write that way. She didn't yet recognize every pattern, but she wanted to. Oh, how she wanted to be able to write and to read in cursive!

Reading was so important in Fiona's family, a lifestyle, really. And there were books upon books in bookshelves all over the house, just waiting to be read. The children were allowed, no, encouraged to explore any book they could reach on the shelves. One day, Fiona asked for a book from an upper shelf and was told that once she'd read all the books she could reach, Pop would consider it. She had no idea the others were out of reach for a reason, but she got to work, reading everything. When Fiona didn't understand something, she looked for an illustration. Pictures always helped. Especially the pictures in Andrew Lang's fairy books. They were just the best!

One afternoon, she found a book she hadn't noticed before, an old and heavy one with thin pages. Almost beyond reach, the book attracted her, so she stood on her tiptoes and pried it from the stack with one finger until she could pull it forward and grab it with her whole hand. Heavier than she had expected, the book almost knocked her down as it fell.

Fiona sat down on the floor next to the book, where it lay, and studied the dark cover of *Gray's Anatomy*. She hoisted the book into her lap and began to flip through the onion-skin pages, some of which she couldn't pry apart. Imagining it was stuck together because the book was so old, she skipped the stuck pages her father had glued together to spare her from seeing anything too gruesome or shocking for a child. Somehow, he had known she'd pry into this book.

The girls had squirreled away so many books in different corners of the house that Mum devised and in-home library card concept that granted them the privilege of borrowing a few books at a time and returning them before they could borrow more. She hoped it would work for record albums, as well, which were mysteriously disappearing from the cabinet downstairs. She loved that the children were so engaged with reading. She simply had to get a handle on the abundance of books being trafficked upstairs.

Eager to tell Pop about their unpalatable pie, Fiona set down the heavy book and rushed with her sisters to greet him when they heard him come through the front door that evening. Soon, they were gathered at the table. As they enjoyed their meatloaf and mashed potatoes with peas, each girl shared something she had learned from her day, before Mum and Pop chimed in with their lessons, carefully chosen to teach something of value to the children.

After dinner, Mum hustled the girls upstairs to brush their teeth and climb into their pajamas. The usual bedtime story wasn't on order tonight because Joel, a family friend and fellow musician, was coming over to play music. Fiona loved listening to the music from a favorite perch on the stairs, feeling safe and secure in her parents' harmony.

Downstairs, Pop made a half-hearted attempt at cleaning up the kitchen, confident Hanna would come along in time to set the place aright. She was, after all, the housewife. This was her domain, not his. The feminist in Wolf never once wondered how Hanna, a trained scientist with a PhD, felt about that.

Joel hadn't yet arrived. Mum was still busy in the kitchen, completing the cleaning Pop had begun, and setting up some snacks for their guest. Pop pulled out some records, so the girls could dance out some of their excess energy. He started with "Your Father's Mustache," a fast, jazzy tune by Woody Herman and Bill Harris, and the girls started jumping around the room. All together, they sang the chorus, "Aaah your fadda's mustache!" You know, thought Wolf, whose hair was growing progressively longer each year, I think I'll grow a mustache.

For the next song, Pop chose one of his Bossa Nova albums; the Brazilian rhythm was still new and quite popular. The girls had a favorite song, one that had been a big hit among Pop's friends since it came out in 1966: "Mas Que Nada," by Jorge Ben. When the song got to, "*Sai da minha frente, quero passar...quero é sambar*," they knew this meant, "Get out of my way, I'm coming through and I want to dance," so, they danced into each other, giggling.

Next came a tango album, Mum's favorite. The sultry music brought her in from the kitchen to wait for a dance with Pop while the girls took turns standing on his shoes to tango with their father. It may have been more tottering than tango, but the girls loved it. Then, Pop reached out and took Mum's hand, abandoning Fiona from his feet, so he could whoosh his wife across the floor, to the delight of his daughters.

The doorbell rang. Pop lifted the needle off the record, slipped the album into its sleeve, and went to the door to welcome Joel. Mum settled the girls onto the stairs so they could listen to the adults play music for a while, as promised, then took out her violin and began to rosin up her bow while Pop warmed up at the piano with a jaunty "Maple Leaf Rag."

The trio then began to play an old favorite: Corelli's Christmas Concerto. The music entranced the adults as much as the girls; soon they were forgotten, and, one by one, they fell asleep on the stairs.

~oOOOOo~

Good morning! Fiona's songbird heart was overflowing as she looked out the window and into a perfectly cloudless sky. "Sooooo fine.... Sunshine!" she sang joyfully along to her little portable record player as she reviewed her belongings in the suitcase Mum had helped her pack. She was going to visit Mother for the weekend. It was summer 1969, and her favorite Beatles tune made her delightfully happy. "Word! Love!"

Fiona shoved her suitcase aside and picked up the special shoebox she had decorated to house letters and other keepsakes. She lifted the sparkly lid and took out the letters Mother had written to her. Her letters, in her neat hand, seemed so loving, so interested, so inviting. Why did Fiona feel so formal around her mother, so removed from reach? She felt as if she needed to be on her best behavior. Maybe, she thought, if she could be very, very good, if she could be polite and helpful and available when Mother wanted her, and out of the way when she didn't, maybe, just maybe, Mother would be pleased with her, and ask her to stay. At least for a while. Fiona flipped over the record. This is the best record ever in the whole world, she thought. And this is going to be the best weekend ever, too. Just wait!

Mum was wonderful to Fiona—kind and affectionate, available and generous with her creativity, her wisdom, and her time. But she wasn't Fiona's mother, not really. She was a step removed, a stand-in. For all her parents' talk about the importance of being authentic, this was one place in her life that wasn't. Someday, Fiona knew, someday, her mother would call for her. And she would go wherever Mother was and stay. I hope I'm not all grown up by then, Fiona thought, unfolding the latest letter and holding it up to her nose. It smelled good. Just like Mother's perfume. It was signed with love, kisses and hugs, and had two underlines under the sentence asking Fiona to come visit again, soon. Fiona wanted that, too. She longed to snuggle into her mother's life, up close and personal, for always. After neatly folding Mother's letter back into its envelope, Fiona tucked it away in her keepsake box.

Though she didn't talk about it much, Fiona was giddy with excitement about spending time with Mother, particularly in a place as fabulous as Fire Island. This highly anticipated trip, one she'd made every summer that she could remember, was her escape from Providence's summer heat, into a beautiful seascape, with 30 miles of soft sand framed by a flat blue ocean on one side, and boardwalks and weathered beach fences on the other. But that wasn't what delighted her. This was a place where Fiona got to enjoy herself as her mother's daughter, and to experience life with her big sister. She'd be no trouble at all. She'd even be helpful, somehow, wouldn't she? Mum thought she was helpful, so surely Mother would see it, as well.

~oO0O0Oo~

Fiona thought her mother was dreamy, perhaps even more so because of her detachment. She idolized the inaccessible beauty of the woman who seemed to be perfectly brilliant at everything. Mother carried herself like the accomplished woman she was—lofty when teaching others, regal when riding horseback, graceful when dancing, lyrical when playing the Celtic harp, professional when at work, and humble when accepting accolades. Fiona had faced plenty of people asking just how proud she was of her mother. In awe was more accurate.

She was right to regard her mother so highly; Peggy was one of those people on whom God seemed to have smiled with a double portion. As a child, she'd been exceptionally intelligent—so smart, the school system where she grew up hadn't known what to do with her. They had simply bumped her to a higher grade as an assistant to the teacher. She'd aced college, even as a single mother, raising Karen. Peggy was singularly focused, and she had the goods to show for it.

Fiona imagined that Karen was equally gifted. Though Mother and Karen were often at odds, Fiona still wished she could be more like them, that her pool-blue eyes would deepen to match their burnt hazel, and her frantic copper-auburn locks would calm down, and darken into a beautiful chocolate cinnamon. She'd blend in deliciously, and they'd know she belonged.

~oO0O0Oo~

Mother, Karen, and Fiona arrived on Fire Island by ferry boat, staring out onto the sea as the sun bounced off the water. Fiona had forgotten her sunglasses, but Karen had offered to share hers. The sun didn't bother Karen's eyes, and she was happy to tan her whole face.

The trio departed the ferry and lifted their bags of food and other belongings into the wagons parked along the pier. No cars were allowed on the island during the summer, so everyone got around by biking or walking and pulling luggage, groceries, or each other by wagon. It was an idyllic place, where life slowed down, with time for sunbathing, beach-combing, and front-porch conversation. Here, on the island, was where Fiona learned more about her mother than anywhere else, as she relaxed among friends, and stories slipped out between sips of cool afternoon drinks.

"Hello, little sparklies," Fiona whispered to her familiar travel companions. Taking in the bright sunlight dancing on the waves, Fiona noticed the sky fill with a delightful shimmer—little sparkles, like beautiful golden firecrackers, seemed to fire off in rhythm with her heartbeat, keep time with her steps as she walked, and sparkle across the water as they drifted toward her very favorite island.

Fiona knew the sparkly specks that clouded her vision well, and they were almost comforting in their familiar regularity; they came with her when she went to visit Mother. This time was no exception.

Nobody had yet made the connection between the arrival of the sparklies and the aftermath that followed—the searing headache and nausea that caused her to curl up in a ball like a roly-poly bug. Wolf and Hanna simply thought she had a sensitive tummy, not understanding that the "sparklies" were a prodrome to a stress-induced migraine. Peggy wasn't so sure it was anything more than nerves. Last time Fiona got "sick," she tried to encourage Fiona to think differently. "Sweetie, why not just tell the yucky feelings to go away, so we can enjoy our time together?" Fiona would have loved to do that, if she only knew how.

Mother had invited travel companions, also. Her college friend Herb and her brother Jim were already at the beach house, having arrived earlier that morning. The men had cleaned and heated up the barbecue, and were just waiting for Peggy's arrival to hand her a beverage and throw some meat on the grill.

Along the way to the cottage, Fiona's Keds kept coming untied; Karen dutifully re-tied them, every time. "Only Karen," Fiona said. "Only Karen can tie my shoes." Only Karen offered. She loved mothering her little sister.

They made their way up the path to the beach-front house. Fiona's multiple trips to Fire Island meant she had some solid memories stored, which contributed to her anticipation and excitement. "We're here; we're finally here," she sang out, spinning in circles with her arms flung wide.

"Come along, Fiona," Mother said, without turning around. Karen looked at her little sister and winked. Fiona dutifully marched along behind her mother and older sister, to the back of the cottage, where Mother was quickly caught up in hugging Herb and her brother. Karen wondered, as she watched her mother engaged in her greetings, whether she and her little sister had just waved goodbye to the last bit of attention from Mother until they were back on the ferry, heading home. She hoped not. Thank goodness for Uncle Jim. He always had time for Karen and Fee.

Jim's well-timed leave from the Air Force was allowing him to spend this weekend with his family. Fiona didn't understand how rare this little stretch of time off was for him, or what it meant to Mother that he had chosen to spend it with his big sister. But here he was, at the grill, regaling everyone with stories of concerts he'd attended at the Fillmore on evenings off with his buddies from the Air Force band. He described his experiences in such enthusiastic detail—the steep stairs up to the box office, the free apples on the way in and the free posters on the way out. At only three bucks a concert, it was quite a bargain, and Jim had seen just about everybody who was anybody perform.

Karen just couldn't get over the Who's Who of musicians her uncle was so casually tossing out: Jefferson Airplane, Quicksilver Messenger Service, Miles Davis, Cannonball Adderley, Jimi Hendrix, Richie Havens, Cream, The Chambers Brothers, The Who, Traffic, The Young Rascals, Janis Joplin, Big Brother & The Holding Company, and more than Fiona could possibly recognize or remember.

"No way! You're making this stuff up," said Karen, clearly

impressed.

But he wasn't. All the concerts were put on by promoter Bill Graham, and he liked to mix it up, pairing very different bands each night. Jim had gotten hooked on the music after attending Graham's first concert featuring the Warlocks, who went on to become The Grateful Dead. It felt weird, he said, to be one of the few guys in the room with such short hair, but the cool thing was that no one cared. No one made him feel out of place, and no one questioned his role in what most felt was such a misguided war.

Herb, a Grand Master chess champion, was in on the conversation but also a little distracted. He seemed excited that another friend, an American chess legend, had promised to stop in later that night to play a quick game of chess. "As if," he had said, "a really good game of chess could ever be quick." He was thrilled when the doorbell finally rang.

Fiona liked her Uncle Jim's crew cut. She liked to run her hand across it, this way and that, feeling the soft or spikey nap. Uncle Jim let her do it for just a moment, then he started messing with her hair, to give her attention and a reason to stop. Since she really liked her own hair just so, that did the trick. She turned her attention to Herb and his guest. "You guys like chess, right? Me, too. One of you guys want to play a game of chess with me? Pop taught me the rules."

"We'd just beat you in a matter of minutes, kiddo. Either of us." Herb laughed while his friend just rolled his eyes and rolled himself a cigarette, "But I'll make you a deal. How about you go to bed now, and I play you a game tomorrow?"

Herb's not half bad, I suppose, thought Karen, observing Herb as he set up the chess board for his game. He's decent to my kid sister, even if he's not going to let her in on the game. She had a feeling he was sweet on Mother. Why else would he come for the weekend? She tried to imagine Herb as her stepfather. He'd certainly be a lot different than Wolf, whom she was glad was gone from the picture. Everyone was different from Wolf. But Karen was quite happy with the one real father she already had, even though he was miles away. And Fiona, who already had two moms, would surely agree that enough was enough. Karen made up her mind, right there and then, to keep an eye on him.

Fiona was watching Herb, too. She wasn't sure how he fit into the family picture. Fiona knew that her mother's side of the family didn't look at life the same way her father's side did. She also understood clearly that Mother and Pop could not get along. "Maybe it's because Mother's family is a bunch of pelicans." She had heard Pop say that, but she didn't understand what he meant. Even if she'd realized he was saying Republicans, Fiona wouldn't have been any more the wiser. Fiona also had heard about donkeys and elephants and how they had parties. As she climbed into bed instead of settling into a game of chess, she thought about people giving tea parties with only animals at the table, and decided grownups were just as silly as kids.

The next morning, as the sun sparkled upon the sea, and the light wind disturbed the grasses growing along the seashore, Fiona awoke to find Herb set up and ready to challenge her in the promised game of chess. Pop had taught her the basic chess moves, but nothing advanced, leaving her thinking she understood the game and could go up against the master. Herb had a choice between two approaches, and either one would teach Fiona a lesson. He could keep it simple, giving her a chance to play out the game and learn about strategy. Or, he could go in for a quick kill and be out on the water with a cooler of beer in no time.

Herb chose the latter. He started by removing all his chess pieces except for his king, queen and one pawn, to start. For a serious player going up against a beginner, this just cleared out the board for an easy kill. But it made an impression on Fiona. Thoroughly outmatched, her experience of chess against Herb was decidedly different than when she played with her father. Pop, also highly skilled at chess, had a different goal: to teach Fiona, not finish her. When he played with her, he would offer helpful suggestions or hints that would help her think, learn, progress. He might clear his throat or raise an eyebrow before a move Fiona was about to make, inviting her to reconsider. He also allowed Fiona to "take it back." Not Herb.

The game was over before it began. Karen, who was pretending to watch television, secretly had her eye on the game. She hated chess. The only thing she found more boring than playing chess was watching others play chess. She had once told Mother it was like watching paint dry upon a wall. But today, she was feeling less bored and more belligerent. She hated it when anyone took advantage of her little sister. She was a bright little thing but, still, it seemed to happen a lot. Karen wondered why and decided it was because Fiona was too curious for her own good. If she'd just stay out of adult conversations and play with her stuffed animals, she wouldn't get caught up in these adult dynamics.

But Herb wasn't all bad. He put the chess board aside, pulled out a deck of cards, and taught Fiona how to do a few fancy shuffles. Then, he got out a leather backgammon board and taught her how to play. He beat her at backgammon, too. Apparently, he wasn't going to learn anything that day. But Fiona sure was.

After a game or two, Fiona grew tired of losing. She was starting to wonder if she even liked Herb. He does buy me ice cream, she thought. And he cooks my steaks how I like them. But he's kind of boring. I like playing chess better with my Pop. With that, she set off to get her bathing suit and get ready for the beach.

After Fiona left the room, Karen swiveled in her chair toward Herb. "You know," she said, "it wouldn't hurt to let her win sometimes, maybe even show her how."

"Wouldn't hurt whom?" asked Herb. "The world is harsh. If she realizes it early, she'll learn how to navigate the realities of life. Trust me; losing at a game she hasn't mastered will help her see the world and herself more realistically. To be successful, she needs to be competitive, which means achieving mastery. It's eat or be eaten. You know that, Karen."

"What if you gave her a taste of winning to help her hunger for it?"

"I'm a realist," said Herb. "And that's not how it works."

"A realist? Get real," said Karen, over her shoulder, as she left the room.

Fiona reappeared with her bucket and beach towel, ready to go make sand castles. "Karen, why don't you take your sister down to the shore to look for seashells," suggested Mother, "or make a castle while we get lunch ready?" Karen knew a babysitting order when she heard one, and it wasn't what she had in mind.

"I just got to the good part in this book," answered Karen from the porch, knowing her mother appreciated reading. "I can see her from here." To Fiona, she said, "Stay up on the shore, away from the water, so I can see you"—more for her mother's benefit than Fiona's.

With a wave of her hand to show she'd heard her older sister, Fiona was already headed down the path to the beach. The fluffy clouds hung lazily in the sky, softening the otherwise harsh sunlight that was putting a sparkle on the sea and in Fiona's eyes. Familiar with her sparkly friends, Fiona wasn't worried by them, but they did make it hard to look at the water, coming in waves upon the shore and seeping into the sand.

"I'm as happy as a clam, I am," she sang in a sing-song voice, to nobody in particular. How do you tell a happy clam from a sad one, she thought. Do they smile? I'm going to find myself a happy clam, I am. Forgetting her sister's request that she stay safely upon the sand, Fiona waded into the water, almost to her knees. The next wave that came rolling into shore knocked her off balance, and she sat down, hard. The water was warm, though, and she scarcely noticed her discomfort as she swished her arms around in the froth. "I am the Phantom Tollbooth," she said, thinking of Norton Juster's fantasy youth novel she'd recently read in her room. Each wave must pay a toll before it can come ashore.

Karen, who'd heard her mother's call to lunch, set down her book and ambled down the path to fetch Fiona. When she pushed through the beach grass, she saw her sister's halo of red poking up out of the water; it looked more like a drowning child than a kid at play. Mother's going to kill me, she thought, as she broke into a run toward the shore.

"I've got you, Fiona," called Karen, as she hoisted her sister out of the water. She grabbed the beach towel and wrapped it around Fiona, then sank down into the sand and held her tight. "You really scared me, honey. Don't ever scare me like that, again."

Fiona had no idea what had scared her sister. She only knew she felt really safe and happy, in her warm embrace. Hoping to linger in her sister's love, she didn't say a word.

Later that day, Herb showed off his chops at the grill, cooking those steaks Fiona liked so much, while Mother steamed some potatoes for mashing. She knew Fiona liked her potatoes with a little well pressed into the middle of her helping for a pool of melted butter. Seated at the picnic table on the deck, with her napkin in her lap, Fiona felt certain she'd never tasted anything better. The potatoes were perfect, and steak was a special treat. Even though Karen had cut hers into pieces for her, Fiona tried to use her knife and fork very carefully.

Mother had recently been to England on a writing assignment, and had come back with some proper English ways, holding her fork with the tines facing down, and not switching her fork and knife between hands as she cut her steak and then pressed it against the back of her fork, with a little potato to hold it, en route to her mouth. This seemed upside down and backwards to Fiona, who had been taught to keep her fork upright to scoop food from her plate, and to switch her fork to her other hand as she used her knife, and then back to her dominant hand to eat. Mother also kept her wrists resting against the edge of the table at all times, whereas Gram had instructed Fiona to keep her left hand in her lap.

Fortunately, Fiona was a quick study, and she watched her mother carefully to adopt her new eating style. Still, she felt clumsy, and Herb noticed. "Hey, Fiona! Looks like you're trying to eat with a backhoe there," he said. "Since when did you become British? Maybe their bad taste in table manners matches their bad taste in food!"

Fiona was embarrassed by being caught trying to mimic her mother; she'd secretly hoped to adopt her mother's ways without fanfare, and didn't appreciate Herb calling her out. She ended up leaving more on the plate than she had put in her mouth. Fiona had been trying to act just right, so Mother would invite her to stay with her forever. Herb wasn't helping.

It wasn't that it would be easier to live with Mother—she was far stricter and far less forgiving than Pop and Mum, who purposefully practiced a limited-intervention approach to parenting, encouraging their children to learn and grow from their own experiences. Mother parented the old-fashioned way. Fiona figured she could step up, if only people like Herb would stop pointing out the ways she was getting it wrong.

~oO0O0Oo~

After dinner, Mother had made it a tradition on Fire Island to bring out Fiona's favorite orange cake by Sara Lee. Mother kept the confection, tucked into its foil container in the freezer, yet somehow the buttercream frosting never quite froze solid. It was cold enough to go down like ice cream, melting deliciously in her mouth, and was finished nicely by the soft orange cake. Fiona asked for a large piece, which she savored slowly, and then Mother offered her another. Fire Island was the only place she would ever be granted seconds—especially without asking.

Fiona reflected on another wonderful day. She was so happy, she wished it weren't coming to an end. After spending the rest of the evening on the deck with the adults, watching the lights from passing boats bounce off the water, and listening to the susurrate waves providing the rhythm to the grown-up conversations, Fiona excused herself even before Mother had to ask her, and went up to bed. Just before she closed her eyes, she said goodnight to the friendly sparklies that had kept her company all day. She hoped it would be lights out for them as well.

A few hours later, she woke up suddenly, unsure of where she was in the dark and unfamiliar room, but she knew, quite clearly, that something was very much the matter. She felt so sick to her stomach, she thought she might throw up. How could my favorite dinner in the world make my tummy so sick, she wondered. After a particularly violent wave washed over her, Fiona sat straight up and, with hardly enough time to lean over to the side of the bed a little, she threw up. "I don't feel so good," she said aloud.

Karen, sleeping in the next room, heard her. Like a loving mother, she came through the door before Fiona could wonder what to do, and walked her little sister to the bathroom, just in time for her to throw up, again. "You're not doing so well, are you, little kitten?" Karen whispered. No, she wasn't. Her stomach still ached, but her head hurt more. Fiona felt like curling up into a ball on the nice, cool bathroom floor.

"Are you all done, honey?" Karen wiped her mouth with a wet washcloth.

"I think so," Fiona whispered.

Karen peeled Fiona out of her pajamas, helped her brush her teeth, and drew a warm bath for her. Once Fiona was safely in the water, Karen went back into Fiona's room and stripped her sheets, using them to mop up the floor. "We can deal with that tomorrow," she murmured. Then she went into her own room and pulled out a soft sweatshirt to serve as her sister's nightgown. The sound of running water had awakened Mother, who was in the bathroom with Fiona, whom she'd wrapped in a plush terry towel, when Karen returned. "She can sleep the rest of the night with me," Mother said.

Fiona had been pleased to have her own room like a big girl, but she was now both delighted and a little nervous to sleep next to the warmth and security of her mother. She padded down the hall after Mother, climbed into that big, warm bed, and closed her eyes. She lay as still as she could, so as not to irritate Mother, knowing she'd already been a bother for being sick to her stomach. This wasn't going to get her any closer to a permanent invitation.

The light was too bright for Fiona to fall asleep, and her head still hurt something fierce, but she wasn't about to bring it up. Mother, keeping a watchful eye, decided on reading until Fiona fell asleep. She was researching the history of the Irish in Iceland, and it seemed, to Fiona, that she read for 500 hours. Finally, Mother gave up, closed her book, turned out the light, and began softly singing a lullaby to her child. "Froggy went a wooing and he did go, uh huh." Mother sang about the frog, his mouse bride, a wise old owl who presided over their wedding, and all the animals in attendance.

As Fiona bathed in her mother's beautiful, clear voice, she felt soothed, no longer upset about getting sick. Gone was all fear of making Mother mad, of ruining her chances at being invited to stay. The song, a swaddling cloth, replaced these feelings with a sense of sacred belonging. Mother felt it, too. That mother-daughter connection. There is no English word for it. In Icelandic, it's Mæðgur: Motherdaughter. Fiona drifted off to sleep before the second verse, sensing what it felt like to be *motherdaughtered*.

~oOOoOOo~

When Fiona awakened in her mother's bed the next morning, she found her bag all packed and waiting for her, and her clothes laid out. It was time to catch the ferry back to the mainland. Looking through the windows of the boat, across the sea and out to the horizon, Fiona noticed her sparkly friends were coming along for the ride. Fiona welcomed her familiar, comforting friends, still not having made a connection between them and how sick she had been the night before.

How could the weekend be over already, she thought, as she watched, not where they were going, but the shore from which they'd come. Fiona dearly wished they'd had more time together, if only to remind Mother what a fun kid she could be, one who didn't get sick all the time.

Once on dry land again, and back at the pre-arranged pickup spot, Fiona saw Hanna, on time and waiting in her car. Thus, began the agonizing transfer from Mother to Mum. Fiona had nothing against her stepmother—she found her kind and calm and seemingly as interested in Fiona as she was in her own little girls. But, at the end of the day, or the end of the weekend, in this case, she wasn't Fiona's actual Mother.

As everyone said their goodbyes, and Karen gave her a hug, Fiona put on a brave face. Deep down, she was devastated, certain she had made a mess of things—a real mess—by throwing up. Again. She hoped Mother hadn't minded too terribly much. She hoped she'd do better next time. She hoped next time would be soon.

Hope can be a dangerous thing, especially when it's built on shifting sands. With every visit and goodbye, the disappointments just kept coming in waves, eating at Fiona's dreams and imaginings like sandcastles, threatening to carry them out to sea.

Fiona walked off with Mum, who was carrying Fiona's bag to

the car. Fiona never had trouble finding it; it was a hand-painted, white Pontiac station wagon, covered in groovy flowers in the style of Peter Max. It always seemed happy, no matter what mood anyone else was in.

Once settled inside, Mum waited to hear about Fiona's adventures, but Fiona wasn't in the mood to share them. She needed to hang onto them a little longer, just for herself, the only part of her mother she would take with her from the weekend. Mum, sensing the child's dismay, promised her a family outing to a drive-in movie the following weekend. A triple feature was playing—*Count Dracula*, *Frankenstein*, and *The Wolfman*—so they'd bring plenty of blankets to huddle up together, and the kids could fall asleep in the back of the car. Fiona perked right up at the possibility.

"Can we have those snowy cap things?" Fiona asked, referring to the little chocolate nonpareils, covered in white sugar sprinkles. "And hot dogs, and maybe some popcorn, too?"

"We'll see about all of that, Fiona." Mum smiled, pleased she had found a way to engage Fiona. "You can rest assured there will be treats. You know how your Pop is."

"Sure, I do." Fiona knew her Pop liked treats at the movies as much as she did. He loved to join in her laughter when the not-so-subliminal advertisement came up, with hot dogs jumping into the buns, and popcorn boxes dancing across the screen. Drive-in movies were, for Pop, the perfect mini-campout. No bugs, plus catering. With movies on her mind, Fiona stopped looking out the back window of Mum's car, and set her sights on the coming festivities.

"Can I be the one to hook the speaker to the window, Mum?" Hanna smiled again, knowing she had done her job to bring Fiona back into the fold.

~oOOOOOo~

As soon as Hanna's car was out of sight, carrying her child back to Wolf's Providence home, Peggy broke down, weeping, as she drove home with her elder child. It saddened her so each time she had to say goodbye to her younger child.

Karen felt the familiar shut-down that happened each time her mother bid farewell to Fiona. Her mother's tears had the same effect on her as her mother's cold goodbye had had on Fiona. The tears felt like rejection. But for Karen, the reason was different. Her pain came from knowing she was an unwanted daughter who had forced a shotgun wedding. In her mother's bitter tears, Karen felt she could taste a distressing message of regret and lost opportunity. Karen also remembered Wolf, and she wondered how Peggy could let Fiona go back to him. Wasn't that dangerous? Karen wondered. Was that why her mother was crying?

So many unspoken, unresolved issues hung between Karen and her mother. The broken shards of their fractured relationship were papered over with a façade of family, with the truth trapped painfully underneath, threatening to cut anyone who came close enough to touch. People just didn't talk about family dynamics; not even the avant-garde, intellectual set did, unless they were lying on a couch entertaining a shrink. Certainly, it would be déclassé to bring up any difficulties you might be experiencing as a single mom, or as a woman trying to break down barriers, thought Peggy. Better to talk about sex and politics or, better still, simply pour yourself a stiff drink or pop a chill pill. Mother's little helpers, as the Rolling Stones so aptly called them. Why shouldn't she take the edge off? So many of her friends did. It's all so bone-crushingly exhausting, Peggy thought.

~o0O0O0o~

Wolf planned to raise his daughters in a barrier-free, gender-blind world. It didn't matter to him that such a world didn't yet exist, hadn't ever existed. Wasn't Bob Dylan telling us how the times, they were a changin'? Better days were dawning. It was a very optimistic attitude, but these were optimistic times. So, when his girls asked if they could be astronauts someday, he replied, "Yes, of course. You can be anything you want to be," ignoring the fact that NASA didn't accept female candidates. If they wanted it enough, things would just have a way of working out. Besides, he certainly wasn't going to be the one to burst their bubble. Rules are subject to change. Rules have exceptions. And his little girls would be the exceptions, if that's what they wanted.

The summer of 1969 was filled with a heady can-do spirit, as families all around the country gathered to watch the lunar landing, the biggest historic event ever televised. Everyone, that is, who had a television. Although Wolf and Hanna had made a conscious decision to raise their family without a "Boob Tube," there was no way any Sprechelbach was going to miss this. It was, after all, *the* lunar landing. Hypocrisy? No, he had decided. Not at all. If there was ever to be a "science is yummy and learning is sweet" moment, this was it. So, Wolf and Hanna simply piled their girls into their hand-painted Pontiac and shuttled them over to the home of a friend. The party—in full swing when they arrived—was an eclectic gathering of friends, family, neighbors, and co-workers of all ages and races. Differences in ideology, gender, socioeconomic status, race, ethnicity, or exceptionality all seemed to pale before the common truth that we were human, and humanity was about to do something extraordinary.

The room was abuzz. Everyone huddled around the television, their plates laden with Jiffy Pop and other treats, and their free hands holding mixed drinks or Tang, the beverage of choice of astronauts, in honor of the occasion. Yet, when the big moment came, the room was so quiet, you could hear, well, a lunar landing.

04 13 23 43 CDR (TRANQ)
I'm going to step off the LM now.

04 13 24 48 CDR (TRANQ)
That's one small step for (a) man, one giant leap for mankind.
And the—the surface is fine and powdery. I can—I can pick it up loosely with my toe. It does adhere in fine layers like powdered charcoal to the sole and sides of my boots. I only go in a small fraction of an inch, maybe an eighth of an inch, but I can see the footprints of my boots and the treads in the fine, sandy particles.

04 13 25 30 CC
Neil, this is Houston. We're copying.

As the room—and the country—erupted in cheering and applause, Fiona realized she'd been holding her breath. She really wasn't sure why: was it the air of anticipation gripping the room, had she been nervous for the astronauts, had she understood this was one of those moments a kid was never supposed to forget? She wasn't sure. But, just as she felt herself relax, and leaned in to watch Neil Armstrong bounce across the lunar landscape, a big brown dog, the fluffiest, most wonderful thing she'd ever seen, came bounding into the room, right up to Fiona, and put his paws on her legs and his cold, wet, black nose into her face.

"Blech. Whoa. Wait. What? Who are you?" Fiona started to laugh as she fell backward, overwhelmed by the excited dog.

"Sorry about that, Fiona. Meet Regis," said Walter, Pop's friend and host for the evening. "Regis means King, but so far, it only suits him in stature. It's actually a pretty regal name for such a sweet, clumsy puppy."

"He's just a puppy? How big is he gonna get?" Fiona was astonished.

"He's not yet two, so still a puppy, but he's pretty much full grown. He has a lot of energy, but he's harmless, sweet as can be."

Fiona, who was sitting upright, buried her fingers in Regis' soft, slightly curly fur. "I don't mind," she said. "He just surprised me." His fur was so soft, it reminded her of Gram's Afghan hounds. Now, those were two regal dogs. This one? Not so much. Fiona decided that's what she already loved about him.

The rest of the evening, as the adults congratulated themselves on the moon walk with too many toasts, Fiona and Regis made friends. Later, Pop and Mum said, "Fiona, what do you think of Regis? Do you dig him? He certainly seems to dig you and your sisters."

"I love this dog," she said, not taking her eyes off him as she spoke. "Don't you love him, Pop? He's the best dog ever. I think he likes me, too. Did you see how he came right up to me?" Holly and Violet also liked the dog; although they were so little and he, so big, they were a little shyer about greeting him.

"Fiona, do you like him enough to take care of him? Is that something you'd be willing to commit to doing?"

Fiona, up and out of her chair, began bouncing like a pogo stick. "Oh, yes! I would take really good care of him! I'd walk him and feed him and brush him and sleep next to him, and I'd…"

"Okay, Fiona; we get the picture!" Pop was amused by his daughter's excitement.

"PULEEAZ, can we have him, Pop? Mum? Oh, my gosh, PU-LEEAZ. Really? It's possible? I'd do all the work and he would never, ever, ever bother you. I would be so good with him, I promise. Cross my heart, Pop."

Fiona knew in her heart and mind, her father wouldn't have asked her about Regis, if he weren't thinking about giving him to her, if she didn't have a chance of bringing him home. Suddenly, she knew he was what she wanted, more than anything. Something to focus on, to take care of, to call her own. Someone who would love her, no matter what. Not even if she messed up on a test or missed a day of school or didn't have what it took to appeal to Mother. Regis would fill a lot of gaps. She was already thinking about making sure his water dish was full, and feeding him just the right amount of kibble, and brushing him—that would take some doing with all his fur. And taking him out for walks, if she could control him on a leash. She might have to sign him up for obedience training, which could be fun…and she would play with him, and he would be her best friend forever.

"Earth to Fiona!"

"Yes, what?"

"Your mind is suddenly up there with Mr. Armstrong. Did you hear what we said?"

It had already been arranged, of course. Wolf's friends were leaving town to pursue a post in Samoa, and they couldn't take the dog with them. This had been a test introduction, to see how Regis did with children, and whether the girls liked him. Wolf turned to Hanna, "Houston, the eagle has landed."

Regis bounded into the back of the Pontiac, and Fiona hugged him all the way home. As soon as he got out of the car, she threw her arms around Pop, and squeezed like she might never let go. "Oh, thank you, Pop! Thank you, thank you! I won't let you down, I promise."

That's quite a promise, little girl, Wolf thought, smiling, but I won't hold you to it.

July 20, 1969 was a historic day for the world and for Fiona. From that day forward, as the world marked the anniversary of the lunar landing, she celebrated the anniversary of the day she brought home her best friend.

All the next week, the mood was light, as Regis brought a new sense of merriment into the house. The kids hated to leave him, even for a minute. In the car, Pop distracted them, with the Left-Right Game, one of Fiona's favorite. Pop had dreamed it up. It involved the driver allowing the passengers to choose the next direction, until the car was thoroughly lost.

"Left, Pop! Go left!"

"No, Pop, go right, go right!"

Pop shimmied the steering wheel, in feigned confusion, as the kids collapsed in giggles in the back. A mother with her stroller pointed at the car. Was it the erratic driving? The hippy-dippy Pontiac station wagon, painted with big flowers and trails of green leafy vines along both sides, festive and fun, like a toy? Was it Pop's big, booming laugh—ha haaaaaa!—that Fiona imagined could be heard for blocks, even with the windows closed? Even driving purposefully, Pop and the kids got stares.

After they'd circled the same block three times, Pop knew it was time to ask directions. "Okay kids, we're officially lost. Who wants to ask for help?" Fiona cranked the back window open and they all yelled out, like a chorus of birds, "Excuse me, which way to downtown?" The woman with the stroller pointed the way, and soon they were back on track, radio blaring. *Monday, Monday* (badaaa, badadaaadum). "Silly radio. Pop, don't they know it's Saturday?"

Back on course, they headed for the family shop. Hey! Had Pop even been lost, at all, Fiona wondered. She didn't wonder long, though. The shop was too exciting. As she headed in and recognized some of the smells—honeycombs, honey candies, halvah, and carob bars—her mouth began to water. Fiona breathed it all in; the store smelled like spices and open bags of pack-it-yourself food. So many wonderful things to eat. There were coconuts, long grain brown rice, lentils, and other healthy foods in the dawn of the "health food" movement. Mum handed them each a chunk of carob, and Fiona scouted the store, to see what was new. There were shelves full of incense, hand-tooled leather purses, and tie-dyed fabric—the same as last time. Then, she spied them: new homespun dolls and purses.

"Hey Mum, Look at these over here! These are new!"

"Do you like them? We are selling them to support social enterprises. The one in your hand is from the Poor People's Co-Op in Jackson, Mississippi."

"Why?" When Fiona asked, as expected, Mum was ready with her story about the great March on Washington, and the effect it had on the Sprechelbach family.

"Fiona, when you were a baby, our hero Dr. Martin Luther King called for a March for Jobs. People flocked to Washington from all over." Mum smiled at the memory. "It was a beautiful August day, 1963. After some incredible music drew us together, Dr. King gave a powerful, stirring speech about a beautiful, shared dream. Well, we were so moved by his call for economic justice, we decided to take action. This store is our response. It's a small step, but it's going in the right direction. Just because you can't fix everything doesn't excuse you from doing what was within your reach." The shop was definitely within Mum's reach. She ran it, because Pop had a full-time job, but they co-owned it: The Cosmic Starshine.

Mum understood her clientele. The shop catered to the young, rebellious crowd of the early '60s. Zig Zag rolling papers and bongs were carefully tucked away behind glass, so they couldn't easily walk away with the customers. The extensive collection of neon posters for sale were best viewed in the back closet with a special lamp to see how they would glow, but they were so intensely colored, they seemed to glow in the daylight without any help. One customer thumbed through them and settled on Ganesh, an elephant-headed deity. "Animal-people are far out!" he said to Mum, as he paid his tab. "And I'll take three packs of Zig Zags."

Far out, or even "far freakin' out" were commonly heard at The Cosmic Starshine. For Fiona, it was a source of endless fascination, and it gave her a sense of belonging to a community, to a tribe. Everyone longs to belong.

After they closed up the shop, they piled into the car, heading for a Be-in at the art museum lawn. "Be-in," Pop explained, "is short for *human be-in's*." As they approached the gathering place, Mum and Pop took time to spread long sheets of bubble wrap along the sidewalk, helping this Be-in be a memorable one. Pop called it participatory performance art. Fiona just called it fun.

Their work done, they headed toward the hill where everyone was gathering for the planned music and poetry readings. Mum spread out a picnic blanket, opened a basket of food, poured out drinks, and lay down to look at the sky. Fiona proceeded to pick daisies and make chains. The crown of daisies in her hair made Fiona feel like a princess. As she lay in the grass, she spied people playing music here and there, and a long group of people holding hands, like her daisy chain crown, just sort of dancing along.

There were a couple of people dancing by themselves. And all around, people were smoking. "Pass me that doobie," said one. "Right on," came the reply. A bit later, "Come on, don't Bogart that joint. It's my last one," was followed by, "I dig you, but if you've got the bread, I can score us a matchbox for five." Fiona didn't quite follow the conversation. She was about to tune out, when she heard them agreeing: "Fan-freakin'-tastic!" She understood that, at least. She understood they were happy.

Fiona surveyed the rolling hills. Everywhere she looked, Fiona saw contented people. Across the way, a woman was beating on a drum, and her kids were dancing to the rhythm. Someone was blowing bubbles. That looked like fun. A couple of people were enjoying a kiss. Gross. Fiona looked away, back to the other hillside, where there were still plenty of daisies. She headed over to retrieve them.

There was work to do.

Finally, as the sun set and the Be-in started to wind down, Mum and Pop packed up the family into the car and started back home. Slowly, stars began to appear in the night sky. Fiona peered up, looking for a shooting star…up and into the cosmic starshine!

~oOOoOOo~

Fiona was already wide awake when Mum popped her head in with a sing-song voice, "So nice to see you smile; it makes the day worthwhile." The family had decided Fiona was old enough to accompany Pop to a protest march at Yale University. Mum would stay home with Holly and Vi. A few friends had arrived, to catch a ride there. Pretty soon, the Painted Pontiac was full of friends who were attending the rally. Mum waved goodbye as Pop headed for Yale, in New Haven, a couple of hours away.

Everyone had their flags, including Fiona. Hers was bright green, with "YIPPIE!" painted in bold letters. Other flags read, "Make Love, Not War" and, simply, "Peace!" Fiona had silkscreened her flag two weekends before, in the family's attic, along with dozens of others her parents had prepared for the Vietnam War rally. She was proud to be considered grown-up enough to participate. The crowd grew bigger and bigger across the campus, with a loud chorus of *We Shall Overcome*.

The plan was to protest the war, and the Selective Service System's lotteries. Young people across the country were angry and unwilling to be dragged into a war that didn't belong to them, to fight and likely lose their lives for the very "Establishment" that had gotten them into what they saw as a wrongheaded mess that had been going on for 15 years with no end in sight. Or, at least, that's how they saw it. Yes, people were mad, resentful, and scared. But there was an excited energy, a curious air of conviction, that made the day seem almost fun.

Fiona sang along with her father, whose hand she was holding with her free hand, while her other hand festively waved her flag. Though her own family was deeply divided about the war, that somehow didn't matter. Pop was a pacifist, she knew, who told her,

"Violence begets violence." That made sense. Whatever Pop did, it must be important and it must be right. He and Mum believed in it, so she did, too. And there were so many others around who seemed to feel the same way. The protesters were bolstered in their beliefs by the strength in numbers and the validation that they were participating in something that really mattered. The police didn't necessarily see it that way. For the time being, they were in position, lined up across the street, but peaceful. Fiona and Pop, deep among the protesters, got to the corner and were moving toward the lawn outside the university's administration building. There were different groups shouting different chants.

"No! No! We Won't Go!"

"1 2 3 4, We don't want to war no more."

"Ho, Ho, Ho Chi Minh, NLF is gonna Win!"

Fiona couldn't quite understand all the words. She pulled on Pop's hand until he leaned over so she could ask her question.

"Hey Pop, isn't it NFL? Hey Pop, Hey…?"

"NLF, Fee, the Viet Kong, the people we're fighting against."

"So, why are they saying that, then?"

That was a complicated question. Pop was in the middle of formulating an answer when the tone of the event changed. Someone had spotted the police line. "Power to the People. Off the Pigs!" the protestor yelled. Fiona didn't understand him, but Pop did. Sensing a clash coming, he didn't join in the chant, so Fiona didn't either.

Suddenly, the police began to approach the crowd, their line pressing forward in measured precision. Some had German Shepherds on short leashes, Fiona noticed, and some sat astride horses. Fiona was focusing on how beautiful the animals were when she felt a sharp stinging in her eyes. She dropped her flag to wipe the back of her hand across her face, but held fast to her father's hand, as he began to run. Moving as fast as she could, with her short legs trying to keep up with her father's long stride, Fiona felt the excitement of the morning turn to terror.

In their flight, they came upon a back stairway. Pop picked up

Fiona and ducked down the stairs, joining several others ahead of him, just as the wild crowd scrambled by. His own eyes raw and filled with tears, he held his hand against the back of Fiona's head, pressing her face into his shirt to shield her eyes. It helped, mostly to make her feel safe in the arms of her Pop. But still, her eyes burned, her heart hammered in her chest, and her ears rang with the screaming, sirens, bullhorns, and barking that would provide the soundtrack to her nightmares for weeks to come.

Moments later, they were back in the car. Pop thought for a moment about the others who'd carpooled. There was no easy way to reconnect, in the chaos, and he had his daughter to think of. They'd just have to fend for themselves. He turned on the radio, and headed off, toward home. He turned the radio on, loud, but not loud enough to drown out the sounds of the clash that was replaying in his mind...or Fiona's. Those were really mean police, really big horses, and really scary dogs, Fiona thought. They were nothing like her first dog, Heart, no matter how much they looked like him. Heart had never scared her. No dog had, until today.

The Vietnam War had started before Fiona was born but was brought into most living rooms across the country every day, in stark and horrifying footage via television news broadcasts. Fiona saw none of this because of Mum and Pop's conscious choice not to have a television; she saw life largely through her parents' lens. This war, her parents had said, was neither justified nor necessary.

Racism is bad, her parents had taught her. Poverty is bad. Science is good. So is honey. And love. "Love, not War," had been painted across so many signs that day, during the demonstration. "Make love, not war. Make love, not war. Make love..." Fiona liked the way that sounded.

Eventually, Fiona and her father made it home, safe and sound. Mum ran a bath for Fiona, who was looking forward to sinking into the soothing security of the warm suds. She was covered, head to toe, in dust. Mum started by giving her a quick shower to rinse off any chemicals from the "unfriendly fire" by the police. Even so, Fiona's eyes still stung. Mum had Fiona press a cool washcloth against them while she waited for the tub to fill. Fiona settled into her cozy bath, filled with the "Mr. Bubbles" suds Mum had poured into the running water. A few minutes later, when Pop poked his head in to check on Fiona, her sudsy little face popped up and said, "Pop, what does 'Off the Pigs' mean?"

Pop looked over at Fiona's forget-me-not eyes, suddenly aware of how much they'd seen that day, and the lasting impact of those impressions. At this rate, Pop thought, she's not going to have that blue-eyed innocence for very much longer. He considered his words carefully, before answering. "That's not something we say, Fiona. It's a form of violence. 'Off' means to kill, and 'Pigs' means police. But that is not how to effect change. We are nonviolent in this family, Fiona. Remember that." This was a satisfying response and plenty for Fiona to absorb as she turned her attention to the rubber ducky that had disappeared under the bubbles in her bath.

~o0O0O0o~

Fiona had no idea her father had ever exhibited a violent streak. It was a closely guarded secret among her three parents, protected by an accentuated propensity for peace. Pop was happy to change the subject.

"Yale was pretty, though, wasn't it?"

"I don't know, Pop, I don't think I like Yale."

"That's fine, Fee. There are lots of other wonderful colleges you will love."

"Pop, will you count to 1,000 for me?"

"In what language?"

"Um, German."

"Eins is one; zwei is two; drei, three…"

Fiona looked up at her father. She was so proud of him. My Pop knows everything, she thought. He's the nicest, smartest father in the whole world. After a while, she lost interest in the numbers he was reciting, feeling soothed just by the rhythm of his voice. The bathwater was cold before Pop finished his count. As he got to, "einhundert, one hundred," he bundled Fiona into a towel Mum had heated in the dryer. Wrapped in the security of her terrycloth robe and her father's affection, Fiona went down to dinner.

Fiona was still sad about losing her flag; she had wanted something to help her remember that important, if terrible, day. But Mum had made her a new one, also green. When Fiona asked her what YIPPIE meant, Mum told her it came from social activists Abbie Hoffman and Jerry Rubin, and stood for Youth International Party, a counterculture movement with no leader and no organization. But, participants had a platform and a voice. Usually, when discussing politics, Pop would say, "Never trust anyone over 30." This was said with a wink since Mum and Dad had both pushed past 30.

As Fiona cleared the dishes from the table to the kitchen sink, the conversation between Mum and Pop turned to the draft. Everyone, it seemed, had friends who were affected.

Pop worked for the government. Involving himself in the new Underground Railroad to help folks avoid the draft would put him and his family at risk of ruin, and included the possibility of a stint in prison. But Pop was considering it, carefully. He loved to say, "Just because you're paranoid doesn't mean they're out to get you." Then he'd start speaking in whispers with friends, and hide the phone in the refrigerator. Fiona simply saw this as another piece of Pop's wisdom. She didn't question who the mysterious "they" might be or why "they" might be out to get her or why the phone should hide in the fridge. And tonight, she was so tired, she didn't even ask for a bedtime story.

"What if I can't sleep tonight?" Fiona asked her Pop, as he smoothed her sheets and reached over to turn out the light.

"Do you have your cardamom bottle?" Pop asked, referring to the bottle of green cardamom seeds Mum had given Fiona that she could open and sniff—a little sleep-enhancing aromatherapy, for when she couldn't sleep.

"What if that doesn't work, Pop?"

"Well, remember that relaxing meditation Mum showed you called the Corpse Pose? You could try lying very still like a statue, playing dead until you just relax yourself to sleep."

"But, what if I get the squirmies?"

"Would you like to have Regis sleep in your room tonight, Fee?"

Fiona looked at the warm brown eyes of the dog she loved, as he stood in the doorway, waiting. She patted her bed, and he responded by quickly jumping up, and settling himself at the foot of her bed. Petting his soft head, she said, "I can just talk to Regis, if I can't sleep." Five minutes later, she was fast asleep.

~oOoOOOo~

Holly and Violet were still too young for school. Most afternoons, Mum entertained them in the living room by reading to them. Fiona envied them. She would rather have had someone reading to her than be writing the story that was due the next day. Though she did like writing, and she had all the materials she needed, she felt a little stuck. She decided music might help. She'd seen Pop turn to his favorite tunes when he seemed stuck. So, she opened the suitcase that was really a portable record player Pop had given her. She pulled out her favorite record album, *With the Beatles*, and set it on the turntable. Lifting the arm, she carefully placed the needle at the start of her favorite song, "It Won't Be Long." Good thing, she thought.

Fiona started to sing along, "It won't be long, yeah..." She loved the song because it reminded her of Mother and Karen, and the day when she would finally be with them. Mother, the famous mystery writer, certainly could have helped her with her story. But she would have encouraged Fiona to come up with her own creative ideas. Karen could have helped her, too. Karen could do anything. She could ride horses, play the guitar, sing pretty songs, write stories, draw—just like Mother. While Mother was a goddess, mysterious and inaccessible, Karen was a shining hero to Fiona. But Karen wasn't there. She was with Mother. Yes, she was with Mother. That's because Mother wanted *her*.

Another song by the Beatles started and her melancholy returned. She thought about the conversation she'd just heard her father having with her mother by phone. Pop had been speaking quietly. But not quietly enough. They were talking about moving. Who was moving. Was Pop? Was Mother? It must be Mother and

Karen. Clearly, they were moving far. Too far for a car ride. Too far for Fire Island. Too far for weekend visits. The next time Fiona saw them would be Christmas. *Might* be Christmas. And then, what? The summer, after that? Perhaps the worst part was that nobody had thought to tell Fiona. Didn't she get a vote? It all felt like too much to Fiona, who picked up her pencil and, finally, started writing.

Onceuponatime, she wrote. All one word. Onceuponatime. And with that, she unleashed a tale of Prince Relavens, a good prince but a sad prince, whose parents had died of "hartattaks" and who had a lovely horse named Spots—because of his spots, naturally—and a golden saddle. She explained how nothing in the world made him happy after his parents died, not even all the gold in the world, and not even riding around on Spots, saving lives. So he quit, and sat in a garden until his beard grew long and white. Fiona wanted a unicorn in the story, so she decided a fairy would ride in and remind the prince that Spots was lonely, so they could all ride and be happy together.

Wow, three whole pages, Fiona thought, as she studied her own neat writing on the pages before her. That's more than the teacher asked for. Fiona hoped her teacher would like it. Not noticing her own sadness and longing pouring out through the pages, she was just glad her work was done.

Placing the pages into her notebook, Fiona slipped her work into her school bag, which she took downstairs to set by the front door, near her coat, ready to dash out the door in the morning to make the school bus. She was all set.

Fiona loved just about everything about elementary school. She loved the big yellow school bus that picked her up in the morning and delivered her home every afternoon. She loved the rows of shiny desks in her classroom and the bright windows that let in the light. She loved poring through her "Weekly Reader," and watching the colorful films that would run from reel to reel and project stories like *Beaver Valley* on the big screen, which was white on one side and had a map of the world, with the United States at its center, on the other. Yes, she loved it all, with the exception of gym class, especially when gym was held outdoors. The big Acacia tree that dusted the playing field with yellow pollen stirred her allergies into a frenzy of watery eyes and sinus congestion. Sneezing her way through gym was not Fiona's idea of a good time.

One day, as she was having a particularly intense allergy attack during gym, which made it hard to breathe through her nose, Fiona got teased for breathing through her mouth. "Hey Fiona, why don't you ever close your frecklebox? Haw haw, can't shut yer yap, huh? Your mouth is hanging open like a dummy." It was the same boy who had not known an answer in class, so she'd whispered it to him and then watched him bask in the glory of his borrowed intelligence. Do I argue? Fiona wondered. Hoping just to change the subject, she called out, "Cut it out." That was like pouring water on a grease fire.

"Come make me! Hey Frecklebox. Hey Freckleface. I know you can hear me. Are you deaf *and* dumb? Oh, I forgot, you're Miss Smartypants Frecklebox."

Fiona, regretting having said anything at all, now did her best to ignore him, but his taunts continued. "Fee, Fi, Fo, Fum. Fiona thinks she's smarter than everyone!"

"Do not," Fiona couldn't help saying, even while thinking, Pop says don't fight back with a bully. And he's bigger than me. I don't think I could beat him. Not on the playground, anyway. Maybe at a game of chess. But this isn't chess. No more talking, she decided. But, it was too late.

"Do so." He said, as he came over and pushed her right into a snowdrift. "Who's so smart now? Smartypants? Soggypants is more like it. Haw haw!" But he had a bit of a surprised look on his face, as if it had been easier than he thought to knock her down and into the drift. He hurried away, and Fiona sat frozen, silently in the snowbank. A few of the other kids looked on, also silent. She was so relieved when she heard the bell ring; she raced back to the refuge of the classroom. But the boy's taunts and actions had released an ugly worm of doubt into her mind. Maybe she shouldn't raise her hand so much. Maybe she should be quieter, keep her knowledge and her ideas to herself. It seemed to Fiona that maybe boys didn't like brainy girls.

Fiona sat on the bus on the way home that day and thought about her family and how odd most everyone thought they were. Was it weird to be smart? Was it smart to play dumb? Do people dumb themselves down, just to be popular? Do they just stop learning things, to fit in? Wow, she thought, I don't think I could do that.

Fiona stared out the window of the bus, so deep in thought she hardly saw the houses and cars as they passed by. She thought about the Red Rover game, and how kids would call everyone but her. Just once, she would to have loved to have heard "Red Rover, Red Rover, send Fiona right over." She would have tried with all her might to break through the barricade of kids holding hands to bring someone back with her to the team that had chosen her. Why, she wondered, do kids choose my grasp to break through, instead of anyone else's? Do they really see me as the weakest link? I try to let go quickly, but it still hurts. Or, why do they aim for me so much, in Dodge Ball? Also, what's so sporting about lining kids up like a firing squad, and then telling them to defend themselves from classmates with crimson cannonballs? Fiona winced, thinking of the long, purplish bruises she sometimes sported on her thighs for days after failing to dodge an attack quickly enough.

Yes, Fiona thought, I hate just about everything about gym class. At least I'm not a jerk to people. I don't push them into snowdrifts and call them names, even people who deserve it. And with that thought, Fiona hit on a plan. She decided to make up some rules for life. Whenever a rough or confusing situation arose, she would make up a new rule to help herself handle it better next time. The first one was about not being like the kid who pushed her into the snowdrift. And what was it that Pop liked to say? Never trust anyone over 30. That's it. That's a good one to throw in, too.

Fiona's Rule #1—Don't Be a Jerk (Even to a Jerk).
Fiona's Rule #2—Never Trust Anyone Over 30.

At dinner that night, Pop asked Fiona about her day. She told him about what had had gone down in the schoolyard with the bully who had teased her in that sing-song voice of his. She told her father how he'd acted like a know-it-all when he wasn't one at all.

"Is there a chance that's exactly why he was acting like that?" asked Pop.

"What do you mean?"

"Well, Fiona, what if he feels uncomfortable for not knowing the answers? What if one way for him to feel better is to put people down who know more than he does?"

"But, that's so mean, Pop."

"I know, Fiona. Some people think they can build themselves up by tearing other people down. Terrible plan. It never really works, either, though plenty of people try."

Pop knew what he was talking about. He'd been picked on, too, for being the smart one at school. All these years later, he could still quickly conjure the face of the school bully who'd twisted his fingers, threatening to break them, knowing how Wolf had planned to be a concert pianist. Wolf thought of himself as nonviolent, but something inside had snapped that afternoon, and he'd fought back, violently, smashing his tormentor's head against the pavement. If the teacher and another classmate hadn't stepped in…Well, he was just lucky they had. And, if his parents hadn't been so well connected in the community, he might have gone on to juvenile hall instead of to college. From where had Wolf summoned that inner wolf of his, the one he preferred to deny or ignore? From his own father. After all, his training ground for how to handle conflict had come in the form of yet another resounding beating from his father, a distant yet demanding drinker, who believed in solving problems with his hands.

Wolf wasn't naturally violent. He knew in his heart he was gentle. His name was a curse from his father, but one he rejected. After all, since he'd reached maturity he'd never hit anyone, had never hurt anyone…except for that one time with Peggy and the baby, an event Wolf had buried so deeply that he hardly acknowledged to himself that it had happened.

Although Wolf had vowed he'd never lay a hand on anyone again, the realization that he had the potential in him to be just like his father had stalked him relentlessly, as if his father were leering over his shoulder. He shuddered at the thought, aware that he'd never truly shake him loose.

Later, while tucking Fiona into bed, Mum brought up the bullying incident again. Mum also understood what it felt like to be put down for being too smart. Fair-minded men had opened doors, and she'd sometimes been careful so as not to outshine her peers too much. She knew the struggle, the inner conflict, wrestling with the decision about whether to play dumb, to keep her smarts to herself a little, or to just be herself. Nobody likes to be bullied or disliked for being different, and it can be exhausting to keep dumbing yourself down just to make other people feel more at ease.

Not all the lessons Fiona was learning in school were easy, and not all were academic. Maybe that was part of the problem. She knew how to navigate her classwork, but not her classmates. And the lesson she'd just learned was a doozy. Mum wanted to soften it.

"Sometimes, what makes you shine," said Mum, sitting beside Fiona, "is blinding to the others. It hurts their eyes. You know when your head hurts, and the kitchen light hurts your eyes, so we turn it off? People like that are just walking around like dark trolls who lurk under bridges. They don't know what to do when a beautiful beam of light comes along and shines in their eyes, so they try to stomp it out. You know, Fee, your father and I love how smart you are. Are you thinking you should hide your light just to make friends with trolls?"

"I don't know, maybe," Fiona said, worrying the corner of her bed sheet between her fingers.

"Well, I hope not. I like who you are and don't want you to hide it from anyone, particularly yourself. You are most beautiful when you let your best shine through."

Mum's soothing and supportive words helped Fiona feel better. "I guess I just need to be who I am, right Mum?" Her stepmother nodded. "But what if I never make any friends?"

Hanna saw the sadness in Fiona's eyes. "Trust me, there are other bright and beautiful people outside of the dark tunnels, up in the sunlit forest. They, maybe I should say, we, tend to find each other. You will, too. Right now, you're home safe with us, right where you belong."

Hanna repeated how proud she was of Fiona, and how much she liked her for who she was. "I think you should wake up each morning and look in the mirror and remind yourself that what you see is more than enough," she said, hoping Fiona would always strive to be her authentic, smart self, practicing the principles she cared about. "Whatever skills you practice, you move toward their perfection," Mum said. "You're already perfectly great, but still you can practice honesty and kindness and peacemaking, and you'll shine more and more brightly. You can always improve your skills, but you can never become more perfect. You just are, as you are. Be your best self. Just walk in beauty. That's what integrity is. If you're true to yourself and others, you've got it. The kid in class didn't have it, but he can't dim your light unless you let him. Shine on, Sweetie."

Fiona thought about that. Maybe, from then on, whenever she was brushing her teeth or washing her face at bedtime, she could remember what Mum had said to her that night about bullies and integrity and beauty, and so many other shining ideals, and it could help her sleep.

Mum kissed Fiona on the forehead, rose to turn out the light, and left, closing the door, quietly. Fiona pulled the covers up over her shoulders and snuggled into her bed. "Shine on." Fiona smiled as she slipped into sleep, safe, satisfied, secure.

Fiona's Rule #1—Don't Be a Jerk. -
Fiona's Rule #2—Never Trust Anyone Over 30.
Fiona's Rule #3—Shine On!

Fiona arrived early at school and sat at her desk, reading ahead in Madeleine L'Engle's *A Wrinkle in Time*, as she waited for class to begin. She'd already read the compelling sci-fi story twice before, and still hadn't tired of it. Besides, she had a hard time sitting idle, especially in school. Other students were slowly filing into the room and taking their seats around her, animatedly talking with each other.

Before Mrs. Francis, her third-grade teacher, could ask the class to stand for the customary Pledge of Allegiance, Principal Siefkin walked into the room. "Good morning, class," he said. "Today, we are conducting a safety drill to make sure we'd all know what to do in the event of a crisis. Right now, I would like you to stand, leave your belongings behind, and file out of the room, behind me, to the basement, in a quiet, orderly fashion."

Mr. Norman Siefkin was the tall, slim principal who spent most of his days in his office, officiating in his sincere suit and striped necktie, and singing his own take-off on a Beatle's song, "PS, I Love You," with PS standing for the public schools. He loved his job, and he loved his school, and he was going to make sure it ran like a well-oiled machine. Today, as he stood in front of her class, Fiona felt his imposing presence and the authority of his deep voice commanding the students to conform.

Fiona tried to follow the rules, to fit in, to do things right. But nonconformity was the watchword in her family. She had two mothers and a father, half-sisters all over the place, a psychedelic station wagon, a natural-metaphysical family shop, no TV, and no set bedtime. Her front porch promoted nonconformity with its purple light bulb, advertising oddity as it illuminated the natural landscape growing wild and free. Just like Fiona's wild and curly hair, that reached all the way down her back, and snarled, when she brushed it. Even her hair didn't like to conform.

Nonconformity was the emblem of the era, but not at this school. Or at any other public school in the city. Fiona desperately wanted to belong, make friends, enjoy being a kid. She also wanted to please her parents and fit in with her family. The principal's announcement of the disaster drill caused conflict in Fiona. The problem was, Pop and the school were at odds, and she knew it. He had taught Fiona that atomic bombs, if they ever were dropped, would vaporize the entire area for miles, so air-raid drills were pointless, "which is why we all must work for a just and equitable peace, Fiona." Yet Fiona's teacher and the administration of her school had the students regularly do "duck-and-cover" drills, just in case.

So, what was she supposed to do? Her father, had he been there, would have said something, she knew. Should she? After a moment of deliberation, Fiona decided to speak up. She raised her hand.

"Excuse me," she said, when the principal didn't call on her. "Excuse me, Mr. Siefkin, but my father says disaster drills are stupid. He says we'd never survive a nuclear attack, no matter where we are, or how well we duck and cover our heads with our hands. He says war is bad, and I have a right not to participate in the drills. Also…"

The principal was unprepared to deal with the daughter of a rebel family; he lacked a response to this bright little face parroting what her Pop had taught her. So, he defaulted to what anyone of his stature would do. He stomped his foot and said, "GO downstairs, young lady. NOW. This is neither the time nor the place for a peace protest."

Fiona was hustled down the stairs with her classmates, her first attempt at civil disobedience an epic failure. Except, of course, that she clearly had been considered disobedient. Mr. Siefkin sure was mad. But Pop had said there was a difference between disobedience and defiance. She wasn't being defiant, which she knew would make an adult mad; she was trying not to obey something her family didn't support. She had engaged in what Pop liked to call "ethical disobedience."

Fiona went into the basement with the other children, and took her seat behind the kid who sat in front of her in class. There she sat, "ducked and covered" on the basement floor, which was as cold and hard as the reality of what had just happened.

A few weeks later, as the semester wound down, Mrs. Francis, handed out honors to select students in the class. Not everyone was listening as intently as Fiona, who was waiting, expectantly, for her award. Not every kid would get one; would she?

"Children," Mrs. Francis began, "citizenship is like a precious gem, a many-sided thing. Participating in the rights and duties and privileges of citizenship requires an understanding of our shared history and hopes. And sometimes, it means taking a stand for what you know is right."

As Mrs. Francis went on and on about citizenship, Fiona began to notice how the big maple tree just outside the window had leaves that looked like wide and thin people, dancing in the wind to the "Maple Leaf Rag." Lost in her wandering mind, she didn't hear her name being called, and hardly believed it when it was called the second time. "Miss Fiona Sprechelbach!" Well, there's only one Fiona Sprechelbach, she thought, so that must mean me, right?

The bell rang, and she skipped off to the school bus with an award for good citizenship, and for making the honor roll for her grades, plus a merit citation for perfect attendance and punctuality. Fiona felt proud to bursting, but she wondered, just a little, whether she had received the citizenship award for expressing her freedom of speech, or despite having done so.

Fiona's (Mrs. Francis') Rule #4—Be a Good Citizen.

Fiona just loved Mrs. Francis, and her citizenship honor had touched something deep within her, rekindling a spark that had nearly been snuffed out in a snowbank, renewing her engagement as an eager student. Yes, I'll still try my best. I'll even try to be a good citizen, whatever that means.

~oOOOOo~

Midwinter in Providence is a cold and bleak time. Fiona, whose pigtails had begun to freeze solid after her swim lessons at the local "Y," thought of the demonstration she'd once witnessed of how a rose, dipped in liquid nitrogen would shatter easily. She wondered, if I snapped my pigtails against this wall, would they shatter? She loved her long, coppery hair, so she didn't try it. Still, she was cold. Really cold. And the hot chocolate Mum had handed her, along with the big fluffy towel she'd wrapped round her body, were only sort of helping to chase the chill.

"Wouldn't it be cool if we went somewhere really warm right now?" Fiona said to Pop and Mum between sips of chocolate.

"It wouldn't be cool; it would be hot." Pop smiled. "Fee, we've been thinking the same thing. In fact, Mum and I are moving the family to India."

"Wait. What? India?" she shuddered, maybe from the cold, maybe from the news. "But that's so far away, Pop. Why India?

When?" Fiona usually knew better than to ask when. Her father's announcements were always accompanied by, "Now."

Like many of their friends, Wolf and Hanna were fascinated by all things Indian, and were moved to action by Dr. Martin Luther King, Jr.'s vision of equality. They felt called to help India's untouchables and widows, who were at the very bottom of Indian society. Wolf and Hanna wanted a world where everyone had a chance at life's best, and they were determined to help bring their vision to reality. Hanna called this work, "Tikkun Olam," or healing the world. She said everyone she knew and respected agreed it was the right way to live.

When Wolf's father had died, he'd left him with a small inheritance. In his father's absence and with his father's funds, Wolf finally had the chance to come into his own, to be his own person, make his own mark. Having lived for so long suffocating under the weight of his father's expectations, Wolf found that even his asthma seemed somehow better. While he felt his feet on the ground for the first time, somewhere deep inside himself he knew he was still trying to please the man who lay six feet under them.

The more Wolf and Hanna had talked it over, the bigger became their aspirations. They recognized the caliber of their concept, knowing it would be one small step for social justice and one giant leap for man—and womankind. Yes, indeed, they would make their mark.

When a few friends expressed their concern that Wolf and Hanna were overreaching, interceding in a place whose culture of ascription had been set in stone for centuries, they closed their ears. The decision had been made. Their calling was to climb out of their comfort zone to create a new life for themselves and the untouchables in India. Bombs away, and fallout be damned. The future belonged to those who dared to dream and then did something about it.

Soon, everything was in order. The Sprechelbach family had taken their photos, received their passports, and scheduled their vaccinations (of which there were many!). The three young Sprechelbach sisters had a sense of what was coming, and they feared it more than the trip that required it. Fiona, the eldest, went in first.

While she was getting her shots, in her dutiful silence, she heard the commotion in the waiting room.

"Help! No! Wait! No! I said, No!" Holly, clung to the leg of the waiting room couch, terrified, and kicking away anyone who came near. Finally, Mum calmed her a little and coaxed her onto her lap. Fiona was done by then, and Holly was next. "Holly," she whispered, as she sat down beside Mum, "the sooner you go in, the sooner you'll be all done, and then you can have a Tootsie Pop."

After all, you're going to get those shots, whether you want them or not, she thought. Just like everything else in this family. Fiona's baby sister, Violet, just buried her head in Mum's shirt. She didn't like the energy around her, but she didn't understand it enough to put up a fight. Yet.

Pop had good reason for his belief in vaccinations. He'd had polio. When he was a child, the prospect of polio terrorized families, and there was little they could do to protect themselves, except send in their dimes to help the researchers work toward a vaccine. During outbreaks, public gatherings were canceled. Fearing contagion, people stayed away from public pools. Pop, who liked the pool, didn't like to be told what to do. Fear wasn't going to bully him out of enjoying life, he'd told himself, as he ignored his mother's warnings and went for a swim. When he was stricken with polio soon after, his mother was inconsolable.

Polio paralyzed. It killed. Sometimes, it stopped you from being able to breathe on your own. As was the custom of the day, Pop's doctors had threatened him with incarceration in an iron lung unless he exercised a lot. Already a little claustrophobic, he'd responded with a near obsession for exercise. Years later, the effects were still in evidence. He'd strengthened his lung capacity and upper body so much that he could still do military pushups, clapping his hands together between each one. And he could lift all three of his girls at once, like weights.

If Pop felt any sense of self-reproach about his risk-taking ways, he didn't let on about it. He focused on what he'd gained from the experience, including his surprising strength. He liked to say he was Popeye, the Inventor Man, (*toot toot*), referring to his favorite cartoon. Popeye would rescue his beloved Olive Oyl from the clutches of bad boy Bluto every time, but only after eating spinach for strength. With his silly laugh and self-accepting, "I yam what I yam," Popeye was not a bad character to emulate, a hero who takes care of his people.

"I survived polio!" Pop crowed. "No child of mine will be at risk of going through that experience." Fiona didn't appreciate his perspective. After all, she was the one on the receiving end of the needle.

Arriving home, Fiona was relieved to find Regis there, happy as ever to see her, smiling right into her face, almost toppling her over in his enthusiasm to welcome her. "Wow, Regis; that's some breath you've got there." Fiona laughed and buried her face into his fur. "I need to get you a toothbrush. How about a biscuit? They're supposed to help." The two trod off to the kitchen together in search of a dog treat.

Regis had been Fiona's best friend since the moment they'd met and in this case, he was a wonderful balm to the whole shots experience. Saying goodbye to him as they headed off to India would be even harder than the shots had been. Mum's parents had promised to take good care of the big dog until the family eventually returned, whenever that might be. They also offered to store one bin of keepsakes and other belongings for each member of the family, plus one suitcase of extra household items. And they'd promised to take care of a beloved jade plant Fiona had won at her school fair.

Fiona climbed up and looked at the top bunk of her bed, overflowing with German plush toys by Steiff—beautiful and somewhat authentic versions of the actual animals they represented. She thought of her bright-red closet, filled with games and science projects. What should she choose to take, to store, to trash? She wondered if she'd have a closet in India, and if Pop would let her paint that one. Red was such a cheery color. She wondered if she should keep her poster of the beautiful Theda Bara, one of the most popular actresses of the silent film era, dressed as Cleopatra, or whether it would crumple or rip if she tried to take it down.

"You, I will keep forever!" she said to her big plush zebra, which had kept her company during her hospital stay as a toddler, and ever since. Down it went, to the bottom of the bin.

2. INDIA

A wave of thick heat hit Fiona when the door of the airplane finally opened. Feeling the need to take a deep breath, she couldn't get one as she stepped gingerly down the mobile stairs. Heat flushing her face, Fiona joined her family as they all walked across the black tarmac to the terminal at Palam Airport, outside of New Delhi. Fiona desperately wanted to hold Mum's hand, to feel the reassurance in her grasp that she was safe, that they were okay in this hot, unfamiliar place, but Mum's hands were already occupied by Holly and Violet. Exhausted and disoriented after 20 hours of flights and airports, the family collected their luggage and made their way through customs, eventually finding themselves outside, at the curb of this incredibly foreign place.

Until she'd left for India, Fiona's life had felt relatively predictable, albeit punctuated by her parents' unusual events and activities. Despite occasional excitement, like needing to flee tear gas at an anti-war demonstration with Pop, she took comfort in her routine. She knew her neighborhood and understood her life at school. She could count on spending Christmas at Gram's, and visiting Mother and Karen a couple of times throughout the year and during the summer. She could count on Mum for a nutritious supper, and on her trusted dog to be waiting for her when she came home from school. Here, she could count on none of those things. At eight years old, she'd been ripped away from everything she knew and understood, with no idea what would happen next. To make matters worse, she still harbored a pain in her backside from all those vaccinations. She felt stiff, sore, and scared. Mum and Pop seemed preoccupied with getting the family out of the airport and over to their new home. Holly and Violet seemed preoccupied with hanging onto Mum. Fiona, feeling insecure and alone, focused on keeping up.

Pop had promised the excitement of a new school, and horseback riding and dancing lessons in Delhi, just like she'd had back home. But this wasn't just like back home. This was nothing like home. As it began to sink in how truly far away she was today from where she'd been yesterday, Fiona found herself longing to turn around. She wanted to hide her face in Regis' fur, play with her friends, make up recipes in Mum's kitchen. She wanted to turn right around and go home.

I'd take the frozen cold of a Providence winter all year long over this Delhi heat, Fiona thought. In fact, that sounds kind of dreamy right now. But I don't think that's the plan.

Fiona had been told she'd be going to school in India this year. That probably meant they were staying in the country at least for an entire school year. In a child's mind, a school year is a lifetime, but nobody was even talking about "just" a school year. In fact, no one had put any sort of timeline on the adventure at all. Maybe they were staying forever. Were they? Fiona didn't know, and she was afraid to ask. If she did ask about whether the move was permanent, she might get them thinking along those lines. She couldn't risk it. She was already pretty sure she didn't want to stay very long.

Pop's obvious delight in having reached the destination where his cultural contribution would take place didn't help Fiona feel any better about their situation. In fact, it made her mad. How could he think it was a good idea to bring us here? What kind of contribution is it if he wrecks his own kids' lives to save the lives of other kids? I don't get it. Fiona wiped the sweat trickling down the side of her face with the sleeve of her shirt.

"Hey, Fee, I have a new word for you," said Pop.

"What is it, Pop?" she shot back.

"Bahut dooer. It means 'far out,' in Hindi."

"Great, Pop," she answered, caring very little. They were certainly far out, but not in a cool way. Not cool at all, in fact.

"Bahut freakin' dooer," Pop mused, "Far freakin' out!"

Fiona rolled her eyes. A station wagon pulled up to the curb to collect their family, driven by two of Wolf and Hanna's friends from home. After hugs all around, they piled into the car, their luggage stowed in the back, and headed toward their new home. Fiona couldn't have been less prepared for the sensory overload. Driving toward the town center, she began to feel dizzy. The mélange of scents, one blending into the other, was overwhelming, particularly in the hot, thick air, as they motored through the stench of an open sewer, and then pungent cooking, and now jasmine or orange, and now cow dung. Through the open window from where she sat in the back seat, she saw signs she couldn't read, colors she couldn't name, strangely shaped buildings against a different sort of beauty in the hills than she recognized in Providence. Every woman they passed was wearing layers of light fabric, in color combinations more exquisite than the last. She heard unfamiliar sounds, too, a cacophony of horns and different engines rumbling against the rhythmic clopping of ox hooves.

More startling were the scenes outside the car window. Here and there were the signs of abject poverty, mixed in with beauty and extravagance. Eventually, the car pulled up to their new home, and got out. Fiona thought she might pass out. She thought of her favorite movie, *The Wizard of Oz*, and wished she could simply click her heels and be transported up and out of India, to be safely deposited in her bedroom in Providence.

As the family walked toward the apartment building, a beggar child approached them. "Memsaab, paisa?" (A penny, Ma'am?) As Mum handed the boy, who appeared to be Fiona's age, a single American coin, the family was suddenly surrounded by other children, pushing and jostling, reaching and requesting coins. Fiona found it difficult to breathe in the crush of children. From everywhere, it seemed, beggars—many of them maimed, emaciated, and appearing weak and ill—reached out for much-needed help. Fiona covered her eyes with her own hands, but she couldn't rid herself of the image of so many grasping hands, some with missing digits, of so many lame children, their barely clothed bodies covered in dust, dirt, and open sores.

Pop peeled Fiona's fingers from her face and enclosed them in his own. Fiona's parents had told her about poverty in America, but this was different. This was in her face. Unforgettable.

India's poverty could eat America's poverty for lunch and still starve.

~oO0O0Oo~

Their new home was a simple apartment by American standards, but it seemed palatial in comparison to the poverty they'd just witnessed. The exterior façade was braced by a rather ornate metal tracery, painted white, which served as adornment and security. Their friends, who'd been living in New Delhi for nearly a year, had seen to it that the family was provided the rare three-bedroom, furnished apartment. Fiona had her own room, as did her parents, while Holly and Violet shared a room. This suited everyone just fine, although Fiona wouldn't have minded the reassuring company of her little sisters.

The apartment was appointed with modern '60s furniture, mostly teak, softened by colorful cushions, and a wicker swing chair hanging from the ceiling in the living room. It had bright windows overlooking a surprisingly lush maidan, or park. Gratefully, it had something called a swamp cooler hanging off one window, to counteract the searing heat Fiona could feel emanating from all the windows at mid-day. And, it had a modest but bright, fully equipped kitchen. Fiona made a snap decision to stay inside the cool apartment for the entire year.

As the day darkened into evening, Fiona went into the kitchen, where she met Mukta, the cook, for the first time. "You can call me Auntie, Auntie Mukta, or just Mukta." Mukta called out, smiling. Mukta had whipped up some eggs and dal—a curried lentil sauce over rice. Fiona wasn't sure about Mukta at first, but she seemed pleasant enough, and she'd made a delicious dinner. After finishing their meal, she and her sisters were shooed off to brush their teeth and get ready for bed. Moments later, as Pop tucked her in, Fiona asked, "How come we have a servant, since this place is so poor? And why are so many kids crippled and sick?"

"We haven't got a servant. Heavens, Fee!" answered Wolf, taken aback by the idea. "We have simply hired a cook, and by doing that, we're freeing your Mum up for teaching while giving someone a good income. And I have no good answer for why so many of the world's kids are crippled and sick. There are bad answers, like when people aren't fair. And also, disease plays a part."

"Like, leprosy?" Fiona asked, shuddering.

"You don't have to fear that. The kids we're teaching don't have it. They've just got poverty, and that's not contagious. I'd give you a book on leprosy, but quite frankly, we still don't know all that much about it. It's hard to study, since it doesn't like to grow in a petri dish. What we do know is that sufferers stop being able to feel pain, and hurt themselves without knowing it. Can you see how pain is useful as a signal? Maybe that'll help, next time you hurt." He was referring to physical pain but alluding to emotional pain. Without waiting for a reply, Pop turned out the light and quietly closed the door.

Fiona closed her eyes, shifting her sight from the dark, unfamiliar space to her own pretty bedroom at home. She wasn't so sure she liked feelings. Especially not the ones in her tummy. It didn't feel quite right.

An hour or so into their slumber, something began to cause the entire family gastric distress. Diagnosis: Delhi Belly. They could have picked it up at the airport, or from the delicious sugarcane juice they'd tried. It was inevitable. The local bacteria, to which people become adjusted wherever they live, were different in Delhi from those their bodies knew and accepted in Providence, half a world away. They spent the rest of that night and the whole of the next week in the bathroom, alternating between vomiting and diarrhea. Mum was particularly worried about the children, and worked hard to keep them hydrated. Pop was worried about Mum, who was as sick as the rest of them but keeping vigil over everyone else.

Pop or, at least his sense of humor, seemed to be the least affected by the bacteria. "No choice but to go with the flow, folks." Fiona, who usually humored her father with a comeback, was in no shape to retort. But, Pop was right. They had no choice but to ride it through. The three girls spent each afternoon, lying tummy down on the living room floor under the breeze of the swamp cooler as it belched out cold, wet air, making the floor cool and damp and inviting. Once Fiona was feeling a little better, she climbed into the wicker swing chair that hung from a heavy metal chain anchored to the ceiling, and twirled a bit, in another act of self-soothing.

On the evening of the first day the family felt reasonably settled in and recovered from their jetlag and Delhi Belly, a meteor shower came through the inky sky, lighting the night. The family climbed up onto the roof to watch. As they lay on their backs, in the cooling air, they breathed a little easier, studying the shooting stars—so many flashing by, Fiona lost count. Maybe India wasn't so bad, she decided. Parts of it were crummy, yes, but this part was pretty cool.

Meanwhile, Mukta settled into a gentle menu, filled with plain dal and naan that everyone enjoyed, to keep the family healthy and feeling well. Fiona particularly liked the lassis, which reminded her of yogurt shakes, only less sweet. They also added probiotics to their daily regimen to try to keep the "good" bacteria strong. Because of their well-founded fears of eating the wrong thing, the family rarely ate out. When they wanted a beverage because of the heat, Mukta suggested Coca-Cola, a safe bet that could, perhaps, aid digestion as well. "Try to buy it frozen." Mukta suggested. "Let it melt as you go."

In time, their tummies adjusted, and the family grew a little more adventuresome. They headed out to the marketplace. Fiona took in the bazaar with its yards of raw-silk fabric on display, and trays of open spices, creating a festival of colors and smells for her senses. She also was fascinated by the array of animals, some for sale, and many that were wandering around, loose, among the crowds. Right away, Fiona spotted a sweet-looking little spider monkey, and made her way over to it. Drawn to the dear face of the beautiful animal, Fiona felt sorry for this creature who was tethered to his perch. She extended her hand toward him, only to have it promptly bitten. "Ow! Stupid monkey!"

Mum turned around at Fiona's outburst. "Everything okay, Fee?"

Offended by the monkey's rebuff of her kind gesture, Fiona assuaged herself by deciding the animal had assumed she had something to feed him. "I'm okay." But was she? She wondered. She'd been bitten by a monkey at a bazaar in India. How bizarre was that? Fiona laughed, despite herself. She examined her finger, turning red and a little blue at the site, but it wasn't bleeding, was it? That can't be bad, she thought, weighing her options. She'd read enough about rabies to know the disease was deadly, but she had heard bad things about the shots. Didn't rabies treatment mean huge needles in your stomach? No, thank you! She thought back to all those shots she'd already had, before the trip. That was enough of that, she decided. Anyway, he's just a pet. If he belongs to someone, he can't possibly be sick, she told herself, wrongly. That was closer to what she wanted to believe than what might be true.

Mum and the girls once again dared to try the local sugarcane juice from street vendors. Fiona thought to herself, If I'm dying of rabies, who cares anyway? The next few days, she checked her mouth for foam. Nope. No rabies.

Although most of the family rallied, little Holly's "Delhi Belly" lingered and worsened. Mukta took it personally, and had been fretting about what she could do for her young charge. She awoke one morning with the idea that some chai tea would help.

Mukta's chai was so delicious, and so very different from the warm chai tea that locals sold to passengers at train stops. The train-stop chai tasted a bit like unfired clay, or maybe simply of sun-dried mud. Holly loved it, but she loved Mukta's best. Somehow, consuming a hot drink made the hot day feel cooler.

Mukta lightly crushed the cinnamon stick, placing her strong fist on the flat of the knife and banging it sharply. Taking the ginger and grating it into the sauce pan, Mukta set the water to boil gently. The cinnamon, ginger, and water made the house smell heavenly. She picked up the saucepan and brought it to the doorway, waving her hand over the brew to help the scent carry. She was hoping the smell could reach Holly in the other room where she was already lying on the floor, tummy down, swamp cooler full blast, letting the cool floor soothe her aching tummy. Poor thing!

Fifteen minutes later, the brew had steeped, and Mukta was crushing 14 green cardamom pods, adding them to the reduced liquid, along with strong black Assam tea. A few minutes later, adding some milk, she said a prayer that the mixture would bring healing. In India, cooks were hired for their loving hearts as much as for their culinary prowess. Mukta had both. As the chai began to froth, at just the perfect moment before it boiled, she took it off the heat. As she let it sit, the smell filled the house. Holly called in, "Smells good, Auntie Mukta!" Mukta smiled as she strained a cup for her dear one. There was plenty for all her young charges.

Later that week, the family would head to the hospital for an X-ray, hoping to find the cause of Holly's continuing woes and get a treatment plan. Until then, this was the only thing Mukta could think to do, to help: give comfort and sustenance. It was no small gift.

Still afraid of the local spicy food, Fiona preferred sweets over the savory fare. Before long, this added up to a cavity, necessitating a trip to a dentist. The dentist took a look and decided the tooth had to come out. If there was Novocain around town, the dentist didn't think it would be important for the extraction of a baby tooth. Fiona disagreed, and cried out in pain as he began pulling. She couldn't enunciate with all the tools in her mouth, but she made herself very clear anyway. "SHTTOPPPPP!!! OWWWW!" she screeched through the dental equipment, attempting to wriggle out of the chair. It worked, for a time. The dentist signaled to Mum and the assistant, and they left the room. Good, Fiona thought, maybe we can leave.

The dentist and his assistant conferred with Mum, and they decided the tooth had to go in one quick yank. Fiona cried out as he wrenched out her tooth without warning. The scream was woven with more than pain; it revealed a terror Mum couldn't take. With a loud crash, she hit the floor, taking the dental assistant to the floor with her. Mum was out cold, the assistant was wriggling beneath her, and Fiona remained in her chair, quivering, her tooth in the dentist's pliers, bloody and gleaming. The dentist was shaken. So was his assistant who, having regained her footing, was trying to figure out what to do. Neither the dentist, nor his assistant, had ever had anyone faint in their office, and they couldn't have imagined it would be the parent instead of the patient. An American parent, at that. Fiona watched and wondered why they were acting like Mum was untouchable.

That afternoon, as Fiona wrapped her tooth in a note for the Tooth Fairy, Pop distracted her from playing with the new hole in her mouth by talking about the history of doctors, dentists, and barbers. He told her how, in some smaller towns, the owner of the local pharmacy or barber shop also dispensed dental and health care, and how the barber pole's red-and-white-and-blue stripes represented blood, bandages, and veins, from a time when the barbers also were the town surgeons. Back then, not much was known about the spread of disease. That got Fiona curious about what had made her family sick. She didn't want to get sick again. With that, Pop waxed poetic about bacteria, mold, fungi, cheese, pickling, and how, when refrigeration was limited, spices can be used to keep food from going bad and to mask the terrible taste of food that has gone off. "No wonder I don't like spicy food," Fiona said to herself, adding, "Do you have any books for me on this, Pop?" As Fiona began borrowing books again, she started to feel a little more at home and a little less lost. With each book that migrated into her bedroom, Fiona became more and more comfortable in her new destination of discovery.

~oO0O0Oo~

"Clang, clang!" The bell echoed down the road. It could be heard for miles. A water buffalo looked up lazily and then returned its gaze downward again; school wasn't for him. But the children came running from every direction. The school lay outside the town center and served a dozen or so local children, as well as about five American kids. Fiona's parents' dream—the forward-thinking school for the untouchables—was being called to session. It was called, "Yes, of Course!"

The name was a bit of word play, a pun on the courses taught in school. It was also optimistic. Of course, women; of course, widows; of course, the children of poverty! They referred to it simply as "The

School," and it offered a practical education based on the philosophy that nurture trumped nature. It was your environment, Wolf and Hanna believed, that mattered most, not your background or caste. Since that philosophy flew in the face of local tradition, the school's savvy local sponsors kept the rhetoric at a minimum. The printed literature in Hindi spoke only of helping the poorest, for charity's sake. Had the city of New Delhi truly understood the founders' aims, would they have allowed them to open and operate...of course? They decided it was best not to test the question.

Although the school offered such interesting and productive classes as yoga and gardening, there wasn't much that was challenging, academically. Sometimes Fiona and her sisters helped the other kids pronounce English words, but mostly they amused themselves by playing with the animals in the school's mini zoo and the local wildlife, also quite accessible on the school grounds. Lizards darted everywhere, and Fiona became quite adept at catching them, particularly when they slowed down to sun themselves on warm rocks.

Fiona's parents gave her a terrarium, and she started keeping a few lizards as pets. "If you pick them up carefully, behind their ears and then turn them and rub their tummies, gently, with one finger," she told Holly, "they get hypnotized, and you can put them in your hair, where they'll stay." Fiona called them her "pet barrettes," and she liked coming up behind Mukta and scaring her with her latest lizard hairdo. Mukta pressed her hand to her heart, every single time, before breaking out in laughter. From the way she keeps doing that, Fiona thought, I get the feeling she'll never to get used to these little guys.

Some lizards were so big and fast, she could only watch them, in wonderment. Look at this brown one, Fiona mused. He's slower. She set herself about catching him, and healing him. She named him Tarzan and decided to nurse him back to health by keeping him cool and quiet, and feeding him bugs. It worked, and he turned green again—for a few days. When he died, she found a little spot for him, out by the old stone fence, and covered him in rocks.

The next day, as she went to put a flower on his grave, Fiona found Tarzan gone. Her friends ran to tell the teachers. Later, Pop asked her what she thought had happened. She shared that he'd probably just made a nice snack for one of the many local vultures on the property. "Right you are." Pop agreed. "Circle of life, and nothing more. What's dead stays dead. Period. Remember that." Fiona made a mental note. Dead is dead. Check. Next subject?

Fiona's fascination with the local wildlife kept her amused, but it made Pop nervous. He didn't mind her love of lizards, but he lost his cool when she tried to rescue a baby bat from a puddle, using a stick and not worrying about whether bats carry rabies. And he lost it again when she came running to him with news of her discovery of "the cutest little rock lobsters" under a rock. How was she supposed to know what scorpions were, if nobody told her?

Pop, who worried that Fiona's interest in animals might lead her to a one-on-one encounter with a tiger cub, a vulture, or maybe a wild pig, tried to redirect her curiosity, inviting her to turn her attention toward ants. These creatures were big and black and plentiful in Delhi. For a while, she was fascinated by their industry in the sandy loam as they moved in and out of their anthill. But, they soon lost their charm.

"Bugs are boring, Pop."

"Did you know, Fee, you can harness the sun to set an ant on fire?"

"That's horrible, Pop."

"On the contrary, it's actually quite interesting. You simply use the convex shape of a magnifying glass to concentrate the energy of the sun."

Fiona wondered if Pop would have been happier with a little boy. Boys liked bugs. She just liked snakes and lizards. She wanted to please her Pop, so she quieted her objections as he pulled a dime-store magnifying glass out of his pocket and extended it to her. "Here, Fee; let's try it."

"Um, not me." Fiona just couldn't bring herself to burn the poor thing. Pop, who wasn't about to let go of a teachable moment, focused his lens on one ant. Sure enough, within a couple of seconds, the ant started smoking. The worst part, Fiona thought, was the sound of the sizzle. Pop asked if she wanted to try it using a twig instead of an ant. She did, and it worked. "It's a good trick to keep in your bag," said Pop, "in case you ever need to start a fire and don't have a match." Fiona, who wondered if she'd be more likely to have a match or a magnifying glass on hand, asked simply, "Ants optional. Right, Pop?"

As Pop headed back to the main classroom, laughing, Fiona returned her attention to the larger, more interesting creatures around her. She couldn't understand her father's connection with ants, or his fear for her safety around more interesting creatures. *I'm a responsible person. And I've never run into an animal that did me wrong. Okay, except for the monkey bite. That darn monkey. Lizards, too; lizards are okay. But not bats or rock lobsters. I already know how to stay clear of those. Lobsters and monkeys and bats. Oh, my!*

~oOoOoOo~

As life settled into a comfortable rhythm, the family made friends in the neighborhood, and began sharing dinners together. And then, the invitations began arriving, to Holi and Diwali parties, birthdays, and even the wedding for a neighbor's daughter. Sheetal, the 15-year-old bride, was a lovely girl. Fiona was dazzled by her dark, mysterious beauty. Besides, she had learned that Sheetal meant "cool," which Fiona imagined must mean she was especially cool. Invited to the third and last day of the traditional Indian wedding, the main ceremony for the couple's wider circle of friends, Fiona's family was abuzz as they headed to the nearby bazaar to hunt for an appropriate gift for Sheetal and her intended, Kumar.

As the family made their way down the center aisle of the bazaar, Mum found an ornately decorated keepsake box the bride and groom could fill with mementos from their wedding. One row over, Fiona spied a beautiful doll dressed in a deep-blue sari, which reminded her of the bride-to-be. She leaned against the stall, counting her coins. There weren't enough. She gave the doll a last, wistful glance, and started eyeing the plastic bindi kits. The one she liked best had many wells of colorful bindi, arranged in a circle, with a clear plastic top for easy viewing. Mum smiled, and picked up four, one for each of them. Mum promised to help them each create the perfect mark in the middle of their forehead, in just the right color to match their saris. That was their next splurge: saris for Mum and her three girls, each with its matching petticoat and t-shirt-like choli. The petticoats, which formed the base, were the first step to dressing. They weren't ankle-length, but the saris would be, once correctly wrapped round the body. Then came the yards of delicious, soft, translucent silk. Fiona's was red and had a tie dye pattern. The family returned home with their packages, just in time to prepare themselves for the wedding feast.

Mukta began the slow, careful work of helping them dress in their saris, wanting them to look just right. She started with Fiona, wrapping the length of silk fabric once around Fiona's skirt. She then tucked it under the wrap. Using much of the remaining fabric, she next made pleats, like a fan, and slipped the edge into the waist. Then, she encircled Fiona's body with fabric and draped the remaining length around her neck, securing it with a brooch, and letting the rest cascade down her back. Fiona was beginning to feel almost majestic.

Mukta returned her attention to the fabric that wrapped Fiona's body, and proceeded to pleat the fabric before pinning it to her left side. Fiona couldn't wriggle out of this if she tried. Mukta helped Holly next, then Vi, and then Mum. If it hadn't been for Mukta's help, they'd have been like boys trying to negotiate the ends of their first neckties, not knowing how much fabric to leave. Dressing up is so complicated, Fiona thought, especially when it involved a sari. Pop, dressed in a dapper gray suit and a bold orange tie, admired his family. Taking Mum's arm, they headed for the door. The wedding wasn't far. As they turned the corner a block away, the unmistakable smell of orange marigold garlands told them they didn't have far to go.

They took their place in the crowd just as the bride and groom were about to arrive. Traditional Indian music rang out, and everyone danced for joy as the couple made their way through the crowd, surrounded by a large group of reveling family members.

The bride was so beautiful; Fiona found her transformation

gasp-worthy. Gone was the next-door teen she'd giggled with over dinner. The goddess of beauty seemed to have stepped in and taken her place. Draped in yards of white silk with delicate gold embroidery, and adorned in layers of gold necklaces, bracelets, and a pair of weighty chandelier earrings, she looked like a storybook princess. Her glossy black hair was smooth under her head shawl, and her hairline was edged in a gold braid, from which hung an ornamental bindi of gold and gemstones. Her delicate hands were covered in mehndi, painted on for the event. The ancient body art, made from dry henna, was likely to last a month or longer. The transformation was much more than skin-deep tattooing. Much more, and much deeper. Fiona felt it and wanted it. How do I transform like that? Look at that chain going from her nose ring to her earring. Oh, I want that!

Fiona thought back to when she'd asked Pop for a nose piercing. Back home, nobody in Pop's circles had a tattoo or a pierced nose, and many adult women even went without pierced ears. His "No!" had been so intense, the finality of it had nearly banished the thought. But not quite. She knew he felt tattoos were for "sailors and jailors," but mehndi was surely different, wasn't it? And anyway, it was temporary. At least he'd agreed to let her pierce her ears, for her next birthday. As Fiona looked at Sheetal, marveling at her transformation, a man in the crowd smiled at Fiona and said, "Perhaps you are next, eh, little one?"

Fiona looked at the man's face and then at her father, shocked. At nearly nine, she wasn't quite two-thirds of Sheetal's age, though if she'd been decked out the same way, she might have looked marriageable, too. This got Fiona to thinking how she didn't want to be married off when she was 15, either. "I'm not even 9, Pop," Fiona said. "Isn't that illegal or something?"

"You mean, would you be a child bride? Well kiddo, child bride is what I'd call an oxymoron. My hope is the practice will end someday, with new perspectives, and maybe an act of Parliament." He looked at his daughter. "But meanwhile, don't worry about what that old fool said. Your old Pop isn't planning on packing you off until you're 70. Okay, maybe 50. And I expect you'll want some say in the matter." He winked, and wandered off to find some food, leaving

Fiona with her thoughts.

Hanna picked up where Pop had left off. She told Fiona how her college friend, Adhita, had come back to Delhi after graduating cum laude, and been very happy by herself for two years before marrying at 24. "Tsk!" clucked a woman to Mum's right. "I pity her poor father. Oh, the dowry for a girl with too much education." She shook her head. Hanna, not wanting to stir up trouble at a wedding, excused herself with a parting word, "Speaking of husbands, I need to go find mine and have some food. Girls, come along now." Pop was in line, with the other men, waiting to take his dinner. Eventually, the women and children were served. Fiona thought, that's backwards. In shipwrecks, lifeboats are filled, women and children first. It might not be fair either, but it's so noble and heroic.

Fiona was pleased to discover that, although the lamb was gone, there was still some butter chicken, and there were still plenty of Gulab Jamun dessert balls left, drenched in syrup. When she finally got to the table, Pop put some of his lamb on her plate. "Finally! I was wondering when you'd get through those lines." he said. Then, he noticed Mum, fuming. "I know you find it weird, and so do I, but maybe women are empowered in Indian culture in ways we don't yet fully grasp. It's so patently obvious that girls and boys are equal that I bet just we don't know the whole cultural story. How could we, right?" He looked over to Mum, who nodded, and continued. "What I do know is that tonight, we're here as guests. Not every moment is a moment for protest."

In the days that followed, Fiona began noticing how men and women behaved with each other. Sometimes, the women trailed behind the men, as they walked. Other times, Fiona noticed, the woman of the household served her husband and guests, but quietly ate her meal, alone in the kitchen while the husband entertained company. Maybe Pop was right, in some other way she didn't see, women came first. I'll keep looking, but so far, what I see isn't for me, Fiona decided. If I ever get married, I'll just be a dreadful cook. That way nobody will get the wrong idea, and banish me into the kitchen, like Auntie Mukta. And anyway, I'll be back in the states. My guy will cook great. Every day for dessert he'll whip me up a Baked Alaska, just like the ones at The Cellar restaurant, but with real American ice cream. I do miss American ice cream. The Cellar Restaurant was a family favorite. They served up beef burgers, the Beatles, and Baked Alaska flambé.

Just when Fiona was feeling particularly desperate for a taste of home, it came in the form of family. Gram arrived in Delhi for a visit. A woman of style, Gram was staying at the sophisticated Oberoi hotel, where Fiona and her sisters got to meet her for tea, wearing their pretty saris. The children hadn't ever seen a hotel so beautiful, with its soaring angular architecture and floor-to-ceiling windows separated by mirrored columns, and the biggest swimming pool they'd ever laid eyes on. As soon as they saw their grandmother, the girls ran into her arms for a big hug. Then, they settled down to their tea and cakes in the elegant lounge, while Mum and Gram caught up with each other.

After a while, Fiona asked Gram if she'd take her to the rest-room, her curiosity and desire to see it more pressing than her need to use it. Having expected it to be opulent, Fiona was disappointed to find the restroom was rather ordinary, kind of like the one in their apartment, only larger. Still, it was much nicer than some she'd seen. Back in the lounge, the subject stayed on bathrooms. Fiona had some sage advice that she needed to share. "Gram, bring toilet paper when you go places. Sometimes there isn't any. Sometimes, you think it's a bathroom but it's just a floor, and a little ditch. And Gram, if you don't have paper, sometimes people use their left hand."

"Well, I don't think I'll be visiting remote outposts, but I'll make sure I'm ready for anything."

"Are you going to the Taj Mahal, Gram?" Violet asked. "One time a buzzard stole my sandwich right out of my left hand there. My hand was clean, though. And then I had a birthday party. You get there by mule, and I rode the whole way myself! It's at the foot of these mountains."

"The foothills of the Himalayas?" Gram laughed. "Your mom wrote me about that trip. I'll bet not too many young women in this world can claim that!"

Holly, not wanting to be left out, added her own riding story, about how, during one of her weekly lessons at the Delhi Children's Riding Club, a pony named Mushroom had taken off down the Delhi streets, with Holly still on his back. Holly described it all, breathlessly. "My word, that's quite a mushroom you rode, Holly, I'm so proud of you!" Gram laughed. "And in the English style, I don't doubt. It's only been 25 years since India's independence from Great Britain, after all. My, oh my, how you girls have grown. And I hear that you're studying dance as well?"

"We are, Gram! We're learning Ga-duck! Want me to teach you?" Violet piped up, about Khatakali—Khatak for short—a traditional Indian dance and classical art form from Kerala, a state on India's tropical Malabar Coast. The dance was a mixture of theater, dance, ballet, masque, and pantomime—and Fiona and her sisters were the only Americans in a class taught in Hindi.

"Maybe later," Gram smiled, slightly overwhelmed at the prospect.

"Gram, wait, do you like clover?" Fiona told Gram how she had discovered a hill covered in clover, with the best little frogs, bright green, hopping among them, under the shade of a walnut tree. There, she came upon a section covered with four-leaf clovers. She was so excited, she wrote a poem! Gram asked if she remembered it and could recite it for her.

"Oh yes, Gram." Said Fiona, eagerly diving in. "I once knew a place where clovers grew four leaves or five, but never three."

"Did not." Holly chimed in. After a brief did-not / did-too exchange between Fiona, Holly, and Violet, Fiona continued with her poem. "Happily, I was a clover, too, and that field was part of me. Now in this field, where clovers are so few and very hard to find, if ever four leaves could give you joy, I'd gladly give you mine. The end."

Everyone clapped as Fiona took a grand bow. "Thank you, thank you ever so much." Then, Gram gave Fiona a hug and suggested Fiona go over to the lobby desk and request a pen and paper, so she could write down her poem for Gram to take home with her. Fiona dutifully got up and went in search of the writing materials, returning shortly with enough for her sisters, as well. While the three girls played with their pens and paper, Mum and Gram took another moment to talk about grown-up matters.

When their visit was over, the girls and their mum said goodbye to Gram and told her they looked forward to seeing her at dinner the following day. It was high noon, and most folks around town agreed with playwright Noel Coward—that only mad dogs and Englishmen ventured out at that time of day. Maybe Americans, too. It was so very hot, Mum could hardly think. Should she call for a car? Take a rickshaw? The girls spied a public fountain. "Oh, pleeeeeazzz, Mummmmy!" Mum hardly had time to say yes. They were already kicking off their sandals and skipping around in the refreshing water, splashing one another with glee. And then, Fiona felt a sharp pain in her foot and looked down to see a swirl of blood coloring the water. She had cut her foot very badly on an unseen shard of glass. The sight of blood swirling, combined with the heat of the afternoon, made Hanna swoon.

Just then, an Indian gentleman happened by. "My good-ness, memsahib, are you quite well?" He was dressed in a cream linen jacket, with a pale blue pocket square in his breast pocket that matched his tie perfectly. Gently grabbing Hanna's arm, he steadied her. Once she was seated safely on the edge of the fountain, he lifted Fiona out of the water, placed her next to her mum, and then pulled out the pocket square and handed it to Hanna, who pressed it against Fiona's bleeding foot. "Alas, little princess, it seems you've found one of Delhi's hidden dangers," he said to her. "Best to keep your sandals on in this world, I dare say, unless you are sleeping, naturally." He winked at Fiona and then turned to hail a bicycle rickshaw driver. With a nod of approval from Hanna, he picked up Fiona and depos-ited her in the rickshaw, next to her sisters, who had scrambled in ahead of her. He offered his hand to help Hanna into the rickshaw, who managed to give him a weak thank you before turning to give directions to the driver to proceed to the pediatrician's office. She was still feeling quite faint.

"Jaldijal, jaldijal!" (faster, faster!) Mum called out, as they sped along the crowded street, weaving in and out of cars, pedestrians, and bicycles, en route to the doctor's office. Watching the passersby took Fiona's mind off her throbbing foot. Peering out of the open side of the rickshaw, Fiona noticed something funny. "Hey guys, check it out. She's wearing only underwear." Some tourist had bought the underpinnings of a sari and, thinking of them as a lightweight skirt and tee, had decided to wear them, on their own. Poor thing, Fiona thought, she doesn't know she's walking around nearly naked. In under a year, she was beginning to see things from an Indian perspective. Then, her mind turned to the absolute stranger who'd just stepped in to help, and the expensive handkerchief he'd given up. As it did, she looked down at her foot, bringing the pain into sharp focus again. She winced. Mum noticed, and decided a distraction was needed.

"Fiona," Mum began. "You've inspired me to write a story. Indialla and the Glass Shard. Our heroine is Indialla. Exhausted from hours of hard labor in the hot sun, Indialla wades in to the fountain of expectation where she promptly cuts her foot on a shard of her shattered dream."

"That's not such a happy tale, Mum" Fiona objected. "I don't think kids will like it very much." Fiona had picked up on Mum's unspoken mood through her story and her voice. Mum didn't have much heart for happy fairy tales, today. Trouble was brewing at home, though she didn't say so. All wasn't right between Mum and her prince charming.

"It's right in line with German fairy tales I grew up with," Mum continued gamely, "Did I ever read you any of the Struwwelpeter stories, back in Providence?"

"Are those the ones with the kid with his head in the clouds who falls into the ocean and drowns, and the thumb-sucker whose thumbs get cut off, and the kid who plays with matches and the next thing you know all that's left are the cats, crying over the burnt-out house, and stuff?"

"The very same. I see they made an impression. Not all fairy tales end happily, but I see that you kids want a happy ending for Indialla. Am I right?" All three kids nodded, so Mum added how a charming stranger was out for a ride on his flying carpet, high above the traffic, so he swooped down and offered her a lift. He delivered her right to the doctor, where soon she was good as new again."

"He really was a nice guy, and we forgot to ask his name," Fiona said, as they arrived at the doctor's office. "It's okay," Mum replied. "He knows we're thankful. Some people come into our lives for the briefest of moments, and are better friends than others you've known for years." Fiona looked down at his blue handkerchief, now mostly red, as she continued to press it against her foot. *Too bad I can't give the man his pocket square back again, and thank him.* She watched as the doctor dumped the nice man's handkerchief into the bin. She didn't need stitches, just a painful antiseptic cleansing, followed by a thick layer of healing balm, and a good gauze wrap.

The doctor gave Mum extra ointment to spread across the cut whenever she changed the dressing. Then she took the sweet-smelling string of little jasmine flowers that were tied into her own hair, and tied it into Fiona's, with a gentle smile. "You'll be feeling better soon, dear one." On the way home, the increasingly familiar smells—now spice, now sewer, now smoke—mingled with the scent of jasmine, and melded into something almost delightful and, at this point in her difficult day, ineffable. Usually very talkative, Fiona found she had no words to describe the diversity of feelings she had experienced, so she just let herself relax in the rickshaw and float along the fragrance.

That night, at bedtime, Fiona decided she needed something really fascinating, to take her mind off her foot, which had started to throb again. She picked up a comic book about the Hindu god Krishna. In this one, beautiful Mirabai was headed into the river to drown herself, having displeased her husband, but Lord Krishna arrived and came to her rescue. *I've heard about telling someone to go jump in the lake before,* Fiona thought, *but I've never heard of anybody listening. She's just nuts. People are so weird!*

Pop came in to kiss Fiona goodnight, and told her she should think about going to sleep, soon. She promised she would, but stayed up another hour or so, reading. Late in the evening, she heard a tapping sound, "ta tappy, ta tappy, ta tappy, ta tappy..." outside her window. Pop had taught her that the now-familiar sound meant simply, "All is well." At night, in their neighborhood, a special private security guard wandered the streets, making that rhythmic tapping sound with his sticks, to reassure residents. Despite their many mishaps, Fiona was beginning to feel India wasn't so bad, after all. Besides, Mum had said that calamities come in threes. After their food poisoning, her disaster at the dentist, and now, her sliced foot, she liked imagining only good times ahead. Forgetting all about Mum's melancholy tone that afternoon, when she finally closed her book, she slipped off into a deep, restful slumber.

~oOOOOOo~

The long rope was pulled taut with a loud, creaking sound and then, "Snap!" Suddenly, they found themselves rising into the air, weightless. All was silence, as Fiona looked down at the sights becoming smaller, below. Tucked into a glider, she and Pop were excited to see the city from above. They were soaring, physically, and she was soaring, too, in her heart. In this moment, she felt free, unburdened and really, really, head-to-toe happy, as happy as she'd ever been. Delhi is beautiful, she marveled. And it was, if you could rise above it, and see it in its full glory. She gazed in awestruck wonder as Pop pointed out the familiar landmarks she had seen from the ground, usually by rickshaw though crowded streets. From up above, the place appeared magical.

To the left, Fiona saw the green, where they'd been to the baseball game and had watched their new friends put up a good fight, before losing to the visiting team. Off to the right, Pop pointed out what they'd taken to calling the "foot-eating fountain" after Fiona's mishap with the shard of glass. Fiona noticed a cow in the street, holding up traffic. They laughed, knowing the drivers wouldn't dare hit it. Was that the cow she'd tried to ride while the grown-ups weren't looking? She'd hadn't told Pop what she'd done at the time, so she bit her lip and said nothing.

The glider banked, and took them right over the bazaar, where she'd been so many times. Fiona could barely make out the vivid yards of silk fabric, the colorful trays of spices, and the pots of fresh flowers, seeing them as an abstraction of themselves from the air. She could almost smell the open spices and fragrant flowers, mostly in her memory. She remembered the spider monkey, the one she was glad didn't have rabies.

A few moments later, Fiona looked down and to the right, and was sure she could make out the Delhi Children's Riding Club. Then, Pop pointed out their apartment, and Fiona noticed the gardens where she and her sisters often played, unsupervised, but safe. The glider pilot pointed out Lal Quila. She remembered visiting the Red Fort monument with her family. Fiona also spied her dance school, where she was studying Khatakali. Fiona tapped her feet in an air dance within the glider, "ta, tay, tay, tut…" Now, she was a sky dancer. Could anything be as wonderful?

Fiona was on such a high, she forgot she was an earthbound creature who couldn't really fly. No matter how free she felt at that moment. Before they turned toward land, the sky darkened briefly, as the glider came under the shadow of a cumulonimbus storm cloud. Fiona hadn't noticed it before. A chill went up her back. They were descending. The ground was very close now. There was no transcending gravity. The illusion of being unbounded from earth's cares had been lost. What comes up, must come down. Always.

The pilot glided to a soft landing, and Fiona and Pop eased themselves out of the glider and shook out their legs to steady themselves on the earth again. As the heat settled into her skin, and the noise of the city invaded her ears, she found she already missed the freedom of flight and the chance to be lifted, up and out, above it all. If only for a moment.

~o0O0O0o~

The family had been adjusting to life in India for more than a year. Just when Fiona had finally found the rhythm, the song was changing. One morning, shortly after her glider adventure, Fiona came out of her bedroom, dressed and anticipating one of Mukta's hearty breakfasts, which she and Holly and Violet ate together before heading to school. But, they were nowhere to be found. Mum wasn't anywhere about, either. Fiona found the cook in the kitchen, but otherwise, she was alone.

"Good morning, Auntie Mukta! Where is everyone?" she asked, seating herself at the counter.

"You'd better ask that of your father, Miss," answered Mukta, averting her eyes.

"They're gone, Fee. Everyone's gone," said Pop, coming into the room. "They've left."

"What do you mean, left? On a walk? To the market?"

"They've gone for good, Fee; I don't know where."

"Without us? Without warning? But, why?" Fiona slid off the kitchen stool and ran out the door and down the stairs, to see if she could catch them. To see if she could get a glimpse of her family before they abandoned her. But there was nothing. No one.

Some life events seem to stop time, for just a moment, or much more than a moment, as if everything is suspended, hanging there between what was and what will be. Fiona, caught in that crossroads, stood in the dirt at the bottom of the stairs, motionless, not noticing the lizards skittering by, the peacock in the trees, or the Hume's Warbler on the lowest branch, just overhead. For a moment, even Fiona ceased to exist.

The clock began again, and sounds of life returned to the air when Pop placed a gentle hand on Fiona's shoulder. "They're long gone, Fee."

"Is that the best you can do? They're gone? What happened, Pop? What kind of fight could you have had with Mum to make her pack up Holly and Vi and split?"

Fiona looked her father straight in the eye, but all she saw there was sadness. He said nothing and simply went inside. Fiona kicked the dirt for a moment. She trudged up the stairs and back into the house to brush her teeth. But there was no toothbrush for her. Wow, Mum must have really left fast, to just grab and run, Fiona thought. I know she'll bring it back when she and my sisters come back.

Mukta promised to get her another toothbrush by evening.

Even more surprising than Mum's unexpected exodus with Holly and Violet was that, for the next week, no one even mentioned them. And Pop had nothing to offer about what would happen next. And then a letter arrived for Fiona from Mum, which explained nothing about what had happened.

17 January, 1972

Dear Fiona,

How are you? I hope everything is going well in New Delhi. Holly and Violet miss you a lot. I do, too. Whenever we see anything interesting, Holly wishes you could be here to see it. We found shoulder bags like Holly's and Vi's, so we got one for you. I'm sorry we took your toothbrush by mistake. Please ask someone to buy you a new one, and remember to use it twice a day. Also, brush your hair every morning. We are staying at an ashram, or religious retreat. Nearby is a city, a new city, called Pondicherry, where people from all over the world are trying to live together in peace and unity. We will visit there soon, and we will write to tell you about it. Its name is Auroville, after Sri Aurobindo, who started the ashram. We miss you, Fee.

We hope to see you soon.

Love, Mum

"We *hope* to see you, soon? We *hope*?" Fiona folded the letter neatly and slid it into its envelope. Is Mum over 30? she wondered. Don't trust anyone over 30. Or maybe, don't trust anyone who leaves you—abandons you—without saying goodbye.

Fiona pulled the letter back out of its envelope, having decided to read it again. She got all the way through the newsy letter, written as if nothing had happened, but got stuck on the last line, "Love, Mum." What kind of love is that? Fiona didn't see or feel love in any of this. In fact, this was the absence of love.

Love doesn't sneak out during the night and take your toothbrush. Love doesn't leave without saying goodbye. Not in the middle of a foreign country. Not anywhere. No. Love doesn't take your little sisters from you. That's not love. That's not what I'd do to *my* kid, Fiona thought. Mum didn't leave Holly and Vi, so why leave me? Oh, wait. I forgot. They're her real daughters. I'm not.

Hanna had simply left, like a thief in the night, leaving Fiona believing her love had been a lie. Hanna hadn't thought to mention that it's against the law for a woman without legal custody of a minor to separate that minor from her custodial parent. That's called kidnapping. Hadn't thought to mention whether she might have liked to bring Fiona along. Hadn't mentioned anything about her feelings, unless you counted the signature block. Fiona didn't.

Who needs a mother, anyway? Fiona asked herself, wrapping herself in an armor of anger, steeling herself against the sting of rejection. But her mind kept returning to the clear, inescapable truth: Hanna's not my mum. Not my *real* mum. My mother's about a trillion miles away, with her other real daughter. Where does that leave me? Fiona wondered. In India, alone with Pop. That's where.

At least Holly and Vi are with their mommy, Fiona thought. They're little and they need her. I'm almost 10, so I'm okay. Deciding she was a grown-up was the safest idea she could muster. To admit she still needed to be something else would have taken her down. Truth was, Fiona also could have used a mommy. Because she couldn't have one of her own, to live with, she decided it wasn't that hard for her to go from missing one mother to missing two. It almost didn't hurt very much more, she told herself.

Sitting on her bed with Hanna's letter, Fiona had almost convinced herself she was fine, until Pop wandered in, looking entirely abandoned and forlorn. As she weighed the sadness in his eyes, she decided, right then and there, she wouldn't ask questions. Clearly, this separation was causing him great pain. No, she'd do her best to cheer him up, as chief Sprechelbach clown and cheerleader. She would work hard to distract him from his sorrows, starting now. "It's okay, Pop. Cheer up. I have an idea. Want to play a game of chess?"

~o0O0O0o~

After a week, Wolf and Hanna spoke by phone. Fiona tried to read her father's face, to gauge how the conversation had gone. She decided it must have gone very well, because Pop asked if she might like to join him on a visit to Pondicherry. Fiona, delighted, headed off to pack. Soon, they'd be visiting the other half of their newly broken family, in a distant ashram.

But first, Wolf had to figure out what to do with their school. He had a feeling they wouldn't be returning to it, which left him feeling conflicted. This school had been his dream—their dream—but with Hanna gone, it no longer made sense. Part of their problem, he realized, had been their very different visions for the school. In their dreams and imaginings, they had seemed completely aligned. Yet, in practice, while their beliefs were still in balance, Hanna and Wolf had envisioned very different curricula. Still, he knew this was only part of their problem. And he realized, if his quest to Pondicherry brought them back together, school be damned. What they had begun, someone else could continue. Life with Hanna was more important to him. Way more.

In record time, Wolf handed over the keys to the school, along with all his hopes and dreams for it, to the folks under whose auspices it was formed as a nonprofit school. The keys were accompanied by a bank note to enable the school to continue operating, at least for the time being. There would be other schools and additional dreams to build. Right now, Wolf's task was to build a bridge.

Fiona understood none of this. As they said goodbye to New Delhi, Fiona felt as if she and Pop were on a quest for a holy grail: family togetherness. She was filled with anticipation and laced with a little fear as they boarded the train for the long ride, more than 1,481 miles. Hanna sure went a long way to get away from us, Fiona thought, as she took her seat next to Pop, and pulled out her book. She intended to look out the window a lot, so she could watch where they were going, and experience the trip to remember later. But, she knew she'd need a break from all she was seeing and feeling along the way. That was when she'd read.

The train ride took a couple of days and, even then, it didn't get them all the way to Pondicherry. Late at night, Fiona and Pop had to disembark and take a taxi for the last leg of the trip. With the sun down, the air was fresher, absent the extreme heat of the day. And, with the wind blowing Fiona's hair through the open window of the cab, the 89-degree temperature and high humidity felt delightful—until traffic came toward them. Then, bedlam ensued as drivers tried to negotiate the narrow road without hitting each other, swerving and screaming words Fiona couldn't—and shouldn't—understand.

Pop ensured that Fiona was given the front passenger seat—the only one with a working seatbelt—which was considered a position of honor. In the most-protected seat in the car, she also had a front-row vantage point of strange performance art: the chaotic theater enacted by the other drivers, many of whom seemed headed straight for them. After a while, Fiona started looking out the side window. That was less scary. Through the darkness, she could make out the names of various shops, cafés, and the many roadside worship stations to various deities, many of them festively lit with white or colored lights. Fiona watched swarms of bats, flying past the lights near the eaves of buildings, and swooping into a scourge of mosquitoes. They passed pedestrians, even at this late hour, and carts being pulled through the night by pairs of water buffalo, sometimes in long lines, carrying gravel or other building materials. The drive was a little too much like an amusement-park ride.

Finally arriving in Pondicherry, Fiona felt everything she'd witnessed along the ride recede into a forgotten memory as the scenery shifted into one of the most serene, picturesque towns she'd ever seen: fresh white walls framed perfect flowering gardens, with lizards darting in and among the plantings, illuminated by low-level lighting. The streets were still; the town was sleeping. Except for the lizards. Whenever her heart sank at the thought of her family splitting up, Fiona promised herself she would let the lizards amuse and distract her.

Pondicherry seemed like the perfect place for a family to heal, to knit themselves back into whole cloth. Fiona felt the town was pretty, peaceful, and filled with possibility. She exhaled as she left the cab, replacing anxiety with hope. Fiona's little sisters were asleep when they arrived, so she would have to wait until morning for their reunion. Hanna gave her a long hug and then lifted Fiona's face to look in her eyes, but said nothing, before showing her to the place where she would sleep. Fiona was too tired and too relieved to be there to puzzle her confused mind much, over Hanna and Pop and what might come next. But she did notice that, while Hanna also looked in Pop's eyes for a moment, there was no hug.

For the next few days, Fiona amused herself with her sisters, chasing after lizards, and wandering the property, while Pop apologized for everything he could think of, and made his case to Hanna about why they should be together. Their voices dropped to hushed tones, as they wandered off, to spend time alone, talking.

Then, one afternoon, taking a break from the tension with Hanna, Pop took Fiona on an excursion to the seaside. Leaving Fiona on a beach towel in the sand, he ignored the signs warning of riptides, and dove into the ocean. Moments later, he was swept from safety, just as the signs had warned, and caught in a riptide, a powerful narrow current running perpendicular to the shore. As he was flung under mighty waves and pulled out to sea, his head slipped out of sight. Fiona, who had been hunting for shells, looked up to an empty sea. Alarmed, she began screaming for help—"Somebody help!"—but the beach was deserted.

Suddenly, she saw Pop's head emerge, watched him take a gulp of air. And then, just as fast, as if he were doing battle with the underworld, another wave swallowed him, pulling him even deeper. Fiona had stopped jumping and was just standing there, horrified. She knew she couldn't go in after her father; he was a very strong swimmer, and she was not. If he couldn't save himself, she knew she couldn't save him, either. She stood there, frozen. And then she once again started crying out for succor. "Help! Somebody, help us!" The beach was deserted, but one person heard Fiona's screams: the most important person. As Fiona screamed for her father again, something inside of him rose up, and he decided to fight for life.

Suddenly, she spotted him, way out to sea, swimming with all his might, parallel to the shore. Once he had swum quite a distance, he made a left turn and began swimming toward the shore. He's swimming! He's coming back this way! He's going to make it! Fiona grabbed her towel and began running down the shore to meet her father.

Wolf dragged himself out of the surf, sandy and pale, his chest heaving. Fiona noticed the chill bumps on his skin and that he had lost his swim trunks. Turning her head away so he could have some privacy, she handed him a towel, which he accepted and wrapped around his waist. "Riptide, Fee. Just like the sign." He'd seen the signs, and gone in anyway, and put himself in harm's way knowingly.

Still, the thought didn't cross Fiona's mind that he might have been trying to kill himself that day. She had no idea how close he'd come to giving up hope. She just thought he was a daredevil.

"Good thing you're a strong swimmer, Pop."

"Good thing," said Pop.

~o0O0O0o~

It seemed pretty clear to Fiona that Hanna was ready to remain at the ashram in India, and would be happy to raise Holly and Violet there. Yet, Fiona kept up hope that her family unity would be restored. She wished on the evening stars about it, and on the moon when she spotted it over her left shoulder. Eventually, her hopes were rewarded. Whatever Pop had said to Hanna, it must have done the trick. One night, after dinner, Pop and Hanna told the children the family would reunite, stateside, but they would go back to the United States via different routes. Hanna would take Holly and Violet through Europe, and Pop would take Fiona through Asia. Apart, again. Fiona wanted to be reunited with her sisters right now, not in a few weeks, but she didn't dare push too hard. She was just relieved and happy to know her family would be together again. Eventually.

How had Wolf worked his magic? He simply had promised to build Hanna an intentional community of her very own, anywhere she wanted in the United States, if only she'd come back to him.

Pop and Fiona set out on their long journey home together. Arriving in Bombay during the wee hours of the night, Pop searched out a 24-hour pharmacist for supplies, so if they ended up getting sick, they could handle things themselves. Finding a 24-hour pharmacist meant waking up the man who slept on the floor inside, so he could open the shop and help them. He was used to this and was most accommodating, but Fiona and Pop were not—they hated having to wake him. The shopkeeper brushed himself off, opened his shop, and sold Pop a remedy. It was neither the first nor the last time he'd have the wisdom to help a tourist digest his culture.

It was still dark as Pop and Fiona wandered through town, and together they welcomed the beautiful, sweet morning as the day dawned with a bright sunrise over the beach. Crabs scurried sideways as the fishermen prepared their nets for the promise of an abundant catch. A feeling of well-being, both physical and emotional, came over them.

Fiona was ecstatic; not only were the Sprechelbachs going to be a family again, but they were going to do so back home, in America. She couldn't wait to sleep in her own bed, eat Hanna's cooking, snuggle with Regis. When Hanna and her sisters left for Europe, it had felt like one more family breakup. No, she told herself. We're just tying a ribbon around the world. Hanna's going one way, Pop's going the other. And the big bow is going to be right there in the States when we get back. She looked over at her Pop, who seemed uncharacteristically silent, and decided it wasn't a good time to share a fanciful image. "A paisa for your thoughts, Pop?" she asked.

Wolf didn't mean to be so glum. And he didn't mean to chase Hanna and the kids away. He still didn't quite understand why they'd left. Living with him was a little like navigating life with an oblivious Einstein—brilliant but socially and emotionally unaware. He didn't push people away intentionally; he just wasn't very connected. He lived in his marvelous head, where he built beautiful worlds. But a relationship can't thrive, all alone in one's head. Wolf knew this, sort of. Over his lifetime, plenty of women had told them so, adding that he could be difficult, distracted, and distant. They came, and they went, and he often didn't know why they did either thing. He told himself he could change his nature, if that was what Hanna needed. But, could he, really? he wondered. He'd moved his family to India, fancying they were strongly united as they embarked on a wonderful adventure. Now, less than two years later, they were leaving, held together by the weakest of threads. Why? None of that really matters, he finally decided. As long as we're together again.

Pop left Fiona's query unanswered. What could he possibly say, to help her understand the situation, when he understood so little about it, himself?

A day later, Fiona and her father arrived in Tokyo. Fiona was amazed at the towering buildings that seemed to converge and eclipse the sky. This is the biggest city I think I've ever seen, she told herself, as they approached downtown. As traffic slowed, she could glimpse the many shops through the throngs of people. So many lights. It was just beautiful! Turning the corner to the hotel, Pop pointed out the plastic replicas of food in the window of a restaurant. "Hungry?" She was. "Okay, we'll eat as soon as we get our room key."

Indeed, the food was delicious—the dinner of fish and rice was the best thing Fiona had ever had in her whole, entire life. Unlike anything she'd had in India. The spices of India, startling and uncomfortable to consume at first, were something she had grown to tolerate, and even enjoy. The food in Japan, by contrast, was amazing. She loved the plain rice and the noodles. The tofu and warm broth were seasoned with "delicious experience," "beautiful place," and "homeward bound." Spiced like that, even a slice of week-old dry toast would probably have tasted amazing. The delicious food seemed to bolster Pop's spirits, also.

Back in the hotel room, Fiona noticed two small geckos, darting across the wall. Could Japan get any more wonderful? She didn't see how. "There's more to Japan than big cities, Fiona," Pop said. Tomorrow, they'd head to Tokyo Station, to board a train for Kamakura. An easy day trip from Tokyo, Kamakura promised bamboo forests, tea houses, and plenty of temples and shrines in Kyoto style, including a giant Buddha. The local street food would be just as delicious as last night's dinner, Pop expected. The street vendors didn't disappoint. With Kamakura having provided an unforgettable taste of what a deeper exploration of Japan might hold, Fiona and her Pop returned to their hotel in Tokyo, exhausted and satisfied. After trying one last unsuccessful time to catch a gecko, Fiona drifted off to a contented sleep.

The day before their flight home, Pop bought Fiona a kimono, and the saleswoman helped her to put it on, tying her obi—the sash that holds the kimono closed—in her family's customary way. As she and her Pop left and made their way down the street, Fiona smiled and bowed at the people passing by. "Poor little thing," one elderly woman said to another, "She is all alone with her father." And she decided to provide just a taste of mothering, within the bounds of protocol: she adjusted Fiona's obi. Two blocks later, another kindly, elderly woman came over, and bowed to Pop, and asked if she might correct the obi. She was offering a little kindness, while remaining respectful of another family's honor. After retying the sash differently, she went on her way. And before they got to the hotel, a third grandmother followed suit. She hoped the underlying message she was sending with her fussing got through. Pop laughed and just took it in, deciding it was just a cultural thing. Fiona, who hadn't known how thirsty she was for these sweet sips of maternal kindness, drank it all in.

Fiona and Pop arrived at Tokyo Airport with plenty of time to spare for their flight home. Pop put Fiona in charge of the timekeeping, and proceeded to lie down for a little shut-eye. Fiona began reading her book, checking her watch, regularly. She was mid-sentence when, over the speaker, a voice crackled a call. Some poor passenger was about to miss their flight. Between the speaker's low quality and the accent, Fiona couldn't quite make out the name. It sure sounded like Sprechelbach. That couldn't be right. According to her watch, they had plenty of time, didn't they?

"Oh, no! Maybe that's us!" She gasped. She listened intently, hoping for a repeat of the familiar call, something like "Wolf Sprechelbach, please make your way to your Japan Airlines gate for an on-time departure," but she heard nothing of the sort. Then, she looked down at her watch again. Plenty of time. Yes. They were fine. No wait…they weren't okay at all. Her watch had stopped.

What time was it? She had no idea. And with that one, horrible thought—the thought of, "I have no idea what time it is and I might be the reason we're not going home"—time seemed to stand completely still. "Pop! Pop! Wake up! I think they just called our names. My watch is dead. We're late. We've gotta run!"

Pop sprang up, disheveled from where he'd been lying, across two of the seats at the JAL ticketing area. Frantically, they started dashing for the gate. When they got there, it was nearly empty. The only person who remained was the attendant. She saw the panicked Fiona, near tears, and picked up the phone. Whatever she said, it must have been good. The next thing Fiona knew, she and Pop were walking down the stairs to a traveling stairway. As soon as they were on, it started off, full speed, for the plane, which had paused in its tracks. Moments later, the door was opened, and they were up the stairs and inside.

Fiona's heart was beating so fast, she could hear it in her ears. And Pop, she knew by the look of him, was freaked. He'd put her in charge of the time. What a time to have a watch breakdown. Would he be mad?

Before they'd caught their breaths, the stewardess came by with a ginger ale for Fiona and a scotch for Pop. He hadn't even needed to ask. She smiled and said, "Maybe later I can show you around. Would you like to see the upstairs of a 747?" With a wink, and before Fiona could answer, she was gone again.

It felt like forever before Pop said a word. Finally, having collected himself, he spoke. "Well, that was a close one. But here we are, next stop Honolulu. Flight looks pretty empty, so maybe ask the stewardess if you can stretch out on a few of the seats, after you get that tour, eh my Fab Fee?" And with that, Fiona knew that Pop wasn't mad.

Fiona looked out the window at the beautiful, clear blue sky. She'd been expecting the familiar sparklies that had so often accompanied her on airplane flights in the past. Where were they now? She searched the sky. No sparklies anywhere. Well, so what? They'd find their way back to her, she knew. They always had, before. Meanwhile, all was well with the world. She and Pop were going home—even if she wasn't quite sure where that would end up being, exactly.

Landing in Honolulu, Fiona felt tired and disoriented, and hardly knew where she was. But something stirring inside her soul said she was home. Back in the USA, Fiona and her father disembarked from the plane, and stood in the long passport control line, before wandering down the corridor to baggage claim to gather their luggage. They just had to go through customs before they could return their bags and get ready for the next leg of their journey. The customs officials took a long look at Pop, glanced at each other, and apparently decided to take a slow, thorough look through their suitcases. Pop's early 1970s appearance had changed dramatically from his carefully groomed 1960s persona.

With his long hair and well-past-five-o'clock shadow, Wolf now sported an impressive horseshoe mustache, which he'd grown in part to amuse his children. Though he wore khaki pants and a button-down short-sleeve shirt, the collar was open, and he had finished the look with a rough-hewn leather belt that had a metal buckle shaped like a peace sign. His hair, disheveled from the long flight, was wavy, making him look a bit like Einstein with a hangover. And like Einstein, he hadn't bothered with socks. Nothing in Wolf's appearance would signal his Ivy League background or that he'd been responsible for highly classified work for the military. Wolf played the part of a mad scientist well, as did so many of his peers who'd heeded Timothy Leary's call to "tune in, turn on and drop out." Pop looked to have been transformed by the times, and perhaps not for the better.

Their suspicions aroused, customs officials took him at face value and decided to search everything. Like it or not, appearances matter. After they were pronounced free to go, Pop hastily shoved their belongings back into their suitcases and forced them shut. Walking away, Fiona could overhear the customs officials calling for the subsequent person in line. "Next." Exhausted, Fiona and her Pop made their way to the gate to catch the final leg of their flight.

Peggy's mother, Fiona's Grandma Noni, was waiting for them at the gate in New York. Wolf was too tired to be too uncomfortable about the awkwardness of the situation, and Noni was too polite to make anything of it. She simply drove Wolf into Brooklyn, then spirited Fiona away for a short reunion at her home. Mother would arrive tomorrow to see Fiona for a few days before she rejoined Pop, Hanna, Holly, and Violet—together again—in Brooklyn.

"You must be tired, dear one," Noni said, "I've got your bed ready, and some wonderful books for you when you wake up. But first, I thought you might like some blueberries and cream. Does that sound good, sweetheart?" Fiona was nodding off, but she heard and nodded her assent. Gentle rains played rhythms on the roof as Fiona ate bowl after bowl of blueberries and cream that weekend with Noni and Mother. The scent of her grandfather Papi's cherry tobacco pipe blend wafting from the garden during breaks in the rain contributed to Fiona's happy homecoming. To her, Noni and Papi's home smelled better than all the mizzled maidans in India.

3. HUNDREDS OF ACRES OF MYSTIC

After an exotic-chaotic spell in India, Hanna and Wolf were ready to try their next experiment and move to the country, where they planned to buy and run a communal farm. It was what he had promised her, while in Pondicherry, to win her back. Wolf realized she might want the communal farm more than she wanted him, but it was a risk and an opportunity he was willing to take. What he wanted was her, and he was determined not to screw it up. Again.

Wolf and Hanna had decided to spend the summer with their newly reunited family at her parents' home in Brooklyn, while they mapped out their plan for the commune. Hanna's parents had taken care of Regis, during their year in India, and Hanna now felt certain they'd enjoy spending time with her children.

Fiona was overjoyed to be greeted by her step-grandparents, her stepmother, her little sisters, and her dog, all at once. Holly's Delhi Belly had resolved, all on its own, once they'd returned stateside. Everyone felt fine. Life itself, in that moment, felt perfect. She ran upstairs with Regis to the room where she would stay for the summer. And, there it was, her chest, containing all her favorite things. On the windowsill sat her jade plant from Providence, still alive! It had grown considerably during their absence, and had been transplanted into a larger, decidedly more decorative, pot.

During that summer in Brooklyn, Fiona and her sisters attended a Jewish summer day camp. Neither of Fiona's parents was Jewish, but Hanna was, and she was determined to have her children exposed to her faith tradition. Fiona was starting to notice how Hanna could ask for and get just about anything she wanted from Pop, and he'd acquiesce. Pop was like a puppy dog, lying on his back baring his tummy. Fiona hoped things would balance out, soon, and the old self-assured Wolf would re-emerge, the leader of the pack.

Each morning, a bus came by to pick up the girls, just a few doors down at the corner, and deliver them to camp. There, they learned about Abraham, Isaac and Jacob, and Noah, mostly through songs that carried Yiddish rhythms and vocabulary. Fiona particularly liked the song about Noah and his ark, partly because she knew the story, and partly because she loved the rousing melody. Often, she found herself setting the rest of her day to the soundtrack of the song, "So, rise and shine, and give God your glory, glory…children of the Lord." Fiona, who constantly had a song in her head and could "change the channel" as she wished, liked having this tune as her inner jingle. She decided it was a perfect summer anthem.

Just as much as the music, if not more, Fiona liked the other kids and the activities they did at camp—the swimming, hiking, horseback riding, even sitting at the picnic tables, weaving colorful lanyards out of plastic cords. So long as it was outside, Fiona was game. The nicest kids seemed to be those who rode the bus with Fiona and her sisters, but maybe that was because they got to know them better and continued to play with them in the neighborhood. And play they did. They swam in the pond or the club's pool. They gathered together for games of Tiddlywinks, pressing one bendable plastic disk into another, trying to flip it into the central tub; or games of marbles. They took out the Mr. Potato Head pieces, to see who could put together the funniest plastic potato personality. And back at the house, they watched a lot of TV. Lots of *Perry Mason*, because Grandma thought Raymond Burr was such a dashing fellow. And lots of *Get Smart*, Fiona's favorite, thanks to Barbara Feldon's portrayal of Agent 99, a smart and savvy woman who knew how to get a job done. Cases got solved. Evil plots got foiled. American optimism reigned supreme. It was all so gloriously simple and playful, and Fiona reveled in the opportunity to relax in a place that felt so safe and familiar.

Pop's birthday that summer was celebrated with a festive dinner, staged in the dining room, with cloth napkins, china, and silver flatware for the occasion. Hanna's parents didn't get the chance to celebrate with their daughter's family very often, so they went all out. Everyone, even the three girls, got their own lobster, presented with whipped potatoes, and drawn butter on the side. Hanna and Pop helped the girls crack their lobster, and let them focus on the rich meat of the lobster tail. The dinner was served and dishes cleared away by a maid, who later brought in a brightly lit birthday cake. Fiona thought Pop looked a little uneasy, and she imagined it was the unspoken American caste system of the upper-middle class being served by a maid, even though he'd seemed fine having a cook in India. "Everyone deserves the opportunity for honest work," he'd said. Maybe he forgot. Or maybe he just didn't like blowing out so many candles.

As she looked around the festive room and absorbed the merriment among her family, Fiona realized she'd be very happy if her parents decided to settle right there, in Brooklyn. But that was unlikely, she knew. This was too good, too easy, too "establishment," Pop would say. They were going to act on Pop's promise to Mum of starting an intentional community. And soon.

~o0O0O0o~

Wolf was full of contradictions. He was a man who, being happiest in his mind, tended the landscape he found there. Never before had he shown any interest in actual farming. He had no farm skills, and had little interest in what he considered brutish, outdoor, physical activity. Yet, he was prepared to invest the rest of his inheritance, $20,000, on a down payment for a farm. The idea of saving some of his money for a rainy day hadn't occurred to him. Or maybe he saw the present moment, the need to save his marriage to Hanna by buying her a farm, a colossal downpour.

Jobs were tight, but Wolf had tentatively arranged for a consultancy in research and design, which he hoped would support the farming venture. Beyond that, he had no backup plan. For a man who loved saying, "Never assume; it just makes an *ass* out of '*u*' and *me*," his plan was paved in poor assumptions about how it would all work out for the best. They plowed forward, identifying an area outside of Harrisburg, Pennsylvania, about 350 miles southeast of Providence, as the ideal location for their farm project.

Halfway through the summer, Wolf and Hanna packed up the kids and the dog, and drove to Pleasance, where they stayed with the Drakes, who were family friends, while searching for properties to purchase. They couldn't stay in the Drakes' house, already full, with two adults and four kids. Since there was "no room at the inn," the family stayed in the Drakes' barn, with the cats. They'd gotten used to rustic restrooms in India, so an outhouse was just fine with them. And, as soon as the girls were shown the rope swing over a swimming hole, where a stream got very deep, wide, and warm, they were happy to stay behind while their parents scouted properties. All summer they swam, swung, and sunned themselves, largely unsupervised.

During the afternoons, the Drakes invited the Sprechelbach girls inside the house to watch TV. They didn't get to choose what was on, and many of the family shows looked nothing like what they knew about family life. Barbara Billingsley of *Leave it to Beaver* and Donna Reed of *The Donna Reed Show* portrayed feminine, even-tempered housewives, in their shirtwaist dresses and pearls, keeping a lovely home, polite children, and happy husbands. Such a different world from the one they'd left behind in India. Was this the USA? Could such strange and beautiful women, and handsome, clean-cut husbands really exist? When they sat down together for supper and family togetherness, Fiona had a hard time watching without squirming. It was attractive yet foreign, everything she wanted and nothing she understood. Two shows Fiona absolutely couldn't bear to watch were *Green Acres* and *Petticoat Junction*, both set on the farm. Fiona agreed with the glamorous Eva Gabor's Lisa Douglas, stuck on the farm in *Green Acres*. Farm life wasn't her calling. I'm with Lisa, Fiona thought to herself. I'd rather be in New York, or any other city. Heck, I'd almost rather be in Delhi. Almost.

When Wolf and Gram talked about the move, Gram was beside herself. "I have a bad feeling, Wolf. If you try hard enough, son, it's said, you can finally succeed at failing. When you're as smart and well-educated as the two of you, the odds are with you. Doors open for you. Why are you trying so hard to be downwardly mobile? Give up this folly, son, and come back to the city, where you understand how to navigate life."

Wolf dismissed the concern with a bland reassurance. "Mother, it's going to be fine. You'll see." Then Gram reminded him that he had said that about India. She needn't have. He hadn't forgotten, and nobody likes an "I told you so." But it was good to hear that her door was always open.

Ultimately, Wolf and Hanna invited their girls to join them on their search. The real estate agent took them to see various cozy, cheery houses, where Fiona could imagine herself living happily ever after, but Hanna showed no interest. Then, the agent pointed out an octagon house they all loved, but it wasn't yet on the market. Would they wait for it? Should they try again, tomorrow? The day was almost over when they arrived at what Fiona thought was the worst possible option: a tumble-down Victorian house, with peeling paint and smashed-in windows, some of which had plastic sheets taped over them to keep out the cold. No one had even tried to hide the fire-singed pillars on the front porch.

Fiona imagined a "Munsters-meets-Addams Family" house, about 10-years post abandonment, after the "creepy and kooky" were long gone, leaving only the ruins. When Fiona peeked around the back of the house, hoping for a pretty yard and maybe a swing set, where and her sisters could play, she saw a moss-covered graveyard instead. Fiona just stood there and watched the nightmare unfold.

Trusting she didn't have a ghost of a chance of selling this classic haunted house, the Realtor almost hadn't shown them the property. But Hanna clearly loved it. "Hey, far out; there are sinks in every room. How cool is that?" Fiona wondered why there were all those sinks, and why the house had such a large porch. The porch was for sleeping in the fresh air, Pop explained. The sinks were for the private patients. The house had been a sanatorium for tuberculosis patients to come and live out their last days in the healthy countryside.

Other potential buyers must have been put off by the prospect of a house with such an unsavory past. Perhaps it was the graveyard out back. Or maybe it was the level of neglect and disrepair. The house had been vacant a long time and bore the scars of abandonment. There were wasps' nests, some still in use, under the house. In addition to the non-functioning plumbing, the electrical wiring was worn, most windows were broken, and the roof leaked.

The Realtor called out, "Watch out for that hole in the living room floor, there. See it?" The charred hole, where someone might have lit a bonfire, opened the living-room floor right through to the ground, below. The Realtor had shared rumors that local kids had been the culprits, or it could have been someone seeking shelter for the night.

At first, Wolf wasn't convinced. "Yeah, but the plumbing upstairs is shot. What good are sinks if you can't use 'em? And, there's no water heater."

Hanna wasn't going to be dissuaded by anything. "Right on. Whatever we can't fix, we don't need."

Wolf laughed. "I see it. How could I miss it? Let's check out the back." Just off the kitchen, he opened a door with a broken glass panel, to survey the tangle of foliage stretching beyond the graveyard, as far as the eye could see. "Shooweee!" He whistled. Three hundred acres. Just think what we can do with that."

Hanna surveyed the acreage with the look of love. "It'll be our Hundreds-Acre Wood!"

More like our Hundreds-Acre Horror, Fiona thought. What we can do out here is bury the dead. Or, at least, our dreams. She shuddered.

"Wait; it runs right up to rolling hills. There's definitely some mystique about this place, isn't there?" crowed Hanna. "Let's call it the Mystic Meadow!"

Wolf's consultancy job had fallen through, but they went ahead with the purchase anyway. After all, both Hanna and Wolf imagined that any employer would jump at the chance to hire either or both of them, given the chance.

Pop must really love Hanna to go to this length to win her back, Fiona thought. It's definitely a big price to pay for whatever he did. She just didn't understand why she had to pay penance, as well.

~oOoOOOo~

Wolf had been right. The sinks didn't work because the plumbing was shot. But, it wasn't just upstairs, as he'd surmised. He twisted the handle of the faucet over the kitchen sink downstairs, releasing just a trickle of rusty water. "We'll have to fix that," he said. "Put that on the list, Fee. Along with a better antenna for the TV." Hanna's parents had sent an old black-and-white set along, and it picked up three or four stations, but only when the antenna was set up just exactly right. Having a television was a departure for the family, but Fiona wasn't about to argue. There was nothing else about the house she liked.

If Hanna, a microbiologist by training, was even a little creeped out by the place, she didn't let on. If Wolf, who'd grown up in a house with a germaphobe, was at all disturbed by living in a former sanatorium, he didn't show it, apart from pointing out necessary repairs.

Wolf's grandmother, Lala, had stayed at home while his parents both worked. Having lost seven siblings to the Captain of Death, all within weeks of contracting the acute and deadly, "galloping consumption," she was determined that her grandchildren would all live to adulthood. She was so obsessive, Wolf often saw her picking out dirt from between the floorboards by hand, and washing down the walls with bleach. It wasn't about godliness, it was about control, and keeping TB—then the leading cause of death—at bay. Putting their faith in science, Wolf's parents also gave generously to sanatorium projects and health-related causes. When Wolf contracted polio as a child, Lala grew even more compulsive, and they gave even more generously.

Was this, now, a morbid fascination for Pop? Fiona heard him say, "TB or not TB, that is the question." She didn't laugh. She didn't find it at all amusing. Disease isn't funny, she thought. Surely people have died in this house. In this very room, I bet. She looked over at the little sink in what was now her bedroom, which indicated it had been a patient room. She shuddered. She looked out the window to the yard where the poor souls had been laid to rest, and their dead dreams before them. Their headstones, weathered and worn, had fallen over, and their carved names were obscured by moss and mud, hiding their lives forever. Fiona suddenly wondered if their souls were restless in this God-forsaken place. She wasn't sure she would ever sleep again, either.

Fiona had a feeling this house might consume her. She also realized her little sisters would react to their "new" home however she did. So, if she didn't want them to be scared, she was going to have to suck it up. After all, Pop and Hanna loved the house and everything about it. Papers were signed, the deal was done, and their fate was sealed. Well, Fiona thought, it could be worse. That's always true, until you're dead and buried. Nobody's got TB, at least. It could be worse.

Wolf repaired Mystic Meadow's plumbing, at least the line running to the kitchen sink, so the family had running water. But that was pretty much the extent of his handiwork. He was conserving cash now that he didn't have the safety net of a consulting gig, and he decided against investing in a water heater. The water could just run cold. If anyone wanted a hot bath in the chipped, clawfoot tub from a different era, they could boil kettles of water on an equally antiquated Wedgewood stove that also served as the building's sole heat source. It looked like it was straight out of the 1888 Sears, Roebuck & Co. catalog. Fiona was small enough to slip between the stove and the wall behind it, very carefully, so as not to burn herself. There, she could get nice and toasty—practically the only place in this house where this was possible. With no insulation, the wind whooshed through the broken windows, vibrating the Visqueen sheets stapled over them. It wasn't so bad, come summer.

Friends from the family's Providence days—some of whom had followed them to India, intrigued by Hanna's "back-to-the-land" concept—began arriving at Mystic Meadow. Living spaces were divided up to accommodate everyone, but Fiona had a room of her own. Her little sisters shared a room, which they preferred. All the grown-ups were "aunt" this or "uncle" that. No one paid rent, but everyone pitched in a little, cutting firewood, planting and grooming the community garden, or co-parenting.

The residents of the Mystic Meadow made a lot of things by hand—to make money at the local home crafter's fair, to save money, and to further their intention to return to a kinder, more simple, handmade existence. Fiona liked this about the people she lived with—well, the women, anyway. They were the kind ones, the industrious ones, the ones who really tried living out the utopia they imagined. Sometimes, they created tooled-leather craft items like belts and handbags. Fallen logs retrieved from around the property became wall art, trays and coasters, and sometimes, simple furniture. They also created tie-dyed clothing and pillows, filled with natural cattail "fur." Those who didn't know how to knit and crochet soon learned. Everyone had projects going. Fiona had already made a few headbands for Christmas presents to send to Mother, Karen, and to Gram, and was working on her first sweater.

One of their first big projects was to plant 1,000 trees. Fiona was surprised by how small the trees were when they arrived. She could hold one cupped in her hand. Something about holding a tiny pine tree in her hand felt momentous. "Grow steadfast, sweet thing," she whispered to each little tree, "and someday you will be the tallest tree here." They couldn't all be the tallest, she knew, but that didn't stop her from encouraging their potential.

It was hard work, planting a grove, but together, they got it done. In the meantime, one member of the crew got a downstairs bathroom by the kitchen up and working. Fiona hoped she'd never set foot in an outhouse again.

Eventually, the people of Mystic Meadow got to know a few of their neighbors, including a friendly farmer up the way. Soon, he invited some of them to his property, to help bale hay and earn a little cash. Fiona tagged along, curious about hay-baling. As soon as she arrived, a calf caught her eye. She grabbed onto the corral fencing, planning to climb up to get a closer look. As her grip locked around the rail, the flow of electricity was paralyzing. "That's a city-girl mistake there, kid," the farmer called out to her, flipping the breaker switch. "You okay?"

Rubbing her hands to abate the tingling feeling that remained, she nodded her head, yes, but her heart was racing from the jolt she'd just received. She felt a little like crying but thought she'd better not. Still, a tear escaped.

"That feeling will pass," said the farmer, kindly. "You don't look like much of a tomboy, kid, but you seem to like exploring. Well, here's another tip. Don't you try catching any snakes around these parts. We've got rattlers and copperheads roaming the range. I've heard tell that copperheads bite more people than the rest of 'em, but they'll leave you alone if you don't bother them. Mess with 'em, and they'll strike. You can't win in a snake fight, just sayin'. So, leave 'em be. If it's animals that interest you, stop by anytime, and help me with the cows. Okay, kid?"

Fiona nodded her head, no problem. Exhausted, hungry, and still a little stung, she decided to head home. She told no one but Regis about her adventure with the fence.

~oOoOoOo~

Inspired by the hay-baling, one of the new residents decided to try mowing the front lawn, which had grown as high as summer wheat. He'd found an old rotary mower in the shed and, with a little elbow grease, had gotten the thing moving. He stopped, short, when he spied something in a thicket. "Hey, Fiona," he called out. "Come take a look at this."

He had found three baby mice, so fresh they didn't yet have hair. He called out, "The best-laid plans of mice and men…"

"Gang aft agley," Fiona finished. "Often go wrong." She'd read John Steinbeck's *Of Mice and Men*. Yet his prophetic statement—or poet Robert Burns', from whose poem the phrase was borrowed—had never meant so much as it did now. "Can I have them?" she asked. "I've already got all the gear for them." She was right. She been given a laboratory mouse as a pet once, and she still had the cage. "I don't see why not," said Hanna, who had followed Fiona out into the yard to see what they'd discovered.

Nobody thought the newborn mice would survive. Except Fiona. But, they did. For weeks, her room smelled like sour milk, as she gave them saucers of milk to drink. When they had not merely survived, but thrived, Fiona declared herself the "Dr. Doolittle" of Mystic Meadow. I've really got a way with animals, she realized. Maybe I should be a country veterinarian. Or, maybe an animal activist like Jane Goodall. Either way, she thought, animals are the absolute best thing about my life right now.

~oO0O0Oo~

Wolf decided the family needed a new car to replace the old family car, which as he'd put it, was "toast." A member of the communal farm had driven the car into a tree, and totaled it. When Fiona asked Hanna why the guy didn't just get Pop another car, she simply said, "It doesn't work like that here, Fiona."

Still, Wolf felt he needed wheels to get himself to the store and the kids to and around town, and he knew he was the only one on site willing to do anything about it. One afternoon, he bummed a ride into town from the neighbor farmer. Just hours later, he drove up in his new, albeit heavily used, car. Maybe he'd been inspired by the creepy Victorian he now called home at the Mystic Meadow, or by the hit TV show *The Addams Family*, or maybe he got a good deal. Maybe it was just his nature. Wolf had bought himself a hearse.

Fiona found it a fitting vehicle for a family whose play yard was a graveyard, but she couldn't say she liked it. Everyone else thought it was fantastic, cool, counterculture or, at the very least, funny. "Can we go for a ride?" the kids said, in chorus.

"Sure, why not?" said Pop, pleased at the response to his new ride.

Wolf and Hanna climbed into the front seat, and the kids scrambled into the open expanse in the back, and lay down, planning to rise slowly, in hopes of scaring anyone they passed on the street. "Bwa ha haaaaaa, I vant to suck your bluuuud," they joked to each other. It didn't occur to the children that their cruise through town could be deathly upsetting to passersby, and the adults didn't clue them in. For a while, Wolf felt smart and savvy for buying that old hearse, following the laws of supply and demand. "The price was right," he said. "After all, who wants a used hearse? We do, that's who."

The hearse's novelty wore off quickly when Wolf noticed how much gas it guzzled: about 12 miles to the 40¢ gallon. Hearses also had a bad habit of getting stuck in the mud on the farm. Shortly after buying it, he traded it in for a gently used purple pickup truck, which turned out to be far better suited to work on a farm—and still managed to turn a few heads.

~o0O0O0o~

Fiona and her sisters spent a lot of their time with the farmer up the road—in the dell, Fiona liked to say. Fiona had been thrilled to witness the birth of a calf. Knowing how much Fiona loved animals, Hanna had given her a copy of *All Creatures Great and Small*, by James Herriot, for her birthday. Pop gave her a professional-grade microscope and a full set of slides. Many hours slipped by as she studied them. A chemistry set she'd been given for Christmas, helped her while away her hours. Today, Fiona was playing with the chemicals. Her favorite was everyone else's least favorite: chemical "rotten eggs." Oh, this is going to be great! Mixing up her stinky brew, she decided she would surely be a fabulous chemist like Marie Curie when she grew up. When she was done, she took her brew downstairs to share the joy.

"Hey, everyone, smell this. Guess how I made it?"

Nobody took much notice, except Pop. Fiona's father, who knew his chemistry, still gamely asked, "How'd you whip that up, Fee?" Smiling, he added, "Hey, good thing you don't go to school; you wouldn't want to take after your old man that way, and get in trouble."

Was it a good thing? questioned Fiona. But she knew the story. When he was a boy, Pop and his older brother had put limburger cheese on the school radiators. It made such a stink, all the kids had to be sent home. "Boy, did we catch hell for that one," Pop said, his laugh escalating to a roar. His laugh could wake the dead, she thought.

"What's so funny?" Fiona asked.

Pop collected himself and then told her, between fits of laughter, how his older brother also had gotten into trouble for dipping a girl's pigtail into an inkwell. "I think he liked her."

"You had inkwells in school, Pop? You must have lived in *Little*

House on the Prairie."

"Very funny, Fee."

"Very funny way to like a girl," she answered.

Another Thursday evening rolled around, and it was time for the weekly meeting at the communal farm. Fiona headed to the living room early to grab her favorite spot on the big ottoman situated strategically over the large hole in the floor. It wasn't that it was the most comfortable spot—quite the contrary. She simply liked its central location and that she didn't have to share it with anyone. She worried a little about falling through the hole to the ground below, so she settled in gingerly. As it was the coldest spot in the room, thanks to the air that came up from below, she bundled up in extra layers on meeting night.

Sitting by herself, as opposed to deep among the others on the couch, meant Fiona was in the best place to catch a breath of fresh air; all the smoke shrouding the meetings made it difficult to breathe. It didn't take long for someone to light up and, not long after that, someone offered her a toke. As usual, she shook her head and passed the joint, clasped within surgical scissors, to the next person. Then, the person who'd made the offer tapped her shoulder again and leaned in, as if to whisper something important. Having held his breath to get the best buzz, he said, "Whooooooo-eee! Grass isn't always greener, right kid?" And, in so doing, he'd let out a huge puff of smoke right into her face, her nostrils, her mouth. Fiona hadn't seen it coming. Hadn't had time to take a deep breath of fresher air to tide her over until the fog settled. "Very funny!" she huffed, blowing and waving away what she could. "Give a kid a break, already."

Fiona was no stranger to marijuana, having grown up in a cloud of pot smoke. And she wasn't even the youngest kid in the room, at 11, to be offered a toke. Not by a lot. But that didn't mean she liked it or wanted it or planned on becoming a pothead someday. She had come to loathe the sickly-sweet smell that accompanied that constant fog in the living room for the way it made her lungs feel and for how stupid it made the grownups act.

The weekly meetings were supposed to be the place where

people could speak freely. They'd been envisioned as a time when an entire group of like-minded, communal spirits could come together to air grievances (Fiona found this funny. Why would like-minded, communal spirits have grievances?) and assign duties such as composting and watering the garden. She, for one, had grievances, which she mulled over silently. Maybe it was because she wasn't completely like-minded. Even the notion of a weekly airing of grievances annoyed her. That seemed like the perfect setup to encourage conflict. Why not hold a weekly appreciation gathering? Don't people mostly get what they're expecting to see? Betcha I could think of something to appreciate. Not the fact that I always seem to get compost duty, which is such a stinky job, but I bet I could think of something.

Introverted Fiona was aggrieved by the sheer number of people around the house all the time, many of whom didn't seem to her to be carrying their full weight. If some of the grownups paid as much attention to what needs doing around here, she thought, as they do to getting the seeds out of their joints, more would get done. It also seems to me that Pop's footing all the bills. How is that fair? She wanted to defend her father, but she knew he wouldn't appreciate her assessment. She held her peace, suspecting the "open and honest" thing was really only open to adults anyway. Any complaints kids might have about adults had a way of boomeranging back, so kids said very little about their elders at the meetings. Mostly, it was adult against adult, kid against kid, adult against kid. Commune equality is a sham, Fiona decided. Here, as anywhere, some people are forever more equal than others, and the biggest bully wins the playground toy. They told us kids that we had an equal voice, but that's a crock, and commune equality is a sham. At least we get to leave after the first hour.

She was hoping to get through the hour without a new grievance being lodged against her. The previous week, a kid had complained that she hadn't shared her guitar. It was true, she hadn't. After all, it was a real one, a special birthday present, and Pop had told her she must care for it, respect it. Considering how often people wrecked things around the commune—Pop's car, for instance—she felt justified in squirreling it away in her room, where she was trying to teach herself how to play it when no one was looking. When the grievance was raised, Pop had come to her rescue, saying, "A guitar isn't a toy. It's a musical instrument, to be safeguarded and cherished. Fiona is taking her responsibility seriously, and she doesn't have to share her guitar if she doesn't want to. Next subject."

Living at Mystic Meadow was like having 10 parents, none of whom cared what she did, unless it made them mad. Today, one of them was mad. "Fiona, you need to think about what you say, watch your mouth, be more careful," boomed the aggrieved adult.

"What do you mean?" Fiona considered herself very careful with her words and deeds.

"The other day, when the neighbor visited, you picked a piece of wild grass and pretended to take a toke off it, saying, 'This is what hippies smoke.' That was pretty fucking dangerous. You can get us into a shitload of trouble talking like that in front of outsiders, kid. Not cool. It wasn't even funny."

"The neighbor thought it was. Besides, he called me a little boy. That wasn't funny or even nice, was it?" Fiona looked over to Pop for a rescue, but he just looked down, as the lecture continued.

"Don't change the damn subject on me, kid. That's not what I'm talking about right now. I'm talking about living consciously, being careful with your words. Are you even fuckin' listening to what I'm saying here?"

"Yes."

"Yes, what, Fiona?"

Does he really expect some salutation, like uncle, or sir, Fiona wondered, like he was the school principal or something? Really? "Yes, I think everyone knows what you're saying. I get it. They get it. You want me to kowtow. But get this: you're not my Pop. You're not the boss of me. You're a hypocrite. You say don't lie and then you get all freaked out if I tell the truth. And still you think it's fine when you joke about the Beatles' glass onion bong, or them taking a toke on *Rubber Soul*. Just not me. Why? Because I'm a kid? Fuck that. Fuck you!"

When Fiona's f-bombs started falling, Pete simply said, "Go you to your room, kid, now!"

Fiona knew an order when she heard one. "Gladly," she said, and stomped out of the room, muttering, even though it wasn't one of her parents who had given her the command. At least it got her out of there.

This whole place is totally messed up, Fiona fumed, as she stomped up the stairs. She forgot all about the wild animals she liked and the swimming hole and the horses and the beaver dam upriver. Right now, she hated everything about Mystic Meadow and her weird life, and anyone within earshot was going to hear about it. I don't need to calm down. I won't calm down. I am NOT going to calm down. I'm going to EXPLODE! She opened her window and screamed. Loudly.

"GAAAAAAAAARRRRGHH!"

Fiona screamed at the top of her lungs for as long as she could keep it up. At the same time, in her head, she started to hear a horrible little mantra, "Fuck everything." She repeated it, silently, over and over, until it started to become almost audible to her, ultimately reaching the same fevered pitch inside her head as the scream itself. Nobody came in to stop her or see how she was doing. She could not stop the voice, nor could she stop the scream. They had welled up from somewhere deep inside, and once given voice, they just took over.

Downstairs, the meeting continued. "You were out of line with my kid, Pete," said Wolf. He took a hit off the joint and handed it back to him. "You took it too far, man. What's up next for discussion?"

Eventually, Fiona stopped yelling, but only after her voice had given out, and so had she. She sat down on her bed and then slid down onto the floor, where she remained, thinking and not thinking, for more than an hour. She told herself she didn't care that nobody had stood up for her, or come to check on her. She didn't need any of them, and didn't want anyone intruding on her room, her space. It was the only place in the entire house where she could find refuge.

Fiona kept her room neat and tidy. Organized. Controlled. There was a place for everything, and everything was in its place. Maybe she'd always been that way, but these days she was approaching her straightening up with a feverish intensity. She didn't worry about the rest of the house; it was hopeless, and she couldn't handle that level of chaos. But, in her room, she kept things shipshape. If she'd had a bucket and bleach, she might have taken to washing the floorboards, just like Lala, or Cinderella. She had a feeling poor 'Ella had felt the same way she did, banished to her room but, finding it her only place of solace among the little mice and birds she'd befriended, she'd kept it pristine.

Even during her meltdown, Fiona hadn't thrown or broken anything. But her world felt upside-down anyway, and she was having a hard time getting it back aright. As far back as she could remember, she'd never lost it like that, never been pushed up and over the edge, to have everything she'd so carefully stored inside spew out like that. She didn't like it. Not one bit.

Tomorrow, everyone will be all weird, Fiona fretted. And now, I'm just like them. All ugly, loud, and out of control. And what did it get accomplish? A fat lot of nothing. That's so nowhere. As she looked around the room from her vantage point on the floor, she was pleased that her life still looked tidy on the outside. Inside, though, she was a mess. She looked over at Regis, who had dutifully followed her into her room and had weathered her storm.

"At least I've got you, my friend!" she said, to the big shaggy dog lying beside her. He'd kept her company through all her bellowing and was, she imagined, quite relieved she'd finally stopped her tirade and was paying attention to him. She grabbed her copy of *The Lord of the Rings* off her shelf, slid up the side of her bed and climbed on top. She'd escape into reading.

"C'mon, Boy, get up on the bed with me." Fiona patted the bed, and Regis jumped up and settled in next to her, resting his head on her leg. "Who's a good dog?" Fiona didn't have to tell her dog how much she hated the world of Mystic Meadow. She just knew Regis understood. "You hate it here, too, don't you, Regis?" Soon, Regis and Fiona had fallen fast asleep, one hand on her book, the other hand securely around her dog's neck.

The following morning, Fiona awoke, still dressed and with her arm draped around Regis, on top of her bed, where the two had abandoned the upset of the night. Up before the birds, the sun, or anyone else in the house, she and her dog slipped silently outside to head up to the clear stream that ran right through the middle of the Mystic Meadow property. She imagined she might catch a crawfish or maybe a salamander to play with. She and Regis wouldn't have to come home all day, with sweet water from the stream and biscuits from the kitchen. Besides, there were plenty of blackberries to pick, if she got hungry. Maybe she'd come home, maybe she wouldn't, but she needed the day, at least.

A few hours into her adventure, the sun, already high, had dried the dew off the leaves, and the day was warming up nicely as the girl and her dog lay down in the thick moss by the banks of the stream. It felt like a soft, cool bed, soothing Fiona in the heat of summer. She folded her hands behind her head and looked up at the clouds, watching their slow progress across a blue field, wondering what shapes they would shift into next. Now there was a duck. Now a squirrel. And now, a dragon, chasing after a flaming pearl. Before he could catch his little cloud-pearl, it was gone again. Clouds were like that. Was wisdom?

Fiona and her sisters had discovered abandoned railways in the wooded glen, which ran out across the meadow, and they liked to skip lightly along the tracks, arms outstretched, like gymnasts on a balance beam. But the tracks led into a tunnel that was too creepy to enter when Fiona was alone. She decided against it, choosing, instead, to check on the beaver pond farther upstream. A couple of industrious beavers were often at work and, if she was very quiet, they were willing to continue their work, uninterrupted by her presence. They reminded her of *Beaver Valley*, the nature film her teacher had shown at her school in Providence. Watching the beavers sounded like fun today, and Fiona guessed she wouldn't be missed around the house. Certainly, she didn't want to go back. Not yet. Not ever, maybe.

I wish I'd brought along something to read, she mused, patting Regis absentmindedly, as he slept beside her. There weren't that many books in the house, but she could have grabbed a *Mad Magazine*, *Mother Jones*, the Whole Earth catalog, or some *Zap Comix*. Some of the characters in the comic strips—The Fabulous Fury Freak Brothers and Mr. Natural—looked like they'd feel right at home with the gang at Mystic Meadow.

Fiona fingered the moss beneath her hand, enjoying the cool, soft texture. It reminded her of her mother—she wasn't sure why. Maybe it was the loveliness of the moss, which she likened to her mother's graceful sophistication. She found herself wondering what Mother would think of Mystic Meadow and all the people living there. If she knew about this, surely, she'd send for me, Fiona thought. Fiona studied the clouds again, wondering if Karen could possibly be looking up into the clouds at the same time. How cool for Karen, living in a pretty room, in a proper house, with polite people, Fiona thought. Even though she's older than me, she might not even know what grass is, except for on lawns. Hey, ignorance is bliss. It would have been so cool living with Mother, growing up with Karen, and being a member of the blissful ignorance crowd.

It wasn't until the sun began its descent, and the air had cooled to a comfortable chill that Fiona decided to make her way back to Mystic Meadow. Once inside the house, she was puzzled by how the grownups ignored her, acting as if nothing had happened. Something certainly had for her. Hanna invited her to join her in the attic, where some of the women were knitting.

Fiona hesitated at Hanna's invitation. She had no way of knowing the adults hadn't given her rage a second thought. They'd moved on, and expected her to do the same. Hanna turned, smiled at Fiona, and beckoned for her to follow. It was enough to lure Fiona into the attic. As she came into the room, she saw her younger sisters already at work. Simultaneously they looked up, smiled at their sister, and returned their attention to their work. Fiona sat down, soothed by the serene atmosphere in the room. Apparently, no one else was interested in revisiting the weekly meeting any more than she was.

Instead, Hanna had some big news for her. Wolf and Hanna both believed they could do a better job educating their children than the local schools could. Not having degrees in education did not deter them. Just as in Delhi, where they'd kept their kids away from the private, expatriate school to attend their alternative, nonprofit school, they wanted to provide another unique educational experience at the commune. The Pennsylvania education authorities had other ideas. One month after the start of the conventional school year, Wolf and Hanna were told their girls would be required to attend public school.

Hanna had summoned Fiona to the attic to explain to her that she and her sisters would be going to the school in Pleasance, joining their friends, the Drakes. Fiona found that she was secretly glad. Maybe even relieved. It would be good to get away from the commune, at least for a few hours a day.

~o0O0O0o~

As much as Fiona hated the weekly Mystic Meadow meetings, she found a different sort of meeting she loved once she started going to school again: the weekly Girl Scout meetings, which took place on Mondays after school, in the home of one of her classmates' parents. It gave her a chance to meet other girls her age and earn and collect badges Hanna taught her how to sew onto her dark "Scout-green" sash. She was hoping someday she might get the Girl Scout doll, but at least she had the uniform, whose green shirtwaist dress with elastic belt, yellow bow tie with the green embroidered GS trefoil emblem, and dark green beret told everyone at school that she belonged. In her uniform, she was just like the other girls; she was one of them, in fact. As a Girl Scout, her life didn't just pass for normal, it really was normal—for two hours every week.

Fiona's troop still went by the old 1913 Girl Scout Promise. "On my honor," Fiona repeated, holding up three fingers, together with the other girls, "I will try, to do my duty to God and my country, to help other people at all times, and obey the Girl Scouts Law."

Today, the Scouts were learning how to stay safe during a disaster, such as the flash flood that had recently happened one town over, sweeping cars and cows down river. The Scouts would earn a badge for their lessons. "Be Prepared," said the Scoutmaster. "That's our motto."

I like it, Fiona thought, realizing it really was one of her life mottos. It had to be, she reasoned, growing up in such an eccentric family under such unpredictable circumstances. She liked it so much, she added it to her own rules for life:

Fiona's (Scouting) Rule #5: Be Prepared.

The Scouts had just received word that Scout camp would be offered that summer. They hadn't been sure. The Scout campground in New York had been hit by flood waters that had reached seven feet high against the walls of sturdy buildings, leaving behind a trail of mud and silt, as they receded. Farm and domestic animals had died. Cars had been overturned and carried away. At the campground, the stream had overflowed its banks, washing away the road and bridge. Their Scoutmaster had wondered what this would mean for their own plans, and whether the organization would shuffle campers across multiple states, change the dates, or perhaps cancel the camps. But, the Scouts were assured it all would be rebuilt in time to open all the campgrounds, as scheduled. Everyone was thrilled.

Times were changing for girls in the 1970s, and Girl Scouting was keeping up. Though the path to Eagle Scout remained closed to girls, Fiona still hoped she could be one, someday, somehow. In 1972, while Fiona was still in India, they had updated the Girl Scout Law to remove the part about obeying orders and instead asked only for respect for yourself and others and for authority. Scouts still pledged to be honest, fair, cheerful, friendly, helpful, considerate, and a sister to every Girl Scout. Fiona was sent home with a flyer about the Girl Scouts and their historical timeline. Pop chuckled as he read over the changed Girl Scout Law, thinking, "Good for them."

"What do you think of the new Girl Scout Law, Pop? They blew up the bit about obeying orders. And they lost the bit about being a friend to animals."

Wolf regarded his child, thoughtfully. "I like it. You're still a friend to animals; it's just that they say it as protecting and improving the world around you. That's good stuff. And when did you ever hear anyone in the Sprechelbach family tell you to blindly obey orders?"

"Never, Pop."

"But respecting someone in a position of authority makes sense.

It's like if you're in a choir. You need to follow the conductor. You can't make a good choir if you're reading ahead to see if you agree with the lyrics, and not honoring your agreement to sing the songs along with everyone else. But the conductor can't overstep by telling you to commit murder or do something else that's against your conscience, either."

"You're preaching to the choir, Pop."

"Hahaaaaaa! Seriously, Fiona, there's a difference between positional power and real authority. Authority is earned. What do I keep telling you, Fiona? Thoughts are free."

"Wow, all this 'cuz the Girl Scouts stopped saying we have to obey orders?"

"Absolutely."

"Thoughts are free," she returned to his message. "Like the song you love so much, about thoughts being free, right? I like the sound of it in German, but I understand it better in English." Sensing an invitation, Pop launched into the song. "Die Gedanken sind frei…"

"I know, Pop, I know. Darkest dungeon, doesn't matter, thoughts fly free, right?" Fiona asked, hoping to be spared the remaining verses. "Thoughts tear down the gates, so renounce your sorrows. I get it."

Pop cut short the song and reminded her how the popular protest song had been banned repeatedly since 1848, so it was important to know it and sing it sometimes, to remind yourself of your own inner freedom. Pop's ideas made sense, but it surprised Fiona that her father would ever consider trusting or following anyone in a position of authority. Especially these days, what with Watergate and everything. She didn't think her Pop trusted anyone, really.

~oOOoOOo~

The summer of 1973 was exceptionally lovely, particularly for Fiona, who was embracing Girl Scouts, and busying herself with gathering badges. For Wolf, the summer was a different story. He fettered himself inside, uncharacteristically captured by the television, which aired all 250 hours of the Watergate hearings, investigating alleged "dirty tricks" by Richard Nixon's campaign during the 1972 presidential election. The questions on the minds of all adults as obsessed as Wolf were posed by Republican Senator Howard Baker: "What did the President know, and when did he know it?"

Wolf was enthralled by *Washington Post* reporters Bob Woodward and Carl Bernstein's investigation and the ensuing national scandal. He became particularly excited by one exchange between Senator Fred Thompson of Tennessee, and White House aide Alexander Butterfield, on wiretaps. "Are you aware of any listening devices in the Office of the President?"

"I was aware of listening devices. Yes, sir."

Wolf had long been concerned, paranoid actually, about the possible presence of wiretaps, which was why he'd sometimes put the telephone into the refrigerator, trusting the "cold storage" would keep others from listening to discussions he didn't want overheard. He'd been most concerned when working on secret projects for the government and had once been approached by a spy, whom he had turned in to authorities. Now, hearing that his own president was engaging in the practice of recording conversations without participants' knowledge, he was thunderstruck. "Far Freakin' Out!" he said under his breath, "Far Freakin' Out."

Wolf had become a disappointed idealist; this was hard to bear. One of the news anchors noted that Nixon was a Quaker. "Quaker my arse," said Wolf to the television set, as if he were part of the conversation. "If Nixon's a Quaker, I'm a monkey's uncle. He's morally bankrupt." Wolf also talked to Fiona, bringing her into the discussion. "Power corrupts, Fiona; you can't trust anyone in a position of power," he said. "Remember that."

It sounded to Fiona as if Pop's Rule had just shifted to simply, "Trust nobody. Period."

Unlike her Pop and other adults, Fiona paid Watergate very little mind. The idea of trusting nobody resonated with her, though, especially since the disastrous weekly meeting. She wanted to steer clear of the folks at Mystic Meadow and avoid any more grievances on either side. With 300 acres, creating distance wasn't hard. Eventually, though, she got bored just walking around by the stream, catching salamanders, and climbing trees. So, she invented a game.

"Okay, Regis. I'll be the scientist, and you be the lab assistant. Got it? Great! Now of course you know about the scientific method. You can't be a lab assistant if you don't know that."

"Rrruff!"

"Who's a smart dog? You are. Yes, you are, you good boy! Now, let's think of an experiment we can run right here by the milkweed, where nobody cares what we do. Now, what should it be? Any ideas?"

"Rrruff, grruff!"

Just at that very moment, Fiona caught sight of a bewitching zebra spider. Seeing it sparked an idea. It involved milkweed, zebra spiders, and songs.

"That's it Regis! Oh, you're such a smart dog! We'll divide this milkweed into two sectors. Spiders eat the pests that hurt the crops, so we'll move them all over here and call it the treatment area. It's area S for Spiders, Songs and hey, for Sprechelbach, too. It'll be the very famous Sprechelbach Spider Song Experiment. We'll sing to the spiders and the milkweed. You can howl along if you want. The other area will be the control, where nothing happens."

There were lots of zebra spiders, and they kept finding their way over to the control area, so there was plenty to do, while singing to the milkweed. Fiona sang all her songs from choir, plus a few Cat Stevens' songs as well. Regis tagged along quietly, barking happily on occasion, but not howling unless Fiona started howling first. The experiment amused Fiona and Regis for an entire month, but with nothing much to show for her efforts, she began to lose interest.

One morning, Fiona opened the door off the kitchen, letting Regis bound outside ahead of her, as she trekked out to her experiment site. "Hey, Regis, let's go check on the crops." Fiona surveyed the wild milkweed growing by the stream on their land, while Regis chased a butterfly. "What do you think, Regis; do you see a little difference?" Regis, responding to his name, wagged his tail, as if to say, "Sure! Absolutely! Area S is taller and greener! We did it! Hooray!"

Or so Fiona chose to think. Pop had told her she couldn't prove things with science, only disprove them. She wasn't quite sure what that meant for her milkweed experiment. Had she really proven the naysayers wrong? People who said that songs and spiders have no influence should take a look for themselves!

"You really did see it, too, right Regis? Me, too. The plants with more spider friends grew taller." She used both hands to pet Regis' face and, still holding his head in her hands, said, "You are just the best lab assistant a scientist ever had, Regis!" After pausing a moment to let go of Regis and reflect, she asked him, "But, was it the singing or the spiders that helped? Or, maybe it was something about combining them? Looks like we'd need another experiment to refine our data, huh Regis? We'll leave that to another researcher. You hungry, Boy?"

Whatever Regis had or had not understood about the experiment, he sure knew the word "hungry." "RRRUF!" Off trod the two scientists back to the house, so she could feed her dog, have a little something to eat herself, and reflect upon her scientific studies as she finished packing for summer camp. "I am so ready for camp, Regis! No flood waters and not even Watergate could keep me from going to Girl Scout camp!" Fiona held up her three fingers in earnest. "Scout's honor!"

~o0O0O0o~

Girl Scout camp was everything Fiona had hoped it might be. It was picture postcard perfect. She learned to whittle, and to start a fire from nothing but kindling. Her favorite part was dinner: the fire-roasted hotdogs, jammed onto a stick and blackened over the fire. She liked baked beans, bubbling in an iron pot, hanging over the flame. She loved both the red Jell-O and the ice cream, both packaged in little plastic cups with cardboard lids. But not everyone agreed about the food. "Spam, again?" One kid asked, in frustration, "Are we going for the world record for how many ways we can cook Spam, or just how many days we can choke it down?" Fiona didn't mind Spam, especially grilled. I'm going to remember this summer as the best one yet, she thought, as she speared her friend's piece of Spam with her fork and took a bite.

It was almost time for the Haunted Garden. The counselors, teenagers just a few years older than Fiona, had set it up just down the path from the central campfire and bungalows, in a clearing at the edge of a wooded glen. They had invited the campers to explore it at twilight, after which they'd return to sing songs and enjoy S'mores around the campfire. Yep, good fun. A spooky adventure.

I'll act afraid, Fiona thought to herself as she walked along through the grasses at the end of the path toward the Haunted Garden. I like the counselors, and they're trying to show us a good time. How scary could it be? The Haunted Garden was at the crest of a hill, a good distance from the campfire, and it took a lot longer to get to than it did to walk through. The counselors had timed it perfectly so that by the time the girls arrived at the Haunted Garden, dusk had fallen. Hiding behind trees, the counselors did their best to make creepy night-in-the-wilderness sounds—barn owls hooting and wolves howling, and even an attempt at a screech owl and maybe a bear. Fiona and the other campers laughed and screeched in feigned terror, until, soon enough, they were through the garden and headed back to the campfire.

As the light dropped to near darkness, the mood subtly changed. It felt unsettling to walk back through the woods, with no visible grown-ups. The shadows in the trees and the sounds echoing through them made everybody jumpy. Fiona heard a stick snap behind her. One of the campers yelled, "It's a zombie, like, from *Twilight Zone*." After a few moments in frozen silence, they all started running for their lives, disappearing in the distance. Fiona, realizing she was quite alone, stopped short, unsure of what to do next. Her heart was pounding and her skin, clammy. Should I yell for help? she asked herself. I don't want to alert the zombie, and I sure don't want other kids thinking I'm being silly or stupid. She took out a compass from her pocket, although it was too dark to read it, and she wasn't sure which direction the camp was, anyway.

Just then, a firefly appeared in the dark, lighting a glow on the compass. After a moment, it vanished. Then another lit the night, and another. There weren't enough to light the way, but they lit up her soul. Just a few little fireflies, flickering in the dark, and Fiona felt she could breathe again. Wait, Fiona thought, this isn't a zombie movie. This is summer camp. And hey, isn't that the campfire over there?

It was. It had been there, all along for her to see, had she thought to look in the right direction. Relieved, Fiona walked on to the campfire for ghost stories. No matter how scary the story, nothing further spooked Fiona that night. Not after the fireflies. Later that night, tucked into her bunk, Fiona pulled out the journal Hanna had given her as she left for camp. "Fireflies are so beautiful," she wrote. "Like little fairy lights in the night. I wonder what it would be like to be one." As she drifted off to sleep, she thought about fireflies and lighthouses, flickering on and off as they lit the night, cheering up the darkness, spreading hope and wonder, and banishing fear. People talk about trying to be a candle, but that's just impossible. Who can shine brightly like that all the time without melting away? I want to be a firefly, lighting pathways now and then, as often as I am able, when it matters most. Maybe I should change my rule about shining so it isn't just about me shining on, Fiona thought. It'd be better if it could be about shining out for others who need light.

Fiona's Rule #3 (Modified for Fireflies)—Shine ~~On~~ Out!

Fiona was thinking back to that night of the fireflies at summer camp as she looked up at the falling leaves floating down around her. There was a chill in the air that signaled it was now fall and winter was around the corner. She knew it wouldn't be long before it was time to tap trees again. Oh, maple syrup, she thought, imagining it seeping into the nooks in her waffle and mingling with warm butter. During harvest, she especially loved the part where they'd take a bit of the hot syrup and pour it onto the snow, and then set it alight to watch it sizzle in rainbow colors.

Just then, she noticed a parade of wooly bear caterpillars inching their way across the road. Fiona decided to stop and help them across the road, to safety. Regis sniffed at the wooly bears and then went over to the grass embankment to lie down while she worked. He didn't see the appeal. "Here, little guy," she cooed, letting the caterpillar crawl onto her hand. "How long a winter will it be this year?"

Fiona studied the fuzzy orange center and two black ends on the caterpillar as she carried it carefully across the street. She was thinking about the legend of the center stripe being a winter weather predictor: the longer the stripe, the bleaker the winter. "You say it's going to be a long winter," she said to the caterpillar, as she set him down safely. "Is it a consensus? Let's see what your friends say." Fiona amused herself for quite some time that afternoon, helping the caterpillars, one by one, making sure they didn't get confused and turn around to try to go back across the road.

"There were 12 mostly black caterpillars, and two were more orange," she told Regis, as she finished her errand of mercy. "That's it then. The Wooly Bear Weather Report tells us it's going to be a long cold winter." She slapped her thigh, alerting Regis to get up and join her as they headed home, their work done for the day.

Why did the caterpillar cross the road? she thought as she went inside. I have no clue. No idea why we do what we do. I guess it's just our nature. She patted Regis on the head and went into the kitchen to get him some food.

Things were starting to look up, Fiona felt, as she watched her parents settle into life at Mystic Meadow. It certainly hadn't been her choice to move there, but she had begun to think she could live just about anywhere, endure all kinds of conditions, just like a Wooly Bear could.

~o0O0O0o~

The long winter the Wooly Bear had predicted started with words in the night. Fiona couldn't help hearing their muffled voices from her room, where she lay tucked into bed, one moment safe, secure and sleepy, and the next, not. She couldn't make out exactly what they were saying to one another, but she could tell they weren't happy. Oh brother, the airing of grievances was her last thought before finally succumbing to sleep. But it was much more than that. These were, at least to Hanna, irreconcilable grievances.

The angry words of the night were followed by packing in the morning. This time, unlike in India, Fiona was awake to watch it happen. It was obvious; Hanna was embarking on another separation.

Fiona understood by now that a separation between her parents was accompanied by a separation between their children. Once again, Hanna, Holly, and Violet were leaving her without her. Without a word. Without a promise or a plan or a prayer. Once again, she would be left behind in the oddest of places with Pop. From Fiona's perspective, Hanna was simply leaving again—without explanation, without asking Fiona if she might want to come along, without a proper goodbye—and she was taking Holly and Violet with her.

Once again, Fiona soon received a package in the mail. This letter from Hanna wished her a happy Christmas. It included 10 dollars cash and a hope that Fiona might spend the money on something that would bring her some joy, not save it, as Hanna imagined she'd do. The box also included the scarf that Holly had been working on at Mystic Meadow for her big sister. Fiona snuggled into it, missing her little sister. At the bottom was a wooden box that Violet had decorated for her. Fiona held it close. She stashed Hanna's cash inside the box until she could take it to the bank where she had her very own savings account. She'd save it, just as Hanna expected she might. She was going places in life, she knew, and that required saving for a rainy day. Or rather, a rainier day. Although today felt soggy enough, she predicted more storms ahead.

Every time she turned on the news, another headline rained down. One refrain, "Oil prices up again today," sounded like a broken record, as reporters explained, again and again, rapidly escalating gas prices. "Employment disappointing," rang out another. The economic weather was new and different, but one thing was familiar: times were hard. With stagflation in the air, every day was a rainy day across America.

Without Hanna, Holly, and Violet, life on the farm was stagnant, too. The farm's mystique was ebbing away. It had never been Wolf's dream. Hanna had been the life blood of the place. What's to become of a dream, without its dreamer? The dream dies. Just because the last nail hadn't been driven into the coffin didn't mean the patient wasn't terminal. After Hanna left, one by one, the others started leaving, too. Eventually, just one person, a fellow folks called Buddy, was left living in the house with Wolf and Fiona. There were also a few people—those who hadn't been an integral part of this back-to-the-land project—still living in trailers on the property's edge.

A second, chatty letter arrived from Hanna, asking after all the good people at Mystic Meadow. She wondered whether Fiona was doing any sledding this year, or tapping trees, and how she was enjoying Girl Scouts. She even asked about Regis. She also shared a description of the beauty and ruggedness of Canada, where they now lived, telling how they'd tramped through the woods and done some skiing. Though she signed it with love, Fiona didn't know how to feel about it. She wondered what Hanna meant by, "Give my love to everyone." Who was everyone? If Pop, why not say so? And if she loved Pop so much, why leave? Fiona took a sip of her mint tea. As the broken leaves settled on the bottom of her cup, she leaned back and surveyed the bleak and barren landscape outside the kitchen window. Empty all the way to the road.

What does she think? Fiona wondered. Does she think this is some sort of mystical meadow paradise she's left us in? She set the letter down, deciding she'd read enough. She'd keep it, of course. She'd add it to her collection of letters in her keepsake box: letters from Gram, and letters from Mother; the other mother figure who seemed to be able to love her only from afar. Everyone's so loving, in letters, Fiona thought. Letters are such a cop-out. Maybe love's like Pop's joke about theory and practice. Love's great…in theory. In practice? Splitsville.

She went outside and stood below the big maple, feeling the chill in the air. She wondered: if she spread out everyone's letters across the ground after a fresh snowfall, drizzled them with maple syrup and lit them, what kinds of colors would arise? Black, she thought. Everything would just go up in smoke.

~oO0O0Oo~

It was another cheerless, frigid morning. I wish the school bus came this far, Fiona thought, glumly, considering the day. Wolf's pickup truck had broken down—again. Had Fiona's parents chosen to send her to the school within her district rather than the one the Drake kids attended, school would have been an easy bus ride away. Wolf never took the easy route, and the consequence was that Fiona missed a lot of school.

"Hey, Fiona," Pop joked, "When you're old like me, you can tell your kids how you had to hitchhike 25 miles in the snow, uphill both ways, just to get to school?"

"Very funny, Pop," she said. "I have a feeling my kids would think it's just about as funny as I do." She was thinking, If I survive until then. She was telling herself she was strong—and knowing she'd had to be for a long time. She needed to believe it. Snow and hitchhiking aside, she also was telling herself how much she liked school, how it was almost worth it to trek to campus where the teachers appreciated her, just to have some hours of normalcy and accomplishment every day.

One morning, Fiona was told to report to the principal's office at lunchtime. Walking down the hall toward her office, she worried nervously about what she could have possibly done wrong. She was at first relieved, then excited, to find it was simply because she'd done exceedingly well on a national, standardized test. She had no way of knowing the extent of the principal and her teacher's shock and awe that a child from such an "odd, deprived" household had done so well. And they had no way of knowing that in and through all the oddities of her life, Fiona had been garnering an education most people had no way to access.

The principal, clearly elated with Fiona's achievement, handed her a single, long-stemmed, deep-red rose. Fiona thanked her and secretly loved it—but she didn't want the other kids to see it. She hid it inside her locker until after the final bell rang.

"What's the rose for?" Pop asked Fiona as he picked her up after school. When she told her father the news, he didn't seem to share her excitement or surprise. "Of course you did well, Fiona; I expect no less from a Sprechelbach," he smiled—forgetting his vow to raise his children free from burdensome expectations. "And I have my own surprise for you. Your chariot awaits." He gestured toward his pickup truck, which he'd spent the day getting up and running again with the help of a neighbor. He hoped it would at least make one more round-trip, before it gave out completely.

Fiona was happy to have a ride home from school, but she was disappointed in her father's reaction to her achievement. Couldn't he, for once, share in her excitement instead of simply telling her it was expected of her? Deflated, Fiona slumped into the seat of the truck with a "humph." Looking over at her, Pop said, "Listen, Fiona, don't separate yourself." Fiona sat in silence during the ride home, wondering what that was supposed to mean. When Fiona got home, she took a cup from the kitchen, filled it with cool water, and headed upstairs with Regis to do her homework.

What Pop didn't explain was that he, too, had scored fabulously well on tests. In his case, it made him feel different from his peers. Being an outlier was the equivalent of an outcast, to Pop. But to Fiona, who already felt like she had a scarlet "O" on her forehead, the results pointed to the possibility she could perhaps fit in and succeed. Same experience, different takeaway, and neither understood each other's viewpoint, because they weren't talking to each other very much anymore.

~oO0O0O0o~

Pleasance School gave Fiona much more than an education. It was a place to go, a place to belong, to participate, to feel normal. A place to build a birdhouse in woodshop, and make disgusting stewed prunes. A place where sewing bright yellow bell-bottoms and a matching vest with a polka-dot satin lining counted as home economics. But it was choir that Fiona loved, best of all.

Even the dumb songs are fun to sing, Fiona thought, as the choir spelled out the letters for C-O-F-F-E-E, and continued with, "Coffee is not for me." The teacher let the kids laugh, hoping the song's deeper messages about choices, discipline, and moderation might sink in better that way.

"Class, we have two new songs today," the teacher called out, as she began handing out the sheet music to "God Bless America" and "Sunrise, Sunset," from the musical *Fiddler on the Roof*. These were just three of many, carefully selected, songs about life, death, patriotism, and wellness, chosen by a teacher who trusted in the power of music to form a helpful scaffolding for life.

As Fiona looked down at the music for "God Bless America," she felt her emotions at the base of her throat, like a lump. No way I'm going to cry. She thought. No freakin' way. She'd missed the States so much while in India that any song about America would likely have had the same effect.

"Students, choir must do more than teach you to sing," she said, as she stepped back to the piano. "It must help strengthen the moral compass." It was an open secret that the music selections all had a bass line of messaging running through them. And, as the children sang, their voices harmonizing with their classmates, each song subtly influenced their thinking.

For select students, the school offered another moral-compass opportunity: opt-in religious studies. "Pop, I have an idea." Fiona broached the subject with equal parts trepidation and intent.

"What's up, Fee?"

"There's a class at school I'm interested in taking, but students have to be Catholic to take it. Can you sign this paper, saying I'm Catholic, so I can investigate the subject?" The school had a program where Catholic children could leave the campus for an hour a week for religious studies, known as catechism. Fiona was intrigued, so she was asking her father to sign a permission slip.

"Let me look." Pop also seemed intrigued, which felt promising to Fiona. Open to his child exploring different perspectives, he checked the box identifying Fiona as Catholic, and signed his name. "Fiona," he said, looking up from the form, "Do you know the one about 'What's black and white, and black and blue?'"

"I know, Pop, a nun falling down some stairs."

"And what's black and white and laughing?"

"The nun who pushed her." With that, he fell into sharing a string of bad jokes, clearly conveying his lack of reverence for the topic.

The nuns welcomed the children with cookies. They were dressed just as Fiona had expected, except that around their waists, they wore a belt of large wooden rosary beads over their habit. They talked about peace, love, and justice. They taught them prayers to recite in the quiet moments of their day or just before bed. Some lessons, the students learned through fun activities, like a coloring page with Psalm 23: "The Lord is my shepherd; I shall not want." The nuns seemed especially fond of the Hail Mary, which they recited using the rosary beads. They wanted to impress on the children that Mary could intercede, when asked for help. And every time they met, they emphasized hope and faith, "Faith is the substance of things hoped for," and reminded the students to hold onto their hopes and dreams. Without fail, they reviewed The Golden Rule, "Do unto others as you would have them do unto you," paired with Jesus' Great Commandment, which they summarized as "Love God, Love People." When they spoke about their worldwide projects on behalf of the poor, Fiona could see they were living out their beliefs. Being loving beats just not being a jerk, she thought, and decided to change her top personal rule accordingly.

Fiona's Rule #1 (Modified)—Love God, Love People.

The nuns spent one class screening the film version of *Godspell*, the rock opera by Stephen Schwartz. Hey, Hebrew. Cool! Fiona thought, recognizing the Sabbath blessing used in the sharing of bread and wine in the Last Supper scene, reminding her of her time at Jewish summer camp. The music in *Godspell* was exciting, as were the visuals: full of hip-looking crowds tripping through junkyards and construction sites, including the unfinished Twin Towers in New York. All those ideas make sense, Fiona thought, as she packed up her things and said goodbye to the nuns before heading out the door.

"Day by daaaaay, day by daaaaay," Fiona sang, swinging hands with a classmate as they made their way along the road back to school. "Three things I praaaaay..." Fiona loved learning about peace and love and the arts and crafts that went with that. And she loved eating popcorn and hanging out with the nuns, watching movies. She even liked knowing the nuns were praying for her and the other kids, even though she knew that Pop would say prayer was unscientific.

~oOoOoOo~

One of the trailers, deep in the woods, that still had occupants in it was lived in by Noah, a some distant relative of Hanna's. Noah went by the nickname Red, after Eric the Red, the Viking invader. Red was older, taller, and stockier than Pop, and altogether more menacing. With his long, burly orange beard, bushy red eyebrows, and hot-headed temper, he fit his nickname well. Word was, he'd once had a full mane of shockingly red hair, before he'd shaved it all off. Now, he kept his head bald and shiny. With the right cap, he'd be a perfectly menacing, red-bearded Santa, Fiona thought. She could hardly remember what Red's wife and kids looked like, or if she'd ever seen them leave the trailer. They mostly kept to themselves. But not always.

One evening, Red stopped in for a visit, and it was obvious he'd been drinking. Fiona had seen people get drunk plenty of times, and noticed that it affected different people differently. Pop got talkative, slightly silly, and sleepy. She hadn't spent enough time with Red to know what to expect. If she had, she'd have known to look out for violence. She might have guessed it anyway; Red struck Fiona as scary on a good day. Today, he seemed louder, more hostile, and downright sinister. Drunk and riled up about who knew what, Red was a fearsome presence. As he towered over Pop, fists raised, Fiona thought, Pop, why are you reasoning with him? That only works with sober people. She watched as logic and reason utterly and completely failed to assuage the situation. Before she knew it, and for no reason Fiona could conjure, Red picked up the television and hoisted it over his head.

Fiona watched, dumbstruck, as their television went flying through a living room window, shattering the pane and destroying the television. As it landed with a crash, on the front porch, Fiona's heart was beating so fast, she forgot to breathe. Uncle Mark, another trailer tenant hold-out, who was on a long evening stroll with his son, heard the commotion from far up the street. They stopped in their tracks and looked down the road to the Sprechelbach home just as the glass shattered. "Daddy, daddy! They threw their TV out the window! Why did they do that, daddy?" Mark's little boy asked.

"I don't know, son. I don't know," Mark answered, shaking his head, as he ushered his child on by. He wasn't going to get involved in the fray. He had a child to protect.

Fiona wanted to run over and look through the jagged glass to the damage below. But, she didn't dare, choosing instead, to remain rooted to her spot behind the upholstered chair. The noise of the shattered glass seemed to break through Red's rage, and bring him back to reason. Abruptly, he turned around and left. Quietly, Fiona tiptoed up the stairs and into her room, closing the door behind her. She slept fitfully that night, in fear that Red would decide to come back. She had a feeling he'd continue to drink until dawn.

The next morning, surveying the damage to the already ramshackle house, Fiona was relieved that no one had been hurt—physically, anyway. She was no longer afraid; she was angry. That was a brand-new storm window, whose shards she was now sweeping up. Gram had given Pop the money to put it in, to help bring a little warmth to the winter, and Fiona had watched Gram's money go right "out the window," along with Fiona's best source of entertainment and connection.

A drunken, alcoholic rage had confirmed that Red—a supposed member of the family—could transform into an unrecognizable, menacing stranger. She was not safe. Yet Pop was allowing him to remain in their lives. Yes, he's family, Fiona thought. But he's downright dangerous. Doesn't that trump, well, everything? Where are the boundaries? Rural Pennsylvania could get Eskimo-cold in winter, but living with this kind of violence sent a chill to the very center of Fiona's bones. New windows could offer no shelter from the familial storms of Mystic Meadow. This winter, hell just might freeze over.

Wolf wanted—needed—a break from the violence, from the sense of loss he was experiencing as he was forced to envision a life without Hanna. He needed a break from the responsibility of holding everything together in her absence. The next night, he went out on his own, leaving Fiona in the house, without him. She wasn't alone, he reasoned, since Buddy, the last remaining member of the commune and a reclusive kind of guy, was home. Buddy was an odd-looking dude, Wolf knew, with his sparsely scattered hair, wild eyes, and stoop-shouldered gait, but he also believed him to be harmless. Buddy tended to keep to himself. It would be fine to leave Fiona with him, Wolf told himself. Maybe because it would be, maybe because he needed it to be, maybe because he didn't think it through.

It wasn't okay. Not even close.

Buddy turned from the window, where he'd been watching Wolf's truck disappear down the dirt road. "Hey, Fiona, come over here. Wanna play a game?"

"Okay, I guess." Fiona really just wanted to read, in her room. "What kind of game?"

"It's make believe," he said. "You like make believe, don't you? Here." He handed her a glass. "Here's how it works. You drink orange juice, I drink beer. And we make believe you can drink me under the table."

"Very funny, Buddy."

"Yeah, I'm just playin' with you. Go get the orange juice out of the refrigerator, and we'll play."

Fiona did as she was told. The orange juice was cold and sweet, but it had a kind of funny taste to it. She wasn't sure she liked it. Still, every time Buddy toasted her, clinking his beer bottle to her glass and telling her to drink, she sipped some more. Buddy was insistent that she finish the glass. "You're way behind, Fiona. I've had much more than you. C'mon, drink up!"

Fiona had no idea how much of that juice she drank, but she found herself wanting to just close her eyes and rest her head on the table. And then her world went black. Fiona had no memory of how she got up the stairs and into her room, out of her dress and tights, and into her bed.

She woke up the next morning with a splitting headache and wondered if the sparklies were going to show up. I don't feel so great, she thought. Looking at her rumpled sheets, she realized the flower pattern was a little blurry. Her heart sank as she realized she'd thrown up on her favorite blanket, the one Karen had given her. "I wish my big sister were here. She'd help me feel better, and maybe help me clean up this mess."

Fiona folded her soiled blanket, knowing she'd need to wash it right away, before the whole room started to smell. She tossed it onto her chair where, she noticed, her pajama bottoms had been flung over the arm. She looked down at herself and back to the chair. That's weird? Fiona tried to think back to the night before but couldn't remember any of it. As she continued to try to remember, a new wave of nausea rushed over her, and she threw up, again. She felt sick and achy all over. Her head still hurt, but so did her whole body, really. She sank down into her bedcovers and let herself drift back into sleep.

Later that morning, when Fiona was downstairs washing her blanket in the bathtub with some boiled water from the potbelly stove, Pop came in and asked her what she was doing. "Laundry, Pop. I'm not feeling so good but I've got it covered."

Wolf looked at the bathtub and stated the obvious. "Bit of a mess there. Did you get sick last night, Fiona?"

"Buddy asked me to play a make-believe game. He gave me orange juice, and he had beer. We were supposed to see who could drink the most. I had some, but I really don't remember what..." Wolf was gone before Fiona could finish her sentence. He found Buddy in his room.

"What the hell is wrong with you, man?"

"Nothin' a couple of brewskies won't fix." Buddy offered him an open bottle. Wolf slapped it to the floor.

"Hey, that's good stuff you're wastin.'"

"You're the one who's wasted. What the hell were you thinking, engaging Fiona in a drinking game? You don't give alcohol to a child, you sonofabitch. She's hungover. That's not good for a growing brain!"

"It was orange juice, Wolf; she's a ham, and you're over-reacting."

"Orange juice! A kid doesn't puke in her bed over orange juice."

"Maybe she has the flu," said Buddy, opening another beer. "Don't believe me? Go check the juice for yourself," he added, knowing he'd already poured out the evidence the night before, and Wolf wouldn't find a thing if he went looking.

Wolf stared at Buddy a moment and then let it go. He had no way of knowing what was true, and it just didn't occur to him that anything untoward could have happened to his child in his absence. Maybe because he needed her to be okay. Maybe because he didn't think it all the way through. Maybe because he couldn't.

"All right, man; gimme one of those beers."

~oOOoOOo~

From then on, whenever Wolf left the house, Fiona made a point to tag along with him, even though she hated to go out on school nights. Even though she knew how late her father would stay out. Fiona needed a vigilant parent, now, more than ever. But vigilance had left Mystic Meadow, and she'd taken Holly and Violet with her.

Whenever Fiona tagged along, she brought her homework, and a library book or two, and installed herself in the kitchen, where the light was brightest. Some of Wolf's friends kept a horse out back, and she and the other kids often amused themselves riding it until darkness fell, or until they got tired of being knocked off. This horse didn't much care to be ridden, and would regularly head straight toward the low branches of the nearby crabapple trees to free himself of pesky children.

One such evening, when Fiona had finished falling off horses and puzzling out her homework, she wandered from the kitchen to the living room of the house where Pop was partying with his friends. Peering through the veil of pot smoke shrouding the room, she found her father and asked him, politely, if they could go home. Isn't this a little backwards? she thought. Shouldn't Pop be the one making me go home early from a party with my friends? She tugged on her father's sweater. "Pop, check out the time. It's really late."

"Don't worry about it, Fiona."

"But Pop, it's a school night. I'm tired. Can't we just go home?"

"C'mon, now, Fiona. You're the one who wanted to tag along." Pop was getting annoyed. He took a hit off the joint passed to him, waited, and then spoke through clenched vocal chords. "If you're sleepy, why not curl up on the couch?"

Yeah, she'd invited herself along. She almost regretted it, but she wasn't about to stay home alone with Buddy again, either. Fiona longed for old times, when Hanna would tuck her into her pretty bed, smoothing the bangs from her forehead, before reading her a bedtime story. When she conjured up the scene in her mind's eye, it seemed more like a bedtime story than anything that had ever really happened. Had life ever been that simple?

Fiona looked at her father, who had already returned his attention to his friends, and then slunk over to the couch and grabbed a woven throw blanket. Nobody noticed as she brushed off some tortilla chips, curled up at the edge, and drifted off to sleep, downhearted and certain she was going to miss yet another day of school.

~oOOoOOo~

Fiona and Karen stayed in touch with each other through Gram, knowing she'd forward their letters from wherever Fiona or Karen happened to be staying. Karen, was now living in Colorado. A single mom, just like Mother had been, she was raising her toddler son, Chayton. When one of Karen's sweet, sisterly letters arrived, Fiona ran to her room, and read it avidly. Wow, Fiona thought, biting her lower lip. She says she's sorry things are hard for me sometimes. Just thinking about her older sister being far away but caring about her made her throat hurt. Fiona read on.

"She's the first person to believe me, Regis!" Fiona exclaimed aloud, startling her dog, who jumped off the bed. "I just knew she would, though." Noticing how startled Regis was, Fiona patted the bed until Regis jumped back up, and settled in again. "And you believed me too, don't you? Doggus woggus shnoggus, who's a good boy? Listen to what she says, here. She says there's stuff going on in the unseen realm, and mostly people try to ignore it or try to convince themselves it's not there. But once you know, you can deal. She's got all sorts of ideas for us. "

Fiona read on silently as Karen's letter described a few tricks she could try to help uplift an oppressive space, including burning some dried sage like incense at each corner of the room, or imagining herself covered in a blanket of light, to blind anything that likes darkness. At the end of her letter, she advised Fiona to turn over to her higher power anything that felt impossibly hard for her to tackle alone, saying "I can't, but you can." That was something Karen had learned from an AA meeting. She added, "Fear Not!" and "Blessed Be!" before signing off with "loads of love."

Fiona pressed her sister's letter against her chest, then folded the letter neatly and returned it to its envelope. A fortune from a fortune cookie fell out of the envelope, as she did. How'd I miss that? She wondered, as she read the fortune. It read, "More than a platitude is an attitude of gratitude." Well, that was silly!

Fiona was both buoyed and soothed by Karen's concern. When she asked her father about her, he hinted that Karen was struggling a bit, as a single mom. He was right. It wasn't easy for Karen, working nights as a bartender, forever in search of childcare for Chayton, and functioning on too-little sleep as she rose with the dawn—and her toddler—to feed him breakfast and start his day. But, Karen didn't dwell on it, at least not in writing. Instead, she filled her letters with encouragement, conveying her own unspoken rule, "Lift others with your words," and reminding Fiona not to be afraid of life.

Fiona's (Karen's) Rule #6: Fear Not.

On the rare occasions when Wolf was present and available, he was good company for Fiona. But that wasn't too often anymore. He didn't seem to care much about food these days, and he'd never been one to enjoy setting foot in the kitchen to prepare a meal for anyone. That task had belonged to Hanna and the other women at the commune. After seeing "that little slip of a thing" become wan and even more waiflike, the matron who served lunch at Fiona's school sensed something was up at home. She started giving Fiona bigger and bigger portions. For Fiona, lunch couldn't come too soon. She didn't notice the volume of food on her plate, but was focused on how delicious it all tasted; she merely scarfed it down, leaving nothing on the plate. Today was Wednesday, Welsh Rarebit day. Fiona thought she'd never tasted anything so good. She cleared her dishes and handed her tray to the matron, who quietly handed her a little bag. Fiona looked up at the woman and then into the bag, where she saw some biscuits, an apple, and a small carton of milk. Feeling too grateful to be embarrassed, Fiona smiled at the woman and accepted her gift, glad she would have something for later.

She headed over to the school auditorium to catch a film her school was showing. It was a horror flick, *House of Usher*, based on Edgar Allen Poe's "The Fall of the House of Usher." Fiona would have found it creepy anyway, but Poe's house hit a little too close to home for comfort. She'd been hoping for something uplifting, that would give her a great escape from her life, not take her deeper into the darkness of Mystic Meadow.

~oOOoOOo~

Wolf was losing the farm. Even Hanna's staying couldn't have saved it, but now the bankers were coming. Hanna's father had heard about the foreclosure and offered to pay the rest of the mortgage in one $20,000 lump sum, and take the property into his own name for safekeeping. A man of business, he knew how to run things without sacrificing them. He meant to care for the property—upgrade and maintain it, bring out its value—and find a way for Wolf to stay on. He didn't want a farm, but he'd stepped up anyway. Wolf, though, was too proud to accept. After a while, Hanna's father quit trying to convince him, and no one else came to Wolf's rescue.

Surveying the property, Wolf shuddered at the enormity of his felt failure. He'd failed to sustain his relationship with Hanna and her dream of living in harmony on a communal farm. He had failed to locate any alternative employment after his consulting gig fell through. He could barely keep himself and Fiona fed; he certainly couldn't afford to feed a big dog like Regis. His cousin Mark offered to take Regis off his hands. Wolf had agreed—a deal brokered behind Fiona's back. It had to be done, but he had no idea how to share the news with his daughter. He knew it would break her heart. And that, he realized, would break his.

Pop sat down on Fiona's bed that evening, and patiently listened to the chirpy voice recounting her day to him. She was so optimistic, forever finding reasons to remain hopeful, to see the best in people, places, and situations. Yet, when he broke the news about Regis, he watched her light go out.

Fiona absolutely couldn't believe what she was hearing from her father.

"You're an Indian giver!" she fumed.

"Fiona, that's an outdated, inappropriate phrase," said Pop.

"Yeah, well, the settlers gave stuff to the Indians with one hand, and took it away with the other, didn't they?"

"That's not exactly what that means…" Wolf realized a moment too late that this wasn't the right time for a history lesson or a political debate. Chastened by his child's tear-streaked face, he got up off her bed and silently walked out of the room. He simply had no solution, nothing to give or say to her. She wasn't wrong. He was taking her dog, and seriously eying her bank account. There were no words for that. It was indefensible, and he knew it. He did just what his own father would have done: drowned his thoughts in some Crown Royal.

Fiona hugged Regis all night, weeping between moments of sleep. The next day, she stayed home from school to play with Regis. They went out to the wooden ruins at the edge of the property, where there had once been some structure, maybe a barn. She sat down in grass to talk to her dog. She thought about running away with him, but she didn't know how to take care of herself, let alone a big dog. They spent the day together, walking along the abandoned railroad tracks, playing fetch with an errant pinecone, and cuddling. All too soon, she knew it was time to get back to the house, so Pop could relinquish Regis to Uncle Mark.

"You're a good dog, Regis. You're going to be okay." Here she was saying goodbye to her beloved big dog for the second time since first falling in love with him at the lunar landing party. While she'd been able to hold out hope during the rugged separation during the family's journey to India, this time it seemed quite final.

When Fiona and Regis got back to the house, Pop was waiting for them in the truck. Although he was irritated that she'd been gone so long, he didn't show it. Instead, he opened the tailgate, and Regis dutifully hopped into the back. Then he opened the side door and helped Fiona climb into the cab. No one said a word on the drive to the trailer where Mark and his family were staying.

Fiona thought about staying in the truck, about keeping her eyes closed and not having to see Regis leave her life. But, she wanted to touch him, to look in his eyes, to bury her face and her hands in his wooly fur one more time. "I love you, Regis," she whispered into his fur. "You're my best friend. I love you, Boy." Her tears disappeared into his thick coat.

Pop put his hand on Fiona's shoulder, signaling it was time to go. She patted Regis one more time and, without looking at her father or Mark, she got herself back into the truck and looked at her lap, sobbing. Mark held the dog's collar as the truck pulled away and disappeared down the road. Fiona never looked up. She felt her heart shattering into a million pieces, piercing her with each breath, like shards of broken glass.

Arriving home, she climbed out of the truck and ran over to the big sugar maple tree in the yard. She climbed up into the solace of its branches and sat in its embrace until bedtime, watching the ants crawl across the bark, and picking apart a leaf.

~oOoOOOo~

The following day, Pop let Fiona go over to her friend's house to help take her mind off Regis. She had begun the visit by talking about Regis for the first hour. Her friend had been a willing and sympathetic audience to her story, and it had been soothing and a help to Fiona to share her grief. Pop's truck pulled into the yard around four o'clock to pick up Fiona and bring her home. She still wasn't speaking to him—only the essentials—so it began as a quiet ride across town. Fiona turned on the radio and messed with the receiver nob until she heard something familiar: "American Pie" by Don McLean. Yay, I love this song. Fiona thought, tapping her fingers on the dash...and music hasn't died yet.

About 100 feet from the train tracks, the brakes went out on the truck. Fiona could tell Pop was starting to panic. Just then, she heard the whistle of the oncoming train. Pop pumped the brakes, but nothing happened. The truck continued to move forward, toward the tracks. Fiona could see the train in the distance. She started whispering the Hail Mary the nuns had taught her, "Hail Mary, full of grace..." Pop leaned across her, and opened her door. "Okay,

Fiona, get ready to jump." She kept on praying, her heart racing. Just as Pop was getting ready to call it and push his child out the door, the truck slowed down and came to a stop.

"ooooWOOOoooooooooooo."

The train rushed by, the whistle, changing its tone as it passed. Only then, did Fiona start to cry. Pop put his hand on hers and closed his fingers in a gentle grasp. She looked in his eyes, as they both caught their breath, hearts racing. "It's okay, Pop. We're okay." But things were far from okay. These days, from her vantage point, the whole adventure in Pleasance was like riding in a purple pickup truck without brakes, heading for a rendezvous with some oncoming train.

Wolf stopped driving his purple truck, leaving it to weather in the yard. He stopped going much of anywhere, really, except to hitchhike to and from school with Fiona. Things turned even bleaker at home. As Christmas approached, Fiona wrote an early letter addressed to Santa and left it out where Pop was likely to see it.

Dear Santa,
It's fine, here. Don't worry about bringing any presents this year. I don't need anything anyway.
Love,
Fiona.

Fiona had long since stopped believing in fairy tales and Santa, but she wrote about them for school assignments, and people still kept giving her reasons to believe in hope. At school, her teacher took to slipping snacks into her desk, augmenting the food the kindly lunch matron continued to send her way. Nobody asked anything about her life. They didn't need to ask. They could see hardship in her tiny frame and the unwashed clothes she wore, repeatedly, to school. And they quietly acted.

~o0O0O0o~

It had been a good day at school, and Fiona was out on the school playground, awaiting her father. Earlier in the day, her story, "The Wings" had earned her a golden star. It glistened on the page, just like the wings in the story she'd written about finding. She'd imagined that when she'd donned them, she'd shrunk to the size of her pet mouse, so she'd made a saddle of hay and blue jeans, and put the wings on her mouse. Riding the mouse took some doing, and she'd sprained her ankle learning how, but ultimately, they'd reached another side of the world, where she could live in a nest, fed by birds. Well, Fiona thought, staring at the shiny gold star, I wrote that we may be there, still, but if we were, I wouldn't be so cold!

It had snowed the night before, and Fiona was getting colder by the minute as she waited, blowing into her mittens to warm her hands. She wished the numbness would set in, so she didn't have to feel the sting of the cold. Sitting on a swing on the empty playground, twisting back and forth in the seat as her feet traced a Figure 8 in the snow, she looked over to the other swing, and whispered under her breath, "It sure would be good to have some company. Does anybody even care? If the nuns are right and anybody's out there, just make the swing next to me move, so I can feel less alone out here." In that moment, the swing moved, slightly, for the first time since she'd been sitting there. Fiona gasped. Then, she laughed at herself for having such a thought. It was probably just the breeze. Who, besides toddlers and nuns, believes in invisible friends! Good thing nobody was around to see me talking at swing sets.

Just then, Pop showed up, rubbing it hands. "Sorry, Fee. It was hard to catch a lift. How'd it go at school today?" he asked, his words a visible fog in the cold, winter air.

"Fine, Pop," she answered, as they trudged to the main road to hitch a ride home. It had been a great day at school, but she didn't say so; she didn't feel like sharing it. He'd just say, "Of course, Fee, I expected no less," anyway. So, why bother?

Soon, a neighbor picked them up. They climbed into the truck's warmth, gratefully. Once Fiona got home, she slid off the truck's high seat to the ground, and headed upstairs to do her homework. As she opened her workbook, her eye wandered to the chemistry set, sitting on the shelf at the side of her desk. Maybe just one experiment, she thought. Measuring some baking soda into a test tube, she added a little vinegar. "Ha!" She squealed in delight as she watched

146

the chemical volcano froth over the edge in a sea of soft bubbles, leaving harmless salt-water. The idea of mixing an acid and a base and getting simple, salty tears got Fiona thinking. She started wondering aloud about the chemistry of sadness. Strangely enough, she thought, chocolate doesn't neutralize sadness as might be expected. She wondered, isn't sadness caustic? And isn't chocolate an acid? Maybe they weren't equally strong. Not having any chocolate to test, she moved back to her homework again.

The afternoon was still young, so Fiona decided to head over to see Jules and Pam, the couple who lived almost a mile up the road from Mystic Meadow. On any other day, she would have gone for a romp along the plowed tracks across the meadow with her beloved Regis. But now instead of Regis, there was a gaping hole in her heart. So, she thought she'd treat herself with a kind couple who had a TV and never seemed to mind if she stopped in to watch it with them. Today was a particularly cold day, and the snow was high. The trek to their home would be worth it, though, for the company, the entertainment, and the pretzels and hot chocolate she knew they'd have for her.

After receiving Fiona with warm hugs, Pam seated her on the hearth cushions before a roaring fire, from where Fiona could see the television perfectly. She disappeared into the kitchen and returned, shortly, with a bowl of twisted pretzels and a steaming mug of hot chocolate, topped with mini marshmallows. An hour passed quickly as Fiona watched the afternoon programming and chatted with her friends during commercials. They seemed to take such interest in Fiona's schoolwork, which inspired her to share "The Wings" story with them. When she finished recounting the tale, they clapped their hands and told her how clever and insightful she was. Fiona wished she could stay in that warm, encouraging home forever. But once Pam began setting the table for dinner, she knew it was her cue to head back to her own cold, lonely home. Besides, it would be dark soon. She would have given anything for an invitation to join them, particularly as she smelled the aromas wafting from the kitchen. But they didn't extend the offer. Instead, just as Fiona was heading toward the door, Pam handed her a bag bulging with half a loaf of fresh-baked bread and some cheese. "Take care of yourself, sweetie," she said, giving Fiona one more hug.

The sun was just beginning its downward descent as Fiona pulled on her bright-red snow pants, her boots, mittens, and coat. Then she wrapped her favorite scarf, the one Holly had made for her, around her neck. Most kids out in the country wore bright colors as protection against the non-locals. They rented snowmobiles for their sport hunting sessions, and they often drank and drove erratically. Despite the obvious signs posted against it, they would trespass on private property. Parents feared they'd shoot anything that moved. Wrapping their kids in bright colors was the protective armor parents hoped would keep their kids from being confused for deer. Most of the time, it worked. Particularly when kids went out in groups. But today, Fiona was on her own, and it was starting to get dark.

As she trudged home, the snow fell above her from a dark, heavy sky. Fiona sensed an odd, metallic taste in her mouth. Pop had said it was from the pollution humans keep dumping into the atmosphere. The particles get mixed in with the snow and fall, with it, to the ground. Fiona was getting tired, and she wasn't even half-way home. Knowing she had to keep going somehow, she decided to make a game of it. Now think! How many steps until you get home? 2,400? You can do that. No problem. Let's see, how can you make that number seem smaller. Just count every six steps. What's 2,400 divided by six? 400. See? Much smaller. Anyone can do 400 sets of steps. Let's do this! One, two, three, four, five, six, 399. One, two, three, four, five, six…398. One, two, three, four, five, six, 397…

Fiona soldiered on, by sixes. Then, as the wind picked up, swirling the flurries and making it harder to see, she tripped on something hidden in the snow. Falling flat on her face, Fiona lay there for a moment, startled by the jarring fall and the cold snow against her cheeks. She sat up. Suddenly she imagined Pop on the sofa back at Mystic Meadow, in the deep sleep of a heavy drinker. If I stop right here, I'm done for, she thought. No one will come looking for me, unless there's a snowmobiler out, in which case they'd probably be drunk, mistake me for a deer, and shoot me. How weird would it be if a snowmobile showed up right now? She knew it wasn't likely.

One of the bigger snowflakes sparkled in a last remaining ray of sunlight as it melted on her eyelash, and as it disappeared, it put her in mind of a friendly firefly she'd met at Girl Scout camp another time she was alone and afraid. Not everything that's scary in life is deadly, she remembered. Deciding she was okay, and the snow-covered rock or root hadn't done her any harm, she took a moment to raise and lower her arms and legs, making an angel in the snow. It's the least I can do, to show my gratitude, she thought.

Wouldn't it be great if instead of a rock or a root, it had been a Hobbit, straight out of J.R.R. Tolkien's fantasy novel? What if one had popped up from Middle-earth to befriend Fiona and escort her safely home? Fiona lay there in the snow, mid-angel, enjoying the fantasy. No, today was a day without Hobbits. Plenty of snowflakes, though.

Another big snowflake cluster flew into her eye and, as she brushed it away, it melted. It reminded her of a teardrop. Heaven's frozen tears. She thought about crying, even thought it might be appropriate. But her tears would turn into icicles, and then her face would freeze and shatter into a million pieces. Way to crack a smile, she thought. And then, she laughed out loud. Oh, Pop would love that! I've got to get home and tell him my joke.

Fiona gathered herself and continued her slog home. She really didn't like this trek, even though it had been worth it to get some warmth at Jules and Pam's home. She didn't like the life she was lead-ing, so far and away from the dreams she'd once held about being her mother's child, living in a more normal world. It had been so long since she'd pondered that dream, she'd all but forgotten it. It didn't seem to fit anymore.

Her new dream was to hang in there, to tough it out until the age of emancipation. That was the dream of freedom that kept her hope alive, and hope was what kept her going. Sometimes, she even al-lowed herself to envision the day when she and Karen could share a small mortgage on a modest cottage somewhere, waiting for the day when Holly and Violet would finish college and join them. Eighteen wasn't so many years away, was it? It sure seemed distant. Maybe she could make a break for it at sixteen. Just a few more years. Just a few more steps…

Fiona was getting fatigued. I could just lie down right now and sleep in this pure, white snow, just dream my way to that warm house with my sisters, she thought. I could give up right now. The bright colors of Holly's scarf caught her eye, halting her thoughts. Wait. It's going to be great. We can all move to California or back to New York City or Providence or Philly. We have choices. We could live anywhere. Fiona thought a moment. Well, not anywhere. Not India, and not here, at Mystic Meadow, heavens forfend—a favorite phrase, like "heaven forbid," she'd learned from the nuns. But we could live just about anywhere else, as long as we're together. So, everyone has to hang in there, to grow up strong and smart, so we can get there. So we can live together. So we can be safe.

Fiona didn't lie down again. She kept going, counting her way along the snowy trail, toward her new dream. Where was I? One, two, three, four, five, six, 100. Getting closer! One, two, three, four, five, six, 99…

Just as the sky turned dark, too dark for a child to be out on her own, really—but there was no one to wonder—Fiona's frozen fingers reached for the handle of Mystic Meadow's front door, unlocked, of course. Nothing worth stealing remained in the house. She knew there wouldn't be much to eat. Maybe some cereal. Likely no milk.

Most evenings, she found Pop deep into his bottle of booze, and sinking lower and lower into his grief. Everything seemed to ransom his focus from food…and Fiona. But tonight, as Fiona left her snow clothes in the chilly front room and slipped into the kitchen, her heart leapt when she heard the snap and crackle of logs burning. Pop had lit the potbelly stove!

"Hey, Fee! Just in time for some of my famous soup." Fiona could hardly believe her eyes as she watched Pop stirring his homemade chicken soup on the stove. When he was up to cooking, he pretty much relied on two recipes: one for roast chicken and another for the chicken soup made from leftovers. Some days there was chicken, then chicken soup, then nothing. But today, there was something. There was soup, and there was Pop to share it with. Fiona opened the fridge, wondering if there might be milk to put in her tea. Today was her lucky day.

"Oh! I almost forgot!" Fiona pulled out the bag she had carried all the way from Jules and Pam's. She unfolded the edges and pulled out the half-loaf of fresh bread and the cheese. "Look, Pop! Tonight, we have a feast!"

By the time Fiona had finished washing the dishes and cleaning up the kitchen, she found Pop asleep on the couch, hands locked behind his head, as they so often were. She smiled at her father. He didn't mean any harm; he just wasn't very good at the traditional mom role. They needed someone else to complete them. Both she and Pop knew they needed Hanna and Holly and Vi, but lately, they didn't even talk about them. Fiona knew her father had been feeling down, and he'd been spending a lot of time on that sofa. But tonight, he'd come through. The soup tasted great, and it had warmed her in many ways. Fiona heard the whistle blow on the kettle she'd set for tea. She looked out the window as she waited for her tea to steep, happily watching the falling snow from inside. She loved it when she had a warm home, with a warm meal waiting for her. It was so unexpected these days.

The next day was a Friday, and Fiona was looking forward to visiting her friend's house after school, which was on the school bus route. It was a special treat for Fiona, who thought about how she loved riding school buses—probably because she so rarely had the opportunity to sit in community with her classmates. Fiona was boarding the bus with her friends when she heard Pop's voice yelling, "Fiona. Get off that bus at once." He hollered so loud that every child on the bus fixed their eyes on Fiona. Slowly, she made her way off, mortified. What did I do? Fiona wondered. Did Pop absent-mindedly forget the plan? "Absent-minded" was the phrase Fiona used to explain her father's constant mental state to herself and, sometimes, to her friends. Yes. Fiona thought. Pop just forgot. That's it.

But, that wasn't it, at all.

As she climbed back down the bus steps and went over to her father, he told her he needed her money. All of it.

"But Pop," she said. "All I have is what I've saved in the bank." Fiona had saved every penny from every allowance from the days when she'd received a monthly amount, plus every cash gift she'd ever received. Reaching a grand total of $100 had made her very proud and had given her a sense of security. Until today, that is.

It was just after the New Year, and school had started up again. Fiona had been avoiding talking about Christmas with her classmates, as Santa had taken Fiona up on her offer that he could pass by the Sprechelbachs this year. She knew money was tight. She didn't know that things were this desperate. Walking to the bank, Pop told her that they were leaving the farm and moving back in with Gram. Pop had already given the school notice that Fiona was being transferred to Philadelphia in the middle of the term.

Fiona and Pop walked silently through the snow together to the local bank, to withdraw her life's savings. I will not cry, Fiona told herself, as she dutifully signed the piece of paper the teller slid toward her. But, when Pop snatched away the money, five crisp $20 bills, before she could even have the dignity of giving it to him, she had a hard time holding back the tears. Fiona noticed the teller looking at Pop and then at her, detecting a hint of pity in his eyes. She pretended not to notice. If she did, she really might cry, and she couldn't have that.

Next stop, U-Haul. After that, Fiona stayed in the truck while Pop, money in hand, disappeared inside a liquor store. Moments later, he emerged with a few bottles in hand, each tucked inside a plain brown wrapper. That weekend, Pop packed up their few belongings and helped Fiona do the same, including her guitar, a few toys, and some clothes. Together, they set out for Gram's house in Philadelphia. After that mortifying scene on the school bus, Fiona was relieved that there was no time for goodbyes.

4. CITY GIRL

The moment Wolf's truck pulled into the driveway of Gram's house—having made its final excursion—Fiona felt she could exhale. Fiona loved Philly. To Fiona, the city truly lived up to the meaning of its name, "The City of Brotherly Love."

She ran up the front stairs of the house, threw off her warm outer clothes, and rushed into Gram's arms. Wow, Gram, smells great! she thought. Gram had, of course, been cooking. Pretty soon, she was seated at the dinner table. She looked at the meal Gram had prepared and set in place for her son and granddaughter.

A platter of green bell peppers stuffed with ground meat, mixed with tomato sauce and rice was set in the middle of the table. Gram's meals centered on beef. Having raised hungry sons, she was an expert in satisfying growing appetites with hearty fare. Her thrifty trick was to buy half a cow from the butcher—220 pounds of beef— at a time. Her secondary freezer in the basement could be counted on to contain plenty of ground beef, steaks, roasts, ribs, brisket, tenderloin, and so much more.

Warm white bread sat steaming in slices in the wicker bread basket. Salad, made from a wedge of iceberg lettuce, drenched in a mock Thousand Island dressing made from a mixture of ketchup and mayonnaise with a little pickle relish stirred in, sat at each place, next to a glass of soda pop. Fiona smiled at her grandmother, delighted, and sat down.

Gram's house had been built for an opera singer, and the massive "great room" had three couches along its lead-lined, soundproof walls. The room was so big that, during the holidays, Gram put up two Christmas trees, one freshly cut, and the other, artificial. Gram had kept her trees up past the traditional 12th day of Christmas, just for Fiona, who found the sight utterly magical as she came into the dimly lit room. The tree lights cast a soft glow and added a sparkle to all the ornaments. It seemed new to her, every year, and she gasped when she saw it, enchanted, as if for the first time.

The great room also had a chess table off to one side, with the chess board etched right into the tabletop, its carved pieces in place, and formal chairs ready and waiting for a game. The airlock entry led right to the great room, so kids could kick off their boots in the mud room and scurry straight into the warmth of the house. And, if it wasn't warm enough, Fiona was allowed to light a fire in the huge fireplace, with newspaper, kindling, and logs at the ready. Out back, there was a large, landscaped yard, which Gram's gardeners kept in impeccable shape, with seasonal gardens, a gazebo for gathering in the summer, a sheltered dog run, and vines, which produced huge, wild, dark-purple, sour grapes late in the season. They were as big as eyeballs and about as appetizing. A long driveway concluded, to the right of the yard, near an old wooden swing set Wolf had played on as a child. The whole place felt like heaven on earth to Fiona. At long last, she felt at home.

Gram's house was made of Wissahickon Schist, the distinctive sparkly bedrock underlying much of eastern Pennsylvania, and it contributed to Fiona's belief that this really was a magic castle. With a film projection booth in the attic, plus a filled gumball machine and retired carousel horse, the home was a warm and welcoming place for kids. The house crested Chestnut Hill, within walking distance of Wissahickon and Cresheim creeks, full of exploratory fun. Coming home, even their muddy feet sparkled. "It's magic helping dust!" Gram would say. "Very good for the roses. Stomp your feet hard to get as much of it off out there for them as you can, before you come indoors." A little dust would inevitably stay with Fiona's shoes for luck, making its way through her socks, leaving her feet sparkling.

It's magical—like Dragon and Tank, Fiona thought. Dragon and Tank were Gram's two Afghan hounds who ran like the wind and loved and guarded Fiona, the house, and its grounds. Ever eager to greet her, but taller than her, their jumps sometimes knocked her down. Yes, they were fabulous, but they were also undeniably odd. Dragon had the habit of meeting Gram in the kitchen and "helping" her empty the groceries. She was especially fond of egg cartons, retrieving them and carrying them gently in her teeth to her basement lair, safe on the washing machine. Tank was even stranger. If you didn't smell like a Sprechelbach, or if you surprised him, Tank might bite you. Fiona noticed folks walked across to the other side of the street when she walked Dragon and Tank. Good thing they did, she thought. Really good thing. Fiona loved the two dogs, and as she spent time in their presence, she felt the well of loneliness and grief at losing Regis begin to fill.

Fiona was elated to find herself in a gracious home, with heat and running water, a place where she could sink into the soft bed in her pretty room and sleep soundly, where she could feel comfortable bringing friends, where she knew she would eat regular, wholesome meals, where simple rules of civility like table manners were expected. Gram noticed that Fiona was underweight, even for her small frame. Rather than mentioning it and risking trouble, she simply set out to resolve it. She kept snacks at the ready, some of them healthy and some of them treats, as she rightly assumed her grandchild had missed out on those, as well as more nutritious fare. For her part, Fiona luxuriated in Gram's bountiful meals and loving care, but she couldn't stop wondering how long this idyllic layover would last. She took to hiding little items of food—a jar of honey at the back of her underwear drawer, for instance, as if she were a squirrel preparing for a lean winter.

Fiona settled gratefully into the security, the stability, the structure of Gram's house. She hoped it would be a while before they had to leave—she'd had enough of leaving for a while. Even when invited to sleepovers, she didn't seem able to bear leaving Gram's for a full night. Gram stayed awake and dressed, ready for the phone call around eleven in the evening, when Fiona would "have allergies" or some other concocted reason to have to come home early.

In the ensuing days, Fiona settled into a comfortable daily rhythm. Although there were the hounds to play with, Gram wanted Fiona to have something to call her own, so she bought her a Wooly Bear hamster Fiona named Boo. Fiona was delighted. Gram also fostered Fiona's artistic sensibilities, just as she had among her own children. Fiona was enrolled in art lessons at the art museum, and she was accepted into the Philadelphia Girls Choir. Her voice had been so clear, so pure, so true at her audition that Gram had pulled a lace handkerchief from her handbag to dab at tears as she listened to Fiona's *a Capella* rendition of "Somewhere Over the Rainbow." Fiona just loved that song, and the promise it held of some faraway world where life was beautiful. Of course, birds don't fly over rainbows, Fiona told herself. That's just an optical illusion. It's a nice idea though.

Fiona sang her way through the spring season, entertaining seniors at centers and retirement homes all over town. Sometimes she took the descant or lead soprano part and, on occasion, she was given a solo. She felt both surprise and elation, watching certain seniors lean in and really listen and smile. Sometimes they sang along with the choir. Afterwards, Gram or Pop often took her out for a special pancake supper at iHOP. Fiona loved the fluffy pancakes the size of her plate, and no one ever commented when she poured on a little too much maple syrup from the little metal pitcher, and let it soak in before taking her first bite.

After dinner, Fiona would settle in underneath the grand dining table at Gram's, where she liked to hide out and do her homework. She had realized, the first time she burrowed under that table, that she could see the television from her little cave. The adults, enthralled with their evening shows, took no notice.

On Saturdays—cartoon day!—Fiona would plop herself on the couch to watch *The Rocky & Bullwinkle Show* about a silly moose and a super-savvy flying squirrel, who tangled with the dastardly Boris and Natasha Badinov, and the *Fractured Fairy Tales* that followed. Her second favorite cartoon show was *Underdog*, about an unassuming beagle who, once he had on his cape, became a superhero. Whenever he'd say, "There's no need to fear; Underdog is here!" Fiona would recite it with him, rejoicing in simple good guy/

bad guy stories where the good guy wins.

~oOOoOOo~

How long has it been? Fiona wondered, shaking her head. She'd spent a weekend with Mother right after coming home from India, but it had been years since they'd had a good, long visit. Fiona could hardly contain her excitement. Much as she would have liked to be heading to Mother's home in California, that's not where Fiona was going. Instead, today, she was flying to Nashville, Tennessee. Peggy taken a deep dive into the New Age and was also fascinated by Eastern religions. She had arranged for them both to participate in a week-long retreat at an Indian swami's ashram. Sri Sri Svarbhānu, or Swamiji for short, was said to have hailed from the foothills of Nepal, and to have tamed tigers and caused eclipses with his presence alone. Much of his past was as veiled in mystery as he was. Perhaps that's what the mystery writer in Peggy found so intriguing. She imagined Fiona would love the experience, having spent time in India, and they'd have a great time at the retreat together.

Did I forget anything? Fiona wondered, looking at her open suitcase. Did I pack my toothbrush? Paste? Fiona had packed and repacked her bags, somewhat out of compulsion but mostly due to excitement. Of course, she had her toothbrush. And her toothpaste. And her hairbrush. She had everything she thought she might possibly need. And then some. The day had finally arrived. Fiona examined her suitcase one more time before zipping it shut and heading downstairs and out to the car. She wondered how Mother's formal dining ideas would square with ashram food. She wondered if she'd know what to do, how to behave. Would she, could she measure up? Well, I'll do my level best, she vowed.

Pop punctuated his farewell with a fabulous bear hug, lifting her right off her feet and almost taking her breath away. "Love you, kiddo." "Love you, too, Pop." Fiona felt so grown up as she waved goodbye at the gate and followed the stewardess, who was escorting her down the jet bridge and to her seat in the coach section. She loved feeling so independent.

She's so beautiful, Fiona observed as she admired the tall, dark-haired stewardess, imagining how glamorous her job must be. If I were only pretty, like Karen and Mother, Fiona thought, maybe I could be a stewardess, too. She knew Pop was counting on her—grooming her—to become a scientist, but right now, Fiona was fixated on the pretty woman in the smart suit and pretty pumps, with the gracious hospitality and kind smile. She tugged at her seatbelt, just as the stewardess had demonstrated, until it was tight enough for her to feel secure, and then peered out the small window by her seat. She loved the takeoff most of all, hearing the run-up of the engines, and feeling the lift-off as the plane departed the runway and headed up through the frothy white clouds. She knew they were made of chilly water but, as the plane moved softly through them, they seemed more like cotton balls or cattail tufts, like the kind that grew in abundance back at Mystic Meadow. She could imagine herself wrapped inside them, rolling around in her deliciously fluffy bed, and floating in the thin air, somehow warm, soft, safe.

As she continued to look out the window, enjoying her candy-cloud reverie, Fiona noticed the old familiar sparklies were along for the ride. She'd missed them. But here they were, once again, accompanying her on a visit to Mother. They seemed to enjoy keeping her company on such trips. She enjoyed watching them—they were so beautiful and dazzling. She didn't know enough to understand what they might signify.

After the seatbelt sign had been turned off, the stewardess invited Fiona to come up front to say hello to the captain, giving her a pin-on set of pilot's wings. As the captain showed her the cockpit, Fiona imagined she might like to be a pilot more than a stewardess. Although she'd never yet seen a female pilot, it didn't occur to her to question the possibility. Of course, women were pilots. Why wouldn't they be? Fiona could imagine herself in this role, navigating that huge dashboard, safely getting folks to from one place to another, with the utmost of professionalism.

The flight was going by quickly. She found she'd outgrown the gifts the stewardesses brought, and wasn't much interested in the movie that was being projected on the screen at the front of the cabin. Looking out the window again, Fiona's thoughts wandered to the quality of time, and how sometimes time seemed to move so quickly. In particular, every single visit to her mother seemed to end almost before it began. What was up with that? I bet before I even blink, I'll find I'm right back on this plane, headed home. Pretty pointless. I mean, did I even experience it? Why even go? Fiona began feeling sad about the ending of a trip that hadn't even begun. Although her capacity to entertain herself with nothing but her fertile, active mind was a blessed antidote to boredom, it was also a curse. She was missing the passage of time by thinking about it instead of participating in it.

Fiona gazed out at the clouds below, and watched the sparklies dance before her eyes. By the time her plane started its descent, Fiona realized with a start that she'd almost forgotten her favorite part: counting down from when they got close to the runway to the landing, seeing if she could judge when they'd touch the ground. Ten, nine, eight, … I'm getting to be a pretty good judge of timing, she thought, having reached zero just as the wheels hit the ground, feeling the rush of power as her body pushed forward against the power of the brakes, with only the seatbelt holding her in place.

Mother met Fiona at the gate. After a quick hug, a pause to appraise her daughter—how much she'd grown, how pretty she looked—she hustled Fiona off to baggage claim to collect her suitcase and hurry over to the rental car Mother had parked just outside the terminal. The plane had been late. They were late for registration. They had to hurry. Fiona caught on quickly, and started to walk as fast as she could. Putting her suitcase next to Mother's in the trunk, she climbed into the car, and settled in for a quiet, hour-long ride to the ashram on the outskirts of town.

Fiona had guessed correctly that Mother had imagined the choice of a retreat would be fun for Fiona, but she wished Mother had asked her. Had she been asked, Fiona would have suggested just about anything else over the ashram, especially if that "anything" took place in California. She'd have suggested Fleishhacker Zoo or the planetarium at the California Academy of Sciences, in San Francisco. Fiona had read about them in library books. Or maybe there was an aquarium or an ice cream parlor or even Mother's office at the college where she taught writing. Anything but another Indian ashram. Mother, though, was really looking forward to the retreat, so Fiona kept her opinions to herself. I'm game to give it a go, she decided. At least we're stateside.

Mother had brought along some of the swami's bathwater to drink, to help them "get closer to enlightenment." As thirsty as she was, Fiona declined the offer to try it. When they finally pulled up to the ashram, Fiona was relieved to find that, unlike Mystic Meadow, the grounds were lush with manicured plantings, and very pretty. They hadn't been there five minutes when a runner told the gathering crowd that it was time for meditation. Fiona's mind had been running amok all day, so she really didn't mind meditating, which she had learned to do in India. It was often superior to interacting with whomever was around.

Before long, Fiona met a girl, a year or two older, who went by Shakti, a name she'd been given by the swami. She told Fiona it meant "the female principle of divine energy, especially when personified as the supreme deity." Fiona considered her new friend's words for a moment, impressed. She then shared with her some stories from her time in India, and asked Shakti what her story was. "I've been here about two years, I guess. Lately, I've been meditating a whole lot, and I've been seeing this phoenix floating over my head. That must mean something, right?"

Fiona couldn't see the phoenix but Shakti said she could tell it was there, out of the corner of her eye. It had been hanging out for about a year, she said, keeping her company. Fiona thought of imaginary friends she had had over the years and understood, instantly, how reassuring that could be. Shakti also impressed Fiona by telling her she could see people's auras and that Fiona's was purple, one of Fiona's favorite colors.

Once she had taken Fiona into her confidence, Shakti showed her the gold necklace the swami had given her. "It's real gold and everything." They admired it together. Fiona liked knowing that the swami gave special gifts and meaningful names, but she wondered why he did. "He gave it to me after we spent some special time together, just the two of us, if you know what I mean." Oh, thought Fiona. That's why.

Fiona didn't want any golden gifts, but she thought it might be nice to have her own bird, at least while she was there, or any kind of benevolent friend, really. For now, she had Shakti. Bird, bird, bird, Fiona's inner voice cooed. Maybe I'll get an invisible bird, too, with enough meditation, she thought. Bird is the word. Mostly, it's nice having someone to hang out with, even if we are mostly sitting silently.

~oOOoOOo~

No mythic phoenix or any other invisible creature ever appeared for Fiona. Instead, what showed up was a head cold, complete with earache. Mother was sick as well. In fact, Mother might have been even sicker. Fiona looked at Mother, and thought she might have been a shade greener than she'd ever seen her. Mother spent most of the rest of the afternoon running to the bathroom.

Mother didn't feel up to leaving the ashram grounds in search of a doctor's office for either of them. Surely, she said, someone could help heal them at the ashram. Fiona desperately wanted to see a real medical doctor with a framed degree on an office wall, but she took one look at Mother and realized that wasn't about to happen. She crossed her fingers that maybe one of the other retreat attendees was a doctor or a nurse. The closest approximation they could find was a first-year chiropractic student attending the retreat. "Do you think you could help my daughter?" she asked weakly. "I'm sorry, it's a touch of flu, I think. I need to go back into the room a bit. Fiona, come on back when you get a chance." With that, Mother headed again for the facilities.

Fiona followed the young man down the hall until they found two empty chairs. They sat down, and he adjusted his collar. Wasn't it getting hot in here? He'd never treated an ear, before, and the prospect was making him sweat. But, the child looked sad, and she was in pain and he felt it was his duty to help. He wondered whether some chiropractic pressure on the head might help relieve the pressure. He asked her to turn her head left, then right. Noticing she turned a bit more freely in one direction than the other, he grew bolder.

"Now, Fiona, I would like to try a manipulation. Okay?" he asked, as he tried the simple manipulation he'd learned in class. The sudden movement added insult to injury. Fiona heard the crackle of her spine, but she also felt a sharp pain, like a bolt of lightning, in her ear. Whatever he'd done, she wished he hadn't, and her yelp let him know immediately that his attempt at assistance hadn't worked out as he had hoped.

Fiona looked up at the young chiropractic student in disbelief. She'd come to him in pain, hoping for help. Now, her ear not only wasn't better, it was a whole different kind of worse. Had he meant to break her ear? No, she had to believe he hadn't meant to harm her. She needed to hold that thought, just as much as Shakti needed her phoenix. Somewhere deep down inside, she didn't want her last remaining trust in grown-ups to burst, along with her eardrum.

Fiona realized how much she missed Gram, who would have taken her to a doctor. A kindly one, who would have looked inside her ear with a light and would have helped her feel better. Fiona felt that going to the doctor would have been the right thing to do. But she couldn't think about it. She was going home the day after tomorrow, anyway. She'd see Gram soon enough. Fiona went to her closet-like room to lie down, and there, she spent the rest of her time at the ashram. Mother eventually recovered enough strength to go out and buy them a loaf of Sara Lee raisin bread, a comfort food that tasted a thousand times better than any of the Indian food served in the cafeteria, and she and Fiona feasted on it in their remaining time together.

"How are you feeling?" Mother asked, as Fiona lifted her suitcase into the trunk. Fiona, who'd been trying not to think about her ear, winced a little. "I'll live." Wanting to be reassuring, she added, "Seriously, I'll be fine, Mother. No worries."

Driving to the airport, Peggy found herself having difficulty focusing on the road. "Let's hope we're not pulled over for driving under the influenza," she joked. Fiona had to laugh. This was a side of her mother she'd rarely seen, and she liked it. Then she noticed that Mother was tapping some rhythm on the steering wheel. "What are you tapping, Mother?"

"Just trying to focus my attention. It's an old jump-rope ditty your Noni taught me. 'I had a little bird whose name was Enza. I opened the window and in-flew-enza.'" At that, she broke into a coughing fit so intense, Fiona wondered if she might lose control of the car and drive off into the embankment.

Fiona reached over, and felt her mother's forehead. "Hey, you're pretty warm. Maybe after you see me off, you should go see a doctor."

"I'll live." Peggy laughed. "But that's enough talking, for me, I think."

They arrived, and parked, and Mother accompanied Fiona to the gate, asking, weakly, "Do you have everything?" Fiona nodded in the affirmative. When the time came to board, Fiona departed her mother without looking back, convincing herself her mother would be waiting and waving, had she turned around to look. In the event, she was. As soon as Fiona took off, Peggy turned around and headed right back to her room, to bed. Fiona made her way to her seat and leaned her head against the cool window. Fiona and Peggy, miles apart from each other, had the exact same thought at the exact same moment: "Well, what a disaster of a visit that was."

No one warned Fiona how excruciating the plane ride home would be with a ruptured eardrum. Every shift in altitude, every stretch of turbulence affected her, and she spent most of the flight leaning forward, pressing her hand against her ear, silent tears coursing down her face. She wasn't sad. It just hurt like the dickens.

The stewardesses governing the flight tried to help her by giving her gum to chew. It didn't help, but it was something to do, at least. She quietly accepted, and noticed them quietly conferring, their faces registering concern. They really didn't know how to help, so they spent the flight bringing her cookies and soda. Fiona tried to show interest, but she just wanted the ordeal to end.

Landing was agonizing, but the pain receded again by the time they had reached the gate. Pop, waiting for her at the gate, gave her a great big bear hug, then noticed her red, distressed face and asked, "Missed me that much, did you?" Fiona didn't answer. Instead, she offered up a weak smile, and they were on their way. What could she say, really? She didn't want Pop to lose his temper, maybe get self-righteous about how he would have done better. Instead, as soon as she got home to Gram's, she went straight up to her room and buried herself in her soft, warm bed. She didn't even come down for dinner.

She wasn't hungry.

Gram and Wolf gave each other worried glances across the table as they ate.

The earaches lingered for months after that fateful trip. Once she realized they were not going to subside, she finally confessed her pain, and Wolf quickly took her in to an ear specialist. They were relieved when he declared her eardrum healthy and her hearing normal. "Your ear infection seems to have healed up nicely, young lady," the she said. "But, ears are sensitive. Traumatize them, and they can remain vulnerable for a while. Until the sensitivity subsides, I recommend aspirin and a heating pad or ice pack, whichever brings relief."

On the drive home from the doctor's office, Wolf noticed how thoughtful—pensive even—Fiona looked. "A penny for your thoughts?"

"How about a dime?"

"Let's see what you've got."

"I'm thinking about time. How it works. Why is it that when you're looking forward to something, it can seem like forever to get here, but then suddenly, it's over? You know how Einstein talks about time as a dimension? Maybe you can twist it, or bend it, or stretch it, so the uncomfortable stretches that feel like they take forever are, in fact, longer. Or what if time's a hologram, and everything's been set down? Everything that ever happened or will happen. So, you're traveling along the hologram experiencing it as forward motion, feeling like you're making progress, but what does that matter to the hologram?

Wolf smiled, in anticipation of the sort of delicious conversation he loved best. "Well, Fee, this might even be worth a quarter. So, you probably feel like a needle on a record player, just playing the song. Is that right?"

"Yeah, kinda," she said. "But I'm not saying we go around and around. We're facing forward, thinking we're making progress, getting somewhere, and things are getting better. But, are we? Maybe we're just like ants, marching along some twisted, infinite-loop, Möbius strip of time, trying to dodge the cosmic magnifying glass."

"Hmm. Sounds rough for the ant. Well, there are lots of theories about space and time, Fee, and what you choose to believe influences who you are and how you live your life. So, if you believe you're just an ant on a treadmill or a needle on a turntable, then you don't have any sense of personal power. That's not very healthy."

"But, really Pop, maybe that's all we are. Where have we gotten? And what kind of personal power does a kid have, anyway?"

"You make choices every day, don't you? And your choices lead you in one direction or another. You're directing your potential, Fee. That's powerful." Wolf glanced over and saw that his answer wasn't satisfactory, and there was no wonderful "Why, Pop?" forthcoming. He forged on. "Did you know there's a kind of needle that actually writes the songs into the grooves of the record? It reacts to the sound waves, and sets down a permanent recording. Think about it. Even with a conventional recording, the record isn't worth much until someone sets the needle onto the vinyl, to bring sound to the song. You know that dog, Nipper, who listens to his master's voice, coming out of an amplifying cone on a Victrola? Long ago, to make the recordings that play on those Victrolas, people used to speak into cones like those. Someone made those sounds in the first place."

"You could be that someone, Fee, writing a song and setting down a new composition for that needle to play. You know, get into the groove."

"Yeah, right, Pop. That's a good one." Fiona shrugged and looked out the window, pretending she didn't want to know more, but she did. Actually, she knew she'd love to write and record a song for the needle.

Wolf continued, on the hunch that she was still interested. "You think I'm kidding, Fee, but I'm serious. That's a good theory of time and space to live by: What you choose to believe influences who you are and how you live your life," he repeated, for impact. "If you don't like mine, pick another that helps you move forward every day."

Fiona continued to look out the bus window, feigning boredom, and took in the kaleidoscope of images whizzing past the window.

Wolf glanced at his daughter who, he could tell, was quite done with the subject. He decided to lighten things up. "So, I have an important question for you. Fiona…" He took her silence as tacit permission to continue. "How does Einstein start a story?"

Fiona looked up. "That's your important question?" She knew the answer. She felt sure she knew all Pop's jokes. "Once upon a space-time…" She gave him a lackluster smile as he continued. "And everyone knows why he threw the clock out the window." Together they shouted out, "He wanted to see time fly!" Pop added, "Badum-bum!"

"I've got a joke for you, Pop." Fiona was happy to switch directions and go down this path with Pop.

"Let's hear it."

"Why's that clock so tense?" Wolf thought for a moment and then shrugged. "It's all wound up! Get it, Pop?" What Wolf appreciated most about her joke was how it had brought a smile to her face and returned the mirth to her eyes. He was ready with a comeback. "So, if the clock got better," he asked, "Was it past tense?" Fiona laughed, the pain was forgotten for a time, and the jokes kept coming: What time is it when a clock strikes 13? (time for a new clock); when a duck wakes up (the quack of dawn); when a dead clock is dead right (I don't know, but even a stopped clock is right twice a day). "Well, Fee," Pop finally said, as they arrived home, "I guess you know all my jokes."

Later that evening, Wolf poked his head through the doorway to Fiona's bedroom as if he had something important to say. "You know, Fabulous Fee," he began, "it's really true; the best thing—the only important thing I've ever done is to raise you up to the fine young woman you've become." Fiona rolled her eyes, though she knew he meant it. That was his truth. Usually, he only said this sort of thing when he'd been drinking. It was nice to know he felt that way, even when sober.

~o0O0O0o~

When Wolf wasn't up in Gram's attic, surrounded by a slightly sweet and smoky haze that Gram did her best to ignore, he was somewhere else in the house, smoking his unfiltered Camel cigarettes. It didn't occur to Fiona to wonder what he did with his days; Gram kept her too busy with her own days to think about it. Had anyone looked over his shoulder, they'd have seen that he was writing query letters in response to job postings.

Sometimes Wolf would send Fiona up the road to the corner store to buy him a carton of cigarettes, with enough extra money to buy herself some chewing gum. He joked, "Hey, Fiona, would you walk a mile for a Camel?" Fiona didn't think to wonder why Pop didn't just take a nice walk and buy his own cigarettes or why the shopkeeper was willing to hand a carton to a kid who was too young to smoke. She was happy to walk down to the market, for the spare change which, of course, she saved.

Gram bought a Habitrail for Fiona's hamster. Boo also was the proud owner of a clear plastic ball. Once inside, he could run around and around to his heart's content, free from his cage, but still safe. Gram's Afghan hounds were also entertained, though a little frustrated by the hamster rolling around the floor inside his ball, safe from their jaws.

After Fiona woke one morning to find that Boo had quietly died in the night— without any help from the hounds—Pop and Gram helped Fiona bury him at the foot of the old tree behind the house. Gram told Fiona the story of the rainbow bridge. "Our beloved pets are in the happy hunting ground, over the rainbow bridge. They're the first to meet us after we pass over to the other side. So, even if we can't see them anymore during this lifetime, we will reunite with them, in the sweet by-and-by," she said. Fiona suppressed the urge to tell Gram that dead is dead, and that's that. Gram meant well, after all. Fiona sank into an upholstered chair and absently fingered the silky ear of Dragon. "Whatever you do, don't get sick, Dragon," she said to the dog.

Gram regarded the child for a moment and then disappeared upstairs, returning shortly with a small box. "I think you're ready for this now, Fiona. Your Gramps bought one for each one of you girls before he passed away." Fiona opened the box and found, nestled in the cotton, a single pearl on a gold chain as thin as a wisp. Fiona had never owned such a beautiful, grown-up, precious item before. It almost made her forget about Boo. She knew she would cherish it forever.

"Fiona, do you see how translucent the pearl is? It reminds me of you. Beautiful and unique." Gram helped Fiona fasten the chain around her neck, and Fiona ran off to find a mirror in which to admire the beautiful necklace. Her eyes and nose were still red from crying, she noticed, but the pearl necklace was oh, so pretty. Gram really knows how to soften sadness and make me feel special, she thought.

"Gram, can I wear my new necklace to school?" Fiona had shown up to breakfast the next morning, proudly wearing her pearl necklace as she finished eating in time to get to school early. She had recently been made a crossing guard. "Maybe you want to keep it in your jewelry box, where it's safe, so you don't lose it when guarding or bang it during gym class," Gram replied. Fiona dutifully removed the necklace and returned it to her jewelry box, which was shaped like a house. When she opened the lid, a ballet dancer popped up and pirouetted to the strains of "Somewhere Over the Rainbow." Gram had looked long and hard to find a jewelry box with Fiona's favorite song, and Fiona felt her pearl necklace was the perfect treasure to hide in such a special box.

Fiona hurried away to her crossing-guard duties. She was looking forward the steaming cup of hot chocolate she and the other guards would be given at the end of their duty. As she stood at her corner, her thoughts kept returning to her pearl. It seemed to embody all that was beautiful and precious. Fiona loved every single thing about her life in Philadelphia at Gram's.

Wolf, however, wasn't loving it. He was bored, he was too old to be living under his mother's management, and he had begun to feel like a ne'er-do-well. He resented staying with his mother, and her relationship with Fiona simply pointed out his own failures and what he couldn't provide as a father. He had put the word out that he'd be happy to do any sort of consulting. Although Wolf specialized in ocean sonar, he wasn't seaworthy himself. Still, he decided he'd take whatever gig came his way. Soon, he was invited to take part in two back-to-back sailing trips.

On his first trip, Wolf accompanied a crew that was filming a documentary about the many accidents and lost ships around the Bermuda Triangle, in the western part of the North Atlantic Ocean. He was hoping something "interesting" might happen. Luckily—or unluckily—depending on your point of view, the trip was uneventful. On his second trip, he accompanied a crew in search of sunken treasure. Nothing had happened in the Triangle, so what could possibly befall him during the short sail between Ft. Lauderdale and the Isle of Shoals, off the coast of New Hampshire? Lots, it turns out. In a bad thunderstorm off Blackbeard Shoals, Wolf lost his footing, and hit his head on a winch. The captain radioed the Coast Guard, and he was rescued in a medevac copter. Although he was ready for duty the very next morning, the captain took one look at the scientist on the pier with the bandage covering his head and ordered him home.

Wolf landed a job "anywhere but here," in Detroit. He was elated. He was going to do better, be better. Gram made a solid case for Fiona staying on with her, but Wolf wouldn't hear of it. He knew her reasons, and most of them were valid. But he couldn't stand the thought of leaving Fiona behind, of losing the last member of his family. Gram held her peace. She knew her bright but beleaguered son, and suspected they would be back.

~oO0O0Oo~

Here we go again, thought Fiona, as they headed off the plane to collect their luggage. Wolf would be working at a research lab in the heart of the city. Wolf had spent the months they'd lived in Philadelphia reeling from the defeat of losing his family and his farm. His outlook improved with the new job and move. The hopeful mottos on Detroit's flag, Speramus Meliora and Resurget Cineribus, spoke of hoping for better things, and rising from ashes. That bodes well, thought Fiona.

It was 1974, and Fiona was about to turn 12. While they were getting settled, Wolf and Fiona stayed with the same family friends who had picked them up from the airport when they'd arrived in

Delhi. They couldn't get over how much she'd grown and how hearty and hale she looked. Her father, not so much.

Before starting his new job, Wolf set out to make it a special summer for Fiona, beginning with an air show. He bought her a model Fokker Triplane they could build together, and Fiona was excited to see a real one, up close and powerful at the show. As they sat in the kitchen gluing together the intricate model, Pop began regaling Fiona with shaggy dog stories that meandered pointlessly before ending with a pun. By this point, Fiona had them all memorized.

"So, Fiona, once the Sisters of Mercy..." Pop started.

"I know, Pop." Fiona interrupted. "The koala tea of mercy is not strained! Badum bum. Now let me guess, the next one will be about the Irish Rary Bird and the steep cliff. It's a long way to Tipperary, right?"

"Ha haaaaa! You're a mind-reader, Fee! But do you know the one about that Fokker was a Messerschmitt?"

"I didn't," Fiona laughed, "but you just told me the punch line."

Fiona's spirits soared. "Oh, Pop! Let's fly in a hot air balloon! They're selling tickets. It'll be just like when we went in that glider in Delhi. C'mon, Pop!" The tickets for a guaranteed ride were too pricey, Pop said, but he bought two raffle tickets for a couple bucks each, and Fiona crossed all her fingers and toes. When they didn't win, she must have looked so disappointed, having anticipated hearing her name, that the pilot was touched, and offered to take her onboard anyway. Fiona didn't weigh much, he said, so she wouldn't unbalance the balloon. It wouldn't be just exactly like Delhi—Pop wouldn't be with her—but it would be wonderful. Wolf didn't have the heart to tell her no.

Fiona climbed into the gondola with the raffle winners and waved goodbye to Pop. Tiny flicks of black soot floated down on her pink sweater like backwards snow as the pilot revved the burner, adding heat to the air inside the balloon. He pulled up the ropes and coiled them at the base of the gondola as it lifted higher, gently gliding through the air along with the currents. Inside the balloon, there was no breeze at all. Only the occasional roar of hot air, and beautiful silence. Fiona felt herself floating over cornfields and drifting above dense trees. When the heater wasn't blasting heat up and into the body of the balloon, the only sound was the flutter of the balloon itself. Fiona felt she'd found heaven as she sailed peacefully across the sky. It was all so perfect, until a dark shadow crossed her mind. Too bad times like this never last. She brushed the thought away, like one more fleck of hot, black soot. Well, I'm here now, she affirmed. I'm here, and I'm not going to let anything ruin my ride.

Wolf watched as the balloon and its precious cargo drifted out of sight. He waited, as eventually, darkness fell. Most folks had left the air show. Where was Fiona? Wolf began to imagine that she'd wound up wrapped around a treetop somewhere. They'd simply drifted farther than planned before landing in a distant cornfield. The pilot had radioed for the van to retrieve them. The ride back to the fairgrounds in the back of the van took longer than the flight itself had taken. Fiona had a great time, sitting on the hay in the back of the van, holding on while they bumped over the dusty road. Back at the fairgrounds, Fiona raced over to her father, her face flush with excitement. "Oh, Pop, that was fantastic. Sorry we're a little late," she said. "Time gets away from you when you're just about in heaven. You should have seen it, Pop! It was amazing!" It hadn't registered with her that he'd been frantic, or concerned about what they might do to get back to Detroit if they missed the last bus back. He needn't have worried; one of the other riders noticed they didn't have a car, and offered them a lift. The summer was off to a great start.

~oOO0OOo~

"Hey, Pop, guess what I saw today?" Fiona and her father tucked into the TV dinners balanced on their laps while they sat on the floor of the living room in their Detroit apartment. They were watching *Star Trek* on their new television set—one of their few possessions.

"What'd you see, my Fabulous Fee?" asked Pop, as he peeled back the foil on his Salisbury steak dinner with peas, mashed potatoes, and a dome-shaped blueberry muffin he would save for Fiona.

"They're selling some used furniture down the hall. It's only $25 for the whole living room set. It's got a coffee table we could use right now, plus a sofa, two side tables, and a comfy chair. Can we buy it?

I can already picture where everything will fit. What do you think, Pop?"

"I don't see why not," he answered without giving the matter much thought. They had come to the unfurnished apartment from his mother's lovely home with nothing but their suitcases. Before they'd moved in, he had made sure there were mattresses, a kitchen table and two chairs, and a small color TV. That seemed to him to be all that was needed. Fiona, though, thought otherwise, and Wolf didn't mind obliging her. By the next evening, the father-daughter duo were the proud custodians of a living room filled with avocado-green furniture. Fiona felt so proud, she convinced herself she'd never seen anything quite so groovy and hip.

Their now-groovy apartment was situated in a cluster of high-rise buildings in downtown Detroit. So many families lived there that it merited its own dedicated school bus. Wolf wasn't bothered by the constant noise, the mingling smells, or even the roaches that infested the incinerator chutes. As an adult who'd spent years in New York City, Wolf was comfortable with urban life. Fiona was not. She'd had very little familiarity with apartment living—except for that short time in a spacious, well-furnished, and quiet apartment in a tony section of New Delhi. This was not that.

School days scared Fiona. She was hoping for a growth spurt, but was still the smallest kid in class. The second week of class, she was surprised in gym class when, out of the blue, she was punched in the stomach and slugged in the back by two bigger girls. They yanked her stuff out of her locker, pushed her books off the bench and said, "Strong's better than smart, Stupid," as they disappeared down the aisle. Fiona sat on the bench where her books had been, too stunned to cry. The gym teacher came into the locker room after she failed to show up for roll call and asked her if she was okay to participate. Fiona made a weak excuse about a bum knee, and sat out the session. Maybe bullies are like hornets, Fiona thought. Maybe if I just ignore them, they won't sting me again. On the bus ride home, she felt a sense of vigilance, as if she might be punched in the stomach again, at any moment.

Fiona was used to the rambling space of houses. This high rise was nothing like their cozy cottage in Providence, Hanna's parents' lovely home in Brooklyn, or Gram's big, beautiful house in Philadelphia. Here, she couldn't play in the neighborhood as she had in India, or run free in the wilds of Mystic Meadow. Despite that scary sanatorium-turned-horrible-house, she did miss its welcoming outdoors. This was entirely different. Cooped up in a tiny apartment on an upper floor in a high rise, Fiona felt as if she were in jail—but a reverse jail, where the bad guys were outside, and inside was the only place where it was safe. She also felt she was struggling to breathe.

A sticky humidity lay heavy over the apartment. On especially hot nights, when Fiona was no more able to draw sleep up around her than her covers, she stole away to the kitchen. A loafer stood at attention at the doorway, unfazed by the sweltering heat. Having outlived its original purpose, it had found new life in serving death to vermin. When she'd been very little, visiting Mother and Karen in New York, Karen had taught her all about the Roach Shoe. One of Mother's old shoes had been dedicated to cockroach patrol. Fiona had squirreled away the information, in case she ever needed it. She was glad she had listened closely.

Taking care not to wake her father, Fiona retrieved the shoe, quietly striking the ground a few times, hoping it would be enough of a warning. Looking away to avoid seeing an expected mass exodus, she turned on the light. After a few moments, she made her way over to the fridge.

As Fiona opened the door to the freezer, a thrill of cold air rushed over her face. She reviewed the contents; plenty of TV dinners for the week. No worries. Better not let them thaw. She tiptoed back to bed, where sleep finally took her away from the sweltering heat, for a time.

Wolf noticed Fiona's discomfort in the apartment and imagined it must get worse when she was there alone, after school. He had no idea about the bullying. One day, he came home with what he considered the ideal solution to keep her company and help her feel safe: a de-scented pet skunk. Whether he thought a skunk would keep intruders away or simply that Fiona would think so, his daughter thought it was pure genius. Her Pop had brought the natural world, the animal kingdom, indoors. Fiona named her skunk Hogan after the afternoon television show *Hogan's Heroes*, because he really was her hero. Soon after Hogan's arrival, the bullying stopped.

When Fiona and her father took Hogan for his first visit to the veterinarian, they learned he was a she. Even so, Fiona kept her name. She loved having Hogan, both to keep her company and for the protection she felt she provided. The vet had told Fiona to avoid feeding her skunk grapes or raisins. "Don't worry," Fiona replied, "we're boycotting grapes." Fiona secretly hoped Pop might take her to DC for a rally she heard was happening, because Cesar Chavez would be there, and she'd love to meet him in person. That'd be so cool, she thought.

"Hogan, I love you," Fiona said, hugging her new friend tightly. "You're my very special guardian. I love that people are afraid of you. And I love how you think bugs taste delicious and how you get rid of all the gross little things that crawl around here. You're like an anteater, only better." She had learned that skunks enjoyed cockroaches and spiders, along with the cat food she fed Hogan. And Fiona simply hated bugs—except ladybugs and butterflies. And fireflies. Mustn't forget those.

Fiona allowed Hogan to roam freely around the apartment, and took no exception to the piles of poop she found in random places. She just quietly cleaned up after her, and flushed the droppings down the toilet. It had occurred to Fiona that, although she was fastidious about her own cleanliness and that of her room, keeping everything in meticulous order (including hanging her clothing by color), she didn't seem to mind scooping skunk poop. She certainly didn't want to do or say one thing to jeopardize Hogan's welcome in their home.

Fiona watched as Hogan made a small deposit in the middle of the living room floor. "I'll clean up your mess as soon as I finish my homework, Hogan." She took out a pencil from her pencil box, sharpened it, and got to work, while Hogan scampered around the room. It was hard to concentrate with such frivolity, but Fiona finished her math and science homework in record time. Then she cleaned up Hogan's mess, and decided to give her a bath, so her fur would glisten. Whenever her fur got wet, even though she'd had her glands removed, she still smelled of skunk. Hogan didn't appreciate being doused in the tub, and she stomped her feet and raised her tail, threateningly, and pooped right into the bath water. Having finally succeeded in cleaning up both Hogan and the bathtub, Fiona wrapped her pet in a bath towel and lifted her out of the tub to get her all fluffy and dry, when the slippery skunk slunk out of the bathroom.

Hogan romped around the living room as Fiona gave chase, shaking and spraying water everywhere. Fiona might have been worried about the mess had she not been laughing so hard. Besides, she knew Pop really wouldn't care—or notice. And she'd have it all cleaned up well before he ever came home.

Whether Fiona was ever in any actual danger in her apartment complex or not, she inarguably felt safer with a skunk. With Hogan draped over her shoulder, she felt secure from the perceived threat of bullies and bad guys, thieves, and thugs. Nobody else knew Hogan wasn't "loaded." Only Fiona and her father knew her scent glands had been removed; Fiona wasn't about to tell anyone else. "Perception," Pop had said, "is a very important tool."

When Pop got home, he started their dinner by pouring a can of Campbell's chicken noodle soup, followed by a can of water, into a pan, which he left simmering on the stove. Meanwhile, he stretched out "for a moment," with his hands behind his head, on the couch in the living room. But a moment stretched into much more than a moment when Pop fell fast asleep.

A sound sleeper, he wouldn't have heard a timer had he bothered to set one. When all the liquid in the simmering pot had evaporated, the pot itself began to burn, sending black smoke billowing out of the kitchen, and setting off the smoke alarm.

The firemen arrived quickly, before the red-hot soup pan set fire to the place. Fiona came out of her room, where she'd been studying, when she thought she smelled smoke. Coming into the black smoke, she instantly began to cough. First, she felt fear, then disappointment in her father. That shifted to embarrassment when she saw the handsome firefighters dash through the doorway. In the eyes of one of them she noticed a sincere kindness and concern. She sensed that he somehow cared about her and wanted her to be okay. This made her feel better, safer, and more secure than even her skunk had.

When I grow up, she thought, maybe I'll be a firefighter.

~oO0O0Oo~

A few days later, Fiona came home from school and found a letter on the kitchen counter, addressed to "Miss Fiona Sprechelbach." Recognizing the handwriting on the envelope, she knew it was from her Uncle Joe. Her heart soared. Fiona had written to him recently after hearing the news that he had come dangerously close to dying from devastating injuries sustained in Vietnam. Mother had contacted Gram about her brother's injuries, and Gram, of course, had told Pop, who had shared the news with Fiona.

Fiona loved her family—all sides of it. She was enthralled with the idea of family roots and the tree that grew from them, up and out to the various branches that reached far and wide. This was where she sought a sense of togetherness, a place of belonging. Despite the fact that the Vietnam War had created a rift and regardless of the fact that Fiona rarely saw many members of her wider family, Fiona felt a closeness to everyone in her extended family tree. She felt so bad for Uncle Joe, perhaps dying in that hospital bed, that she had written him her most carefully crafted letter, ever.

> *Dear Fiona,*
> *Thank you for writing to me in the hospital. I am doing much better. I'm not sure why I survived. When I woke up, I couldn't feel my legs, and I wasn't sure what would happen next. Then someone said, "God sent you a get-well card, and that's all you need to know right now." And now, I have your beautiful get-well card, too.*
> *I know how your father feels about the war. The war is complicated. Yet I spilled my blood for his right to be an idiot. But you're not an idiot, Fiona. I know you're a thinker. Do yourself a favor in life and don't jump to conclusions about stuff you don't understand. Life's not black and white, Fiona. It's a sacrifice to be of service, and choices are hard. Think about that, next time you march. And do me a favor. Go look up the word entitlement, and think about what it*

means. Look up Semper Fi, too.

I was sorry to read about the passing of your pet hamster. I'm sure you did your best with him, and I still think you're going to grow up to be a very fine veterinarian. I know you asked for a photo, but I don't have a one to include for you. This is not the way I want you to think of me, anyway. Ask your mother; she might have one lying around somewhere that you can have. Write again soon, if you get a chance.

   Love,
   Uncle Joe

Fiona pored over the letter many times, and asked Pop, without showing him the contents of Uncle Joe's message, to fill her in about Joe's war history. Pop gave her an abridged version, based on what he'd heard, and what he believed she could or should understand.

Joe had served in the reconnaissance Marines, later called Special Forces. He was a "tunnel rat," part of an elite group of six who went down into the tunnels in Vietnam. Like a complete city underground, said Pop, these expansive tunnels housed hospitals and stores and kitchens and rooms filled with beds—and they were booby-trapped.

Uncle Joe and five others, including a Navy Corpsman medic, had worked together as a team, in a group that was like the Navy Seals. There had been a big explosion from a mortar blast, and Joe was found unconscious and quite torn apart. Rescued by comrades who had presumed him dead, Joe had been kept in a medical coma, during which he'd undergone several surgeries before awakening at Oak Knoll Naval Hospital in Oakland, California. He'd lost five months of his life, but he had not lost his life. He had a stainless-steel sternum and a significant scar running down his chest. He had been devastated to learn he could not move his legs. He was still hoping to regain the ability to walk. Uncle Joe had received five Purple Hearts. In many ways, Joe was extraordinary. Even Pop had to admit that.

Still, Fiona couldn't help feeling a little hurt that Uncle Joe had called Pop an idiot. Keeping the contents of his letter to herself, Fiona decided to get out the dictionary and look up the words "entitlement" and "Semper Fi." Entitlement, she saw, meant "the fact or sense of having a right to something." She wondered if Uncle Joe thought America felt entitled to the freedom he'd been fighting for. She didn't find Semper Fi in the dictionary, so she asked Pop. He told her it was short for "Semper Fidelis," the Marine Corps motto that means "Ever Faithful." Fiona thought the motto fit Uncle Joe quite well. She planned to tell Uncle Joe how proud she was of him in her next letter, although she thought better of sharing that pride with Pop.

~oOOoOOo~

Within the next few months, the war that had divided Fiona's family and the nation drew to a violent close as the North Vietnamese troops captured Saigon, and South Vietnam surrendered. The Americans withdrew. Fiona watched it unfold on the small television screen, forming her understanding based on what the news channels shared. The war became more real for Fiona than it had during her correspondence with Uncle Joe. Looking at the television, she imagined the soldiers were uncles, brothers, and sons, just like Joe.

I wonder what Uncle Joe would want for Christmas, Fiona asked herself. She was already squirreling away little gifts for Christmas. "Aunt Em loves sunset postcards," she remembered of her father's brother's wife. "Maybe that's something aunts and uncles share in common." She had a few pretty cards saved up, so she made a mental note to ask Mother whether her younger brothers might like such things. She had her own personal wish list, as well. This year, she was eyeing a beautiful eight-inch Victorian doll, a redhead like Fiona, named Jody. The doll came with a dainty parlor that included a grandfather clock, player piano, purple sofa, rocking chair, telephone, and miniature tea set. Jody's pet dog, painted on the outside of her parlor, was forever caught in the act of jumping after a butterfly. The J. C. Penney ad promised an old-fashioned experience, "just like it was when grandma was a girl." It had been years since Fiona had played with dolls, but this one awakened an old dream. Looking at Jody made her yearn to touch her dreams, to imagine them with skin and pantaloons and a fabulous hat. Gram still had a grandfather clock. Had she owned it since she was Jody's age? Fiona wanted to imagine her own life, set in Gram's calm, loving world.

Gram hadn't shared any of the triumphs or tragedies from her youth with Fiona, so all Fiona could conjure was a fabulous fantasy, a world of refinement, of music, and stability. It was an ideal world, courtesy of the Ideal Toy Company. What a perfect name for a toy company, Fiona thought. "Hey Pop, look at this beautiful doll," Fiona began her pitch. "Isn't she wonderful?" Fiona cooed, knowing her father would rather she fell in love with something scientific. Pop put his perspective aside, though, when he saw the delight in his daughter's eyes. "She's only $15.87; you save a whole dollar when you get the doll and the house, together. That's a pretty good savings, I'd say. Fifteen bucks, for a doll and a house and a piano and everything. Where else can you get a piano for so little? It's a little piano, so it won't take up much room or be noisy at night. And I'm thinking she's a collector's item. An investment. Santa could put her under the tree and surprise me. What do you think, Pop, could we?" As Fiona pretended to swoon over the ad, Pop agreed to spring for a taxi and take Fiona to purchase this dreamy new doll his daughter had her heart set on.

Heading out to the mall that Saturday, Wolf seemed increasingly uncomfortable as the meter clicked away in the taxi. Fiona had miscalculated the distance. A $15 doll was quickly becoming a $30 adventure. Once Fiona got the doll home, Pop's disapproving glance made her begin to regret the adventure. That was stupid, she thought, eying the box. From now on, I'll just keep my wishes to myself. I'll find a way to buy myself something without help. Squirrel it away somewhere secret. Maybe I'll even wrap it, and open it on the very day. But I won't put anybody out.

Fiona's plan helped her feel both satisfied and smart. She was already making sure Pop wrote out the rent and utility checks each month and got them in the mail on time, so why not take charge of her own joys, as well? This way, Pop could still enjoy giving her what had delighted him as a child—things she didn't care about much—and still be sure to have something that made her happy. Pop won't disapprove, and I won't be disappointed. It makes sense, she thought. She felt her hero, the logical Mr. Spock from *Star Trek*, might also approve. By sticking to logic, she kept herself from feeling the sense of isolation and loneliness that stalked her decision.

Fiona looked over at the colorful box housing her doll and its Victorian house. "Pop's going to wrap that up, and now I don't even care about her anymore." She realized. But when Christmas dawned, she found she did still like Jody, and all she represented. Jody didn't get played with much, but she got posed, and somehow her presence mattered, motivating Fiona through the school year and out into the freedom of summer. Next year I'll be a teenager at last, Fiona thought. And I'll be in the 8th grade. "Not too long until I'm off to college. Right, Hogan?" Hogan sniffed her agreement.

During the first week of her second summer in Detroit, Fiona joined her father at work. She whiled away the afternoon in his workshop, crafting metal animals out of soldering wire. The activity didn't hold her interest or attention for long, so she trotted over to Happy Tails, the pet store where Pop had purchased Hogan. It was just down the street from his office.

"Hi, Fiona," the owner sang out, easily recognizing his frequent visitor. She had taken to stopping in every afternoon to pet the puppies and check on the exotic animals.

"Hi, Dan," she responded. "How's Rudy today?" Rudy was the name she'd given a certain ferret she'd fallen in love with the moment she'd met him. Before Dan could respond, playing his part in the identical dialogue they exchanged each day, two teenagers walked in, asking if he had a job opening. As Dan handed each of them an application, one asked how much he paid. "Not hiring," he answered, and sent them on their way.

"Hey, I'll work here," Fiona said. "And you don't even have to pay me. I'm here all the time anyway: I catch a ride with my Pop when he comes into work. I could come in all summer. You know how much I love animals, Dan, and I'm very neat and polite and always on time. You can count on me like clockwork."

Dan thought for a moment, considering Fiona's earnest offer. "If it's okay with your dad, it's okay with me."

Fiona felt richly rewarded by getting to spend each day caring for Dan's animals, and by helping customers—it more than made up for the lack of pay. She cleaned cages, fed animals, swept the floors, and restocked shelves. Within a week, Dan let her handle the cash register. When he poked his head out of his office to supervise her, he noticed how carefully and confidently she handled the animals when showing them to customers. He couldn't imagine how she knew so much about them. "The kid's a natural," he said, under his breath and returned to his desk in the back.

Downstairs, where customers were not allowed, the shop kept dozens of hamsters, mice and rats in cages, as well as guinea pigs and lizards of all kinds. After a rodent or lizard was purchased upstairs, Dan went downstairs, selected another, and brought it to a display cage upstairs. Fiona was grateful the animals let her move among their cages, cleaning their spaces and replacing their bedding and their water. Maybe they're grateful I'm taking care of them, she thought.

"Atchoooooooo!" she sneezed. "I've got to go outside for a while, okay, guys?" Fiona said to all her companions. She took her work very seriously, even though it was kicking in her allergies something fierce. When she wasn't blowing her nose, wiping her eyes, or taking Sudafed from a little bottle of bright red relief Pop had purchased over the counter, she remained devoted to her job.

When she came back inside, her eyes and head feeling once again clear, Dan asked, "Do you think we should take out the Nile Monitor for a while?"

"Awesome!" she answered. That was Fiona's cue to jump up on a stool, so her toe wouldn't become a snack. Dan opened the door to the cage and, together, they watched the Nile lizard chase around the shop floor. After the lizard had had his exercise and Dan had returned him to his cage, he came back with Rudy, the beautiful golden-brown ferret Fiona had been obsessing over.

"Fiona, you've been doing such a great job for me," Dan said, handing her the ferret.

"Are you going to clean his cage, Dan?" she asked. "Can I hold him while you do it? I'll be very careful with him."

"I know you will, Fiona. That's why I'm giving him to you."

"What?" She looked down at the fuzzy animal in her arms and back up at Dan. She wasn't sure she understood.

"I'm giving him to you. If it's okay with your dad, I think you should take him home with you."

"Seriously?" She looked at his little face and said, "Did you hear that, Rudy? You're finally coming home!"

~o0O0O0o~

Pop could hardly say no. Fiona had been talking about Rudy for weeks; she was smitten. Now that the summer was ending, and with it her job, Fiona would have had to say goodbye to Rudy. Instead, he had come home with her. She'd named him Rudy, having read "Rikki-Tikki-Tavi" a short story about a young mongoose in Rudyard Kipling's *The Jungle Book*. She knew a ferret was different than a mongoose, but Rudy had reminded her of the story.

Although Rudy was new to Fiona, and his fur was softer than Hogan's, she made a promise to herself to love both pets equally. Compared to Rudy, Hogan was slower and more plodding; Rudy was bouncy. He could pop nearly two feet into the air, but also liked to burrow into the woven couch. Hogan had gentle claws, whereas Rudy's were razor sharp, although he rarely used them. With Hogan and Rudy, one on each shoulder, she felt safe and empowered moving through the apartment complex. People gave her wide berth to avoid the menagerie they saw coming their way. Fiona considered her pets her very own security patrol, and one creative form of self-defense. With the help of her exotic animals, Fiona had securely transitioned from the *Green Acres* of Mystic Meadow to the urban jungle of America's "Motor City." Once again, she'd found her way.

Out of the blue, Pop announced that they were heading to Toronto, for a quick, visit with Hanna. A girl needs to be prepared, Fiona thought to herself, packing. The train ride from Detroit to Toronto took just shy of five hours. Four hours and fifty-one minutes, to be exact. Fiona knew this. She had the timetable from the train station. She'd wanted to bring Hogan and Rudy, and had made a very convincing case to Pop about hiding her pets under her seat, hoping nobody would notice. If they did notice, they'd be a hit anyway. Who wouldn't love to play with a skunk and a ferret on the train? But Pop didn't bite. Technically, one wasn't supposed to bring feral animals across borders. "Fee, ever heard the one about young gulls crossing sedate lions for immortal porpoises?" His punch line, Fiona knew, signaled the end of the conversation. Both animals were left in the kind care of Dan.

Fiona and her father checked into the hotel near where Hanna, Violet, and Holly were living. Fiona had known for only two days that they would be going to visit them, and she could only wonder, after all this time, what had caused Hanna to want to see Pop, and why they were going. Pop had told her nothing except to pack for two nights. The fractured family met up at a pop-up street fair in Toronto, a kind of neutral place with plenty of distractions. The rides were for younger kids, but Fiona was so glad to have time with her younger sisters that she didn't mind. This fair's a gas, Fiona thought. Especially the pony ride with the fuzzy model horses with their long manes. As Holly and Violet rode round and round in the ring, Hanna noticed Fiona eyeing a dappled model horse and bought it for her, as a belated birthday present. Fiona felt she'd treasure it forever. Later, after the family sat down to dinner together at Hanna's apartment, Hanna presented Holly with a dramatic, flaming Baked Alaska for her birthday. Fiona was having so much fun, she hadn't noticed whether Pop and Hanna had taken any time to talk. As far as she could tell, everyone was getting along, at least.

At the end of the second day, as she was packing her bag and preparing to leave for the train station with Pop, Fiona was hoping—she felt almost sure—that they'd all reunite somehow, as they'd managed in the past. Just not today, I guess. When Fiona and Pop got to the lobby, Hanna was there, with Holly and Vi. Hanna gave Fiona a good, strong bear hug, and said, "I love you, honey." Then, there were more hugs all around. The girls all smiled when the grownups shared a shy goodbye kiss, and an impromptu tango, to the music that was playing in their heads, and nowhere else. Then Fiona and her Pop hopped into the waiting cab, and headed off to the train station.

On the train home, Fiona was feeling giddy at the prospect that Pop and Hanna might reunite, and she and Holly and Violet would be together again. Fiona would have tasty dinners at the table with her family. The house would be clean, the furniture would match, and there would be a mother in the house to provide affection and all the girl-things Fiona needed. Lost in her musings, Fiona gazed out the train window, seeing nothing. Tonight, the house would be silent. Knowing they'd arrive home late, Pop had arranged for Dan to bring Hogan and Rudy to the apartment the following morning. Fiona would have preferred to come home to their comfort and affection. No worries, Fiona thought to herself. Tomorrow they'll be back home. And, who knows. Maybe one of these tomorrows, Hanna will be, too!

Over the next couple of weeks, Fiona didn't dare ask her father how it was going with Hanna, and he didn't say a thing. She wished on every evening star, and hoped with every fiber of her being, for a family reunion.

One evening after dinner, as Fiona was sitting on her bed between Hogan and Rudy, doing homework and Pop was in the living room, reading, the phone rang. "Hello. We're looking for Dr. Wolf Sprechelbach, husband to Dr. Hanna Sprechelbach. Would that be you, sir?" asked the voice on the line.

"This is he. Who is calling?"

"This is the Toronto Police Service, sir. Are you sitting down, sir?" Pop sat upright and set down his book.

"Yes, yes. What is this about? Tell me."

"Sir, I am sorry to report that Mrs. Sprechelbach was killed tonight in what appears to be a random act of violence." Wolf dropped the phone. For a moment, he sat motionless, almost as if he hadn't heard the horrible news. A weight settled into the room that threatened to crush him and everything in it. He felt as if he couldn't breathe. Not asthma. Worse. He felt certain the news was going to kill him, too. And, in the moment, he would have preferred that.

Fiona, hearing the phone clatter against the table before it landed on the carpet, came into the living room. "What's going on, Pop? Who called? Is everything okay?"

Wolf turned toward his child with a look of torment in his eyes that told her nothing would ever be okay again. He looked like he was going to collapse, right then and there. Instead, he gathered Fiona into his arms and sobbed, quietly, "Hanna's dead, Fiona. She's dead." Then he got up and walked right out of the apartment, saying nothing more than, "I'll be back."

With a new clarity, Fiona now understood that even when things were bad, they could always get worse. I take back my wish! She thought, desperately. Yes, I wanted my sisters back, but not like this. This is like an evil monkey-paw answer to a kid's wish.

It wasn't long before Pop returned, with a set of keys in his hands. He had rented a car and, despite the heavy storm that night, he insisted on driving to Toronto. "Pack your suitcase, Fee; we're leaving in five minutes."

"What about Hogan and Rudy?" she whispered. Pop looked at her for a moment. "We'll call Dan from the road. I'll hide a key." Fiona didn't argue, didn't ask to bring them with her. This was not a time for asking.

Fiona and her father set out in the rain and drove all night toward Toronto, tears coursing down Wolf's face as he drove, in silence. Wolf kept on driving, stone faced, until "Fire and Rain" came on the radio. When James Taylor crooned, "I always thought that I'd see you again," Wolf lost it. Sobbing violently, as Fiona had never seen him do, he could hardly see the road through his tears.

"Hey Pop, why don't we pull over? Pop? Hey, Pop?"

Finally pulling over, he said, "Maybe I'll just shut my eyes for a few minutes." He slept for what felt like hours. Fiona did not. She just sat in the dark of the highway embankment, alone with her thoughts.

Wolf had shielded Fiona from the horror of Hanna's death. All she knew was that there had been some sort of violence, and that Hanna had died. Not knowing any of the details enabled Fiona's fertile mind to run amok with possibility, tormenting her, as she tried to imagine what had happened.

Who could hate Hanna? she thought. It must have been a stranger, someone who didn't know her at all, who took her life, who had robbed Holly, Violet—and Fiona—of their mother. Everyone who knew Hanna loved her. Especially Pop.

Despite having a mother who wrote sinister mysteries and often thinking about gruesome scenarios as a result, Fiona hadn't imagined she'd find herself stepping into one. She didn't know the full story. She just knew that a melancholy darkness had fallen over the family and, by extension, her world. That same weekend, the news had reported a number of deaths: suicides, murders, and accidents. Some of the incidents had been racially motivated, some involved domestic violence, and a few were simply tragic accidents. These violent occurrences were much more common in the United States, particularly in big cities like Detroit, than in Canada. Fiona found herself wondering what was in the atmosphere to cause so much trauma in one weekend, having no understanding that it happened, somewhere in the world, every hour of every day.

The funeral was open casket. Pop and Hanna's parents had consulted with the experts, who felt it was important for the children. Hanna's was the only real coffin Fiona had ever seen from close up. It was a smooth black and lined with cushioned white silk, and appeared comfortable for Hanna, who looked to Fiona as if she were only sleeping. Fiona had half expected—wanted—her to wake up.

Fiona and her father couldn't have imagined their family would be unsafe in Toronto. Is anyone truly safe, anywhere? Fiona wondered, shivering in her discomfort. What Wolf didn't tell his child was that Hanna's death had been a tragic accident: an unsupervised child in the next-door apartment was playing with his father's gun when it had gone off; the bullet shot through the wall, killing Hanna as she slept. A saving grace was that the girls were spending the night at a friend's house when tragedy struck. Pop eventually explained to his daughters, only very briefly, that there had been a gun accident. Nobody thought of grief counseling to help the girls with their feelings, though Gram suggested karate lessons might be cathartic. No, everyone agreed, best not to mention it.

The only respite from the unrelenting anguish came from Pop's brother Eric's wife, Aunt Em. Emily hailed from Britain, and was the kind of woman who faced her own tragedies with a stiff upper lip. But her heart bled for the suffering of others. She set about baking as soon as the funeral was over. Then, she packed up the car she had rented for the occasion, and headed to Detroit. She would see to it that there was plenty of food in the freezer, and that her nieces wouldn't starve. Uncle Eric was busy with work, so Em drove alone from Indianapolis with a car filled entirely of food and ice. She drove without stopping, to ensure the food stayed cold.

Arriving at their apartment, she knocked on the door, brightly. Smiling, she asked, "Hey girls, want to help your auntie bring a few things in from the car?" Hugs conveying grief, relief, and warmth were exchanged, and, soon, the fridge was filled to overflowing with delicious treats. The frozen foods were thoughtfully labeled. Fiona spied one in front that said, "Hi, I'm a stroganoff; pop me in the oven at 350 for 30 minutes."

Aunt Em stayed for a couple of days, providing the sweet support of a desperately needed motherly presence. She took the girls around town in a car she had trouble driving, thanks to the unaccustomed power brakes and steering. Jerking along the streets, she lurched forward and stopped, like a jellyfish swimming through the ocean, and it made the girls laugh. Aunt Em's short visit helped restore a sense to equilibrium to their lives, providing balm for the badly hurting souls of three bereft young girls.

Wolf, who remained overwhelmed with grief, commuted to work every day. In some ways, it was easier than spending time attempting to mother his motherless children. After work, he sometimes walked with them to the local diner. By mid-evening, he needed relief. Strong relief. Often, he sat on the couch, staring unseeing, at the television. Later, when he went to bed, he frequently took a little something to help him sleep. The ensuing "cocktail" of comforts made him impossible to awaken, come morning.

Fiona worried. One recent weekend, just two doors down, paramedics had come and had wheeled away a neighbor who had died from an overdose during the night. Fiona overheard one paramedic say to the other, "Third one this weekend. Something's up." The paramedics had their ears to the street, Pop had said, and seemed to know when a new wave of drugs had hit the neighborhood, or when the concentrations had increased, surprising addicts and resulting in a wave of overdoses. Narcan could sometimes save someone who'd OD'd, but only when the paramedics arrived in time. This time, they hadn't.

Fiona wondered what it would be like to be a paramedic. She tried to imagine how she would deal with the traumas they had to face. Maybe if she followed that road, she could save people's lives. That'd be great. And if she could somehow save Pop, that'd be even better.

As she watched the paramedics leave that night, she thought about that neighbor, a boy not much older than she was, maybe 15 or so. She hadn't known him well, just enough to be bothered by his loud music, but seeing a sheet leave on a stretcher, and knowing a kid was underneath, was jarring. Kids die, too, she thought. Not just old people. She knew this kid had overdosed on something. Heroin, probably. She hoped Pop wouldn't ever get himself into trouble like that.

She had reason to worry. Moe and Traz, the dealers in the building who supplied Wolf with his pot, were hanging around a lot. When they heard of his estranged wife's death, they offered to lift the pain off Wolf's shoulders. They weren't being altruistic. They saw a prospect, and they knew how to mine it.

"A horse with no name? I think I'll pass," Wolf initially answered them, referring to a song by the band America, and to the equine nickname for heroin. He was tempted, though, to take them up on their offer to relieve the excruciating pain in his heart. Every day, the temptation grew stronger.

With a watchful eye on Pop, Fiona now had to take charge of her two younger sisters as well. "Did you make your bed? Brush your teeth? Pack your lunch? How about I brush your hair, and then we can head to school?" she'd say to her sisters every morning.

Fiona was trying hard to mother her sisters as much as they would let her. At bedtime, they were more open to her directions and affection. Almost teens themselves, and with psyches impacted by the sobering that comes with traumatic loss, they often felt they were quite grown up. Less so at night, particularly when they missed their mom. Eventually, though, the three girls fell into a soothing routine that included a bit of TV after the brushing of teeth.

This Wednesday evening began like any other, but then the doorbell rang. Wolf, feeling the need for some strong relief, had invited in Moe and Traz. The three of them disappeared into the bathroom, presumably out of sight of the children. Curious, Fiona sneaked over and pushed the bathroom door open slightly, to see them setting about their business. When one of them looked up, and saw her peeking in, she quickly moved away. A few minutes later, Pop was stretched out on the living room couch, out of pain, and the two guests nodded to Fiona as they left.

Poor Pop. He'd be fine in the morning, she thought. He always was.

Fiona and her sisters had eaten their TV dinners and they were watching an episode of *Star Trek*, while Fiona whittled away at a piece of wood for a box project she was working on. The knife got stuck. Pulling as hard as she could, Fiona yanked the blade out of the wood only to jam it into her other hand, between her thumb and forefinger, hitting an artery.

As blood pulsed out of the wound in time with Fiona's heartbeat, Holly and Violet started shrieking in terror. Fiona was strangely silent. She, too, was afraid, and a little angry at herself for making such a mistake while whittling. Her heart began racing and the pulsing blood quickened. What if she couldn't handle this situation on her own? What if she couldn't fix it? Her hand, in this state, kept Fiona from calling Gram for advice. And Gram wasn't close enough to help her deal with something like this, anyway. Pop, zonked out on the sofa, clearly wasn't available. Trying to rouse him was like trying to wake the dead.

"Is Pop dead?"

"No, Vi, Pop's not dead." Fiona replied, weakly, "He's just sleeping." As she wrapped a paper towel from the kitchen around her hand, Fiona tried to reassure her sisters that everything was going to be all right. Although she absolutely didn't know this for a fact. "I'm just going to go into the bathroom for a while and put on a Band-Aid. Okay?" Fiona didn't want to worry her sisters. Even if they weren't so little anymore, they didn't need this sort of bloody mess; they'd just lost their mother, hadn't they?

Fiona thought about whom she might call on for help. The neighbors across the hall? They seemed pleasant enough. But what if they're not home? Or what if they yell at me or call child protective services on Pop? She didn't want what outsiders to become involved with her situation. They were all safer, she decided, keeping the door closed. Darn it all, Fiona, she told herself. You really shouldn't have been whittling! That was an idiot move, dumb ass! You created this problem. You think of a solution.

She closed the door to the bathroom. Kick it into gear, kid! She told herself, surveying the bloody mess around her. Then, she started mopping it up with toilet paper, and flushing it away. When it was looking better, she ran her hand under a little water, wrapped it as best she could with a washcloth, and pressed her thumb into her index finger, trying to stop the bleeding.

The next day at school Fiona went to see the school nurse about her hand. Shocked and alarmed, the nurse gasped, and then asked Fiona what had happened.

"Well, I was whittling some wood for my school project," she began.

"Unsupervised?"

"Well, my dad was under the weather."

"How so?" The nurse was beginning to piece together the puzzle.

"He's been, well, he's been pretty…he's sick. Anyway, can you help?" Fiona stammered.

While treating the wound, the nurse scolded Fiona for not seeking adult help. She told Fiona she could have lost the use of her thumb had she cut a tendon—something Fiona already understood from years of poring over Pop's anatomy books. The nurse also told

Fiona she could have gotten into real trouble had she lost more blood. Something Fiona also had considered. Fiona decided to say, simply, "Thank you, ma'am," and accept the brusque woman's help. The nurse dismissed Fiona but not before telling her to return to her office the next morning, so she could check her hand. As Fiona collected her backpack, she noticed the nurse writing in her chart. She wondered what those notes said and whether they could be worse than the accusatory thoughts that still plagued her, reminding her just how much she fell short. What worried her more, though, was who might read her chart.

Fiona and her sisters were doing their level best to raise themselves in a near-impossible situation. Fiona knew that. She just hated it when she didn't execute flawlessly. She imagined Pop was doing his best, as well, and she forgave him when his execution was anything but flawless. He was trying, but it was all too much.

Seeing his daughter's bandaged hand might have been the final catalyst. He finally relented to the calls from his mother, who had invited him to bring his girls home for the Christmas vacation, and forever after. The girls shrieked with delight—which told Pop he'd made the right decision. Fiona was elated. She was getting what she wanted most for Christmas: a safe, secure sense of family, and a loving, willing woman to take the heavy, self-assumed mantle of "surrogate mum" off her shoulders.

At school, Christmas was in the air. Fiona could see it in flocked office windows and in the handmade decorations that filled the windows of each classroom. She could sense it in the chill air that hinted at the coming of snow. She sipped it in the hot chocolate she and her sisters made from single-serve packets, using water they heated in the kettle on the stove before school. And, she could hear it in the songs she sang in the school choir. It was going to be great. How could it be otherwise? Even the date is great, Fiona thought. 12.25.75. What a cool number. Fiona and her sisters knew that, by the time that date rolled around, they'd be safely back in Philly with Gram. Maybe for good, this time.

Fiona had been selected as a soprano soloist in the Winter Concert, and she needed to memorize and polish Mozart's "Ave Verum" in Latin, so she practiced every day, every chance she got, even in the bathtub, where the acoustics were great. She felt quite honored to sing this song and, as she focused on the words, the throbbing in her still-healing hand seemed to recede. Fiona loved reaching for the vocal heights as she sang, and practiced the passage over and over, to make sure she would hit the notes, just right. She practiced the other pieces too—Vivaldi's "Gloria in Excelsis," a Mozart "Alleluia," and, of course, the obligatory Christmas carols. The rehearsals sometimes ran long, but they made her feel less tired, not more. She thrilled to hear voices all around her, singing harmonies. Choir was one part of school she truly looked forward to, with pleasure.

At home, Fiona and her sisters distracted themselves from their memories of Hanna by trying to think of a Christmas present that might cheer up Pop. They settled on a piñata. Since they couldn't easily buy a ready-made piñata, they decided to make one out of papier-mâché. They blew up a big, red balloon and tied the end in a tight knot. Then, they cut strips of newspaper and dipped them in a bowl with a solution of water and flour, which they'd borrowed from their neighbor across the hall. Flour wasn't much of a commodity in their apartment since Pop didn't bake. Gone were the days of homemade delights, warm from the oven. That had been Hanna's territory, and they'd long since eaten through everything Aunt Em had brought them.

The girls carefully laid the strips of wet newspaper over the balloon, and set it to dry. It took them three balloons to get it done; the first two popped, mid-project, leaving them covered with glop, and giggling. They kept the mess up on the counter, so the pets wouldn't go after the piñata before it dried. Finally, after the third try, they had a solid, hollow ball, allowing them to pop the balloon, themselves. They painted their piñata with bright poster paint Fiona had borrowed from her teacher. Ultimately, they cut an opening in the bottom and inserted gifts Fiona had bought with her meager savings—things they thought Pop might like to find inside for his present: a can of olives and a can of herring. They also added a few chocolates; they hoped he might share those.

While their hands were still covered in sticky glop, the phone rang. Fiona wiped her hands on a towel, and picked up the phone from the receiver where it hung in the kitchen. It was Mother calling from California, with a Merry Christmas gift of her own: an offer Fiona could hardly believe. An offer Fiona had long since given up hope of receiving. She'd thought she'd finally buried that dead dream, and here it was on her doorstep, alive and kicking, inviting her to ask it into her heart again.

Peggy had been thinking over Hanna's tragic death and considering the consequences. She felt it was her time to step up to her role as Fiona's mother. She had no idea how Fiona might respond, but she could, at least, ask. Peggy wasn't as afraid of Wolf as she'd once been. The words tripped off her tongue. Why not finish out your school year, Mother asked, and join me out here in California for high school?

Yes, Peggy was inviting Fiona to come live with her—Fiona almost had to pinch herself. Did Mother just say, "Would you like to come live with me in California?" She had indeed. "That sounds great, Mother! Outstanding!"

But as Fiona hung up the phone, one thing perplexed her. High school? Does Mother not know how old I am? Fiona didn't want to jinx the offer by saying anything, so she stayed mum about the undeniable fact that she was in 8th grade. In Philadelphia, that would mean facing another year of junior high. What Fiona didn't know was that in California, high school started in the 9th grade. Yes, Mother knew how old her daughter was, after all.

Fiona's head spun at the drastic change in her fortune. In a matter of weeks, she was moving back to Gram's in Philly. And, in a matter of months, it looked like she'd be moving once again, to California! Merry Christmas.

~o0O0O0o~

Moving day arrived. Wolf packed up the kids and drove back home to his mother's house. Once again, it was in the dead of winter, with snow flurries obliterating the view across the wide windshield of the U-Haul truck he'd rented to haul whatever would fit. He stowed his girls, zipped into flannel-lined sleeping bags, in the back with the boxes. The cold cut through Fiona and her sisters like a crisis all night long, and they burrowed deep inside their bags. Fiona breathed into the bag hard, as if blowing up a hot air balloon, squeezing her eyes closed and hanging onto the promise of a cup of cocoa and the warm fire Gram could be trusted to have, waiting.

The cold kept away the thoughts, but her heart was still heavy, having just said goodbye to her beloved Hogan and Rudy. They weren't welcome at Gram's, so Dan had graciously offered to take them back to his pet shop. Just as Wolf reached the Philadelphia suburbs, engine trouble brought the trip to a sputtering stop. Wolf knocked on the door of the closest house—it wouldn't be the first time he'd relied on the kindness of strangers, or the last. The strangers generously invited Wolf and his tribe in to wait in the warmth of their home. Wolf's youngest brother, Zeb, was driving out from the city to help fix the truck and retrieve them. This was the uncle Fiona knew least well. He'd just returned from a stint in Zaire with the Peace Corps. Though Fiona couldn't remember when she'd ever seen him before, his face looked strangely familiar. All the Sprechelbach boys had a certain look about them. Big forehead. Wild hair.

The girls drove the rest of the way to Gram's in the comfort of Uncle Zeb's warm station wagon, with Wolf following behind in the now-running U-Haul. Wrapped in her sleeping bag like a flannel burrito in the back seat, Fiona wondered, once again, what it would be like to live with Mother. Having all but given up on her lifelong dream, she was having trouble conjuring up a mental picture, now that it was close to becoming real for her. She eventually managed envisioning a beanbag chair—a pink one she could sink into to read in the silence of her own sanctuary.

When Christmas came, Pop was genuinely delighted with his gift. And he did share the chocolates. In turn, Gram and Pop gave Fiona, Holly, and Violet matching black turtlenecks, which they found very *Mod Squad*; they felt like actress Peggy Lipton in the popular TV show. The three sisters pushed aside their feelings of loss long enough to revel in being together and to find joy in having put a smile on their Pop's face.

~oOoOoOo~

It was a lazy Sunday morning, and Fiona awoke feeling sluggish, again. She was feeling a little bloated, as she often did after having eaten too many of Gram's stuffed peppers and delicious, sweet küchen. Looking down at the thin, blonde cover girl on the *Teen* magazine that lay at her bedside, she thought, I've got to make a change. I need to start getting prepared for my move.

She wondered if there was any way to get a jump on it and become a California girl before she even got there. California girls were cool. Fiona had seen the films. They were free. They had long, corn silk-colored hair, and cotton shifts skimming their slim, sun-kissed bodies. Certainly, some of them were surfers. A surfer girl? Fiona? In her dreams. But maybe she could get the look without having to swim with sharks.

Fiona's hair was already long, but it wasn't sleek. And she'd have to wait for some sun to get a true tan. But she could mimic California culture by controlling what she ate. She imagined that meant no sugar and no caffeine. Didn't California girls drink sodas? What about meat? She should probably become a vegetarian. Yes, definitely. Starting right this minute.

Resolving to transform herself with her own new "California clean and healthy" diet, Fiona went downstairs to make herself a cup of simple tea.

Pop called it her "twigs and berries" diet. Better than seeds and stems, she thought, picturing the roach clips and half-smoked joints she detested; much better!

"Your daughter's gone a step beyond vegetarian, Wolf," Gram laughed, thinking about how Fiona had decided she shouldn't eat meat or sugar or fat or dairy or white bread…basically anything Gram defined as food. "She's a 'breath-arian.'"

"Grammm…" Fiona feigned indignation. "I resemble that re-mark. Anyway, I'm an arbitrarian! Puhleeaz!"

Fiona, who was secretly delighted that Gram and Pop were interested, decided it would hurt their feelings to tell them that this diet, in her mind at least, was purely "SF Bay Area-ian."

It wasn't that she wasn't eating; there was a lot of salad involved, and a lot of tea. Her stomach wasn't empty, but she wasn't getting much nutrition, either. It takes knowledge to be a successful vegan, and Fiona didn't have even the basics.

Fiona was determined to succeed, and found it relatively easy. At first. After two days of eating like a rabbit, though, it became clear that her unaccustomed diet had taken its toll.

That afternoon, as she entered the dining room, the space became a little hazy and then lost all its color, fading to black and white as the details of the room seemed to zoom away. Like Alice spiraling down the rabbit hole, Fiona found herself suddenly off balance as she crashed into Gram's porcelain teacups.

Fiona sat on the floor, collecting herself and the teacups, amazed she hadn't broken anything. She looked up to see Gram's two Afghans staring at her, their narrow heads cocked, quizzically. "Lucky thing you guys were the only ones who saw that," she whispered, as she got up from the floor, petted the dogs, and put the teacups back in place. Fiona wasn't certain how the adults would react, and didn't want to give them excuses to keep her in Philly "for observation," even if she might need it.

Fiona decided right there in the dining room that her California-girl makeover didn't need to be about food right now. Surely there were kids with all sorts of diets in that "free-to-be-you-and-me" state. Best to wait until she got to California to go all wheat germ-granola.

She opened the refrigerator door, pulled out one of Gram's leftover bell peppers and wolfed it down, cold. For good measure, she grabbed a bottle of the Vernors ginger ale Gram had brought back as a special treat from a recent visit to Cleveland. At that moment, the fact she was famished, combined with the love she knew her grandmother had thrown into the pot, merged into the most delicious meal she'd ever tasted. Gram should really enter the county fair, Fiona thought, replacing the tin foil on the plate before placing the remaining leftovers back into the fridge.

Feeling satisfied but disappointed in herself for letting hunger demolish her diet, Fiona flicked off the light in the kitchen and took the stairs, two at a time, up to her room. She slid her Simon & Garfunkel album, *Parsley, Sage, Rosemary and Thyme*, out of its sleeve, and set it on the turntable. She played "Patterns" three times before lifting the needle and setting it on the edge of the record, to hear the whole album through, from the top. She flopped her back onto her bed and lay, with her hands behind her head, just listening, trying neither to feel nor think.

Fiona finally flipped the album to hear, "Flowers Never Bend with the Rainfall," before switching the album to *Bookends*, to hear "America," "Fakin' It," and "A Hazy Shade of Winter." Just before she slipped off to sleep, she pondered how Paul Simon's thoughts could so completely match her own.

The next morning, feeling a lot better, Fiona took a bit of Gram's delicious küchen cake from the kitchen counter, and headed out for a long walk, thinking about her impending move. As much as Fiona would miss her grandmother once she went to California, she was most concerned about Holly and Violet. She was worried about how they would do without her.

Fiona imagined falling into a fairytale with them, where they could magically transform themselves into a crown of violets and holly berries to be woven into the mane of a white Pegasus-unicorn that would carry them to Berkeley at bedtime whenever they were lonely. There, they'd transform back into human form, sharing tea and conversation before returning safely home again by morning. Daydreams aside, she planned to ask Mother if she could invite them for a visit once she got settled and made sure it would be a happy place for them. Heck, a happy place for her.

Fiona dusted off her old daydream about sharing a home with her sisters. They could all attend college out there. Why not? In her mind's eye, she conjured up an idyllic sunny yellow Victorian cottage, complete with lavender and white trim, a gingerbread roof, a roaring fire, a view of the Bay, and two cats in the yard. The two cats came into her imagination uninvited. She didn't mind them, as long as they didn't come inside and kick up her allergies.

Fiona kept on walking until the wind whipped up. She glanced at her watch. Two hours had gone by, and she realized she hadn't left a note. She decided she'd better get home quickly, before she was missed. Gram was waiting for Fiona when she got there. She gave her granddaughter a hug and then nodded toward a small box sitting on the table, addressed to Fiona. It was from Mother and had arrived by special delivery, right after she'd left for her walk. Fiona gazed down at the box, fingering the edges, and noticed the local florist's return address. Then she looked up at Gram.

"What do you suppose it is?" she asked.

"It's from the florist. I can't imagine why, though," said Gram. "It's not your birthday, not Christmas."

Fiona tore back the flaps of the cardboard box and lifted out a smaller while box. Cautiously she opened the lid and looked at her grandmother before she peered inside. There, she found a ceramic teacup, containing a tiny arrangement of beautiful little red roses. Fiona gasped.

So did Gram.

"Is there a card? What does it say?"

Fiona's face blushed like the roses, "Nothing, really."

"What do you mean, nothing? What does it say?"

The florist's card simply said "Congratulations, love, Mother." Grandma knew why, or guessed. "You have your period? Why didn't you tell me?"

Fiona averted her gaze. "Shhh, please, Gram. Don't say that! Say moon time or something. That's what my friends all say."

"Moon time? As in, that time of the moon-th?"

"Moon time, maybe because you go crazy like a werewolf, beforehand."

That made Gram smile, just as she'd hoped. She hadn't meant to slight Gram. She just didn't want Gram talking about, well, *those* sorts of things. Gram didn't use the right words. She was just too clinical, or else she used farmhand stories, and none-too-subtle ones, at that. That talk about birds and bees, and about how boys won't buy the cow if they can get the milk for free…I mean, talking about all that with your grandmother? Gross. I mean, Gram is way too old to understand me and my generation.

Fiona hadn't appreciated the many times Gram had suggested she start wearing a bra. She didn't think she needed one, anyway. Gram seemed to think she'd feel more like a woman, all grown up, wearing one. In a harness? I think I'd feel more like a broodmare. Didn't Gram know about women who were burning their bras, and claiming their freedom?

"If you buy me a bra, I'll just burn it," she had said, before storming out of the room. And now, here she was with Gram, on these very private subjects again. This was awkward. Fiona loved having shared a confidence with her mother and treasured her teacup, with its blood-red buds. It was a beautiful symbol of the blood-tie between mother and daughter. But as far as keeping a confidence, Mother might has well have sent up flares. Now everyone in the household would know her most private business.

Though it was now an open secret, Fiona still tried to be private about her moon time. There was one, glaring signal that betrayed her, however. The day before her "moon time," she would be visited by strange sparklies and a weird, shapeshifting amoeba. They clouded her vision, signaling a storm ahead. She called it PMS, for Painful Moontime Suffering.

"Argh, just kill me now," Fiona writhed on her bed, hardly able to think, so great was the pain exploding in her brain. Migraines were like that. Every time. Whenever she got one, Fiona felt like a butterfly with a pearl-pin pushed through it—only still alive. Right now, the pain was running right through her left eye into her brain. She couldn't move, didn't want to move, and any sound, any slip of light, was excruciating. Everything hurt. All that existed was pain.

Fiona rolled off her bed and slunk into the bathroom. Without reaching for the light, she settled in front of the toilet, pressed her hands against the cold porcelain and waited, wondering if this would be one of those episodes where she vomited until her ribs hurt. She grabbed three towels. One, she spread out on the floor. Another, she rolled up for a pillow. Another, she used for a cover. Curled up this way, she often dozed off to sleep. This time, though, she entered a surreal experience. Doctors call it Alice in Wonderland Syndrome, and rightly so. It felt to Fiona as if she had a tiny body and a huge head. Her hands seemed small, too small for usefulness, so it was wonderful and strange that she could still reach out and pick up her towel without difficulty. Space didn't work logically. Nothing made sense, nothing seemed real, except for that railroad spike through her eyeball. She got up and reached for the miles-away door with her miniature hand. Even though the size of her enormous head clearly exceeded the doorway opening, she made it out to the top of the stairs without a problem. The magical geometry of it all was making her seasick. "Hey, people…hey anyone…hey, help!"

Pop heard, and came running. He pressed his regular-sized hands against what Fiona perceived to be her couch-sized forehead, and somehow it covered the expanse. No fever. Good. "Migraine?" Fiona nodded. With a quick, "I'll be right back, kiddo," he sped down to Radio Shack to pick up a few components, and then returned home and took out his soldering kit. He quickly built Fiona a biofeedback machine.

"The idea here, is to help you slow your pulse, warm your icy hands, and cool your head," he whispered to his daughter. "This will help bring circulation into your fingers and reduce the blood flow in your brain. Give it a whirl, and you'll be feeling better soon."

Fiona didn't really care about the science behind it; she just wanted to feel better. And, she did. A little. Eventually, her head and body returned to their normal sizes, and the pain subsided. Until the next time.

~oOOoOOo~

The country was celebrating the bicentennial that summer, and there was no better place to be than Philly, the country's first capital city. Gram spent most of the summer holed up in the Carter/Mondale campaign office, stuffing envelopes and making calls in preparation for the November election. Wolf and the girls flew kites, had picnics, watched fireworks, and generally enjoyed the break from school, mostly ignoring the elephant in the room: Fiona's impending move.

Fiona pushed closed the lid to her suitcase, sat down on the bed, and looked out the window. California. Would moving to California fix anything? Moving all over the place hadn't worked out all that well for Pop, she thought. He thinks you can solve a problem by leaving the problem behind. How about me? Will it work out better for me? How am I so very different? Or, will I just fall back on Gram, over and over again, like Pop?

She cranked up the volume on the stereo. Her thoughts were going in circles, and she wanted it loud enough so she didn't have to hear herself think them. Downstairs, the family was treated only to the pounding baseline. Over and over again. Thud-thud-thud, thud-thud. Think it's over? Think again. Thud…

Gram glanced over at Pop, sighed, and decided it was time. After rocking three times, she hoisted herself out of the heavy upholstered chair and shuffled over to the staircase. Cupping her hand round her mouth, she called upstairs to Fiona. Twice. She hadn't imagined Fiona stood a chance of hearing her over the concert coming out of her room, as "Oh What a Night" started up, again. The kid had probably set the record player on repeat. Gram just didn't feel like hauling herself upstairs to stop the racket. With another sigh, she resigned herself to the hike.

"Hey Fee, "How about a different song for a while?" protested Gram, as she leaned against the doorframe, watching her grand-daughter fiddle with her things. "Do you want to talk about any-thing? Are you doing okay, honey?"

"I'm fine, Gram," Fiona mumbled into her suitcase. "I'll change the record." Without looking up, Fiona reached over to the turntable, lifted the arm with her forefinger, and set the needle on a different song. Gram shook her head, pressed her hand against her ample breast, and departed the doorframe to head back downstairs. Fiona shoved the door shut with her foot, switched the record to "Welcome to My Nightmare," by Alice Cooper, and amped the volume. If Gram complains, I'll put on Kiss, she told herself. Maybe she didn't want to hear the words goodbye. Maybe she didn't want Gram being so nice. Maybe she didn't want any thoughts about staying in Philly to intrude on her beautiful plans.

~oO0O0O0o~

The time for goodbyes had arrived. There could never be enough hugs, Fiona thought, embracing her Gram, then her sisters, in the strong bear-hugs that were the Sprechelbach family tradition. Pop drove her to the airport, and saw her right to the gate. She waved goodbye to him, and he to her, until they were out of sight of each other. Seated in her window seat, she looked out the oval window, to see him standing there still, waving his farewell.

5. MOTHER

Fiona sat on the wooden swing and felt the ragged hemp of the ropes, rough against the palms of her hands as she rocked back and forth, digging her heels into the dirt. Her eyes wandered around the tangle of garden—to the weathered guest cottage, detached garage, and her mother's Berkeley bungalow that, at least for now, she would learn to call home. The house was bordered by a rippling creek in the back. Fiona could smell the raspberries, ripe on the vine, where they grew along the creek's banks. She really was here.

Fiona admired the wild energy of the garden making its way across the yard, and appreciated the metaphor she found in its freedom and the experiences she anticipated in the bohemian community of Berkeley. She was particularly drawn to a rosebush, consuming half the house and exploding with a riot of tiny pink buds.

"I really should cut that thing back before it takes over completely," said Mother, who had wandered out into the yard, having noticed her daughter had disappeared.

"Oh, I don't know," Fiona said. "It's kind of spectacular. Do you ever bring any into the house? I can imagine filling every room." Mother considered her daughter for a moment. "Take as many as you wish," she said with an amused smile. "I'm sure they'll look lovely in your room." Remembering her promise to her father, Fiona felt they'd also look lovely in her hair. That thought brought back a distant memory of weaving daisy chain garlands as a little girl. Things were sunny back then, too, she thought, at least for a little while, I guess the Byrds were right in their song: To everything there is a season. Fiona's mind drifted to the physical and emotional distance that had grown between herself and her Pop over the past few years. It was the sort of chasm she felt certain couldn't be bridged with flowers, and that sad fact colored her joy with a hint of melancholy.

Fiona picked up her luggage from the foyer and followed her mother up the stairs to her new room. There, she found a twin bed, a simple dresser, a desk, and a shelf for her things, all in a sleek, minimalist, Swedish style. The space was spare, but she appreciated having her own room and trusted, in time, she could make it feel familiar. Perhaps she'd start with a few roses.

A box from Gram, which had arrived before Fiona, packed with some of her favorite books, photos, and knickknacks sat, unopened, in the corner of her room. She stared at the box a moment, picturing her grandmother, who had so thoughtfully and carefully gathered Fiona's most precious pieces and had sent them along, despite her reluctance to let Fiona go so far away from her warm embrace. The box was a symbol and reminder of the security she had left behind and the safe space that waited for her should she decide to return.

Fiona slid her finger under the taped edges of the box, pried back the flaps, and pulled out a book, a well-read copy of *Wind in the Willows* by Kenneth Grahame. She fingered the worn edges of the cover and set it on her night stand. A bookmark would take the casual eye to her favorite quote about heeding the call to step into your new life before the moment passes. I love that book, Fiona thought. Someday I really must go messing around on boats. If the author thinks it's that great, there must be something to it. I'm sure I'll have a better time of it than Pop did.

~oO0O0Oo~

Although Fiona hated the dentist, she knew that the picture-perfect California girl had beautiful teeth, so when Mother made an appointment, she didn't resist. Ever since Mother had made the appointment for a routine checkup and cleaning, though, Fiona had begun suffering nightmares. Fiona couldn't imagine the experience would be any better than any other dentist, just because it was

Mother's dentist. Until she saw him. This young man was teen-idol gorgeous. His skin was tan against his white coat and Colgate smile. He had Paul McCartney hair and Paul Newman eyes, and a voice that came out like music. Fiona could have sat there all day, gazing dreamily into his eyes as he checked her teeth. She hardly noticed her discomfort and ultimately was pleased to be pronounced good to go, until he mentioned her wisdom teeth. Although she was still young, it was clear all four were impacted, sideways, and showing no signs of emerging on their own. If she wanted to avoid problems later, they had to come out.

What kind of problems? Could she have a moment to think about it? Dental work was painful. Was it really and truly necessary? Fiona had spent her entire young life working diligently to become knowledgeable. The last thing she wanted removed were her four talismans of wisdom. Where was the wisdom in that?

Mother didn't like to let problems persist. The following week, she dropped off Fiona at the endodontist's office. This doctor wasn't as handsome. He wasn't as personable. But when he put that mask over her mouth and nose, and told her to breathe in, it really didn't matter. Opening her eyes later, she thought, that wasn't so bad at all. Not until the next day, when her cheeks swelled up to the size of a chipmunk with a treasure trove. Mother responded by babying her for three days straight, plying her with ice cream, applesauce, and chicken-bone broth. While she was recovering, she passed the time reading. She'd already read all the books she had brought from Philadelphia. So, as she was accustomed to doing, she borrowed books from the "house library," squirreling them away in her room. She chose some New Age titles, plus works by Dickens, Dostoyevsky, and Shakespeare, a poetry anthology, a Physicians' Desk Reference, and a copy of *Our Bodies, Ourselves* that had caught her attention.

"Looks to me like you're planning on a rather long recovery," said Mother, as she surveyed the stack of books beside her daughter's bed. Fiona had gathered them, hoping to distract herself for a while. After her mother left with her abandoned lunch tray, Fiona pushed the books aside and decided to write a letter to her younger sisters, back home. Out-of-state calls were expensive, but at least she could write.

Within a week, Fiona's face had returned to a shape she recognized in the mirror, but her mouth was still a bit raw, and ached. She wasn't sure she was quite ready to face the world. Deciding a little sunshine would do wonders for her healing and her head space, she parked herself in her little piece of paradise—the warm, fragrant oasis of her mother's backyard, near the pool.

Tucked into a chaise longue beneath a light blanket, she closed her eyes and let herself feel the warmth of the sun and the comfort of the chaise. She breathed in, slowly, spelling the word *p-e-a-c-e* in her mind, held her inhale a moment, and then slowly released the air, again spelling *p-e-a-c-e* on the exhale. During her third drag of warm air, she felt the ground begin to roll beneath her in the most peculiar way. It felt like someone was shaking out an Oriental rug, with her still sitting on it.

Oh, wow, she thought. This is not good! Is this an earthquake? What if this is the Big One? Just when she started to get nervous, the gentle rolling stopped. Fiona lay back against the chaise and closed her eyes. She could still feel the sensation of the earth rolling beneath her.

Fiona went inside to turn on the television, looking for word of the earthquake in on the TV. Nothing. "You won't find anything, hon," Mother said. "Around here, earthquakes are normal. Smaller ones don't make headlines."

Fiona didn't find that very reassuring. She had heard the reporters talking about earthquake preparedness and how it was impossible to predict when the next quake would strike, and how serious it might be. She thought about packing a little box by her bed, with shoes, a flashlight, a first-aid kit and maybe her teacup. But she did little more than think about it.

She did call her Pop to tell him all about the quake. He answered with his usual enthusiasm, "Hey, Fabulous Fee!" His familiar voice did more than anything to reassure her of her safety in the world.

The next weekend, Mother took Fiona horseback riding in Berkeley's Tilden Park to soothe her spirits. She had already told her mother how much she loved horses and unicorns, though she imagined a horse was much easier to come by. Fiona was hoping Mother would ride with her, particularly since her mother was such an experienced rider, and Fiona hadn't ridden through the wooded trails of Tilden Park. But her mother seemed content to wait for Fiona in the car, taking the opportunity to get a little work done. "Why don't you incorporate a horse into your next mystery story, Mother?" Fiona suggested. Mother nodded, absently, shooing Fiona off to her riding adventure so she could turn her attention to the piles of work that sat in the back seat.

On the way home, Mother stopped by Mr. Mopps, a popular toy store on Grove Street, where Fiona could pick out a Breyer model horse to add to her collection and commemorate the day. She appreciated how Mother didn't hint that high school girls might be too old for collecting model horses. How could anyone grow out of something so beautiful? That night, just before slipping into sleep, Fiona glanced over at her new horse before turning out the light, and realized she was beginning to feel at home.

~oOoOOOo~

Peggy, who was used to her solitude, began spending more and more time out in her writing cottage in the backyard. One evening, captivated by the storyline in her latest mystery, she fell asleep at the typewriter. Awakening to birds singing, she realized she actually liked it better in the cottage than the house. Rubbing her neck, she realized she had a solution to a problem that had been nagging at her.

It wasn't easy being a single mom, and writing for a living. She had considered renting out the cottage, then rejected the idea with a shudder. She couldn't do that. Where would she write? Where would she work through the night, without disturbing anyone? Peggy reasoned that her most creative work came when she was alone with her thoughts. As a mother, she knew she had another mouth to feed, and she needed to make the most of her writing to create income. She'd given up on the idea of rental income until this morning. The solution was as clear as the morning sky: she'd give up her bedroom to a renter, and move out back. It would lighten the burden substantially, and bring in a steady income.

Peggy wasted no time. "This is going to be good for my writing," she told Fiona as she packed up her books and a few clothes, and carried them to the cottage. "That and the rental income are going to be really good for our bottom line."

Although Peggy's writing income was supplemented by her teaching job at the local junior college, it wasn't a lucrative gig. She was paid only for the time she spent in front of her class, not for the time she spent creating her curriculum or grading the fruits of it. When not busy reading student papers, Peggy worked on her novels, a task that called for uninterrupted concentration. Peggy kept the teaching job, despite its arduous hours, for the prestige of being a professor. But one can't live by prestige alone; wasn't that how the saying went? She also did some editing for a local magazine, which brought in a small but steady paycheck. All of this required quiet, dedicated focus. This focus, over years of hard work, had brought her a certain quality of life. It had also instilled a taste for solitude.

Peggy needed to produce, or she'd be another starving writer. She'd "been there, done that." There was no way she, or anyone in her care, would ever want for anything, ever again. Somehow, she'd managed to muddle through with Karen, but this was a whole new chapter. She intended to do better, and often repeated the affirmation that told her so: Every day in every way I am getting better and better. This was a step toward better. It was better to rent out a room in the main house than sacrifice what had proven to be an ideal writing space out in her delicious cottage. It was already beautifully furnished with a futon, a night stand, and a lamp, plus a small sofa and an upholstered reading chair. She had imagined she'd simply use the cottage as a day office, and the spare furnishings reflected that. Now, it was to be her home.

Peggy stepped through the wet grass with one more box of books, headed toward the cottage. Yes, the studio would be fine. She already spent many nights out there, after all. She liked to write on into the night, sometimes nodding off, other times plowing through until the morning light reminded her it was time for coffee. Her typewriter was perfectly perched on a wooden table by the garden window, her preferred workspace.

The cottage didn't have a closet, and there was no room for a rolling rack, so Peggy would keep most of her clothing in the main house. She would keep most of her life in the main house, really—dining and spending "quality time" with her daughter.

Extra income. Space. Solitude. Sitter. Why hadn't she thought of it sooner?

Fiona said she understood, and was even the tiniest bit flattered that her mother trusted her enough to move out and across the garden, leaving her largely to her own devices in the main house. But mostly, Fiona didn't understand. Not really. It was hard not to take it personally, when it was. Personal. I move in, Fiona thought. And you move out. I came all this way because you invited me. What gives? Is it me? My very presence? Or, did I maybe do something wrong here, and you just haven't clued me in yet?

~oOOoOOo~

The quiet in Mother's house became a deafening solitude. Fiona tuned it out by turning on the TV. But, when it came down to it, even when Mother was in the house, in the kitchen making tea, Fiona felt lonely. She was almost looking forward to a renter moving in.

That evening, Mother was headed out for a workshop. Mother didn't trust Fiona to stay on her own yet, so she arranged for one of her college writing students, a fellow who called himself "Bear," to come hang out with Fiona for a few hours. Mother described him as "big and scary on the outside, but a teddy bear, really." Fiona wondered if she'd have felt safer alone. Pop's choice for a sitter had been unfortunate. Would Mother's judgment be any better?

Just before it was time for Mother to leave the house, a motor-cycle roared into the driveway. As Fiona watched from the front window, a burly guy swung his leg over the bike, pushed it back until the kickstand engaged, and lumbered up the walk to the front door.

"What's with the nickname?" Fiona joked as she took in the full measure of this overgrown teddy bear. Bear simply smiled and turned his attention toward his teacher. "Hey, Dr. S."

"Come on in. Feel free to talk shop, but she can write circles around you," said Mother as she went out the door.

Fiona and Bear studied one another for an awkward moment before he offered to take her across the bridge to Tommy's Joynt for a burger.

"On your motorcycle?" she asked, intrigued. She liked the idea of a ride, but she liked the idea of not being alone in the house with a bear even better.

"Sure. Unless you'd rather walk, but they might be serving breakfast by then," he joked. "It's pretty cold on the back of the bike, Fiona. Go put on something warmer."

She rushed upstairs to retrieve her heaviest East Coast jacket, and they were on their way. Even with a huge helmet encasing her head, she felt free, with the wind blowing into her face and the radio blaring as she held on tightly to Bear.

Fiona leaned out to the left to look at the lights in town and feel the breeze as they roared across the bridge.

"Cut it out, Fiona," Bear called back to her. "You want to take this thing down? You're pulling me off balance." Fiona hadn't thought of that; she only needed to be told once.

"Tommy's Joynt has the best burgers ever," Fiona gushed to Mother, who was there in the living room when Bear delivered her safely home, three hours later. And Bear's cool, Fiona thought to herself. What was I worried about?

In the end, Peggy couldn't bring herself to rent out her bedroom. She wasn't quite sure why. Maybe she just didn't like the thought of someone sleeping in her bed. Maybe she didn't want some stranger down the hall from Fiona. Whatever the reason, she decided to rent out the garage, instead. To make it livable, she enlisted Bear's help. He, in turn, called two friends. It was not a big project, just a little sheet rock, a few lights, and moving in an old shag carpet from her bedroom that had seen better days. In less than a week the work was done and rented out to one of her students. Peggy could have moved back into the main house. Although she kept her bedroom filled with her things, and her clothes in her closet, Peggy still slept in the cottage.

~oOOOOo~

Despite her immersion in her new writing space, Peggy was aware that Fiona was lonely. One day, she came home with Tugs, a golden retriever she intended to try out on the household. Her poodle, Tink, was so bonded to her that he rarely left her side, desperate to walk with her or wait by her feet as she wrote. Tink was ancient, and Peggy knew he wouldn't last much longer. She also knew Fiona needed a companion in the house, and decided a dog was just what she needed. One of her students was giving away a golden retriever. Perfect! In a flash, it was all arranged.

"Oh, what a dear dog," Fiona gushed. "His coat is so soft. Look; he's such a love. Don't you think so, Mother?" "Hey Tugs. Can you sit? Can you shake?" Tugs obediently sat, and lifted his paw. Fiona was in love. She called him upstairs and patted her bed. Needing no further invitation, he jumped up and sat there while she got ready for bed. She fell asleep next to Tugs, his head on her pillow.

The next morning, Fiona awoke with her lungs, tight and heavy. Her eyes were swollen nearly shut, and she sneezed six times in succession. She wandered downstairs, and Tugs followed. Fiona found Mother making orange juice in the kitchen.

"Looks like you're allergic to golden retrievers," she said, surveying her daughter's red, swollen eyes. "Do you have any Sudafed handy? If not, I think we have some in the medicine cabinet in the upstairs bathroom."

Fiona ran upstairs for her purse. She was never without her little red bottle of Sudafed. She twisted off the cap, shook out two, and swallowed them easily. It helped with Fiona's allergy symptoms, but little could quell the disappointment in her heart. When Mother took Tugs out to the car later that morning, Fiona stayed upstairs, poring through her photo albums for old pictures of pets she'd loved in the past. She felt a crushing pain in her chest, which had nothing to do with allergies.

Peggy called Tugs' former owner, who reluctantly took him back, and quickly set to work researching hypo-allergenic dogs.

There were none available for rescue from shelters. It looked like locating a puppy might take a few weeks, and she needed to distract her daughter from the disappointment. She glanced at her schedule; no time for horseback riding this weekend. On Saturday, she was taping an interview, and on Sunday, she was running a writing workshop. Why not invite Fiona on Saturday? It'd be a lovely "take your daughter to work day," just like those they'd had together when Fiona was little. Maybe she could even arrange for Fiona to have a few moments in front of the camera as well. Time in front of the camera could be great practice.

A few calls later, it was all arranged. Saturday morning, Fiona awoke and went downstairs to see a video camera all set up for recording. The kettle was already hot, so she quietly made herself some tea, and then watched, in awe, as Mother dazzled the camera. Then, shocked, she found herself in the hot seat. When she shared with Mother that she wasn't sure she could do it, Mother told her to just project confidence, remembering that confidence is being aware of what can happen if you fail but choosing to move forward, anyway.

"So, Miss Sprechelbach, how does it feel to be a world-renowned journalist and writer?"

"Most excellent indeed," Fiona deadpanned for the camera, "Fabulous!"

"And what would you say was the secret of your great success?"

"Ah, that's like asking how do you get to Carnegie Hall. You practice."

"Well, thank you so very much for your time."

Mother whispered in Fiona's ear "Now here's where you say, 'thank you for having me,' and you smile at the camera and show those pearly whites."

"Thank you for having me."

Fiona ran right upstairs to her room excitedly to journal about the experience. She was bitten by the bug. "A writer, I will be!" she wrote, in her most fancy script. Then she called Pop. When she'd talked about studying writing, though, he scoffed, "Who put that idea into your head? Your mother? How could you consider something so banal? You've got a mind for the sciences, Fee. Never forget that."

Wolf could hardly believe what was coming out of his own mouth. Everything he'd promised himself he wouldn't do to his daughter, he was doing, and he couldn't stop. He was just so mad that his ex could have warped his daughter so quickly. "Don't you have any goals? Goals of lasting import, for the benefit of humanity? Don't you want to win the Nobel Prize?" No, Fiona realized, I really don't. That's your dream, not mine. You can go win one yourself, if you want it so much. Don't put that on me. She thought all that, but what she said was simply, "Right, Pop. Science rules. I get it."

Just days later, Mother showed up with another puppy, a lovely black poodle. "She has hair, not fur," she said, "so you shouldn't be allergic to her." Fiona gathered the fuzzy pint-size pup into her arms and said, "I think I'll name her Starlight."

The poodle warmed in Fiona's embrace, but she seemed even more interested in Tink. "That's okay, I guess," Fiona said. "I can go to school without worrying that Starlight is lonely since she has Tink to keep her company." Secretly, she hoped Starlight would love her most of all, the way she already adored her new pet.

~o0O0O0o~

Fiona woke with the sun, so happy to be alive and living in Berkeley. Tucked into the fresh sheets on her own bed, in her own room, upstairs in Mother's spotless house, she reveled in the indulgence.

Fiona luxuriated between the covers for a moment, breathing in the familiar fragrance of Mother's laundry detergent, before getting up slowly and sitting on the edge of her bed to admire the light streaming through the window, and the view of the garden, beyond. Then she made her bed, as nicely as she could, and skipped downstairs to find Starlight.

Even her precious hypoallergenic poodle, with her soft hair, was pristine. Starlight was on day 10 of a two-week treatment for a coccidian protozoal parasite, but the vet had told her this kind wasn't the kind people get, and Starlight seemed to be feeling well.

As soon as she saw Fiona, Starlight started dancing at the door, asking to be let out.

"Just a minute, little one," Fiona said, as she reached down to pet her curly head. "I need to get a baggie in case you poop out there. The last thing Mother needs is to step on one of your little gifties on the way in from her studio."

A moment later, the pals had traversed the stone steps and onto the grassy expanse of Mother's back garden. Fiona admired Mother's rose bushes, blooming across the side of the house, while Starlight did her business on the lawn.

"Good girl, Starlight; good girl," Fiona said, as she slipped her hand into the baggie, turning it inside out, before she stopped to collect the little dog's deposit. Just before her fingers closed around the poop, Fiona glanced down and jumped back. Yikes, I almost touched it. Oh, that's so gross! Fiona felt her stomach heave. Fiona wasn't faking it. She was grossed out to the max.

Starlight's poop was alive with what looked like partial strands of angel hair pasta. Worms. Starlight had worms! Her beloved little buddy was filled with vermin, and now, maybe Fiona would be, too. Not because she had touched them. She hadn't even come close, really, but because she'd been carrying Starlight around. Oh, my Gawd! Fiona shuddered.

Starlight ran up to Fiona and sat, like a good girl, waiting. But the affection she was so used to receiving from her person was not forthcoming. Fiona could hardly look at her cherished dog.

"What's all the racket out here, Fiona? You're probably disturbing the neighbors and, worse, you're definitely disturbing me," said Mother, emerging from her studio. Fiona, normally so concerned about pleasing her mother and remaining in her favor, couldn't focus on that right now.

"Worms, Mother! Starlight has worms!" Fiona recoiled from the offending product, the back of her hand pressed against her mouth.

"Stuff happens, Fiona, whether it's with kids or pets," said Mother, as she pulled the baggie off her daughter's hand and used it to scoop up the poop. "We simply take care of things. The vet will probably want to see a sample to find out what kind of worms we're dealing with, here. You get Starlight, and I'll bring this."

"But, Mother…" Nothing seemed to faze Mother, whereas Fiona didn't even want to pick up Starlight. She still loved her; she just didn't want to touch her. Not until she was pronounced pestilence free.

"Fiona!"

Fiona grabbed a towel and picked up Starlight with it, holding the little bundle at arm's length as they walked to the car. Mother grabbed her purse and a larger, opaque bag, into which she secured the sample. They drove the short distance to the vet, with Mother and Fiona in their seats, and Starlight on Fiona's lap, happy to be going for a drive.

The veterinarian's office was closed.

"Don't they know dogs get sick on Sundays, too?" Fiona asked, rhetorically.

Without a word, Mother put the car in reverse, pulled out of the parking lot, and drove across town to the emergency vet. It was open, but they didn't carry de-wormer medication, as they dealt only in emergency-triage type of care. "But this is an emergency!" Fiona groaned, near tears.

"Pull yourself together, Fiona," said Mother, in a voice suitable for Sunday prayer. "Just take a breath."

Fiona tried, but because of the little sample they'd brought along, the car was starting to smell of pup poop. Fiona rolled down her window and exhaled. You can't catch worms from the air, can you? She wondered. No, of course not. Sheesh!

The emergency veterinarian took the sample into the back, and gave it a look, confirming that the protozoa had been contained, but that Starlight had caught a tapeworm, likely from eating a flea. The vet explained to Mother that Starlight was now shedding live tapeworm segments and Mother could get an over-the-counter remedy at the pet store, which was still open. All they had to do was give Starlight the medication and, for the next few days, the little host would poop out her unwanted guests.

"You mean we're going to have to see this again?" Fiona's voice was a blend of exasperation and disgust.

"Who's we?" said Mother. "She's your dog, your responsibility. You will be taking care of Starlight."

Fiona decided she'd fallen into one of mother's creepier novels, and she couldn't find her way out. It reminded her of the sci-fi novel *Dune* by Frank Herbert, which she'd read in middle school. The story featured Paul Muad'Dib, a rider of enormous worms, called Shai-Hulud, which meant, "thing of eternity," in Arabic. How fitting, Fiona thought. Going through this ordeal with Starlight is going to feel like eternity.

During the drive home, Fiona pulled her sweater down over her hands, so she could pick up her puppy without physically touching her. Mother sensed her distaste.

"Fiona, get over it. She's sick and she needs you." Mother said. "When animals are sick, that's when they need us, most. You know that."

Fiona said nothing, but scrunched her nose in response, following her dog into the kitchen to give her a dose of medicine. Then she went into the bathroom, to wash her hands, and headed up to change into clothes she could bleach, and maybe to have a shower. As the day wore on, slipping into evening, Mother called Fiona from her room, asking her to wash up for dinner and come downstairs to set the table.

"Okay, just please tell me we're not having spaghetti or white rice," Fiona said. "Like, ever again."

"It amazes me that you survived your stay in India," said Mother, "when you have such an aversion to facing a little dog feces at home. Surely you saw worse, there."

"You have no idea," Fiona said. "And anyway, maybe that's why."

Fiona had learned a lot about hygiene since India. For example, she'd learned to wash her hands while singing a tune that took about 60 seconds, like "Happy Birthday," or "Twinkle, Twinkle," inventing new lyrics. "Twinkle, twinkle little star; parasites are best in jars; off my dog and off my hands; getting healthy's in our plans; twinkle, twinkle little star; bleach and soap will get you far!" she sang out cheerily.

Fiona loved hot soap and water. The problem was, it didn't love her back. She was washing her hands so often and so hard, her skin was starting to peel. As she wiped her hands on a paper towel, she noticed how red and raw they were.

"Oh, Mother, look at this. Do you think maybe it's latent leprosy?"

"Yup, bad case of Med Student Syndrome. You're a goner," Mother deadpanned, "I'll give you two hours to live, tops."

"Seriously, Mother."

"Seriously, Fiona. Try some hand cream."

~oOOoOOo~

Knowing that her older sister Karen had attended a Catholic school growing up, Fiona was more than excited to begin Presentation High School in Berkeley. The only thing she knew about the place was that it was run by nuns, and the students wore uniforms.

Mother decided to use the occasion of the uniform purchase to teach her daughter about frugality, by taking her uniform shopping at local thrift stores, including Goodwill and the expansive Value Village warehouse in Richmond. Fiona, who'd once decorated an apartment for $25 and appreciated the value of a bargain better than Mother could ever know, was delighted by the values. Not being fashion savvy, though, she wasn't very selective with her clothing selections.

Fiona didn't know much when it came to the details of her older sister's life. She didn't know about Karen's routine run-ins with the nuns, or the regular finger rapping or the paddling with what the nuns liked to call the "Board of Education." She just knew that she wanted to have as much in common with Karen as possible. She also wanted to do well, to please Mother. Being good in school was an important part of who Fiona was in her family of scholars. But she also wanted to fit in and make friends. That wasn't happening.

Uniforms were supposed to help put students on equal footing. They could also diminish you. Uniforms, Fiona soon learned, were not uniform at all. It mattered how old the required sweater was, and Fiona's was obviously ancient. It mattered whether a skirt or a sweater was the right length, and Fiona's fit the written requirements but not the unspoken ones. The white collars on her second-hand button-down shirts were the wrong shape and size. And shoes, it seemed, were more important than anything. After just a few days on campus, Fiona was certain there must be an unwritten rule book about shoes. The requirement for dress shoes was interpreted widely. Girls who were cool could get away with baby doll patent-leather Mary Janes, particularly if they were platforms. Otherwise, girls wore leather loafers, with pennies or tassels or trim. Fiona had Mary Janes, but they felt wrong in some unfathomable way. Before high school, she'd never really bothered with her looks. With her bouncy ginger hair and startling true-blue eyes, she was used to people responding to her, not what she was wearing. Not here. Here, she couldn't catch the beat.

Mother seemed to know the unwritten rules for adults. That's why she drove a vintage Mercedes. Her choices in her wardrobe, jewelry, and transportation all communicated style, power, and elegance. They whispered, softly, "I have arrived." It's funny that I'm her daughter and I've got none of that going on. If only I could figure out how to convey such a feeling, Fiona thought, wistfully.

Because Fiona spoke with a touch of a lilt from her time in India, a kind of ineffable not-from-here accent that had amused her parents, her classmates thought her aloof, and stuck-up. They dismissed her as a shabby snob with no fashion sense, and gave her the nickname "Professor Mouse." At first, Fiona had been touched, assuming they were referring to her petite size and the diligent way she paid attention in class, raising her hand often, and completing their copious assignments so neatly and thoroughly.

Hadn't that been in admiration for how well she was doing in school? But then as she sat on her bed, her books strewn about her as studied, she got to thinking. Maybe they meant "mousy." And maybe, even in a private Catholic school, it wasn't cool to be bookish and brainy. After all, nobody liked the curve-raiser on tests who, just by existing, makes it that much harder for everyone else.

Fiona was once again flying solo, an alien from some other planet who had somehow made a crash landing in a foreign place she feared might never feel like home.

Where would home be, anyway, for a Professor Mouse?

~o0O0O0o~

In the evenings, after she'd completed her homework, Fiona liked to pull out the cardboard "memory box" in which she stored things that mattered, like the rabbit's foot keychain Gram had given her for luck, the now-dried petals of the tiny roses that had first filled Mother's teacup. That was where she stashed away all the letters she had received over the years. Sometimes, she would bring them out to read the words of encouragement they contained. She also found some solace in her weekly calls back east. Over the phone, she enjoyed Pop's delight in her nicknames. Maybe he was just trying to lighten things up, but his jokes about nuns really did seem to help somehow. This led to a litany of knock-knock jokes, which ultimately made Fiona laugh and helped her feel a little better about her life.

Maybe it wasn't so bad, she thought, as she hung up the receiver. She thought about the beauty of her mother's home, and the lovely neighborhood surrounding it, and Mary, the one friend she had made, who lived just two houses down. If only we went to the same school, Fiona sighed.

Mary didn't attend a private school but went to Berkeley High. Mary introduced Fiona to her friends—classmates who didn't seem to notice that Fiona was different, mostly because they all were. Fiona formed the impression that everyone who was cool went to public school. She longed to spend all day with these new friends, to be part of the universe that was Berkeley High.

One Friday evening during dinner, Fiona gathered her courage and said, "Mother, what if I were to try public school? It would save you a ton of money and driving time since it's pretty much walking distance, I think." Mother sat silently for a moment, then surprised Fiona when she said she'd consider it.

Fiona didn't even need dessert that night. She knew better than to press her mother any further. She did an extra good job on the dishes, and went up to her room to give Mother time to think, while she started imagining her new life.

The next afternoon, Mother's dance group was coming over to the house. They were going to practice some New Age movements that had been choreographed by a self-avowed Russian mystic a few decades earlier. The simple, almost robotic, ritualized steps set to music were easier than Indian dance, although less interesting, Fiona felt, watching through the window as they moved together in the yard. Mother romanticized those New Age teachers, especially those who laid any claims to Sufi lineage. The Sufis were known for their mystical Islamic belief and practice in which Muslims seek the truth of divine love and knowledge through the personal experience of God.

The teacher who led Mother's dance class also held "work weekends," which promised an altered state through silent physical labor and sleep deprivation—a classic brainwashing technique, if you asked Fiona. Whereas Buddhists have walking meditations, these were working meditations, a kind of pay-to-play dynamic, through which leaders got a lot of free labor.

"Fiona, it's important to make something of your soul." Mother had said, having fixated on the idea that your soul doesn't exist until you create it. "Right, Mother." Fiona had agreed, amiably, though she wasn't quite sure she did. She had even once accompanied Mother to one of the weekends. She'd endured it for two hours before quietly leaving to escape the tedium. She might have stayed longer, to help build an orphanage or something, but not just to fix up some guy's private property, and not even have the pleasure of talking to anyone while doing so.

Looking out at her mother, now, it crossed her mind that these hypnotic robotics would work well with the Hare Krishna tabla drums, finger cymbals, and chants. She smiled at the mental mashup.

Fiona kept her distance from what she and her friends called the "mystic crystal crew," a term they'd borrowed from the 5th Dimension's song, "Aquarius." They'd heard all sorts of stories about problems with various guru figures. One of them was a bit too affectionate, even with boys. Another had a huge fleet of fancy cars. All of them seemed to preach about the release of material goods and obsessions, which meant releasing goods and services in the guru's general direction. Fiona worried about the risk of getting pulled out in the undertow against her will, if Mother got too swept away by any of them.

"I'm going over to Mary's," Fiona called out to her mother during a break in the music, and headed out for a few hours without waiting for her mother's reply. She planned to be home by dinnertime.

Tucked into the privacy of Mary's pink bedroom, Fiona and her friend talked at length about the weirdness going on in Berzerkeley, like the leader who'd banished negative words, even labeling a stretch of seven days, commonly called a week, as a strong. "I guess that means they believe it is positive to be strong and negative to be weak," Fiona reasoned. "But the weak shall inherit the earth."

"The meek," said Mary. "The meek shall inherit the earth."

"Okay, same difference..." Fiona acknowledged, staring down at Mary's magazines. The last thing she wanted was an argument. An old local newspaper with the groovy name of *Right On!* and an intriguing cover article on Bourgeois Zen caught her eye. She was about to ask Mary if she could borrow it, but Mary wasn't done with her thoughts.

"Nope, not at all," Mary chimed in, "Meek is having your own strength under control. Not weak. So nope. Totally different. But I see your point about messing with reality using words."

Finally. Fiona thought. Something I can agree with. "Yep. Like I was saying, words matter. But in the end, they're just words."

Mary's voice fell to a whisper, as she told Fiona about her bandmate Mattieu, and how his family was trying to get his older brother back with the help of a deprogrammer after he fell in with a cult. Mary said groups like these had ways to separate people from their past and those they loved, so their entire life's history didn't seem real any more. Fiona sat, spellbound by what Mary was saying, until she caught a glimpse of Mary's clock radio. She leapt up with a start, grabbed her coat, and said, "Gotta go! It has nothing to do with the conversation, really. Talk soon, Mare. Peace out!"

Certain she'd catch hell for being late to dinner, Fiona pedaled her bike as fast as her feet would allow. *Too bad I can't redefine time!* Fiona laughed to herself. Parking her bike against the side of the house, she suddenly thought about Daylight Savings Time and how humans really did redefine time, simply by changing their clocks. *As if we could*, she thought, slipping into the house through the kitchen door.

Mother's class had run long, so dinner was late. *Whew! Dodged a bullet*, she thought, as she opened the flatware drawer and proceeded to set the table, without being asked. During dinner, Mother asked if Fiona was interested in attending a training with her.

"So, Fiona, it's a little like est, the Erhard Seminars Training. It's called The CASST Process. Let's go take it together. It's just two weekends, and it's totally transformative. Life-changing, Fee. My treat."

Fiona's thoughts raced. *So, I bet they'll make you hold your pee while yelling at you to break you down, so they can brainwash you. Sounds like a laugh riot.* Then, she offered up her best, undeniably academic, reason to pass on CASST weekends—exams. Big ones. Huge.

"You know I have to study, Mother."

That ended the conversation. Peggy didn't believe Fiona for a moment. Although Fiona was conscientious enough, her studies wouldn't keep her from anything she really wanted to do. But how could a responsible parent argue with a daughter who was talking about excelling in school? And the last thing Peggy wanted attached to her hip during a CASST weekend was a kid who didn't want to be there. In the interest of self-preservation, she let it go. Maybe she'd put off undergoing the CASST Process for a while, herself, until Fiona could go with her.

As soon as she'd done the dinner dishes, Fiona picked up Starlight and headed up to her room. She set the beloved dog on her bed, put on her headphones, turned on her record player, pulled out *Innervisions* from its white sleeve, carefully blew off the dust, and set the needle down on the first track of side two. Stevie Wonder is always grounding, Fiona thought. Even when he's talking about higher ground. Then, she picked up Starlight, and lay back against her pillows, grateful she had dodged not one, but two, bullets that day. Maybe three.

Fiona transferred from Presentation to Berkeley High right after the Christmas holiday, having finished one semester at the private school. Sitting in the high school office, looking over the freshman schedule, Mother suggested Fiona sign up for orchestra.

"Sure," she said. "Why not?"

Having been granted her wish to attend public school, Fiona was determined to be a model daughter. She was being exceptionally agreeable these days, particularly for a teenager. Yet when they met with the orchestra director, he told Fiona that many of the instruments were already booked, including her first two choices, flute and violin.

"Everybody plays flute, so you'd never get a position in an orchestra unless you're the best of the best. What about viola?" he suggested. "It bears similarity to the violin, and violists always have a place at the table." At the mention of viola, Fiona's spirits sank. Wasn't the viola the brunt of everyone's musical humor? But Fiona was bent on being amenable. And it was Mother who made the decision, with a simple nod of her head.

Besides her music classes, Fiona looked forward to an ambitious assortment of classes for her first semester at Berkeley High, among them advanced levels of math, English, and social studies. Mother also arranged for Fiona to take weekly private lessons with Boris Żywny, a viola teacher who hailed from the USSR. Boris didn't say where, exactly, he was from in that large union. He didn't talk about his past or what had brought him to the United States.

What did he leave behind? Fiona often wondered as she watched the maestro tuck his viola under his chin and, with pride of posture and passion in his eyes, begin to play. And why is he so reluctant to talk about it?

When she called her father later that evening, she told him about Boris Żywny and how she imagined there was a great story behind him. She also imagined, once she had become a famous storyteller like Mother, maybe she'd be the one to share his secret with the world.

"Bet you thought I'd never pick up a viola, Pop." Fiona laughed. "To tell you the truth, neither did I. But right now, this is as close as I can get to a violin." She imagined her father was biting his tongue as they chatted, keeping himself from voicing any viola jokes.

"Come on, Pop, not even one joke for me tonight? Toss one in the fire."

"Ha haaaAAAaaa! That's great, kiddo," Wolf laughed in response, "That's one way a viola surely beats a violin. They burn longer. I'll give you that."

Hearing her father's laughter through the receiver warmed the room and made her enjoy him and miss him all at once. Still, she smiled.

Boris Żywny had a decidedly different sense of humor than Fiona's father. Some say humor represents pain plus distance from it, but Boris' brand of humor was in-your-face pain, up close and very personal. He used insults to get his students to pay attention.

"Get your shoulders out of your ears, Fiona!" he muttered in a stage whisper even though nobody was in the practice room but the two of them. "You've got a shoulder rest for a reason. Use it! And don't choke that viola." He tapped her shoulder with his bow, with an "Ahem!"

Fiona, who had been wondering about ditching that very shoulder rest, piped up, "But, Mr. Ż., the concertmaster doesn't use a shoulder rest, so maybe…"

Seeing where her thought was headed, Boris cut her short, "You want pain? Bend that long swan's neck over a viola until you're old like me, and you'll get it. Don't worry about the concertmaster. That mushroom-head's got a stubby neck. Maybe he'll be okay, maybe not. Not my student, not my problem. You try that, and you'll end up in a world of hurt. Believe me on something: suffering for your art is overrated. Sounds romantic now. At my age, not so much. You're no toadstool, missy, so don't act like one. Now, less talk and more playing. From the top, please. And this time play like a swan, not a hobbit."

Secretly, Fiona both dreaded and enjoyed Mr. Ż's zingers. They cut into the heart of a girl who was trying so hard to master the viola, but they also made her laugh and try harder. And, occasionally, when he took aim at others, she knew it was just to help her succeed. Fiona imagined this tactic was better used by sports coaches to motivate their teams.

Boris tailored his slights to his students. For students who played sports, he used sports metaphors. For those who loved *Star Trek*, he dipped into sci-fi similes. Some kids liked cars. Fiona took to writing down the most creative ones. Who knows, she thought, maybe I'll be a viola teacher one day and need them. Taking pen to paper, she wrote, "Drop the Vulcan neck grip and stop strangling the thing. What did that poor viola ever do to you?"

She could hardly steady her pen, quivering as it was from her giggling as she wrote how he equated her playing with terrible driving. My upbow staccato notes, apparently, sound like jalopy horns. Oh, and it's shifting, not double-clutching. I didn't know that! Fiona laughed out loud, this time so hard that tears started streaming down her face. Oh, and then he said, 'Take charge and drive, already!' as if I could do that, Fiona mused. He should be a stand-up comic! Smiling, she wrote: "Ż is for Zinger: You're taking so much liberty with the timing, it's making me seasick. You sound like a drunken sailor. Weigh! Hey! And up she rises, early in the mornin'."

Boris meant well enough, but when Fiona shared his litany of insults with Gram and Pop, they didn't agree. "Too bad you're not here, Fiona. Teachers here at Curtis Institute of Music teach the best and brightest," said Gram, "They don't resort to such insults to bring out excellence in their students."

Fiona, knowing that was probably true, almost added, "But I'm not at Curtis, am I?" Deep down, Gram's comment hurt her, too. After all, she wasn't at a great conservatory; she was just in high school. Maybe you had to be there, she thought, to get how funny they were. His words still rang out, in her head. "Where are you, Fiona? Have you left the building? Who was in charge of that set of notes? You were! Tune back in, and get in tune! And by the way, you were purely channeling Satan on that double-stop. Whoa! Talk about trumpets from hell! What's that you're trying to play, the theme from the Czech wrestling team?" Fiona wasn't sure what compelled her to immortalize these put-downs in her journal, but she felt the need to do it. Shaking her head, she realized she couldn't remember any of the good things he'd said, though she knew he'd said as many positive things as bad. Those probably wouldn't be as interesting anyway, she reassured herself.

It was getting late. Fiona had finished her math and other assignments, and now turned her attention to the social studies homework she'd been dreading. Her assignment involved researching and presenting some aspect of American history. There was no assigned length. Instead, the teacher had said to just think of it like a comfy skirt: not so long that you trip on it, not so short that it doesn't do its job covering what it should. Fiona had decided she wanted to write about the Vietnam War, which had ended the year before she came to California. The country had been in that war for almost her entire life.

All that evening and late into the next day, Fiona pored over her books and took notes. She hand-wrote some concepts, then took out a piece of blank paper, rolled it into her typewriter, and tried to just write, as Mother did. Nothing.

Fiona was stuck but the clock was not. It was still ticking.

Fiona decided to head downstairs for a cup of coffee and some Fig Newtons. Deep down, she was secretly hoping for a little help getting started on her paper. She was in luck. Mother was sitting in the kitchen.

"I have to write a paper," Fiona mumbled into her cup, "and I'm stuck. I checked out some books, but I don't know where to start. I tried. Look." Mother, sensing her distress, sat down.

"Hmm, I sense a bit of your father in these notes here."

"What do you mean?"

"I mean, your father likes to hide behind a wall of words. Intellectuals who obfuscate are a dime a dozen. It's people who write clearly who are rare. The thing is, it's a brave task, writing clearly, because when you do, you risk being understood. Do you see what I mean?"

"Yes, but I don't know what I want to say."

"Yes, that's clear from what I'm reading here. You don't have a point to make, so you're hiding behind words. If you write enough of them down, your paper will be nice and heavy, and you'll get a 'gentleman's B' for the heft of it. You know...for how far it reaches, when you throw it down the stairs."

"Gawwd Mother, do you actually do that with your student papers?" Making light helped Fiona deal with her discomfort.

"Listen, hon, it's not that hard. I'm sure you know the three major sections of a winning paper: say what you're going to say, say it, and then say what you said. But, that's basic. If you want to go for the A, tell a captivating tale. Looks like you've done a ton of research, and all you need to do is choose one main point and drive it home. Think you can do that?"

"I can try."

"Okay, listen, if you want to get real, work from what you know."

"Right, but what do I know about Vietnam? I mean, like, personally know?"

"I mean you can approach this as a journalist. You have uncles who can each give you three very different first-hand accounts."

"I know about Jim, Joe, and Ben." Fiona replied. "But I only have a couple of weeks, Mother. I'm not a professional writer like you."

"But, you might want to be one someday. Yes?" Not waiting for a reply, Mother appraised the stack of books on the table and then focused on Fiona's face. "It's a chance to see how you like journalism. You can practice listening skills and the asking of open-ended questions with family members who are on your side. Wait just a moment, I have a letter I've been saving for you."

Mother disappeared into her room, and returned with an envelope addressed to Fiona. "My nephew wrote it to you when you were just four. I wasn't sure you were ready, until now. I'd almost forgotten about it."

Fiona immediately understood this letter to be from the same cousin who'd been a taboo subject, off-limits for discussion. Ted had died in Vietnam, and Fiona had rarely heard his name mentioned, and then only in somber whispers. Fiona opened the letter and read it in silence.

January 1966

Dear Fiona,

Just a quick letter to wish you a Happy New Year! There's so much I want to tell you, though I have a feeling you won't understand until you're older. I want to give you an idea of what life is like over here. One thing I learned real fast was to never let your socks get wet! They give us woven-metal inserts for trench foot, but they didn't do the trick for this lone soldier. I've got a tough case of gangrene, and I'd just love a fresh pair of socks, warm from the drier. I got some in a nice care package from my mom—your Aunt Ce—last Christmas. Here's a picture of me posing with a little box of Trix she sent. Of course, I had to share it with my buddies, since that's just what we do.

Vietnam seemed so far away before I came, and it is way different from home. I don't feel like I'm making this world a better place by being here. I hope, when you're older we'll be back at peace again, like when I was little. War is not the answer, and I want you to grow up in a better world than this.

I don't know when I'll get to send you another letter, so I'll just come out and write this. I think about all of you, every day. That's what I hold on to. It helps me wake up in the morning and face this scene. So, you see, Fiona, you're really an important person to me, even though you don't know me. I hope someday you'll read my letters and know your cousin was thinking of you. Okay, enough of that. I hope you're just having fun being a kid right now, and I hope to write again, soon.

Love,
Your Cousin Ted

Before Fiona could ask how he had died, or tell Mother she was sorry he died, or say anything at all, Mother folded up the letter and put it back in its envelope, in the matter-of-fact way that signaled the Ted topic was still very much off limits. "Okay, let's get this party started. Let me see the books and the notes you have so far. You make us a pot of tea, okay?"

Mother pored through the pages of notes, taken in Fiona's neat hand, and smiled at her daughter's diligence. Then she flipped through a few of the books, while Fiona brewed a pot of jasmine tea. Fiona watched for 25 minutes while Mother put her notes in order, adding some of her own in the margins, and bookmarking important pages in the library books. Then she picked up the phone and called her brother Jim. When the interview was arranged, Mother accepted a fresh cup of tea from Fiona and said, "Get out your tape recorder. I will help you create an outline, to get things going."

Delighted, Fiona pulled the tape recorder Pop and Gram had bought her for her birthday from the front pocket of her backpack. She dropped in a fresh cassette, and waited. Mother signaled when she was ready. Fiona pressed "record," and Mother launched in.

"Now, Fiona. It's good you took typing. If you choose to type this paper, you already know to double-space and indent your paragraphs. Don't skip a title page to save paper. Presentation matters, so make it look good. Set your typewriter for a standard margin of an inch on each side. Some people add just a hair's breadth more, to lighten their load. I'm not saying you should do it. I'm just mentioning that some people do. When they do," she winked, "they take care not to add so much that a teacher might notice."

Mother paused for a moment to assess the pile of books. Then, she began reading off and applying the names of the major authors whose books Fiona had brought home, along with the quotable quotes Fiona had found. She clicked off the tape now and again to find a book, and then continued to talk about what she'd say and do if she were researching and writing the paper. She didn't write Fiona's paper for her, but she pointed the way. It was something only a master can do: give a beginner a taste of what it will feel like when they arrive where they are going.

Fiona found it rather delicious, watching Mother at work. Then, Mother turned off the tape recorder for the last time and turned to her daughter. "Okay, kiddo. That's the easy part. The real work is bringing it to life. Now, go talk to your uncles, then decide what you want to say. Think you can take it from here? If you like, you can use my IBM Correcting Selectric to type up the notes from that recording. It's in the living room. That way, you can use regular paper."

"Thanks, Mother. That'd be great." Fiona was delighted. Mother hadn't ever offered to let her use her typewriter before. It was faster than longhand, and so much easier to use than the typewriters at school. No need for erasable onion-skin paper, either! No wonder Mother is on *The New York Times*' bestseller list, thought Fiona. Maybe someday I'll be a famous writer like she is, and have an IBM typewriter of my very own.

~o0O0O0o~

Uncle Jim roared into the driveway on his motorcycle. Fiona watched from the living room window as he swung his leg over the bike and planted it on the concrete. He lifted off his helmet, shook out his mane of dark hair, and set the helmet on the bike, next to another, before striding up to the front door.

"He's here!" Fiona called to her mother, as she ran to open the door before Uncle Jim had time to knock.

"Hey, Fee, long time no see! Bet you don't remember the last time we were together in person, do you? It was Fire Island. You were pretty young."

"Of course, I remember, Uncle Jim. And I'm ready to roll if you are."

"Well, not quite, Missy," he said, surveying the shorts and sandals she was wearing. "See how I'm dressed? You need to copy me: long pants, strong jacket, and sturdy shoes with socks. On my bike, it's all the gear, all the time. I'll wait while you really get ready."

"I'll be back faster than you can say Jack Robinson!" Fiona raced up the stairs, and only moments later reappeared, dressed in a pair of jeans, a leather jacket, and her paddock boots, laced up high.

"Okay, Uncle Jim?"

"Better than okay," he said. "Ready to rock 'n' roll."

Uncle Jim had suggested Fiona's very important interview take place at The Nut Tree, a 70-acre orchard in Vacaville with a road-stop restaurant, fruit stand, miniature railroad, and an airport. Fiona could ask questions over lunch. That sounded great, to her. Uncle Jim helped Fiona fasten her helmet and climb onto the back of his bike. The engine roared to life, and she could feel the excitement buzz through her body. Off they rode, into the wind, headed toward Oakland General Aviation, the area's main airport, where Jim kept his small propeller plane. Jim just loved the airport, with its three long runways.

They drove up to a locked gate, and Jim got out his key card to open it. They continued along the flight line to the tie-down area, and Fiona hopped off, taking care not to burn her leg on the exhaust pipe. Jim parked the bike right next to the plane, and hooked their helmets to the back. When Fiona asked why the plane was simply tied down and not stored in a hangar, he explained that this was a thrifty choice.

Fiona surveyed the plane. Chains rose from the tarmac and hooked onto the wings. Uncle Jim unhooked one chain and asked Fiona to release the other. She was starting to feel like a copilot. Then Jim unlocked the door and removed the flight control lock on the yoke, a pin that kept it steady. He invited Fiona to follow him as he completed his pre-flight check, moving clockwise around the plane, starting at the left wing. Fiona followed, fascinated by how much there was to check. He checked the gas level, draining any accumulated water from the gas tank in the left wing and then checked the oil. On his way to do the same on the right wing, he checked the propeller movement. He also gave each wing a quick shake to make sure they were securely attached.

Shaking the wings? Fiona felt a flash of fear. Was this such a good idea, after all? I could have interviewed him from the safety of our living room, or over the phone. Still, it'll bring my paper to life. I trust Uncle Jim, and not everything scary in life is deadly, right? I'm just a reporter, on assignment, after all.

"Okay, Fiona, you're curious what it was like for me, right?" Uncle Jim asked, after checking to be sure the tail flight controls moved freely. "I'd like to paint you a picture of just one day in the life of an Air Force musician. A day just like today, only back in 1969. Sound good?" Fiona nodded, as Uncle Jim invited Fiona into the cockpit. As they were settling in, he looked over to see if Fiona had her seatbelt securely fastened. "There are flight controls on both sides of the flight deck, Fiona, but don't touch them," cautioned Jim, "unless I tell you to. Okay?" Without waiting for a response, he called out "Clear!" to warn anyone who might be around that propellers were about to start spinning. Then, he got on the radio to ask for permission to taxi to runway 27 right. "Why 27?" Fiona asked.

"Runways are named for their degrees," he said, "so 27 means 270 degrees, or directly west. If you land the other direction, it's runway 9, meaning 90 degrees. We take off into the wind, and around here, that's usually heading west. Sounds simple, right? Simply follow instructions, just as we are right now, heading to the runway that they've cleared us for. Runway 27. The service is a lot about following instructions and procedures. Like right now, we're about to do what's called a 'run up' to test the magnetos. And before you ask me what's a magneto, it's like a coil on a car. It magnifies the electrical power, so spark plugs spark."

"Am I that predictable?" Fiona asked, laughing. "Okay, here's a question for you, Uncle Jim. What if the test fails?"

"No worries. And, good question! If there's a drop off in power, we taxi back and have the airplane repaired. We don't fly if anything's the slightest bit off or wrong. If any of the pre-flight check elements or the run-up fails, we just don't fly. It's not worth the risk. But don't worry, we're right as rain. And I'll tell you about a different test.

To get my guaranteed assignment in the band, I had to take a test of my clarinet skills. I deferred as long as possible, not considering how they were counting on me for the band. Then, after basic training, when there was a snafu showing Cape Canaveral instead of California, I insisted on my original orders. So, that was another delay. Then, I cut my finger seriously, delaying my service three more weeks. My superiors got fed up, and threw another audition my way. If I didn't pass my Level V test, I could have ended up in the motor pool, meaning the front lines. But, I passed. Nobody was watching the sergeant who tested me. He could have decided to flunk me out of spite, but he was honest, thank goodness. It was the same guy who gave me my entry test, but he'd forgotten me, and I sure didn't remind him. From then on, I did everything I could to win him over. He had other problems to deal with, and I told myself I wasn't going to be one of them."

"Problems like what, Uncle Jim?"

"Like, there was this one guy trying to get out on a Section 8—that means unfit for service—by playing all the music up a half step. It's not an easy feat, and it takes a fine musician to pull it off, as you know from your viola playing, but, man, it made us all sound sour, as you can probably imagine, and that worried us all. You don't want to be seen as a problem. Take it from me. So anyway, I was up early, and hard at work. You know those days when at six a.m. you already know it's going to be a hot one?"

"Well no, not really. Mostly I'm asleep at oh-dark-hundred."

"Not if you join the Air Force, you're not," Jim laughed. "If you're a night owl, like I used to be, it does take some getting used to. But, you do get used to it. Anyway, that day, I knew it was going to be a real scorcher. I'd walked across my barracks to the band room and grabbed some gear for the bus. There was hardly the space for all of it, since there were six of us headed out there. Hold on a sec…"

Pressing his brakes all the way, Uncle Jim revved the engine, switching between two magnetos to make sure there wasn't a drop in RPM between them. The test went fine, and he contacted the flight tower, with his tail number, C117WS, to request clearance. "Oakland Tower, this is Cardinal one-one-seven Whiskey Sierra, ready for takeoff on two-seven right."

The air traffic controller radioed back, "Hold on the numbers." Jim waited a few moments and saw an airplane taxi across the runway ahead. Then the controller said, "Cardinal one-one-seven Whiskey Sierra, cleared for takeoff." Jim pushed the throttles all the way forward, giving the engines full power. As the airplane reached takeoff speed, he pulled back on the yoke, and they lifted into the air. Eventually they settled at a cruising altitude over the Oakland hills, on their way to the landing strip at the Nut Tree, and Fiona sensed the moment was right to continue her interview.

"Out where? What kind of a bus? What gear? I need details, Uncle Jim!"

"Sorry, Fee. It was a two-hour ride out to Travis, in a regular school bus painted Air Force blue. Gear was instruments, chairs, timpani, and music stands. Okay? Hey, why don't you enjoy the view for a while, like we did, on the road to Travis. All the way there, we'd enjoy the view. We'd wave at the ladies, hoping they'd wave back, and we'd listen to the thundering sky from the roaring airplanes flying into Travis. I'll fill you in on the rest of the story over lunch. Yes?"

Yes! Fiona thought. Spread across the open plains halfway between San Francisco and Sacramento, the Nut Tree was only 30 minutes away by plane. Like many small airports, it had its own tower but no controller, so pilots were on their own, watching out for themselves and each other as they navigated the air and looked to land. As they neared the Nut Tree runway, Fiona saw a large windsock, looking like a canvas megaphone, filled with air and rippling in the wind. It indicated westerly winds today.

"I'll bet you're thinking about how great it would be to become a pilot," said Uncle Jim, "so I'm going to talk you through my landing. I'm going to do what I call a right-hand traffic pattern, so I'm downwind, then I'm turning right to a base leg, well past the runway, and right again, to start my final descent to land on the numbers, if possible, at stall speed."

Fiona thought Uncle Jim must be a mind reader. Yes, I'd like to be a pilot, and I do need to know all this stuff.

Uncle Jim approached the runway, watching the VASI or visual slope indicator lights, to make sure he was neither too high nor too low during his descent. He explained to Fiona that the two sets of lights can appear red or white. If the pilot approaches the lights at the proper angle, if his guide slope is correct, the first set of lights appears white, and the second set appears red. If both sets appear white, the aircraft is too high and, if both appear red, it is too low. Then, he approached the runway on the perfect glide slope, landed the plane right on the numbers, and took a taxiway off the runway and over to the tie-down area. He found a parking place for the plane, shut down the engine and, once the propellers had completely stopped moving, opened the door and climbed out. Hooking the wings to their chains anchored in the ground, he put the control flight lock in place, and escorted Fiona to the Nut Tree Restaurant. The restaurant need not have been special, so enchanted was Fiona by her flight, but she found the place charming, with its choo-choo train for little kids, a playground, and a menu that pleased her. She loved the cake-like blueberry bread, baked in the shape of the restaurant's roofline, and the shaped honey cookies, for which the restaurant was renowned.

While Uncle Jim and Fiona stood in line, waiting to be seated, he took a moment to collect his thoughts and consider the rest of the story. He was trying to convey a sense of his time in the Air Force Band. He smiled as he thought back to those mornings when his alarm would startle him out of a sound sleep, set to give him just enough time to catch the bus from Hamilton to Travis. Yes, he thought, this one day should encapsulate my experience. But still, I need to take care in the telling.

Almost everything in the area that went to Vietnam in the way of cargo or passengers went through Travis. The story Jim was about to relate to Fiona concerned some of that cargo: caskets. The experience had affected him deeply, and he wanted to share it. He just wasn't sure if it was to assuage himself or to help Fiona with her assignment. He hoped she could take it. If she was anything like her mother, he imagined she could.

As the pair sat down to enjoy their hamburgers with fries, a chocolate milkshake for her, and coffee for him, Uncle Jim resumed his tale. As he did, Fiona resolved to eat quietly, even to sip her milkshake slowly, quietly, without any slurping. As much as she relished her chance to fly out for a lunch at the Nut Tree restaurant, she was enjoying her uncle's story more, and she rarely took her eyes from his face as he spoke. She had brought a small reporter-style notebook in which to take notes as his story unfolded. He talked too fast, though, and she had quickly given up trying to transcribe the interview. She'd have to rely on memory. So, she paid attention to the things that stood out most strongly, so she could paint the picture again for her classmates. It was something Mother had taught her, about being a good reporter. Most of the time, it works, she thought, it had better work today!

"Arriving at Travis," he said, "I headed toward the mess hall with the rest of the band to get ourselves some breakfast. As usual, some of the guys were nursing some righteous hangovers. Nothing but coffee for them. I was cool, I was clear; I wasn't 21 yet, and I didn't drink. I didn't even like the 'near beer' they served in the Enlisted Men's Club. After breakfast, we piled back into the bus and headed over to the flight line next to a C-130 Globemaster airplane. I was still on 'unloading crew duty' for the day, so I helped unload the truck, then picked up my clarinet and lyre, the mini-stand that attached to it and held my music."

"What's a flight line, Uncle Jim?"

"A flight line is the part of an airfield where planes are parked for loading and refueling. Now, I headed to where the band was scheduled to perform on the tarmac. We formed right along the flight line, not far from the portable bleachers that had been set up for ceremony participants, and waited. It was one of those, 'Hurry up and wait' moments, same as ever. And it was really, very hot, Fiona. Can you imagine us in our full-dress blues, standing out there on that blacktop, in 100-degree heat? We watched the heat waves rising off the asphalt, making it more like 120 degrees. I'll bet you we could've fried us some eggs.

"After about an hour in that hellish heat, moving as little as possible and trying to keep our instruments in tune, people started showing up and clambering into the bleachers to take a seat under an awning. We saw dignitaries and families of fallen soldiers, mostly women and young children. As I surveyed the crowd, I caught a glimpse of one woman who reminded me of your mom, wearing a black veil like Jackie Kennedy did at the President's funeral. That's when the terrible import of the ceremony really hit me. How this music we were playing would be the soundtrack to a powerful memory, how it might resound in their mind's inner radio, forever associated with someone they'd loved and lost. The band leader gave the downbeat with his narrow baton, and we started playing. The ceremony began with the 'Star-Spangled Banner.' Everyone in the bleachers stood as the music reached them to salute the song and witness the first casket being brought off the plane and placed on the ground in front of the bleachers."

"Wow, that's really heavy," Fiona whispered, her eyes becoming bigger and bluer as she took in the circumstance in the story. She had wanted to smile at the image of fried eggs he'd conjured in her mind, and was glad she'd kept her face solemn.

"Every time," said Uncle Jim, "I listened as all the citations were read: Bronze star for heroism, Silver star for some act of bravery, Purple Heart for being wounded or killed in action by an enemy of the country. From the citations, I could pretty much tell how each soldier had died. Then our band would play a service anthem. Depending on which branch of service each fallen soldier was from, we would play the Air Force Hymn, the Navy Hymn, and so on. Everyone in the band knew all the music by heart. And so, we watched, taking in the moment and the emotion as families ultimately were presented with the folded flag lifted from their soldier's casket. It was brutal, every time. But I tried not to think about it and just do my job. It was hardest when someone reminded me of someone I knew. It made it more real. Harder to deny. Do you understand?"

"Mmm hmmm."

"Yeah." Uncle Jim paused, wondering whether Fiona could possibly grasp his point. Satisfied that she was trying, he continued. "And we knew the day wasn't over for these families. Later in the day, trumpet details—soldiers on temporary assignment for this specific purpose—would come down from Marin to Daly City near San Francisco, to play for the burials. Nobody kept count of how many times they'd played "Taps" or "Anchors Away" or the other service hymns. We just concentrated on the music. As each casket was taken away, another appeared in its place. We'd steel ourselves for three hours or more of this process, standing at attention or at parade rest, meaning hands behind our backs and feet 18 inches apart, or playing. I wanted to stay strong."

"Did you?" Fiona pushed the remaining crumbs around her plate, pretending not to be finished with her meal. She didn't want the story to end yet.

Uncle Jim smiled. "I did not. During those three hours in the sun, we could count on at least one of the guys fainting from the heat—we were taught not to lock our knees, which would have guaranteed we'd be a goner—but it never seemed to be a guy with a hangover. They seemed to be the safest, maintaining the slightest weave or wobble, which kept them loose."

"Did anyone fall down that day?"

"Sure did. This one ran longer than usual, and after about three hours, one of the trumpet players went down. Trumpet players stand behind the back row, so I didn't see it happen, but I sure heard it, and so did everybody else. He was a big guy."

"What did people do?"

"Somebody got him to the shade. We didn't call an ambulance or anything. Maybe we should have, but we were almost done. After a while, he came back and took his place. Not long after that, we were given the signal to play the national anthem once again, which signaled the close of the ceremony. For the families of the fallen, it signified the end of a life they were trying to hang onto. For the band, it meant we would soon shift from playing formation to marching formation, leave the flight line, and head back to the bus.

There, we'd load up our stuff, climb in, and take the weary ride back to Hamilton, and the place where we were all allowed to collapse: our barracks. It got to us, which is why so many members of the band drank or got high. Those days out on the tarmac, with so much time contemplating death, the war could feel pretty tragic."

"That does sound tragic." Fiona agreed. "Is that all you did, all the time?"

"Not at all. We had lots of other duties. I was working hard to win over my sergeant," said Uncle Jim, "so I'd begun playing bass for his combo gigs in the Officer's Clubs. And there were parades on holidays, and concerts in high schools.

"Did you ever play for my high school?"

"Not that I remember. But I will tell you one time that's a stand-out, the day after Dr. King's assassination, when we were scheduled to play Sir Francis Drake High School. We generally felt some hostility, but nothing like that day. Listen, Fiona, I'm not complaining. We had it easy. The guys who had it rough were the ones over in Nam. Here I was, with room and board covered, and earning pretty good money, about $100 a month, plus $15 more for each gig. I have absolutely no complaints about my experience, Fiona, as I could have been in one of those caskets."

"I hear you. And you made sure your boss was happy to have you," Fiona offered. "And you tried hard not to fall down on the job?"

"You bet I did. The first thing I did when I got out of the Air Force was call my music teacher, Mr. Geanocos, to thank him for saving my life. So, keep practicing, Fiona. You never know; it could actually be the difference between life and death."

"Nice try, Uncle Jim, but I'm not in any danger of being drafted."

"As I said, you never know." Uncle Jim winked.

Fiona tried to pitch in on the cost of lunch with money her mother had given her, but Uncle Jim said, "Don't worry about it, Fiona. You can treat me after you get your pilot's license."

"It's a deal, Uncle Jim," she said, shaking his hand on the bargain.

"And thank you for sharing your story with me. It was really something else."

"Worth the ride with your old Uncle Jim? You know, you might give your Uncle Bob a call, too. I know he's not nearby, but I'm sure he'd be happy to share his story over the phone. You'd get an even clearer picture by hearing from each of us."

"Thanks, Uncle Jim."

They walked out of the restaurant, back to the airport, and over to the tie-down area, where Uncle Jim repeated the pre-flight steps Fiona had watched before they lifted off in Oakland. As he called them out to Fiona, she tried, once again, to memorize them, making a mental note of the steps involved.

They climbed into the plane, fastened their seatbelts, and Uncle Jim secured the door. After the run-up, Uncle Jim looked at the traffic pattern, to make sure the skies were clear. He taxied out, gave full throttle, and took off. "Keep your eyes peeled for the Mormon Temple, Fiona. That's when we'll call in to the Oakland tower."

While they flew back to the Oakland Airport, Fiona thought about Uncle Jim's experience. She wasn't sure where she'd weave his story into her presentation for social studies class, but she felt quite confident that it was a good fit, for a "Points of View" assignment. Mother was right, Fiona thought. I've got the start of a great story. There are so many opinions, though, and there's still so much pain on all sides. It's not going to be easy, weaving it together into a report for class.

Nearing Oakland, she spotted the temple, and Uncle Jim called the tower, just as planned. "This is Cardinal 117 Whiskey Sierra, inbound over the Mormon Temple, requesting landing instructions." The response came quickly. "Cardinal 117, you're clear for traffic pattern runway 27, right." Fiona now knew what that meant. She was learning so much during their outing. After landing, Uncle Jim contacted ground control for clearance to taxi to his tie-down spot.

When they got there, Jim called in for fuel. He liked to top off the tank, so it would be full for the next flight. While waiting for the fuel truck to pull up, Uncle Jim had Fiona tie down the plane and position the flight control lock. Just before leaving, they placed a sun shade across the inside of the windshield, and closed and locked the door. Fiona felt like giving the plane a hug, out of sheer gratitude for the safe flight and the unforgettable Nut Tree lunch. But, she didn't want Uncle Jim to think she was weird. It's bad enough my Philly family thinks I'm some California twigs-and-berries tree hugger, Fiona thought. I'm not a Plane Nut back from the Nut Tree, although the Plane Nut would be a cool home name for people who are just plain nuts about planes, she thought.

Uncle Jim handed her the extra helmet, swung his leg over his motorcycle, and helped her climb on behind him. With the wind once again in her face, Fiona closed her eyes and thought back on what a wonderful day it had been.

Uncle Jim gave his niece a quick goodbye hug, then messed up her hair the way he had back on Fire Island. "I'm glad we're flying friends, kiddo. You can call me anytime with questions, and I'll try to answer you right away. And, if you're ever in a jam, remember, we're also family."

Just before he rode off on his motorcycle, he pulled a scrap of paper from his pocket, scribbled down Uncle Bob's phone number, and handed it to Fiona. "Talk to your Uncle Bob. He'll have a different take on it for you. See ya around, kiddo."

Fiona wasn't sure Uncle Bob would even know who she was, but she gathered up her courage and dialed the number Uncle Jim had scrawled on the scrap of paper. "Hi, Uncle Bob. This is your niece, Fiona," she said to voice on the other end of the line. "Do you remember me? I'm writing a paper on Vietnam, and I think you were in the Air Force there, so I wonder if you'd have a minute?"

Of course, he knew who she was. In fact, he'd been expecting her call, and he was happy to help. She quickly learned that his job had been to repair airplanes in Thailand, with occasional forays to Da Nang, on the eastern seacoast of Vietnam. Uncle Bob began by talking about how Thailand was "dang hot, and there were a lot of mosquitos." They were all issued quinine tablets as a precaution against the malaria, "for all the good they did," he said. The quinine, he said, had side effects, bad enough that a lot of people stopped taking them, and ended up dealing with the disease instead. Fiona was beginning to get that everyone who went to war was at risk, whether they saw the front lines, or not.

Uncle Bob talked about his assignments to Da Nang. "Typically," he said, "my unit was sent there to repair an airplane after a pilot flying a sortie or specific mission was hit, and his plane was damaged and forced to land at Da Nang." Uncle Bob and his unit got the planes in good enough condition to fly on to the repair depot in Thailand, where they would be restored to fighting shape.

"We'd patch it up quicker than you could say 'Bob's your uncle.' But I think that you're looking for my standout memories, right? Here's one of them. It was the first time I flew to 'Nam, just after I'd arrived in Southeast Asia. I was standing at the top of the deplaning stairs, the gangway of the airplane," said Uncle Bob. "We'd just landed. I was looking out over the runway area, and all I could see were rows and rows and rows of gray boxes. I had no idea what they were and asked one of the crew members what was inside—freight? supplies? The crew member turned ashen and told me they were our boys, waiting to go home. There were thousands of them, Fiona. Uncountable thousands. Endless caskets."

Fiona gasped at the stark image her uncle had conjured up in her mind. All those plain boxes upon boxes, each containing an actual person, like one of her uncles. Then she thought back to Hanna's cushion-lined coffin. She'd never really thought about death before. Not really. Not as a thing. Not on that scale. Fiona began to feel sick to her stomach.

Before Fiona could think of something to say, Uncle Bob continued his story. "Yeah. That was a real eye opener. I'm afraid we all got used to it. And think about it, Fiona; I was just a few years older than you are now. And we had no training in the language or culture of the area, and no way to prepare for all we would encounter. Is this all too much, kiddo? Shall I stop here? Or, shall I tell you more?"

"No. I mean yes, Uncle Bob, please do," Fiona stammered.

"On my third trip from Thailand, and the first time I'd stayed overnight in Da Nang—I preferred to go in, repair the plane, and get the hell out of there—we patched up a jet fighter that'd been hit by a missile and had just barely gotten back. Our work was done for the day, so we had some drinks to, you know, relax and release the tension. It was a pretty simple existence—work, drink, rest, repeat."

"You say it was simple, but to me it sounds intense," Fiona said. Uncle Bob smiled on the other end of the phone, at his niece's insight.

"We got used to it," he said. "Anyway, I was back in the barracks, in one of the many rows of bunks, and I'd just fallen asleep, when… Boom! There was a huge explosion. After drinking, followed by sleeping, I was a little groggy and had no idea what was going on. Someone, maybe an MP regular Army, came running through the barracks, handing out M-16 rifles, and we ran outside into sandbag shelters, and waited. Everyone thought the Viet Cong were trying to take over the base, which they'd attempted to do before. It was just a few weeks after the Tet Offensive, in late January, '68, during the lunar new year or Tet holiday, when the enemy had almost succeeded in a strong coordinated attack against us. Well, we waited and waited and waited for something to happen. The air was thick with bugs, and so were we. There were no tents, and everything was damp. Hot and damp. Everything out there was biting, and the sandbags had creepy crawlers—all kinds of things crawling around.

"Finally, just before dawn, someone came around and told us to stand down, that there had been no attack. It had been friendly fire—that sounds a lot like an oxymoron, doesn't it, Fiona? A fighter pilot had been taxiing for takeoff and, as he made his turn to go onto the active runway, he made a mistake and shot a missile into the ammo dump by the end of the runway. We'd spent the night among wet, hot sandbags, waiting for an attack that never came. Now, that was a good thing, but there were a lot of other places I'd rather have been."

Uncle Bob, wanting to spare Fiona his darker stories, stopped there. "Did you have any particular question in mind for your project that I can help you with?"

"Actually, I do. I'm wondering if you can tell me what you think about the Vietnam War."

Uncle Bob wasn't prepared for that question. "That's a tough one, Fiona. I think you're asking a few different questions with that one. What do I think about the people who sent us over there? About whether it was a good decision? About my serving the country? Or, about the draft? I wonder, does it really matter what I think? I think this paper is about what you think. I will tell you this: I haven't joined Vietnam Vets Against the War, if that's what you are asking."

"That's super helpful, actually, Uncle Bob." Fiona knew she had some thinking to do to reconcile these oral histories and come to her own conclusions. "Okay," she said, "then I have just one more question. Karen said you seriously saw the Beatles once. Is that really true?"

"It really is. And it was in your neck of the woods. Let's see, it was August 29, 1966, so that's more than 10 years ago now. I'd come up from Vegas, where I was in advanced training at Nellis Air Force Base. A friend of mine, who lived out your way, got us tickets over at Candlestick Park. I drove about 12 hours, having left the base right after training the night before the concert. I remember I had a really great car, a pearl-white Karmann Ghia.

"I slept for a bit and then went out to check out the Haight and, you know…"

"To score some pot, maybe?" Fiona was only guessing, but it seemed likely.

"No comment. But I will tell you this. The best thing about going to the Haight was that it couldn't have been more different than Vegas; the complete opposite of everything I'd been experiencing daily since basic training ended. The Haight was great. Everything moved more slowly, and I enjoyed the break. I'd traded the bright lights of Vegas for the psychedelics of the city, which suited me just fine.

"I didn't have much time to explore the neighborhood before the concert, though. We had good seats, somewhere in the middle, I remember, opposite the stage. Had it been a well-behaved crowd, people who'd come to hear the Beatles instead of their own voices, and had there been a decent PA system, it would have been quite a concert. Instead, we got wisps of music through the thunderous, desperate screaming by the rest of the fans. So, we didn't hear much music. It was basically a huge scream fest. But, I'll leave you with this; I did see them. And, looking back on it, that really was historic."

"Thanks, Uncle Bob." Fiona was already wondering how she might weave the Beatles into her oral histories about life and death during the war. In 1969, John Lennon and Yoko Ono had written "Happy Xmas (War is Over)" from their hotel bed. Maybe I'll quote some of that at the end of my presentation, she thought. Or I could sing my report, and accompany myself on guitar. I could start with Peter, Paul & Mary's "Where Have All the Flowers Gone?" and segue into Cat Stevens' "Peace Train," then introduce a new a song about three uncles and a cousin, and end with the Beatles. No! What am I thinking? That's a terrible idea! Worst. Idea. Ever.

Fiona felt overwhelmed by all the new information she'd just learned from interviewing her uncles. They had given her enough to make her question everything she thought she knew about a war she'd protested, even as a little girl. She'd also learned about refugees, who referred to their experience as the American War. Still, she did have a Beatles brag story, which she'd decided to save for the end of her presentation, to leave her audience on a high note.

During dinner, Fiona and Mother discussed Vietnam, but only briefly. Fiona expected her to mother to defend the war. Instead, Mother surprised her. "Fiona, entering Vietnam may possibly have been a mistake," she said, "but that doesn't negate the value of bravery and sacrifice by those who fought there. It's very easy for your father to rail against such things, but they are often more complicated than your father—or most people, I imagine—would like to think." And with that pronouncement, Mother had sparked an idea for a title: "It's Complicated."

As Fiona sat at her desk, rehearsing her presentation in her mind, she realized she really didn't know her classmates, and they didn't know her, and that was her doing. Yes, she'd worked hard to weave together oral histories, observations, and historical facts, her experiences, and even songs. Would they enjoy it? She grew more nervous. As her classmates wandered in, she noticed one boy was wearing his hair in a long neatly plaited braid down his back. He had on a tie-dye t-shirt he might have made himself—like one of many she had made in the past. Maybe we share that in common, she thought. Then again, how would he know that? I'm dressed like a square, straight out of Presentation High. Now, she felt all eyes on her, as she moved to the front of the class. She spoke quietly at first, before all those silent eyes, then more and more boldly, as she connected with her uncles' stories. She wove in the death of her cousin, all those coffins, Uncle Joe's injuries, and pointed out how so many people on all sides had been forever wounded from the experience.

When she finished, Fiona looked around the room at her fellow students, with a quiet smile that she hoped conveyed confidence and invitation. Instead of asking about her uncles, as she'd expected, they launched a sudden attack on her topic and ideas, their words slicing through her like shrapnel. One of her classmates called her a hawk. Another said her mind was brainwashed with establishment apologetics. Hadn't they listened? Hadn't they picked up on how complicated it all was?

Nothing could have saved her presentation. Not even the Beatles.

Gathering her papers, with shoulders hunched, Fiona retreated to her desk and the shelter of her own silence. Feeling smaller and less significant than she had when she arrived, she wished she could just disappear.

As everyone was leaving the room after class, Fiona's teacher, Mr. Pope, took Fiona aside.

"Do you have a moment?" Fiona nodded hesitantly, unsure if she could shoulder any more feedback. "That was an insightful presentation, Fiona," he said. "Contrary to the feedback you got from the other students, it wasn't 'establishment' at all. Remember, the others are exploring the world of ideas, just as you are. It was brave of you to be different from your peers and explore your own opinions.

"Did you notice how many of your classmates shared the same opinion together? They're trying so hard to be different, while still staying part of their group. They're just creating another kind of conformity. It's like trying to be the tall poppy, thinking you're different when you're fundamentally the same thing.

"Listen, Fiona, everyone wants to be unique. Do you want to know how to be truly different? Be excellent. Pick something, anything, and just do your level best to be great at it. Pour your heart into it and be great at it. Excel. Shine. Always do your best. That's how."

Having expected continued criticism, Fiona was floored. As she pondered tall poppies, the rest of his positive feedback about the paper, her delivery, and the way she'd included music almost didn't register. "Um, thanks, Mr. Pope," was pretty much all she could muster.

It was a huge "aha!" moment. At the ashram, Fiona had heard that enlightenment is instant and forever, as if once the truth is seen by the mind's eye, it can't ever again be unseen. For the rest of her school day, everywhere she turned, Fiona was struck by the tall poppies she saw walking down the hallway, each trying to rise above the others to be different, accepted, admired. And yet, the conscious effort to be different enough to be accepted and fit in, really was, as Mr. Pope said, conformity. Same as everyone else...except me, she thought. I am no opium poppy. If anything, I am a rose bush, as tall as a house, with thousands of tiny flowers just everywhere. That's me. Whatever blossoms, I'll make sure it's excellent. Maybe it'll be stories. Stories by the dozen.

Keeping Mr. Pope's words close and her own self-doubt at a distance, Fiona felt, deep inside, a growing sense of "okay" welling up. This was all she needed to know she would be okay at Berkeley High. Not only that, she was going to find her passionate pursuit, something, as Mr. Pope had said, to excel at. Now, if only the other students liked roses as much as poppies, she'd be fine. Being a wild rose wouldn't have hurt her heart so much had she not wanted to fit in, too.

This was one of Fiona's defining moments, and she knew it. But, as they also said at the ashram, "Enlightened or not, the floor still needs sweeping." Here and now, she still had to do her chores, eat her vegetables, go to gym class, and update her wardrobe.

6. SUNNY DAYS

Fiona pulled her three-speed bike out from the side of the house and began her ride to school. It was only a mile down a paved trail that took her through her neighborhood and underneath the suspended BART train tracks, which had effectively connected disparate parts of the Bay Area in 1972. Fiona had worked out a time buffer so she could enjoy the ride at a relaxed pace, pedaling just fast enough to get there on time, without getting sweaty.

Today, she left the house a few minutes early, so she could stop at the mailbox conveniently located along the path, to drop in a letter she had written to her sisters, whom she knew were patiently awaiting word from her, back in Philadelphia.

"Hoooo, hoooo," she heard, just as she came out of the garage. She heard it again. "Hoooo, hoooo." She looked up into the trees, trying to spot the owl. She'd been hearing it for weeks but hadn't spotted him. This time, Fiona was going to figure it out. A black squirrel scampered across the street and up the trunk of a redwood tree, drawing Fiona's attention upward. There, she saw them. A pair of mourning doves. These weren't owl sounds, after all. It was more of a "Coooo, coooo." She realized her assumption had influenced her ear. She'd have to discuss this with Pop.

Well, she thought, it sure beats the caw of that wild peacock I've been hearing in the afternoon. The doves gave her a soothing sendoff, as if they were assuring her that all would be well today. Berkeley felt magical to Fiona, with all its wildlife and wooded beauty. It was so different from the gritty places she'd left behind in her life. In Berkeley, the streets were cleaner, the sun seemed warmer and brighter, and the clouds were fluffier against the blue sky. Yes, Berkeley was a place to feel inspired, like anything was possible.

As usual, PE followed lunch. Who works out on a full stomach? Fiona thought, as she stood in front of a cold, metal locker in the girls' gym, threw in her book bag, and pulled on her gym shorts. Why would they even schedule gym at this hour? This was one aspect of school that made her cringe. She didn't like to sweat, and she really didn't like to dress down in the locker room.

"What day is it?" someone called out.

"Just ask Bethany's butt. Hey, wait, it's Moon-day, get it?"

Very funny, Fiona thought. Yes, Bethany's undies had the day of the week on them, and Bethany seemed to enjoy the joke no matter how many times someone told it. But Fiona just didn't get it, and she was in no mood to care. Fiona had bigger issues on her mind than Bethany's bikini underwear. PE brought back bad memories, and she wanted out. Life so far had left Fiona leery of locker rooms and had done nothing to inspire an affinity for athletics. She had decided to talk with Mr. Bell, her PE teacher, who had mentioned he also taught martial arts. Maybe she could try something different. She wondered if martial arts might be her ticket out.

Summoning up her courage, Fiona headed over to teacher. "Mr. Bell," she said, "Didn't you say you are a sensei?" She watched an eyebrow go up as he took in her question, wondering what would follow. "Aikido is good exercise, right? So, it could be a good substitute for gym class, right?" Mr. Bell listened with a quizzical smile as Fiona proceeded to explain a few Aikido basics that, of course, he already knew. She also threw in that Aikido was a cool way to master the force, like Yoda, since dojos are where you practice the way of harmonious life-spirit-energy, and didn't he agree? She threw so many words at him, she hardly gave him the space to agree. Intrigued by her interest and initiative, he was delighted to help. She'd still need to pass the physical fitness and swim tests at school, but that could be arranged. For just one moment, Fiona was at a loss for words. No more PE! She'd done it. She'd convinced someone in power of something important to her. "Oh wow, thanks, Mr. Bell, that's awesome!" she finally managed. On that simple "yes," Fiona floated her way through the rest of the school day.

At the end of the day, Fiona parked her bike in the garage and ran inside the house to finalize the paperwork with Mother. Not a big PE fan herself, Mother had approved Fiona's plan, and was expecting good news. Fiona breathlessly shared how she'd made her case and won. Complimenting her for her successful implementation, Mother reached in to her purse to retrieve enough cash for a gi—the crisp, white Aikido wrap-jacket and pants—and the first month's tuition. Could this day get any better? Only by sharing the good news over the phone with Pop, Gram, and her sisters, which she ran up to her room to do.

Twice a week after school, Fiona biked over to the dojo not far from home. She had it all figured out, she told her sisters. "I wear ankle tights, and a tube top under my shirt. I can change into my gi without worry." That sounded super-smart, and they decided to do the same thing, for karate class.

The dojo fell silent. A small, frail-looking man stepped before the class and bowed. As she and her classmates returned the bow, Fiona thought, this must be the master sensei. Must be; he looks ancient. Poor thing.

Upon Master Sensei's signal, student after student came at the old man, trying with their might to topple or lift him. Person after person, including Fiona, failed. He was so rooted to the earth, so filled with ki—life energy—that not even the strongest or most advanced student in the class managed to move him.

He's no bigger than I am, Fiona thought. And he's the most powerful person here. That's amazing! Maybe size is irrelevant. Could it be? Whatever. I want what he has. By the end of the day, Fiona's physical confidence was soaring and her dedication had doubled.

Fiona had found a physical exercise class that was equal parts mind, body, and soul. At the dojo, she learned how to fall without getting hurt, and to redirect an attack without harm, using the attacker's own energy. Sensei Bell had told her many times that she could apply the principles of Aikido to other aspects of her life. She now knew he was right.

~oOO0O0o~

Although a classic Berkeley bungalow on the outside, the interior of Mother's house was all modern. Her furnishings reflected the uncluttered aesthetic of a contemporary woman who made her own money, ran her own household, and had no time for fussy, frivolous things.

Every time some called the house, the ringers could be heard coming from three phones: the kitchen wall phone, the living room desk phone attached to the answering machine, and on Fiona's pink princess rotary phone in her room. Fiona had taught herself to wait until the second or third ring to answer the phone, in case Mother wanted to take the call. She didn't want to seem anxious, like a little kid jumping at the first ring, although she always harbored the hope that it was a call from home.

On this occasion, the call came from one of Peggy's students, Tina. Yet to Fiona's surprise, she didn't want to talk with her teacher. A little bird had told her Fiona was interested in messing around on boats. She wanted to know if Fiona would like to go salmon fishing the following morning. It was the most unexpected invitation Fiona had ever yet received. Mother was already agreeable.

The morning would come quickly, thought Fiona, as she tucked herself into bed and tried to picture herself in a boat, in the dark, on the Bay with someone she barely knew. Tina was coming for her at 4:00 am, devastatingly early for a kid—for anyone, Fiona imagined. What a time to wake up, and on a weekend, where reasonable people normally sleep in!

Tina was punctual. A groggy Fiona opened the door and slipped out into the predawn fog without waking her mother. Climbing into Tina's car, she wondered if she'd made the right choice. She could have been up in her room, warm and safe and sleeping. As Mother had also suggested, she was wearing her white, rubber-soled Keds, and had left her purse at home, zipping her wallet into the pocket of a heavy coat she'd layered over her cable-knit sweater. "Good choices,"

Tina said, as she surveyed Fiona's attire. "It's really cold beyond the bridge this time of day." Nothing about the dark, damp air fit Fiona's definition of day, but she understood what she meant. Fiona hadn't thought to bring a hat, but Tina said she had extras below deck. Soon, they were on their way.

"If you open my backpack, Fiona, you'll find a thermos of hot chocolate and some biscuits. We won't want to each too much until we're back on land," Tina told her, "but you need a little something to tide you over and warm your belly."

As the fishing boat steamed south toward Point San Pedro, Fiona started to notice the sky softening from black to a deep blue, and then to a vivid turquoise blue. Tina, who was one of very few women who had a captain's license on the San Francisco Bay, told Fiona the sky was a very good sign. "Red sky at morning, sailors take warning," she said. "Red sky at night, sailors delight. We're in good shape." Tina winked at Fiona, whose own sky-blue eyes held the reflection of the waves. "Better put on some sunglasses, to avoid a headache later on."

As they motored south, Tina pointed out the Farallon Islands and the Red Triangle that stretched from there to Bodega Bay and Big Sur. "We're not going out that far, of course, but it's awesome to see the red waters when they're stirred up from sharks in a feeding frenzy."

Sharks? Fiona felt ill. Tina brought the commercial fishing boat to idle, set the lines off the back, and began slowly trolling for salmon. As the boat rocked back and forth, back and forth in the waves, Fiona began to feel even more queasy. Seeking relief, she climbed down the steep ladder that brought her below deck. Bad idea. Suddenly she felt wretched. "Come back up on deck, Fiona, you'll feel better up here," Tina called over her shoulder. Slowly making her way up the steps, Fiona felt like she might hurl her hot chocolate overboard for the sharks.

"Here," offered Tina, handing her some candied ginger. "This will help. Come sit by me, Fiona, and I'll tell you a story you'll love." Distraction worked even better than ginger, when treating a seasick sailor. She launched in, quickly and without pausing for questions.

"Long ago, on the mystic Isle of Eire—Ireland—lived a curious young lad called Finn McCool, spelled impossibly, so don't worry. Yes, he was your namesake. Now, you just breathe and listen. Breathe, and listen, and chew on the ginger. That's right." Tina spun a marvelous tale of young lad who grew up strong and hale in an enchanted forest under the tutelage of the druid Finegass, near a sparkling stream where the sacred salmon of knowledge swam.

"Seven years they strove in vain to capture the salmon, as it grew fat and wise on the holy hazelnuts that fell into the stream. One day, Finn finally caught him. They prepared a stew, which Finn was to stir. But he had to take care not to taste it, lest all the knowledge meant for the master druid pass solely to the apprentice, Finn, too early. Oh, he was careful, but their cat rushed by after a rat under his feet, upsetting the brew, and as he turned to save it, he burned his thumb on it. Crying out in pain, he put his hand to his mouth, and in that small taste, received all the wisdom at once. Finn grew to be a great hunter-warrior, Chief of the Isle of Ireland, and a sacred sage who shared his profound wisdom with any who sought his insight. And, here, I end my tale," wrapped up Tina.

"Finn McCool," said Fiona, "How cool is that?"

The best part of the story was that Fiona hadn't felt the slightest bit queasy while Tina had been telling her tale. The ginger candy and the storytelling had worked their own magic.

"Did you make up that story, Tina? Fiona asked, transfixed by the ease with which Tina piloted in to her slip, and the speed at which her crew set about resetting the gear and securing the vessel. Tina smiled as she continued to work but didn't answer. Instead, she rewarded Fiona for her participation in the day with a small salmon and a couple of white fish she was told wouldn't be as savory as the salmon but were still worth cooking.

"So, the white fish for sharing, and the salmon for wisdom, right?"

Again, Tina smiled. "It's the first taste that matters. After that, do as you wish." She helped Fiona off the boat and continued to support her under the elbow, as she walked out onto the pier, knowing her inexperienced sailor would likely feel a little off balance in her first few steps. Indeed, she wobbled her way down the ramp to the parking lot, grateful for Tina's support.

As they drove home, Tina asked whether Fiona might enjoy her line of work. Fiona thought about the cold, dark morning and the wind cutting through her like a knife as they motored out into the Bay. She remembered the part about the sharks and shuddered at the thought. She thought salmon fishing probably wasn't the life for her. Still, she thought she'd show some interest, in gratitude for their morning together. "I don't know, Tina. Seems very cool. How hard is it to get your captain's license?" she asked.

"Well, Fiona," Tina laughed, "first you need your sea legs."

Despite what seemed like a full day at sea, Fiona was home by 11 am. This is perfect timing, she thought. I will surprise Mother with my catch and make a salmon lunch for us to enjoy while I tell her all about my morning. She turned on the stove, telling herself the only way lunch with this wonderful fresh fish would be a disaster was if she were to make a mess in Mother's shiny new kitchen. After prepping and drizzling the fish, she set it under the broiler at 450 degrees. It would be funny, Fiona thought, if I burned my hand on the salmon. Funny and cool.

Fiona set the timer to 15 minutes, and turned on the oven light, so she could keep an eye on her project. Once the timer sounded, she opened the oven door, slid her left hand into Mother's quilted oven mitt, and pulled out the rack. With her right hand, she slid a spatula under the salmon to flip it over. As she did, it spat out olive oil. "Yeeowwwwch!" Fiona had not planned on being boiled in oil. She would like to have kept quiet, but it hurt. Just like her mythical namesake, she drew her hand to her mouth and sucked on the burn. Setting the fish on the stovetop, she ran cold water over her burned knuckle.

"What happened, Fiona?" Mother called down the stairs from her bedroom closet, where she was choosing what she might wear at a formal event that evening.

"Nothing, really, Mother. I barely burned my hand, no big deal."

"Run it under some cold water," Mother advised.

"Got it. Doing that. I'm fine. No big deal. I'm okay."

Despite Fiona's reassurances, Mother came into the kitchen to check. She's going to tell me to take a breath, Fiona thought, knowing her mother had the habit of telling everyone to breeeaaaathe when she thought they were upset. Fiona was not wrong. "Breeeeaaaathe, Fiona." Mother said, taking a deep breath for effect. Fiona thought Mother got a "Look into my eyes, you're getting sleepy," hypnotic sort of expression whenever she said it, so Fiona avoided her gaze. Still running her hand under the cold water, Fiona said, "Hey, I'm taking after my namesake Finn, getting a little salmon burn. Maybe I'll be all the wiser for it." Mother rolled her eyes. "The wisdom of Finn McCool? Those are some pretty big boots to fill, kiddo," she said. Then she smiled, adding, "Knock yourself out."

After lunch, Fiona headed upstairs to finish her homework and prepare for the next day. She'd agreed to join a few friends for an odd job, painting a house. Mother, though, called her right down again. She'd forgotten to clean up from her cooking spree.

When her alarm clock went off again the next morning, Fiona threw it across the room. Maybe the wisdom of Finn McCool is telling me I need to find a different job in life than painting houses. This is no way to make a fast buck. There has got to be an easier, gentler way to make it through life than fishing for salmon or painting houses. But, a promise is a promise. I've got to go do this. Fiona rushed out the door, without her usual cup of tea.

Trying to wrestle ancient ivy, with its thick, fibrous stems, from the worn stucco wall before they could even begin painting, did nothing to make the job any more appealing. And Fiona's hands were starting to ache. Parts of the ivy pulled away in large sheets of leafy foliage; other sections remained stubbornly stuck. But all of it left a textured tracery across the surface that needed scrubbing. Note to self, she thought. Never plant ivy, never buy a house that has ivy, and like the ads say, "Kids, don't try this at home." Ivy adheres to your life, Fiona thought. I wouldn't be surprised if it starts clinging to my dreams now, ornamenting the dream about showing up at a final exam for a class I didn't even know I was taking—ivy's the perfect nightmare, the persistent problem you just can't seem to solve.

Eventually, Fiona and her friends did solve the ivy problem, and got the wall painted. But, the painting proved an even less comfortable experience, as she started feeling ill from the fumes. By the end of the day, they'd managed to complete the job and collect their payment, but she was exhausted. She had a sick headache, her hands were red and raw, and the nails on both hands were ragged. Worse, she hadn't practiced all weekend, and her hands ached too much to begin now. Maybe, Fiona thought, after soaking her hands in Mother's Epsom salts and warm water, she'd be able to practice at least a little. She thought about Uncle Jim, and how he'd practiced six hours a day growing up. Maybe that's why he was so good at it. Headache and hurting hands notwithstanding, Fiona was determined to practice, and to do it right. For every mistake she made, she'd stop to play the passage correctly 10 times before moving on in her music. But not right now.

Fiona drew herself a nice long bath, to soak her hands and the rest of her tired body. As she lay back and plugged her ears, she enjoyed the roar of the rushing water. Turning the water off, she rested, listening to the sound of her breathing. Afterwards, she massaged some Skin Trip lotion into her hands, one finger at a time. It smelled the way she'd imagined California would smell, like coconut palms swaying in the wind. Then she slipped into some flannel PJs and, forgetting about her plan to practice, turned on her small black-and-white, rabbit-eared Sony TV to see what was on. She took out an Emory board to buff her nails so they wouldn't snag on a viola string. At least that's something accomplished, she thought.

The weather wasn't great that evening, which wasn't boding well for UHF Channel 44, even when Fiona fiddled with the antenna. The four VHF networks, CBS, NBC, ABC and PBS, were all okay. Fiona searched among them, hoping for something fun. She was in luck. *Kung Fu* was on, with the craziest musical guests, José Feliciano and Cannonball Adderley. Watching them was almost like practicing, wasn't it? She might turn in early, skip *The Tonight Show* and practice in the morning. She turned down the volume on her TV, so she wouldn't disturb her mother, who was writing in her studio. With the concentration skills of a surgeon, Mother wouldn't hear the slight noise from Fiona's TV, she knew, but it felt good to offer a gesture of respect.

Fiona took out her journal, opened it to a blank page halfway through the stamped-leather book and began to write a haiku poem about her reluctance to practice that night. "The shameful student, not mindful of teacher's pains, instead writes poems." Or maybe more accurate, "The hurting hand, too sore to play viola, instead writes poems." More accurate, Fiona thought, but no better. She closed her journal and turned on *The Tonight Show*. Pretty soon, she was fast asleep.

On Monday, in music class, as students were taking their seats and warming up their instruments, Fiona imagined that people around her could hear she hadn't practiced her viola. One person delivered a viola joke in a stage whisper so loud, Fiona knew she was meant to overhear it. Especially since hers was the only viola. She also noticed that some of the violinists were warming up by playing difficult pieces that weren't even on the class program. Fiona couldn't decide if she were playing out her own disappointment in herself for not practicing, or if her classmates really were judging her.

During her next private lesson, Fiona asked Mr. Żywny if he would give her a beautiful, complex passage from the Handel-Halvorsen "Passacaglia" to warm up with, so she could be as cool as the violinists. Mr. Ż was not amused. "You have about five seconds to decide why you are playing the viola," he said. "If you are going through all of this just to impress the violins, then neither you nor I have time for this. If you want to play well, your purpose shouldn't be about showing off. Warm up with slow, long bows and the actual music you're about to perform. Play with the violins, but play well for the audience. Or yourself."

She should have known Mr. Ż. wouldn't stand for string section antics. "How many dead violinists does it take to screw in the light bulb in my basement?"

Fiona looked up at her teacher. "I don't know, how many?"

"Apparently more than eight since that's how many are there, now."

"That's not even funny," she said.

"Neither was your plan to compensate for not practicing your viola by plotting to show up the violin section. Remember, Fiona, anyone who can carry a tune can play the fiddle. It's harder to hold an inside voice and play the viola. You completely misinterpreted the situation because you were disappointed in yourself. You're the superior player, and that's why they tease. Get used to it. Uneasy lies the head that wears the crown."

Fiona had never heard Mr. Żywny say something like that. Suddenly, Shakespeare was starting to make a whole lot more sense.

~oOOoOOo~

In the weeks before Fiona's first class recital, Boris Żywny had become harsher than ever in his exacting demands and relentless criticisms. "I feel like I'm dodging gnats, here, Fiona! Tone. Tone. Where is your TONE? What kind of viola is that, anyway; a monotony or just no-tony? Play your instrument like a goddamn soloist. Where's your ego? Kick it up a notch. Pick a tone that reflects the mood of this piece and stop ducking under it. This is your moment, Fiona, so own it."

Fiona knew her revered teacher was trying to motivate her. She realized he wouldn't push her like this if he didn't think she had it in her, but she'd had enough of his insults. Right then and there, she made the decision that once her recital was over, she would throw her viola into the fire and roast marshmallows with it. It wasn't a Stradivarius, for heaven's sake. And she was pretty sure she wasn't God's gift to the viola. Mr. Ż., however, must have thought she was—or could be, or he wouldn't be wasting his time and ridiculous comments on her. Still, he didn't need to be so harsh. Fiona preferred being motivated by encouragement.

Then came the recital.

It didn't really matter that the orchestra played well. What mattered to Fiona was what she saw when she glanced over at Mother sitting in the audience; she was beaming. Not yet able to assess her own skill on the viola, this was what she needed to believe she had been successful. It was then, and only then, that she let herself enjoy the experience. Fiona knew she had made some mistakes along the way, but she'd remembered Mr. Ż.'s admonishments not to telegraph them to the audience by rolling her eyes, scrunching up her nose or, worst of all, stopping the music. "Be proud of all of it—the whole shebang—embrace everything, including your mistakes!" he'd said. "Carry yourself like an artist, no matter what."

Even Mr. Ż., who surely had heard her mistakes, was full of praise. After the recital, when Fiona approached her mother and her teacher, she could hardly contain her astonishment when he drew her into a bold hug and said, "You were amazing, today, Fiona!" She wanted to remind him that she hadn't had a big solo, but Fiona knew he would shift to disappointment in her if she were to downplay her achievement. "How many times have I told you," his voice rang out in her memory, "learn to accept a compliment with grace!" Regardless of his style, he was trying to teach her to own her abilities—her failures and her successes. Today was a day to celebrate.

Fiona felt the transformation as she took in the experience, transported to a higher sense of self by her performance and by the audience's response, particularly those who mattered to her—her mother and her teacher. As she and her classmates received their congratulations, she stood there, along with everyone else, said thank you, and took it all in. For the first time, she allowed herself to accept her abilities, to know she was good, and to be okay with it.

Having dared to appear on stage, and to have played her heart out in front of God and everyone, including Mother and Mr. Ż., Fiona felt fearless, as if she could do anything. She had just accomplished something real. Something right. Something beautiful. If she could do this, she reasoned, surely she could do more.

Why had it worked? she wondered. Maybe it was because she was playing in concert with her peers, the ones from whom she had recently felt so estranged. But today, they played together. Maybe it was because, for once, instead of concentrating on technique, she had been able to dwell in the sound as the viola became part of her, and she had been singing through herself, through the polished wood, the secure bow, and her whole heart. Whatever it was, she'd had a sip of what it's like to trust in something and let it carry her along. And she knew she wanted more.

No one had been disappointed. Had she ever experienced that before? It seemed, so often, someone in her life was disappointed, most often her mother or herself. Not today. The whole thing had turned into a glorious lesson about life and possibility. In her journal that night, Fiona penned a new haiku about her experience and new-found perspective. "Now the way grows clear, the hand that writes the music reaches out to me." After reading it through a couple of times, and thinking back on her day, she added a little note. "As a poet, I don't know it, but as a musician, I've come to fruition." She thought about drawing a smiley face, and decided it was too junior high. It was nice to feel good about herself, Fiona thought, as she set her journal on her nightstand and slipped into sleep.

~oOOoOOo~

Far out! A date! And I have an entire closet filled with nothing to wear, Fiona thought, as she slid open her closet door and took inventory of her sweaters and skirts and sensible shoes. These are fine for school, but a first date? No way.

Fiona wasn't sure why Brennan had asked her out for a breakfast date—she was surprised. She knew very little about him, except that he was a soccer player, and according to the grapevine, decidedly more devoted to soccer than school. He had a sort of "I'm naturally beautiful, so naturally, I don't care" kind of vibe.

She knew he had noticed her in class, but she was sure that was just because she was smart. Why else would somebody like me? she asked herself, scrutinizing her reflection in the mirror. Fiona decided not to overthink it and ruin the date before it began. Back to giddy excitement and getting ready.

Closing the door on her closet, she decided the answer was in her dresser. A breakfast date calls for tight jeans and the prettiest sweater I can find. She tugged her only pair of bedazzled jeans—she'd used Mary's bedazzler and had created a simple star—out of her drawer, and paired it with the baby blue cashmere sweater Mother had given her at Christmas. She examined her reflection, frowning. I'm kind of meh, but I don't hate my legs, she thought. Maybe I should switch to a skirt. Fiona fingered the soft fibers of her sweater, as she toyed with her ideas and options. She thought about Brennan and his bright eyes and lazy smile. Wait. Save the skirt for a possible second date, she decided. *Bedazzled says "cute," but jeans mean I'm not trying too hard. There ought to be a book on all this. Hey, I'll bet there actually is.*

Fiona laid out her jeans and sweater on her freshly made bed, set her black velvet shoes from Chinatown on the floor nearby, and went to take her shower. She really hated mornings and, after suffering through five school days of waking at the ungodly hour of 6:30 am as her alarm startled her out of her sleep, she particularly looked forward to sleeping in on Saturdays. Yet here it was, 7:00 am, and she was up and on her way to the shower. *Only a breakfast date with Brennan could roust me out of bed before 8:00 or 9:00 or 10:00 on a Saturday,* she thought. *Well, on second thought, Mother often did, for one reason or another.*

Lost in a delicious daydream about her date, Fiona let too much Clairol Herbal Essence shampoo pour into her hand. She decided to use it as a body wash as well as a shampoo, realizing, right then and there that this would be her fragrance for the day. Its distinctive smell would clash with anything else. Gram had given her some great perfumed lilac water for Christmas. That would have been nice, with some other shampoo. Same with Patchouli oil. Hanna had given her a tiny bottle of Patchouli back at the commune, and she'd felt so grown up wearing it. She still had the original bottle; she'd refilled it many times since then. But Patchouli oil could be strong, and some people tended to think it smelled like pot. It could hardly have smelled more different, but because it was strong enough to mask almost any scent, loads of people wore it to hide their indulgences from unskilled noses, forging the association. Fiona had long ago made the personal decision to go with the Patchouli and not the pot, which had a smell she loathed. Lilac water was generally a safer bet, though. And zero perfume, today's choice, was safer still.

Fiona snapped out of her reverie and realized she was going to turn into a prune if she didn't stop daydreaming and get out of this shower. Not a good look for a first date. She shut off the faucet, toweled off, wrapped the damp terrycloth around her body, and went down the hall to her room. She let her towel drop in favor of smoothing on a little body lotion, then picked up the towel and draped it over her desk chair, so she wouldn't have to hear about it later. Grabbing her brush, she ran it through her long, damp hair a little too quickly, snagging it halfway down the length, creating a snarl.

Slow down, Fiona, she thought. Maybe this was one of those moments when Mother's suggestion to breeeeaaaathe would be a good idea. And what would Pop say? "Mellow out, Fabulous Fee, you've got it going on." She looked in the mirror and whispered, "I've got it going on." She slowly worked her way through the snarl, and brushed her hair into a long, smooth ponytail. Then she picked up her ball cap, considered pulling her ponytail through the cap—she liked that look—and then tossed it back on her dresser, choosing a slightly more feminine look over anything too casually sporty. She was going on a date with a jock, so she'd better not signal that she was a jock or a wannabe. Skipping the cap would be more honest.

Five minutes later, Fiona had pulled her bike from around the side of the house and was off, pedaling as fast as she could without getting sweaty.

She parked her bike in front of Fat Albert's, the most popular breakfast joint within biking distance, snapped the lock into place, and ran a hand across her head to smooth her ponytail. The food must be great, she thought, surveying the long line, snaking around the corner from the quaint diner directly across the street from 5th String Music and Mr. Mopps Toys on Grove Street. Brennan was beaming at Fiona from inside, where he'd already snagged them a seat at the front table by a window. Good thing I didn't dress up, she thought, taking in the jeans and simple tee Brennan had on. Mostly, she noticed the muscles giving shape to that t-shirt.

The waitress came by with menus and two cups of coffee. Fiona was a little bit flattered that she assumed two high-school kids drank coffee. A small silver pitcher of heavy cream was already on the table. Fiona watched the cream swirl like a lazy cloud as she slowly poured it into the coffee, using the cream to balance out the bitter coffee taste.

They both ordered hot apple pie, which everyone knew was the best thing on the menu, at any hour of the day or night. She skipped the "a la mode," but when Brennan didn't, she wished she'd ordered her pie with ice cream as well.

The waitress delivered their slices of pie, both steaming, but Brennan's was hidden beneath vanilla bean ice cream dripping down the sides. He looked at hers, and back at his, and laughed. Picking up his spoon, he scraped half the ice cream off his pie and slopped it on hers. She smiled at him, secretly thrilled with him and the ice cream, and they each dug in.

Fiona listened to Brennan wax on about soccer through most of their breakfast. This play and that near miss, his training schedule, and what it meant to play right middle field. He also jammed about his hero, Jairzinho, the Brazilian football legend, about whom Fiona knew next to nothing. Fiona couldn't have cared less.

"So, what about you, Fiona? Do you play any sports?" Fiona appreciated that Brennan had stopped talking about himself long enough to take an interest in her. But even his question indicated how little he knew of her, and how ill-suited they seemed to be for each other. Not a sporty girl, Fiona was not sure how to answer.

"I'm into a martial art called Aikido and the development of the mind-body connection," she said. When he didn't look up from his plate to respond, she said, "And I really love to ride horses. I even collect model horses to enjoy when I'm not around real ones. I've gotten some of them across the street at Mr. Mopps. Do you ride?"

"Nope, not my thing." This was going nowhere fast, as the conversation slipped into an uncomfortable stall.

"Hey, Fee, do you sail? We've got a sweet sailboat." Fiona, who remembered turning green on Tina's boat, imagined it might be fun to set sail on a sunny day with friends, and was excited to suggest they had something in common. She shared stories from her recent salmon-fishing trip. Before she could follow it with her father's adventures on the high seas, Brennan cut in, with a story of his own. "That's so cool, Fee! Listen, you know those guru-type guys you said your mom hangs out with? My older brother has skippered for a few of 'em. You've probably heard of at least one of them. There was this one real character, though. Have you ever heard of those process weekends? You know, like est and The CASST Process?"

"Of course I have! Who hasn't?" Fiona leaned in. "Tell me more!"

"So, when my brother, Jack, was in high school, he had this totally boss job as a skipper for the guy who started one of those. His name was Mr. Kargo. Word is, it was spelled with a K but he changed it to a C to go along with the nickname he took, Cassowary Cargo."

"Oh my gosh, you're talking about that Cass fellow! The same one who founded the Catalyze Anger, Synergize Strength Training Process? Mr. 'The CASST Process' Cass? Get out of town!"

"Seriously. The one and only. Funny, calling yourself The Cass, like some special superhuman thing. I met the guy once. Slicked hair across his square head, three-piece polyester suit, white Naugahyde loafers, big ol' stogie cigar; you get the picture. He looked like a street-corner shyster, the guy who'd try to sell you a watch, or maybe the Brooklyn Bridge. His shtick was that he'd been to Australia and had been given a spirit animal."

"Let me guess which one! Deadly bird. Aims for the guts. Right?"

"Yep. The very same. So, anyway, my brother and the chef would set up the food and then wait. Maybe he'd show up, or maybe he wouldn't. My brother would come home with a ton of amazing food, big trays of anything you'd want. You know, fancy food. When he did show, they'd go out on these super easy sails. He'd smoke his stub, and sit back and talk about this person or that and just laugh. He was rolling in dough. Imagine, and for telling them to go beat a pillow or whatever. Ransoming your rage, he calls it, and of course there's a whole ladder to climb, pay as you go.

"Anyway," Brennan had barely taken a breath, "he offered my brother a job after high school, but only if he'd go through the training. Even offered to pay his way. My brother said no. Turned down a free ride to avoid getting tangled up in the crazy. With people like that, there's always a reckoning. And my brother's no dope. He's got a good nose for shysters. At least that's what I think," he said.

"He sounds really cool. Your brother, I mean. Not the other one." Fiona replied. "I can see the headline, now, 'Skipper Charts

Own Course. Becomes Captain of Own Life.' I like it. Smart move."

Just then the waitress came by with the check and, assuming the gentleman would pay, handed it to Brennan. Reaching for her wallet, Fiona asked, "Shall we go Dutch?"

"How 'bout you take care of the tip," Brennan smiled. Fiona was, once again, impressed. She pulled out a dollar and left it on the table. It was about double what was expected; better to be generous than stingy.

"I sure wouldn't want to bare my soul to someone, just to have him splash it all over as he talked behind my back," Fiona said, as they pressed their way through the throngs of people still waiting for a table. "And although I haven't met your brother," she added, "I already like him." Then, as she put out her hand to shake Brennan's and say goodbye, he took her hand and said, "Hey, why don't you show me some of those model horses you said they sell across the street?"

"Really?"

"Yeah, why not? I mean, if you have time and all."

Fiona's gaze caught Brennan's lovely green eyes for the briefest of moments. Oh, she had time. She had hours upon hours to focus on horses and a handsome boy. She slipped her hand into his and, together, they crossed the street.

Fiona explained the different horse breeds to Brennan, and pointed out which models depicted race horses. "These are collectible. If I take good care of them, I might have something to pass along, someday." Fiona's mind flashed to a warm brick colonial home, Irish setters by the hearth, and a little girl's room with beautiful crown molding, shelves on every wall, each one lined with model horses. "I know I probably shouldn't be interested in these model horses anymore," she said, "but I still think they're just so beautiful."

"I can see that. Why not? Here, I'll show you what I want in here." Brennan showed Fiona his favorite things in the store, including various model-building sets.

"See that tri-plane, Fiona? I built that same one with my dad."

"Hey, me too. Your dad sounds cool if he built models with you."

"Yeah, he's okay."

Brennan walked Fiona back to her bike, helped her unlock it, and then steadied it as she swung her leg over the bar. Before she could ride away, he touched her face and leaned in for a lovely little kiss. Then he winked and said, "Maybe you'd like to come sailing with me sometime."

Fiona pressed her hand into the same spot on her face in wonder as she watched Brennan wander down the street. *Maybe I should go find out a little more about soccer,* she thought.

~oOO0O0o~

By the following Saturday, Brennan, true to his word, had invited Fiona to come sailing with him. She opened her bedroom windows and leaned out to feel the sun warm upon her face, and a gentle breeze lift her hair. *This definitely feels like a sailing day,* she thought.

Fiona had rarely sailed, and had certainly never been sailing on a Soverel-33 racing sailboat. She had no idea what to expect, and she began to feel a prick of fear. Such a vessel calls for a crew of more than one experienced sailor and a rookie, and this one was well staffed. But, Fiona didn't know that. Her fears about what to expect had more to do with heading out on the open sea with a boy she hardly knew than whether she'd fall overboard.

Biking her way over to the Berkeley Pier, Fiona's fears grew. *I really have no business going out on a sailboat alone with Brennan,* she thought. *What if he's not as nice as he seems? What if he's really one of those jocks who's just waiting to take advantage the moment he gets a girl alone?* It's not as if I can dive off the bow of the boat and swim for shore. Fiona was working herself into a frenzy, pedaling slower and slower, eking her way toward a destination she no longer wanted to reach, until there was so little momentum, her bike nearly fell over.

With heart racing, she let the foreboding feeling guide her, as she made a hard-right turn and began biking toward home. Had she gone one more block, she would have reached the pier, where she would have seen her trusted friend, Mary, carrying a cooler filled with food, heading out to meet three more of their good friends. Fearful of the prospect of a private date with Brennan aboard a boat, Fiona had unwittingly just missed out on a party. But she wouldn't know the whole story until Monday, when her girlfriends circled her at school to find out why she'd "jumped ship." Unless Brennan called. Not likely, she thought.

Biking back the way she came, Fiona's heart returned to its normal rhythm as soon as she had her house in sight. I need to calm down, she said to herself. I must be reading too many of Mother's murder mysteries. Then again, Pop says, "Just because you're paranoid, doesn't mean they're not out to get you." See? I was raised to be wary. She brought her bike round back, took her key from around her neck, and let herself into the house.

"Phew. That was a close call," she said to Starlight, as the poodle came scampering up to greet her. Fiona picked her up and snuggled into her soft fur, feeling even more secure now. Starlight didn't seem to mind Fiona's constant cuddling, or the way she tended to carry her around like a plush toy. She liked it. Fiona was her person. Starlight wagged her tail and tried to reach Fiona's face with wet kisses, as Fiona gazed into her eyes, showering her with praise. "Who's a good dog? You are, my little Starlight moonbeam! Okay, let's some watch TV." Fiona hugged Starlight tightly and then set her down on the foot of the bed before she could wriggle free.

Turning her attention to her guitar gathering dust in the corner, she forgot about the television and went over to retrieve the instrument. Sitting on the floor, leaning against her bed, she started fingering "Blackbird," thinking how she'd also like to learn classical guitar. Giving up after her third try, she started in on "The Boxer." Everyone who says the guitar is easy is actually wrong, she thought. She sighed and set it down. Okay, the viola isn't easy either, but at least it's tuned logically.

Five hours after Fiona had made it safely home from her missed sailing rendez vous, the phone rang. Fiona jumped at the sound, sure she knew who was calling. She took a deep breath and picked up the receiver on the princess phone in her room. Brennan launched into tales about the day she had missed. He told her about her other friends who'd gone sailing with him and how disappointed they'd all been when she hadn't shown up. Her heart sank. Just like *Seventeen* and *Cosmopolitan* magazines advised, she'd trusted her gut instead of the guy, but this time, she'd been wrong.

"I am so sorry," Fiona whispered to support her charade. "I woke up with a sore throat. I didn't want to get you guys sick, but I didn't know how to reach you. Will you take a rain check, maybe? Thank you, Brennan; I missed you, too. Okay; better go rest my voice."

Fiona was relieved he wasn't mad. But she was really thinking, Liar! You're a freakin' phobic liar! Why not just admit you're a coward? Hanging up the receiver, Fiona wondered if she hadn't trusted him or if she hadn't trusted herself. What had made her turn a perfectly innocent sailing party into something out of Warren Beatty's *Shampoo*?

Fiona picked up Starlight, sat on her bed, and glanced at the TV. Abandoning that idea, she fiddled with the radio to find the right station with the sort of songs that would fit her mood, and decided to write a letter to Pop. She set Starlight on the bed, went over to her desk, where she picked up her favorite pen and pulled out some stationery she'd been given for Christmas. She climbed back on her bed and leaned against her "study buddy," the plump pillow with arms covered in floral upholstery. Mother had said all the college girls had them in the dorms. The pre-lined stationery was folded over to form its own envelope, keeping everything neat and tidy, just the way Fiona liked it. She thought for a moment before setting pen to paper.

Writing carefully in her neat hand, Fiona told Pop that Berkeley reminded her of San Francisco's Haight Ashbury district and about the Bill Graham "Day on the Green" concerts she'd been to. I'll bet you could get high just breathing in the air at the Coliseum, she thought, grimacing. She knew Pop would enjoy her story, so she tried to make it as descriptive as possible. She decided to add in a little science for him, letting him know she'd kept track of which concert had the thickest air. Not surprisingly, the Grateful Dead concert was in the lead. Fiona and Pop were diehard fans of the band. Diehard. Dead. Grateful. She thought of her parents—Pop was a "Dead Head," a Grateful Dead fan, and Mother liked to "deadhead," to cut spent blooms from her rose bush before they became rose hips. Fiona was in the mood for wordplay, but she couldn't quite come up with it. Something about being "hip." About being a diehard Dead Head. Ah, she was overworking it. She picked up her poodle.

"Someday," she said to Starlight, "snappy little lines will slip right out of me every time I want to be clever." She peered into her poodle's eyes. "But Pop would tell me to let go of clever, and lean toward smart, wouldn't he?" She picked up her pen and resumed writing.

~o0O0O0o~

Undaunted by Fiona's faked illness, Brennan had invited her to watch him play in an informal soccer match with a few friends the following weekend. Eager to see him in action, she headed over to the field right after dinner. She realized, pretty quickly, as she sat in the stands, that she was watching less of the game and more of him. During a quick break, Brennan opened a bottle of orange Gatorade and, before taking a swig, lifted it to her, as in a toast.

"Hey, Fiona; 'bet I can drink you under the table!" he joked. Fiona felt her face drain of color, and a chill run down her bones. She didn't know why, but she suddenly felt dizzy and nauseous. Well, maybe just queasy. Brennan noticed. "Hey, was it something I said?" Fiona had no idea. She had nothing against orange Gatorade. Heck, she had nothing against drinking yourself blotto. She had no idea what was going on inside, or why she was weirding out. She couldn't access the unconscious association between orange juice and predation. It was buried way too deep. Motioning that she didn't feel well, Fiona begged out of the second half of the game. As she pedaled home, with the breeze in her face, she started to feel a little better. Was it the escape or the evening air that soothed her? As soon as she parked her bike against the side of the house, Fiona headed directly to her room and her dog. She feared she might hyperventilate. Brennan was nice, and everything, so why was she being such a spaz?

A few days later, Brennan called Fiona. He told her he didn't think things seemed to be working out, and maybe they should just be friends. Fiona should have been relieved. So, why wasn't she?

She phoned Mary, to help her make sense of the situation. "It's weird, right Mare? I mean, one day he's all into me, and the next day, he's not."

"Do you care?"

"What do you mean? Of course, I care. I guess. I mean, I don't know."

"That's the problem."

"What is?"

"You don't know. Every time he asks you out, you get all excited, and, um, you go. But once you get there, you freak out, shut down and either pull a no-show or go home halfway through the date. What's up with that?"

"I don't really know, actually. I mean, I like him and all, but once I get there..." Fiona was without explanation.

"I'll tell you what's going on. I mean, if you want my input. You know I try to be honest with you, Fee."

"Spill it."

"I think you're doing the guy thing."

"What do you mean? What guy thing?"

"Well," said Mary, "it's usually guys who do this. It's that thing where the guy starts out acting all into the girl, but once she starts showing some interest, he totally freaks out and acts terrible until she gives up on him. You're that guy."

"I am not that guy, Mare."

"Then you explain the seesaw you're on. You might want to look in the mirror, Fee."

Fiona dearly hoped her friend was wrong. But, she had a sneaking suspicion Mary was right. Fiona was frightened. It was way too much for her to accept that a guy that cool was into her. So, she'd thrown ice in his Gatorade. Dang, this was hard.

One Wednesday afternoon after school, Fiona arrived home to find Karen in the living room, with her young son, Chayton. What a wonderful surprise, she thought, but she had a feeling Mother had known they were coming, since she didn't seem in the least bit surprised. Wouldn't she have said something at breakfast? Fiona felt perplexed, but she let it go, so she could enjoy their visit.

The tension was high. At dinner that evening, they politely caught up on how Karen was doing in Boulder, and Fiona learned that the reason for their visit was to allow Chayton to spend some time with his dad. Karen had fallen into the fractured family dynamic—passed from one generation to the next.

As she drifted off to sleep that night, Fiona thought about Karen, who was sleeping just down the hall. There was so much she didn't understand about her older sister. She'd moved away in a mad dash. Why? She was so smart, but she hadn't gone to college. Was that because she'd been a single mom?

Well, I'm not leaving, I'm staying, Fiona thought. None of this rolling stone stuff for me and my kids. I want to gather some major moss. She had already decided she wanted daughters, and, as always, she imagined providing them with the quintessential house with two gentle dogs sleeping by a glowing fireplace—her idealized image of hearth and home. She'd stay put, and her kids would be in one school all their days. She'd choose some cozy neighborhood where they could feel grounded and grow up with a strong sense of belonging.

The next morning, Karen rose early, borrowed Mother's car to take Chayton to visit his father, and promptly plowed it into the concrete roundabout in the center of the street. Fiona ran to the window of her bedroom. And that is precisely why I wouldn't dare drive Mother's car, she thought. It seemed Karen had meant to do it, a Freudian "oops" moment. Anything to stick it to Mother. All her young life, Karen had felt the sting of Peggy's resentment at having to raise her as a single mom. Oops! I didn't mean to smash something of yours, did I Mother? I didn't mean to wreck something of yours just because you wrecked my life! They're playing our song, Mother.

Roundabout. Yes!

Mother's vintage Mercedes. Ouch.

Fiona marveled over the moment of the car crash for most of the morning. She'd never wrecked anything of anyone else's, either on purpose or by accident, as far as she could remember. And, although she'd had words now and then with Pop, it wouldn't have occurred to her to even raise her voice at Mother, let alone smash her car.

Weirdly, Mother didn't say a single word about the car crash. So, for all her drama, Karen got what Fiona was used to getting. Nothing. During dinner, Karen announced she would be leaving after the weekend. Again, no comment from Mother. Nothing. Was she that angry or that over it? Fiona imagined Mother knew the car crash held a deeper meaning, too.

After dinner, Karen left the house to escape Mother's stink eye. "Be a love, Fiona, and watch Chayton for me, will you?" Fiona just nodded her assent, also in silence, as Karen sauntered out the door.

"Tell me a story, Aunt Fee," begged Chayton, climbing into her lap. Fiona arranged his chubby four-year-old legs across hers, gave him a hug, and said, "Okay. Name three things. And give me the name of who you want starring in your bedtime story." Chayton was quiet for a moment and then said, "A rocket ship, a cow, the moon, and my mom."

Now it was Fiona's turn to think for a moment before she launched into her spontaneous story. "Well, Chayton, once upon a time, Karen the Cow wanted to build a rocket ship to sail to the mooooo-oon, to find out whether it really was made of cheese. She was a very smart cow, and had very smart little baby cows…"

When she'd finished weaving her yarn, complete with a pun about how the cow used cow-culus (special math for cows planning their trajectories), Fiona looked down at Chayton, who still looked wide awake. Oops, she thought, realizing she'd gotten carried away in the story and forgotten the purpose of the telling. Guess I should have made it a relaxing story about a cow grazing, watching rockets while falling asleep softly by a stream.

"Can I have a story about Venus and a lion? Can you make up that one, Aunt Fee?"

"Maybe when it's not bedtime. How about a song?" Fiona replied. "As soon as we get you into your jammies and tucked into bed." Fiona got Chayton ready and tucked him into the guest room bed he'd be sharing with his mother, if she ever came home.

"Froggy went a wooing and he did go, uh huh…" Fiona sang her mother's lullaby. singing each verse more softly, until Chayton's eyelids finally closed for the last time. Tiptoeing out of the room, she looked back at her sleeping nephew and thought, I kind of liked that. Karen's lucky.

The next day, Chayton was to visit his dad and spend the night there. Karen wanted to go out, and invited Fiona to come along after she got out of school. Fiona knew what "going out" meant to Karen, even in the afternoon.

Fiona felt as comfortable with the idea as a freshman at the senior prom, but she wasn't about to miss out on a once-in-a-lifetime chance to go drinking with her big sister. After class, she pedaled as fast as she could over to University Avenue to meet up with Karen.

Karen handed Fiona her newly minted fake ID, which she tucked into her wallet just before they walked into a bar on the main drag. When the server asked for their order, he looked at Fiona's face and then down at her ID, and back at Fiona.

"You look pretty young."

"Thank you. Everyone tells me that." Karen winked at the server, who smiled and took their order. Fiona knew, after passing the ID test, she couldn't just order a Coke. The folks at the table next to them had ordered Tequila Sunrises. Karen told Fiona how they were made, how important it was to get the ratios just right, and stir just short of too much, so they'd be beautiful. Karen ordered a Tequila Sunrise. "Make it two," Fiona added.

The sisters sat for quite a while, saying very little, mostly looking around the room awkwardly. There was almost a decade between them, and they had spent very little time together. They really didn't have much to talk about. Fiona would have loved to confide all her feelings in her sister, and ask her more questions than she could remember in the moment. Here was her big chance to have her sister to herself, and she was blowing it with nowhere to start. She was relieved when their drinks came, so she could focus on the color striations of her Sunrise.

Just then, a man approached Karen and tried to strike up a conversation. "I'm with my sister now, but you can call me later." Fiona watched, as her sister wrote down the wrong number and handed it to the man, with a sweet smile. Fiona opened her mouth to correct her, but Karen kicked her, under the table. Oh, my gosh! Fiona thought. Karen actually did that on purpose. Good one! She realized, then and there, how little she knew about adult interactions and how out of place she was: too young to be sitting in a bar, sipping a Tequila Sunrise with her sister. Something about that made her feel giddy. Maybe it was the tequila.

Somehow, the random man's intrusion had broken the ice. Karen and Fiona spent the rest of the evening sipping more Sunrises and talking about Fiona's favorite new film, *Star Wars*. Many of Fiona's friends had spent most of every weekend that summer of '77, waiting in line to see the epic space opera, time and time again. She had seen it only once, so far, with Mother, at the Coronet. She had loved the plush seats and fresh buttered popcorn, and the chance to be out with Mother. But what she remembered most, what she knew she would never forget, was the film. And she remained quite certain, she would never, ever, in all her years, see a movie she liked more.

Karen was kind enough to sit there, sipping her Sunrise and taking in all Fiona had to share. She'd hadn't seen such animation in her tightly controlled, do-gooder little sister before. No one had. Again, maybe it was the tequila talking.

One more Tequila Sunrise, Fiona thought, and she wasn't going to remember her own name. It was time to go. She was secretly hoping Karen might want to see a movie with her on Saturday.

Mother hadn't waited up for Fiona and Karen. Fiona felt relieved that her mother wouldn't catch her with tequila on her breath, but she was a little disappointed to think her mother hadn't been worried. She knew she was out with her older sister, and that should have been the worrisome part. She assumed Mother knew what they were up to, and just didn't care.

~oOOoOOo~

The only film of interest playing on Saturday afternoon was a horror flick at the Rialto, called *Malatesta's Carnival of Blood*. Fiona was fascinated by the tagline, "You'll shriek with horror as you watch his victims take a diabolical roller-coaster ride to a bloody death!" It sounded suitably creepy, and she liked the idea of shrieking with horror alongside her sister. The two of them had squealed in delight as they watched the Beatles on *The Ed Sullivan Show* in their matching pink PJs. Yes, it had been a very different sort of shrieking, but wouldn't this be just as fun, if not more?

Saturday came and went, and so did Karen. She had decided to go out on her own, leaving Fiona with horror on her brain and heartbreak in her chest. After she picked up Chayton in Mother's mangled Mercedes Sunday evening, she returned to Mother's just long enough to pack up their bags and head back out. This time, someone picked them up. Neither Mother nor Fiona asked who.

Fiona was sorry to see her sister and nephew leave, and a part of her wanted to go with them. But she knew, with Karen out of the house, the tension would ease and she and Mother could go back to normal. Whatever that was. Fiona couldn't read the emotion on her mother's face. She got the feeling that Mother was glad to see her go, and imagined she'd be relieved when Fiona moved out, as well. She had no way of knowing what Mother really thought. Mother had a great poker face, and she held her cards close.

~oOOoOOo~

Peggy had been studying a New Age personality theory called the Enneagram, said to be based on an ancient body of wisdom that identifies nine core personality types and how each one sees and interacts with the world. Her teacher, Dr. Judith Prana, was hosting a field trip to the airport—a hotbed for diverse personalities and where people, under pressure from travel, tend to reveal more of their true selves. Peggy had taken an interest in using the theory to interpret the motivations of the characters in her mystery novels, and she was looking forward to the field study. At the last minute, she decided to invite Fiona to come along with her.

Excited to be invited by her mother, Fiona quickly climbed into the car. Mother had decided Fiona was a personality type 3—the Achiever, who is the success-oriented, pragmatic type: adaptable, excelling, driven, and image-conscious. Fiona was curious to find out what that meant for her life.

As Dr. Prana's students found one another at their rendez-vous point outside the United terminal, Fiona noticed members of the Hare Krishna cult assembled nearby, in their orange robes. She knew from her father that these people came together to foster consciousness, but right now, as they clinked their hand cymbals, spun around and chanted *"Hare Krishna,"* they just seemed to be asking for money.

"However conscious they are," Fiona said to her mother, "they certainly don't seem to be self-conscious."

"The trick, Fiona," said Mother, looking over at the chanting dancers, "is not to take gifts from them, or they won't ever leave you alone, asking for a donation."

The class sat down together at a departure gate and began watching the passersby, personality typing each one as they came along. Fiona knew only the definition of type 3, so she just watched people pass and thought about herself.

The Achiever, she thought. I'm kind of like the Avis rent-a-car slogan: "We try harder." I think I can live with that.

Dr. Prana came over to Fiona and quietly appraised her with a critical eye, as if observing a specimen. "She's a 3," she said to Peggy. "An Achiever, all right, but a self-preservation type 3. Mother issues." At that, Peggy snapped her head toward Fiona but said nothing.

"Your mother, Fiona, is also type 3, but a sexual subtype. More charisma." Dr. Prana turned her attention toward Peggy. "You already know that, don't you, Peggy?" Mother nodded in agreement. Having no idea what this meant, Fiona didn't respond, turning her attention, instead, toward the crowd surging through the airport. Still, she continued to listen as Dr. Prana encouraged Peggy to help her daughter identify and work through her "mother issues" by putting her into therapy with one of the other students, supervised by Dr. Prana.

Mostly, Fiona found it fascinating that Dr. Prana thought her "mother issues," whatever they were, lay with Fiona and not her mother. Certainly, there was a connection. She looked around at the other students, feeling mortified, and dreading the idea of sitting with any of them for any amount of time, while taking care not to say too much about Mother. Clearly, this was a lose-lose situation in the making.

In what her mother would call an avoidance move, Fiona returned her attention to the passersby and let her mind drift from the word Prana to others that started with the letter P: pompous, professor, pernicious, pariah, poopy head...She smiled as her assessment of Mother's teacher diminished. Her reverie was abruptly interrupted with another suggestion from Dr. Prana. "Why don't you bring Fiona to the individual session we're having on type 3s this Thursday evening?" she asked. "We could use more representatives on stage."

What? Fiona thought. No way. She looked pleadingly at her mother, silently willing her not to agree to putting her up on stage like some circus act. She said nothing as her mother nodded in agreement, like some zombie. But wait; wasn't Fiona supposed to be all about self-preservation? She turned to Dr. Prana and said, "No, thank you."

Mother placed her hand upon Fiona's arm, and said, "What she means, Dr. Prana, is no problem; thank you."

Fiona slipped her arm out from under her mother's insistent grasp, smiled weakly at Dr. Prana, and died a little inside. If I were Karen, she thought, I would have said a very clear, "No way!" and then I would have gotten up and headed for the car. 'Course, if I were Karen, I wouldn't even have come here today.

Thursday evening came way too quickly, and Fiona found herself on center stage. Man, this is weird, she thought. Everyone is staring at me, judging me, typing me. She looked at the other two guinea pigs sitting next to her and gave them that same weak smile she'd mustered for Dr. Prana. Each was asked to present a brief biography to the audience. Fiona quickly thought of a few simple things that wouldn't reveal too much.

"My name is Fiona Sprechelbach," she began. "I'm in high school. I'm working on my yellow belt in Aikido and am prepping for college." Her words were met with silence. At first.

Dr. Prana launched in about how shallow type 3s can be, confusing achievement with self. Fiona felt the audience stares turn into glowers of judgment, which made her feel exposed, shamed, and sick to her stomach. Once again, the word "self-preservation" came to mind.

"You know," Fiona stood up. "It's not that simple. How can anyone be so simple? You think you can judge someone based on a few words of introduction? Besides, isn't this whole personality thing supposed to be based on ancient wisdom? What kind of ancient wisdom would say that you should label a person just so you can judge them?"

"Classic 3," someone said. "Such ego." Fiona turned beet red and was about to answer, when Dr. Prana called for a 15-minute coffee break.

They don't get it, Fiona thought. They don't even get what they're trying to do. She stepped off the stage, down the stairs, and out through a side door, which led her to her bike. She knew Mother would stay for the second session, but Fiona was done. She was glad she'd planned an exit strategy and had come by bike. And she was glad no one had seen her leave or had tried to stop her.

Despite her relief in escaping the madness, as she swung her leg over her bike, she began to cry. For a lot of reasons, probably, but as far as she knew, for the embarrassment, the rejection, and the mean-spirited behavior by a group of people pretending to seek some sort of enlightenment. Maybe it was disappointment, too. Was anyone good? Was anyone kind?

"That must've felt rough in there," came a voice from the darkness. She had been seen. Fiona, panicking at the thought of being sent back inside, considered pedaling as fast as she could. But the voice had sounded understanding and kind. Stepping out of the shadows was a guy she'd seen in the group during the airport field trip. Bill, if she remembered right. Cute guy. Younger than the rest.

"No, it was fantastic," she retorted. "I wish I could go through it again. Or maybe, I'd rather have dental work, every day for the next month."

"That bad? Nothing is that simple, is it? Which is both the point and the problem."

"The problem," she said, "is no one gets it."

"I'm Bill. You're Fiona, if I'm not mistaken."

"Bill, I'd love to stay and chat about the wonderful evening I'm having," she said, "but I'm not about to get caught leaving and let someone drag me back into that circus."

"So, you're running away from the circus?"

Fiona liked his sense of humor. She also liked that his next line was to ask her out. Suddenly, she wasn't feeling quite so judged or rejected anymore.

"Let's continue this conversation somewhere more pleasant. How about I call you?"

Fiona nodded. She wondered if he would. He did, and they set a date for Saturday.

Bill came to pick up Fiona at 7 pm sharp, wearing tuxedo pants and a crisp white shirt, with silver cufflinks, and a long coat. Fiona thought he looked fantastic with his long, wavy brown hair flowing past his turned-up collar. He escorted her down the steps and out to quite a car. A muscle car. A Pontiac GTO. A statement ride. And she was getting the message.

The car was almost as old as Fiona. But then, Bill was quite a bit older than she. He had already earned a degree from UCLA in musical performance. Fiona was both surprised and grateful her mother was letting her go out with him. She imagined Mother was trusting his personality type, and ignoring his age.

Before they drove off, Bill asked, "Did you remember your ID?" By this, he meant her fake ID. She hadn't forgotten it. "Ever been to Charlie Brown's?" he asked, stepping on the accelerator, hard. Fiona shook her head no. "Then let's go have some fun." The car sped off with such a start, Fiona's head snapped back against the headrest. She knew then she was in for quite a ride.

Charlie Brown's, a popular bar located on the water in Emeryville, offered a beautiful view of the San Francisco Bay and the city beyond. The place had a roaring fireplace, a polished mahogany bar, and plenty of bistro seating near a small stage, where the band *Crosswinds* was playing. The waitress came and, before she could say anything, Bill put down a $20 bill and said, "Two Irish coffees, please." She smiled and asked for Fiona's ID. She looked Fiona in the eyes and said, "You look so young." Fiona, now practiced at her response, said, "Thank you."

"So," Fiona asked, "why Enneagram?" She was hoping to get his opinion of the New Age philosophy that had grabbed her mother by the brain, so she'd know where he stood before she offered her thoughts.

"Yeah," he said. "So, how'd you learn you were a 3?"

"My mom told me."

"Interesting. What do you think you are?"

Fiona hadn't thought about it and, frankly, hadn't paid much attention to the other types. How weird, she suddenly thought, that she'd just accepted the diagnosis. "I don't think I can fit into one neat little box of crayons," she said. "There are too many lovely colors and shades. Maybe I'm a rainbow. Maybe I'm not a number. Maybe I'm a unicorn."

Bill smiled, not offering his own opinion of the personality test or of her. The conversation moved on. Finally, he said, "Come on; I've got more to show you. This evening's just getting started."

They walked back to Bill's GTO. As a breeze picked up, Fiona wished she'd worn a coat, and not just a sweater. But, she'd picked a pretty one for the evening, with beading and a V neck, which she hadn't wanted to hide under a coat. Suddenly, she felt Bill wrapping his jacket around her. More than the coat, she realized she liked the feeling of his arms embracing her. *Maybe that's why I didn't wear a coat,* she thought.

Back inside the car, Bill turned up the heat and navigated onto the highway. Soon, he was parking at Oakland's Jack London Square. He took out a case from behind his seat, and together he and Fiona headed into a jazz club, just across the train tracks. It was different there, much more urban than any part of the Bay Area Fiona knew, but Bill seemed very much at home. Once inside, he seemed to know everyone there. As Fiona moved toward the front of the room with him, Bill found a place to sit with some of his friends. Fiona noticed him quietly open the briefcase he'd been carrying. It wasn't a briefcase at all; it was a trumpet case. Then, he stepped on stage with his trumpet.

Fiona was thrilled to think Bill had brought her to hear him perform. But jazz, really? She hated jazz, even if her Pop liked it.

This band mixed the jazz up with contemporary hits. When Bill began playing "What You Won't Do for Love," Fiona's ears perked up, as she listened and watched, impressed. He played three other pieces after that, and Fiona couldn't help but wonder if he'd chosen his playlist for her. *In my dreams,* she mused.

"What'd you think, Fiona? It's a pretty good band, right?" asked Bill when he returned to the table.

"You were great; amazing!" Fiona said. She'd really enjoyed Bill's music, and she imagined he was used to hearing praise. She cut to the chase and told him plainly what she thought. Because he was good. Great, even. Bill grinned a cat-ate-the-cream grin, and Fiona at once knew that, good as he surely knew he was, he still appreciated her saying so.

Fiona heard "Last call," all too soon. Bill returned his trumpet to its case, and walked with Fiona and other band members out back to a garage, where the others had parked. "Great night, guys," he called out, as they all said their goodbyes and headed their separate ways. On the way home, listening to Miles Davis on his eight-track player, Bill shared how he felt that the secret of Miles' exceptional playing was that he wasn't hiding behind his skill set, and he knew when to juxtapose a simple line against fabulous underlying complexity.

Bill opened her car door and helped Fiona out of his car. Under the glow of a nearby street lamp, she'd been imagining him gently lifting her chin until her eyes met his, then leaning in to give her a soft, slow but simple kiss. Instead he reached out his hand, for a handshake.

"Good night, kid," he said. There was something permanent about the way he said his goodbye. She got the sense he wouldn't be calling again. She wasn't sure exactly how she felt about that. Relieved, maybe. Disappointed, definitely.

Despite her conviction that Bill wouldn't ask her for another date, Fiona found herself listening for the phone to ring. She wanted him to call, but she was okay if he didn't. Still, she wanted to be ready. As she sat in the kitchen the next morning, studying, she jumped when the phone did ring. And she was surprised when she realized how disappointed she was to learn it was Uncle Joe.

Fiona loved her uncle, and just hearing his voice distracted her from her focus on Bill. She was so glad he was home from the war, and was doubly glad that he was recovering from his war injuries. She also was happy to chat, since Mother wasn't home. Uncle Joe launched into his exciting news. He was going to have a clean record. All charges against him had been dropped. "Charges, Uncle Joe?" Fiona had no idea what he was talking about. The last she'd heard before now, he was walking again, and had gone back to college, with help from Uncle Sam. Fiona felt slighted by having been kept out of the loop.

There'd been a demonstration on campus, Joe explained. When protesters raised the American flag upside down—a mark of distress in Joe's eyes but disrespect in the eyes of the law—Joe, and the other veterans who had gone with him to rescue the flag, had been arrested with the rest of the protesters. Fiona listened quietly as he went on to vent about "that draft-dodger college president" who'd had them arrested. So, the college administration had strong feelings about not participating in the war, and her uncle felt otherwise. So did the judge, a veteran himself, who promptly dismissed all charges. "Oh, Uncle Joe," Fiona whispered, "I'm so relieved!"

As soon as she hung up the phone, Bill did call. He'd enjoyed their conversations and wanted them to continue. Fiona was delighted. She told him about Joe and what had happened, adding, "I'll bet my Gram would say, 'It could've been worse.'" It also could have been better, she thought, if only people were willing to talk to each other once in a while.

Fiona cut a miniature pink rose from the bush in the backyard and carefully placed it into a tiny bud vase. It was Mother's Day, and she'd put some concerted effort into making her Mother's Day card. She wanted everything to be perfect. Mother was under a self-imposed deadline for her new novel, and had just come into the kitchen from her writing studio, still scribbling notes on a legal pad.

"Happy Mother's Day," Fiona said, presenting her mother with the card and single rose. Mother glanced at it, smiled, and said, "I'll look at that in a moment, Fee; I just need to finish this thought."

Fiona's heart sank a little, but she knew better than to make anything of it. Finally, Mother set down her pencil and took a sip of her coffee, which had been cooling on the counter.

"How do you write so many books, Mother? How do you think of that many stories? And why murder mysteries?" Fiona asked.

"It gets easier with practice," she answered, and took another sip of coffee. Deciding perhaps that she'd come upon a teaching moment, she added, "The murder, itself, is just a MacGuffin, which means a vehicle for exploring people. It's all about character dynamics, really—the old drama triangle of victim, persecutor, and savior. So, the murder is just the human element that gives me a chance to make the story interesting. Ironically, to come to life.

"Let me know if you think this scenario is plausible. Let's say it's set on Mother's Day. Your protagonist or main character is a young man who decides that rather than help the kids make their mother breakfast in bed, reinforcing their connection, he'll just take the kids out to eat, making himself look like a hero to the kids, for 'giving Mom a break,' while subtly chipping away at the fragile maternal bond. Exchanging obvious 'pity the poor dad' looks with a waitress, he makes sure she will remember him. When he comes home, what does he find? Mother's dead. Conveniently, he has a great alibi. But is he guiltless? Who dunnit?"

Fiona didn't care for the set-up. "I don't know, Mother. It seems to me the guy should've helped the kids pour her some cold cereal or something, and then take them all out. Then, nothing bad would've happened, and he'd be a real hero. Why not make the guy a mensch?"

Mother just stared at Fiona blankly, saying nothing, which told Fiona she wasn't pleased with her idea. Rising to the challenge her mother seemed to have presented, Fiona asked, "Okay, so, how about turning the human element on its head, maybe by introducing aliens? Maybe the father investigates and saves the kids after the mother is eaten by aliens? You'd have a dinner-murder mystery plot twist."

Fiona could see her mother wasn't moved by that one, so she tried again.

"Okay, scratch that. How about a tropical disease, introduced by the government, to take over your brain? And then, there's this hero scientist who…"

Mother cut short her story line. Turning her attention back to her writing pad, she said, "Okay, Fiona, thanks for your input. I've got to get back to it."

Fiona felt confused by the interaction. Why did she even come into the kitchen if she didn't want to talk? Fiona fingered the pretty rose, lingering in the vase and looked at the card she'd so carefully created for her mother—neither even noticed during their brief exchange in the kitchen. This Mother's Day was dying its own slow death, and it was a complicated crime scene.

Fiona was in a mood. And not a good one. Mother's Day might be a cliché started by a greeting card company, but it felt important to Fiona, and the day's events had thrown Fiona into a funk. Fiona decided to call Mary. She never felt lonely at Mary's, except when she stopped to realize this fun-loving family was not hers. She was just reaching for the phone, when it rang. She was not surprised to find it was Mary.

"Hey! I was just about to call you! Wanna get together?"

"Yes, I do," said Mary. "Fee, I need you to come over, right now. It's the dog. He ate…something. We need to get him to the vet."

With Mother's permission, Fiona hopped on her bike and pedaled as fast as she could, down the street to Mary's. Winded, she set her bike just inside the gate and ran up the walk to the front door. Mary's family had long since established that Fiona was family and could just let herself in. She ran to the kitchen, where she found Mary cradling Bailey, her golden retriever puppy, in a terrycloth towel.

"He can barely stand up, Fee. I'm really worried."

"What in the world did he eat?"

"Brownies. Like, all of them. And they were, um…they weren't mine. They came from a friend, someone you know, who left them here. That doesn't matter. They were, um, special brownies wrapped in foil. Somehow Bailey got into them. Can you help me get him to the vet? Mom will kill me if Bailey bites it."

"He's not going to die, Mare." Fiona hoped it more than she believed it, as she helped her friend set Bailey inside the basket on her bike. Everyone knows dogs aren't supposed to eat chocolate, that chocolate can kill a dog, she thought. But I have no idea what hash will do to a dog. Surely the vet will know.

Mary climbed on her bike, and the two friends rode as fast as they could with the puppy to the emergency veterinary clinic downtown.

~o0O0O0o~

Dr. Bishop, the veterinarian both Mother and Mary's mom regularly used, happened to be staffing the emergency clinic that Sunday. He was not fazed, neither by the girls' panic nor the puppy's condition. He'd seen both too many times. When Fiona noticed him glancing from her face to Mary's, presumably studying their eyes, she quickly said, "They weren't our brownies."

"They never are," said Dr. Bishop without a smile, as he tended to Bailey. He gave him an emetic to cause vomiting, and said he'd need to keep him overnight for observation, while he slept off his high. "You know, girls, you put your puppy in considerable danger. No matter whose brownies they were, it was your job to protect your puppy. Do you understand?"

"Yes, doctor," the girls answered, in chorus.

Biking their way back to Mary's house, Fiona feeling relieved, said, "Puppies are so dumb. They go for the chocolate, even though it can kill them."

"Just like people, I guess," Mary agreed.

"Yeah, but people can learn; dogs are just clueless, so they depend on their people. So, a dog can be dumb as a post, so long as his people aren't."

"Okay, Fee, are you saying I'm clueless, or maybe dumb as a post?"

"Ouch, no. No way. Never." Fiona backtracked hastily. "You're going to be a great therapist someday, Mary," Even as she apologized, she couldn't help thinking, *No way I'd ever poison Starlight with hash brownies. Not me.*

Back at Mary's, the girls headed straight for her room and fell backwards together on the bed. "Revive me, Johnny, I'm totally wiped out!" Mary laughed, putting on a Johnny Cash tape. Country music wasn't Fiona's favorite, but she wasn't about to complain, as he crooned "You Are My Sunshine." That song got Fiona thinking about Pop, and how he'd often played it for her, drunk and sappy, and told her how raising her was the only thing of value he'd ever done. *Yeah, right!*

When Mary's mother, Bea, got home, the girls simply told her that Bailey had eaten some chocolate, and the vet wanted to keep him overnight, just to be sure he was fine. Dr. Bishop had been clear but also cool with them, and Mary and Fiona felt he would keep their secret.

"That must have been traumatizing for you two, as well as the poor little puppy," said Bea. "I applaud you for your quick, responsible actions. But I still wish you'd called me. I could have helped." She made a pot of chamomile tea and invited the girls to sit down. "I'm sorry I don't have any cookies or brownies to offer you girls." She smiled, adding, "It seems my dog has wolfed down the whole stash."

Fiona didn't dare look at Mary. She didn't quite know if Mary's mother was wise to them, or not. She guessed the former. Bea was raising her two kids on her own after her husband had been killed in Vietnam, and she was supporting them through her work as a nurse practitioner and classical homeopath. Fiona wasn't entirely sure what all that meant, but she sensed Bea was a wise woman.

"I'm glad you're here, Fiona," said Bea, between sips of tea. "I've been thinking I might be able to help you with your migraines. Of course, you'd have to ask your mother, first." Fiona was open to anything that might help. She borrowed a book from Bea on homeopathy, wanting to know more, right away. "Meanwhile," said Bea, "Why don't you think of those migraines as a pot that's simmering just below boil? A lot of things in life can make us boil over, so you need to focus on what you can control to reduce the heat and help everything simmer down."

Fiona thought for a moment. "So, before my head boils over, I should simmer down? But it's not anger. They just arrive."

"If you tracked them, you might not think that. You might find connections. You might find it worthwhile to stay clear of the things that might trigger a flare-up."

"Such as?"

"You won't like it, Fiona. You start by steering clear of a bunch of things you probably love, and then slowly reintroduce them, and see if they trigger a flare. I'd say for a lot of people, MSG and preservatives are on the top of the list, followed by yeasty bread, gooey cheese, caffeine, bananas, peanuts, and chocolate. Oh, and the nightshade family."

"So, basically everything I love eating. Is that all? What's left?

And, by caffeine, do you mean no more tea? I mean, why even wake up? Besides, it's a monthly problem, so there's nothing I can do about them anyway, right?"

"Well, hormones add a wallop, but it's other things that also fill the pot and make a boil-over more likely. You can also take down the heat. Maybe try that biofeedback machine of yours, or even some quiet time with your dog."

Before Fiona could respond, Mary chimed in. "Too many choices, Mom. Here's a choice, Fiona. We can stay here or head out. Not pizza. I hear you. So, how about The Med?" suggested Mary. "I bet some of the gang will meet us there. Want me to make some calls? We could make plans to go see that new 'Rocky Horror' thing." Fiona had been wanting to see *The Rocky Horror Picture Show*, dressed up like one of the characters in the movie, and throw toast into the air. "Mom, can Fiona borrow some of your old nursing stuff? She wants to go to the show as a nurse."

Bea offered Fiona one of her old nursing uniforms without question. "Why don't you leave it here until you need it, Fee? You don't need to drag it around in your bicycle basket."

"Okay, back to choices," said Mary. "The Med or Zach's house?"

"Zach's."

7. TRIPS

Fiona knew that her friend Zach's parents were often away, which made his house the perfect gathering spot for their small circle of close friends: Becca, Mary, Fiona, Zach, and Quinn. They'd get together on a whim, often for no reason at all. It was enough just to hang out and enjoy each other's company. Zach was the oldest of the group, and he also was the wildest and funniest of the five friends: bright and beautiful, like a comet about to crash land. A former high school football star, he'd lost a hunk of his leg in an accident and was slowly self-destructing, buying himself a wild time with what he considered his blood money: the payout from insurance.

Although Fiona couldn't truly fathom what Zach was going through, she remembered her Uncle Joe, walking again and back in college, working hard to turn his Vietnam tragedy into triumph. Not Zach. And not Zach's parents. Zach had said his introduction to drugs had been at 11, when his dad had given him his first line of coke. Now, it helped him feel invincible, despite his injury. He liked to keep cocaine in a sterling-silver vial, with the tiniest silver spoon Fiona had ever seen, dangling from a chain around his neck.

Sometimes, well honestly, most of the time, when the friends were all together, Zach would take a dollar bill out of his wallet, fold over one edge to keep it in place as he rolled it up into a little straw, then slip into the bathroom to snort a bit of the white powder into his nose, "for luck." As he came out, sniffling, Fiona wondered what kind of luck he expected it to bring.

As soon as everyone had gathered at Zach's, he pulled out his stash, and began preparing a joint. He pulled a bud out of his bag, crushed it, and removed the stems and seeds. Then he joined two Zig Zag rolling papers, and carefully rolled his joint. He licked the edges of the papers, pressed them together, twisted the ends, and held up his masterpiece. Zach considered himself an expert. It was, everyone admitted, nicely done. He'd gotten a lid, about an ounce, of Mexican pot for about $15, which was a lot cheaper, yet stronger, than the stuff he usually got from Oregon or Humboldt County. The stuff gave him a pretty good buzz, which helped him get through the day.

Zach held up the joint, proud of his prowess, his position in the group, and the quality of his pot. "Shall we?" he asked his friends, and then waited for their typically awesome answers. He started them off, looking right at Mary, "Is the Pope Catholic?"

Mary, "Can you teach your pet rock to stay?"

Quinn, "Haw! Hey, do vacuum cleaners suck?"

Fiona, "Do Vulcans live long and prosper? Or wait, what about, Are pies square?"

Zach pulled out a lighter, lit the joint, and took in a long, slow drag. Instantly, his eyes began to water, and his voice came out in a tight rasp. "Hell, yeah, math-head. πr^2!"

"Hey, do we have any pie for later?" asked Mary. "Like, real pie. You know, apple or something."

"Does it look like my mom's the happy homemaker type?" answered Zach. "She wouldn't know a rolling pin if you threw it at her. Might be some leftover Indian food from the other day."

The thought of Indian food made Fiona's mouth water. Funny, she thought to herself. I thought I'd hate it forever, and it's maybe my favorite. "Meh," said Mary. "Let's not and say we did. Got any Cheez-Its or Red Vines or Pringles?" she asked, adding, "You know we're going to get the munchies."

Becca grabbed the joint from Zach, took a deep toke, held her breath a moment, and then passed the joint to Fiona who, as she'd so often done since she was a young child, just passed it along. Some things never change. Like munchies, Fiona thought. Fiona still held her breath—the smell brought up too many bad memories—but these were the friends she knew and loved, and this was their world.

"Anyone ever heard of astral projection?" Quinn asked no one in particular.

"I almost did it, once," said Zach. "I figured it would be a wild ride. But that's not the kind of sex I'm into."

"What does sex have to do with astral projection?" Fiona asked. "Astral projection is about having an out-of-body experience, like through mental telepathy or hallucinogens." She remembered having a conversation about it, over that Tequila Sunrise with Karen. "I promised I'd never try it."

"Promised who?" asked Zach, poking Fiona in the arm. "C'mon, Fee, Who? Who? And why not?"

"Hoohoo. You sound like an owl," Fiona said. "I'll tell you who, my older sister, Karen."

"I didn't know you had an older sister," he said. "I didn't know you had a sister at all. Aren't you an only child?"

"There's a lot you don't know about me, Mister." Fiona certainly felt like an only child, most of the time.

"You shouldn't do that, Zach," said Mary, "the out-of-body thing. I heard about this one person who tried to come back but found her body was possessed by an evil spirit. You can't just leave your body unprotected like that."

"Come on, Mary. You're so superstitious." Zach rolled his eyes, and, another joint. "Next thing you'll tell me is my head will spin around, and I'll spew pea soup like Linda Blair in *The Exorcist*. By the way, don't step on a crack…unless it's cocaine. And then don't step on it, snort it. Ha!"

"You can laugh if you want," Mary answered, darkly, "but if you leave your physical house empty, it's wide open for anyone to take up residence. And, from what I've heard, it isn't easy to get these squatters out. Still, if you summon the Holy Spirit…"

"C'mon, Mary, you're bringing down my buzz." All this heavy talk was bumming out Becca, who threw a pillow at Mary and called her a "jive turkey." At that, all the friends joined in, grabbing and tossing decorative pillows at each other, some of which split at the seams, effectively stopping the conversation with a feather storm.

"Okay," said Zach. "Onto the next subject. Who has something better than astral projection?"

"You have a one-track mind, Zach." Fiona knew Zach had eyes for Becca, and he seemed to be doing his best to seduce her with his bravado. She also knew both Becca and Mary thought Quinn would be a catch, if only he were straight. Fiona, the "bookworm baby sister" to the group, hadn't taken that kind of interest in anyone in their group.

The room fell silent for a while, everyone except Fiona enjoying their buzz, until Becca asked, "Um…anyone ever heard of a key party?" Becca said she knew her parents went to them sometimes. "From what I understand, here's how it works. All the men, upon arrival to the party, put their car keys in a bowl by the door. Toward the end of the party, when everyone is sufficiently drunk and thinking about going home, each woman reaches into the bowl, grabs a set of keys, and heads home with the driver of that car for the rest of the night. What happens, is up to them, and no one is supposed to discuss it in the morning."

"What if they're gay?" asked Fiona.

Quinn was genuinely puzzled. "You mean, like, what if they're gay and married to someone straight? Or, what would happen if two gay guys crashed a straight married-couples' key party?"

"Right. Never mind. Stupid question."

The friends looked around at each other, silent.

Becca batted her eyes at Quinn. "Whatever floats their boat, right?" She loved his shaggy blond, surfer-dude hair and green eyes, and since he was gay, he was safe to tease.

"I don't know, Becca." Mary blushed as Quinn batted Mary's hand from his hair. She didn't like this kind of teasing and she was beginning to like keys and bowls even less. "Women go along, but what choice do they really have if he's the breadwinner? You know why they call it wife-swapping and not husband-swapping? Because it's the woman who gets tossed around. She gets the shaft, if you'll pardon my drift."

"The shaft? That's rich! You slay me, Mary, you really do!" Zach laughed. By now, he was too high and laughing too hard at her unintended joke to listen to or care about what she wanted to say next. But Becca cared. She was having none of it.

"Don't paint us as the victims here, Mary," Becca replied. "We're very free not to fish the keys out of the bowl. We can study or marry or have kids or not have them, as we choose. We need to stand up and be the hero in our own stories. It's about choices. Self-care. That's all I'm saying." She pretended to light up a cigarette. "We've come a long way, baby!"

"You, in a Virginia Slims cigarette commercial," said Fiona. "I like it. We're free to light up and die from emphysema, too." She admired Becca for not just thinking but also voicing her powerful thoughts, standing up for what she believed and how she saw herself. She already knew, for Becca, self-care ran the gamut, from acupuncture to Zen practice, and included sleep, raw food and living in gratitude, plus doing "whatever turns you on," including acid, weed and, apparently, sex.

Fiona was really getting into what Becca had said. It was like her own high. Self-care seemed like an important concept—practice, even—she thought.

Fiona's Rule #7: Practice Self-Care.

As Fiona wondered whether she might be getting too old to be making up life rules, her musings were interrupted by Mary, continuing the conversation.

"Becca's right," said Mary. "Women have rights. No more stoning to death, no more prison for adultery. No more weeks in Las Vegas, awaiting a divorce decree. But, did you know that 20 years ago, a woman could undergo a forced hysterectomy just for disobeying her father or husband?"

"In what country?" said Becca.

"This one, you idiot. I'm not kidding," said Mary. "I read about it in *Cosmo*."

"You're pulling my leg," said Becca. "I don't remember reading that."

"No, truly. Diagnosis: hysteria," said Mary. "Hysteria-hysterectomy; the removal of hysteria. No lie. Just 20 years ago."

"And I thought getting the right to vote was rough," said Becca. "I wonder how many of those suffragettes who had our back, had to lose their womanhood on account of a pissed-off husband. Now, we've got women handing it out to a guy with a set of car keys. Women like to get off, too, you know. Love your neighbor as yourself. That can mean a lot of things."

"That's right out of the Bible," said Mary. "Jesus said it. But can you please not twist it like that? You know it bugs me when you do that."

The conversation was getting a bit out of hand, And the guys, enjoying their high more than the girls or their conversation, had been completely left out of it. Fiona, watching the conversation and the comfort in the room deteriorate, stepped in. "Hey guys, we seem to have spiraled into such a downer," she said. "How about we talk about something else? The weather would be more fun than this. Anything else, except maybe Mother's Day. What do you say?"

Both Becca and Mary sat in silence for a moment before Mary spoke. "Fiona's right. Let's drop it. Is anyone hungry? I know I am. I've got dinner plans with my mom later but I'm hungry now." The mood in the room was already lifting as the friends headed into Zach's kitchen to see what looked good. Nothing.

"Hey, let's all go down to The Med and see what's happening," he said. "We could all use a change of scene, and some chow."

"Maybe they'll have a key bowl at the door," said Becca.

"Let it go, girl," said Mary. "Let it go."

Mary and Fiona settled into their usual table upstairs at Caffé Mediterraneum, joining the rest of their friends from Zach's. "Omigosh, this is heaven," said Fiona, biting into her favorite pastry, a bear claw. It was almost as big as her face, and she was planning on eating all of it. The rich, buttery semicircle of pastry was filled with almond paste and soft raisins, and drizzled with icing.

"Hey, do you think this bear claw is as big as a real bear claw?" Fiona asked, taking a break from eating, to appraise her pastry.

"It won't be by the time you're done with it," answered Mary. "Are you going to save me a bite, or what?" Mary grabbed the pastry from the plate, took a big bite out of it, and passed it to Quinn on her right. "Hey, wait a minute! Give it back." With one swift move, Mary had turned a personal pastry into a communal claw. Within moments, it was but a sweet memory. Fiona considered replacing it, but she knew it would meet with the same end. Next time, she thought, I'll just wolf it down on my way from the counter to the table. She smiled at the imagery that created. Wolfing down a bear. A daughter of Wolf, no less.

~o0O0O0o~

Fiona, who'd missed the Mother's Day breakfast she'd imagined she'd share with Mother, who'd skipped lunch in favor of rescuing Mary's puppy from the pot brownies, was famished. Maybe if I'd had a chance to eat my bear claw, she thought, I wouldn't still be hungry now. But, she was, and so was Mary.

"So, what's for dinner?" As usual, Mary had read Fiona's mind. Since the group was planning to see *Rocky Horror*, and since they all knew so much about the movie already, she'd used a line from the movie. "Meatloaf again?" They all yelled back. Fiona had been hungrily eyeing the toast Mary had left on her plate. She continued the game, "How about a toast?" Mary threw her toast at Fiona, who caught it, smothered it with jam, and took a big, loud bite.

Fiona looked at the faces laughing round the table and thought, these are my people, my real and true friends. They got her jokes, and she got theirs. Their joshing was all in good fun, never mean spirited. They weren't afraid to speak their minds, yet they had each other's backs. They could go deep into dialogue or keep it light. They even shared bear claws; it was almost tribal.

Mid-frivolity, Fiona made eye contact with the "Bubble Lady," a name they'd given to an older woman who was often at The Med as well, blowing bubbles and trying to sell copies of her poetry books. She'd printed them herself, around the corner at Krishna Copy. She seemed more than proud of her work; within those pages one would discover who she was and what she represented. She looked about twice the age of Mother, which meant she might be in her 80s. But, unlike the octogenarians Fiona knew, who wore lace collars adorned with a strand of pearls, the Bubble Lady was decked out in a clownish costume. Fiona kind of liked the baggy pants, paired with a brightly colored shirt, several colorful scarves, and a rakish hat set upon a wild mane of curly red hair. Not for herself, but the look really worked well for this bold woman, who didn't seem to care about what others thought.

But maybe she does care, Fiona decided. Who would dress like that if they weren't seeking attention, if not approval? Besides, she did want people to buy her poetry.

"What's up with the old beatnik?" Zach asked. "I see her, sometimes, over in People's Park." There were rumors about some of the people there having been handed one-way Greyhound bus tickets westward after Medicaid stopped paying for psychiatric inpatients during the "great deinstitutionalization" that began in '65.

People's Park. Fiona felt that deep inner cringe when she thought of that parcel of land "won" through protests a while back, now home to drifters and panhandlers and all kinds of people who just couldn't figure out how to participate in a society any bigger or more complex than that stretch of weeds. Some of them, she imagined, had even stuck around since the Summer of Love.

Like most of her friends, Fiona avoided People's Park. Part of it was a matter of following her mother's rules, and the other part was that she was too scared to go there, anyway. Pop would say they were just people, perhaps more harmless than the guys she'd encounter on Wall Street. Fiona had no intention of going there, either.

She thought about the Joan Baez tune, "There but for Fortune," about how kids like her could just as easily go down bad roads. She hadn't made the connection before this, and she certainly couldn't envision herself being as old or careworn as the Bubble Lady. But, she thought, the Bubble Lady was once young, just like me.

~oOOOOo~

After the movie, Fiona and Mary made their way back to Mary's house, where Fiona said goodbye to her friend and continued pedaling down the street to Mother's. What had begun as a quiet Mother's Day at home had turned into a kaleidoscope of activity and emotion. She certainly understood that it was a wild and crazy time to be alive: a time to think, to believe, to seek.

For now, she thought she might put on some music, and take a long, hot bubble bath. Well, maybe no bubbles this time. She parked her bike and came through the side door, which led to the kitchen. There, in the waning light, she saw the pale pink rose she had plucked from the garden for Mother that morning, drooping in its vase; some of its petals already drying on the counter. Nearby, lay her Mother's Day card. Was it unopened? Fiona couldn't tell.

Today, she thought, was not much of a Mother's Day. Oh well, I dub it "Fiona's Day." So there. With that, her hand hit the counter like a resounding gavel. Mother's poodle raised a sleepy eyebrow, noticed it was only Fiona, and went back to sleep.

Speaking to nobody in particular, Fiona asked, "Anybody need me down here? Didn't think so. Well, I'll be off then," Bowing to the poodle, Fiona added, "Dear sir, I bid you my fond adieu. My lady, would you do me the honor of accompanying me?" She picked up Starlight and wandered upstairs to draw her bath.

~oOOOOo~

The summer days dawned warm and breezy. Zach's parents had been on a vacation for a couple of months, and he, as usual, had the run of the house. Mother was on a fact-finding mission for her newest mystery novel, and Mary's parents were visiting her older brother at college. Becca and Quinn were just as free and clear; somehow, they'd come upon a perfect storm of opportunity.

Only two weekends were left before Zach's parents came home, signaling the end of summer, and the friends planned to make the most of every remaining moment.

The only rule the five friends set for themselves those remaining weekends was to have each other's backs. Even so, they'd decided those lame kinds of questions that sometimes come up for first-timers when tripping, such as, "Hey, what if you're not really here? What if you're in my imagination? What if we don't really exist?" were off limits. It was, after all, so "high school." Still, since they'd promised to avoid putting each other's ideas down. If someone felt like saying "That's so lame," they had to say "Groovy," instead. Most of all, everyone was supposed to have fun.

Fiona parked her bike against the side of Zach's house and let herself in through the side door to the kitchen, just as she did at Mother's. Mary was unloading food, and Becca was making sandwiches. They looked up at Fiona with a smile that said, "Welcome to the club." Fiona set her food contributions on the counter, mostly things that wouldn't ignite a migraine, and went into the living room in search of Zach and Quinn. Mary and Becca soon followed.

Zach was slouched in a La-Z-Boy recliner, strumming his dad's Stratocaster electric guitar. Quinn was hanging out on the couch, rolling a joint and pretty much looking like it wasn't his first hit of the day.

"Quinn, you're stoned!"

"Ya think?" he grinned. Mary had such a gift for stating the obvious.

"That's so..." Mary realized she couldn't finish her sentence. "Groovy. That's so groovy." Everyone laughed.

"What's that smell?" Zach sniffed, as Fiona walked past, "Patchouli? My mom wears that stuff. You know what it smells like? Smells like bad parenting, that's what."

Fiona, mortified, headed to the bathroom to scrub the Patchouli off her neck.

"Come on," said Zach, after Fiona had rejoined the others, "I have a plan."

The friends all crammed into Zach's Honda 600, a hand-me-down from his parents. Their destination, college apartment housing near the U.C. Berkeley campus, was only five minutes away—slightly too far to walk, but within range of the six-gallon gas tank. As the friends piled out of the car following Zach's erratic drive there, Fiona was wishing they'd walked, anyway.

Still not entirely sure about Zach's plan, Fiona followed him and the others up the stairs and into a smoke-filled apartment; its atmosphere was dark and heavy. Zach signaled everyone to wait as he went into the bedroom to transact the deal. Fiona surveyed the room. Over the door jam, someone had scribbled the phrase, "Courage is destiny." It seemed out of place.

Two people were leaning up against the wall. One, as gaunt as any beggar Fiona had met in India, had pinched a yellow rock between two fingers and was slipping it into the stem of a clear glass pipe. The other took a lighter and brought its flame up gently to the black end of the pipe, while the first inhaled deeply, as if the smoke were more precious than air itself. They motioned to her as if to ask, "Wanna try?"

Fiona wasn't sure how to respond. "What is it?" she asked, trying to be polite.

"Crack cocaine. It's just another way to do coke," came the reply, "The high is better. First hit's always free…"

"That's okay, I've got to catch up with my friends anyway."

They laughed and lost interest. A shiver ran down her spine; she wanted to run from the apartment. But her feet remained rooted to the floor. Why? Fear? Fascination? Maybe it was a lapse into that "groupthink" mentality Pop had taught her about, where people abandon their individuality just to belong. A few minutes later, and not a moment too soon for Fiona, they were on their way back to Zach's Honda. "Score!" Zach said, once outside the apartment, smiling broadly.

"I call shotgun!" Quinn hollered, as Zach hopped into his seat and reached over to unlock the passenger door.

"If you go straight a few blocks, we could hit a 7-11," Mary suggested, hopping in the back, next to Fiona.

"Bravely forward, dear." Quinn quipped. "It's not straight, it's bravely forward." Everybody laughed. Quinn was new to being out, and loved reminding his friends that he was gay, as if to remind himself that his friends were still supportive.

During the ride back to the house, Zach explained his plan. "So, 'shrooms this weekend and acid next. Good stuff...It'll be the trippiest summer yet."

Fiona looked at the wrinkled, brown desiccated mushrooms Zach handed her and remembered she'd read how Amanita phalloides or "death cap" and Amanita pantherina or "panther cap" mushrooms could look just like their edible or psychedelic cousins. Death caps, she knew from one of Mother's murder mystery plots, were as tasty as they were toxic. Destroying the liver, they were responsible for more deaths than any other mushroom, by far. She examined one more closely.

At least it wasn't a muscaria, Fiona reasoned, which although quite hallucinatory, was also toxic. No, those were red, and more useful for killing flies than tripping out. She was proud of her knowledge. Yet, without another thought, and well before her intuition kicked in, she popped hers in her mouth, as did the others. They certainly didn't taste like those delicious sautéed mushrooms from Gram's boeuf bourguignon, Fiona thought. In fact, they were kind of grody. Good, she thought, relieved by the disgusting taste. It must mean she hadn't consumed death caps.

"Anybody hungry?" Zach asked, turning the car toward Telegraph Avenue. Fifteen minutes later, they'd parked near People's Park and had climbed out of the car, in search of food. Bad idea. Halfway down the block, Mary said, "Hey, I'm kinda freaking out here. Can we go back, maybe?"

Mary's friends turned around at once, realized she wasn't kidding, and turned back toward the car. Zach headed back to the house, at once. Once safe inside, Mary headed toward the couch, to lie down. Quinn got her a pillow, from the bedroom. Fiona covered her with a blanket, and spent the rest of the afternoon sitting beside her, waiting for the high to pass, so they could go home. A few hours later, Mary sat up. Zach plopped down next to her with a glass of water.

"That was different," Mary said, weakly.

"Okay, maybe it wasn't the best," he said. "Next week will be better. Best trip ever. Everything copacetic. Promise."

Fiona wondered if she should go back to Zach's the following weekend. Her friends seemed so enthused. Even Mary. Why hadn't it worked for her? Zach was especially excited about the acid. He said he'd been told it was as pure as it gets, and he'd paid quite a price for it. They'd stock the fridge and pick out great music. They'd even put super-cool sheet music on the piano, in case anyone got inspired.

When Fiona showed up at the house a week later, ready for the acid adventure with her friends, Zach was in his favorite spot, playing guitar in the living room. His house didn't have a pool, but his parents had put in a hot tub, so Fiona had packed her swimsuit. She had a feeling everyone else would go skinny dipping under the stars, but she wasn't sure she was ready for that. No, she was certain she was not.

It was a beautiful Sunday. There was plenty of food, and nobody would have to leave and interact with anyone outside. In fact, they made a pact that they wouldn't go out for any reason. They didn't have to; they'd planned it all out very well, they thought.

Fiona began to wonder about their commitment to stay in the house all weekend and interact with nobody but themselves. What if she wanted out? What if she got scared? What if she felt claustrophobic and needed air? What if she got tired of hanging out with her wild and crazy group of friends? What if she ended up wishing she'd spent the weekend walking Starlight or riding her bike in the sun?

You blew off the coolest guy and bailed on the most amazing day on the Bay with these same friends, Fiona told herself. You got yourself all worked up, you started second-guessing yourself, and *you turned tail and practically back-pedaled all the way home. Are you really going to do that again? Maybe your gut instincts aren't as finely tuned as you thought. Maybe you should just be gutsy. Go for it, for once in your life.*

With butterflies in her stomach, Fiona eyed the collection of paper squares Zach had laid out on the coffee table. They looked like something you'd give a little kid—temporary tattoos, maybe, or stickers. *This is going to be way better than 'shrooms,* she told herself. *Like Pop says, "Better living through chemistry."* She smiled, thinking of her father, as if he had her back.

"Let's get this party started!" Zach set down his father's guitar, went over and picked up a slip of paper, gesturing for the others to do the same. Each placed the paper on their tongue, smiley face up, and sat back to let the acid take effect.

Nothing. Nothing at all.

In all my concerns, I didn't expect to be disappointed, Fiona thought.

Suddenly, she felt relaxed—no, more than relaxed. She felt euphoric, really. One part giddy, one part silly, and one part purely optimistic. Fiona was inspired, life was magical—she was capable of anything. Intrigued by the colorful little dots that seemed to frame everything in the room, she found them unfamiliar, unlike the sparklies she'd come to know so well, but not threatening. She kind of liked them. Maybe the sparklies and the dots were friends. Or cousins. Kissing cousins. She got up from her easy chair, sashayed over to Zach, planted a kiss on his nose and then giggled. He wasn't startled. Neither was she. "Does that make us cousins, Zach? Are we kissing cousins?"

Fiona wandered over to the grand piano and pinged a note, aware of the aura surrounding her fingers. In a sing-song voice that began with the same note, she said, "My hands are magic!" She leaned in close to the piano and took in a drag of air. "Hey! This note smells like chocolate! Chocolate in the key of G. Who wants chocolate?" She licked the key. "It even tastes like chocolate! It's a chocolate piano! Now that's music to my ears."

"No, this note smells like lemons," said Becca, tapping a different key. "And this one is raspberry! We're in the middle of *Charlie and the Chocolate Factory*. Hey, Augusta Gloop," she said to Mary, "come tell us which one tastes like blueberries."

Mary didn't respond. She was too busy hiding behind the strands of her long, blonde hair, which she had draped across her face.

"I'm gonna go get me some ice cream to go with that piano," said Zach, as he disappeared into the kitchen. He was gone quite a while. When he finally returned to the living room, he was carrying, not the ice cream, but a bottle of beer. "I propose a toast," he said, flinging his arm in the air, which caused him to lose balance and sit down, hard, his beer bottle emptying into the carpet.

"Here's mud in your eye," he said, retrieving and hoisting his nearly empty bottle into the air.

"More like mud on the rug," said Becca, "and you're all wet."

"Jesus put mud in your eye, and you're not blind," said Mary from behind her veil of hair.

"Far out, man! That's so wizard, Miss Mary, Mary, quite contrary." Zach had no clue what her biblical reference meant or that it was one. He was preoccupied with the swimming and sliding of things normally thought to be solid, like the chair he was certain couldn't hold him, and the table whose legs were melting. Like his own were.

"Duck!" Fiona yelled, and everyone did, except Mary, who was already hiding.

"What the hell, Fiona?" asked Quinn.

"Don't you see it?" Fiona was lying on the floor, staring up at the ceiling.

"See what?" came the chorus.

"Duh! The tiger!" she pointed toward the textured ceiling, her finger unable to hold steady. "Up there, look! Wherever it goes, there it is."

Mary, voice muffled from under a blanket where she was now

hiding, asked, "Isn't there a poem about tigers?"

Quinn didn't see the tiger, but he was on board. "Tiger, tiger, burning bright. Hey, if a tiger vanishes in the forest, was it ever really there?"

"If anything vanishes in the forest, who the hell cares?" asked Zach.

"Fiona, give us a little music on that piano before it melts," said Quinn. "Give us a reason to dance, Baby. C'mon, it's time for a little get down and boogie."

"Does anybody really know what time it is?" sang Becca.

"Does anybody really care?" Zach continued the song.

That call-and-response from the song by Chicago struck Fiona as both beautiful and profound. She wanted to play it on the piano, or at least search for a note that tasted like blueberries. She hit on G and took in the fabulous chocolate emanating from the instrument. "Omigosh, I love you guys! Like, I really love you. I love us. You know what I mean? We need to stay friends forever."

"We can't stay friends forever, Fiona," said Zach, who'd noticed his nose was running. "I'm dying. Don't you know that? Can't you tell? I'm melting, right into the carpet." Zach, beginning to panic about his runny nose and to question the source and quality of acid he'd purchased, began a slow wail, that escalated into a scream.

He'd gambled, buying that acid. How could he be sure, as he'd been promised, that the great acid maker—who'd made a local legend of himself selling his wares for local Grateful Dead concerts—had indeed made this particular batch? What if it was a knock-off? What if it was laced with strychnine? "Get me to the hospital," he said, crawling across the carpet. "Get me to the hospital. GET. ME. THERE. NOW!"

Fiona got that Zach was serious, and so did the others. His high had hit the stratosphere. They just didn't know what to do about it. Had he taken more than they had? Together, they decided they needed to get him to Alta Bates Hospital. He didn't look so good. They looked out the window at Zach's car. It was alive; they could see it breathing, but they couldn't be sure where it would take them. They decided to walk.

Thirty-seven minutes later, the five friends stumbled into the emergency room at Alta Bates, all holding onto Zach. The receptionist took one look at the loopy group and knew exactly what she was dealing with. She ushered them into an examining room, and, without a word, pressed each kid into a chair. Then, before leaving, she asked, "How many hours so far?" Best they could tell, it had been four hours.

The attending physician pulled out his pen light and shined it into the eyes of each patient. He realized they were in better shape than they thought they were, better than most of the kids he'd treated, better than those sad cases he had lost to overdoses. Most acid trips he'd seen had lasted only six to eight hours, and if they'd been poisoned, they'd have known about it much earlier.

"I'm Dr. Stu Kadish. Call me Dr. Stu. It's good you came in. You look like bright kids…" he began.

"We are!" said Fiona, "even him." She pointed to the tiger that had followed them to the hospital and taken up residence on the ceiling. "He's burning bright!"

"As I was saying," he pressed his forefinger against his lips, inviting Fiona to be quiet. "You look like bright kids. But what you did today was not bright. You just can't do drugs. You have no idea what they'll do to you. You guys are going to be okay—this time. Another time, you might not be so lucky. You're on a treacherous path, and you have no idea the bad places it could lead. I've seen beautiful kids die from overdoses. I don't want to see that happen to you.

"I've seen bright futures like yours just fade away into addiction. It happens before you know it. I don't like the end of the path I see you taking here, so listen to me. Change your course. And I'll tell you, if I see you in my ER again, I'll turn you in for your own good. You'd better believe I will." He stopped, realizing the limited capacity of his audience.

Fiona knew the nice doctor was speaking, but it all came out like blah, blah, blah. She could sense the concern in his voice, but she was more concerned about the tiger and what it might do. It was like a Japanese origami tiger, just two dimensions of folded translucent paper, but alive, and moving along the ceiling. Then again, Fiona wondered whether it wasn't merely a ceiling tiger, but an inter-dimensional tiger, maybe even a time traveler. She knew it was friendly, but maybe it was tricky, a Cheshire cat of a tiger. She wasn't at all sure it would make a good pet.

She wondered what it might enjoy eating. Where do I buy invisible food? Fiona wondered. And how do I find the invisible tiger-food market? By following invisible signs? As she watched the tiger chase its tail, a thought occurred: what about chocolate music? Would that be good for you, my tiger? She had no idea how to take care of a pet tiger. Even a translucent one. Or an origami one.

Dr. Stu started talking again, so Fiona turned her attention toward him. But she couldn't really see him through all the striations of light streaming out of the ceiling light, putting a soft glow on everything in the room. She gazed up at the doctor's face, realizing the glow was creating a soft halo around his head. She liked him; he looked almost holy, like St. Francis, only different.

"Who are you?" she wondered out loud. "Are you a saint?"

"What?" asked Dr. Stu in exasperation.

Now the center of the good doctor's attention, Fiona felt suddenly safe. And she knew that Mary, sitting next to her with her head bowed in what Fiona assumed was prayer, would feel safe, too.

"Listen, kiddo," he continued, "I'm your doctor. I have a daughter about your age. You need to be careful. Take care of yourself. Think about getting yourself some new friends. This is very important to me. Are you hearing me?"

Fiona's mind began to wander, considering whether all doctors were saints, and wondering whether any saints had children. His message was almost missed in the mental mist. Almost. What did get through loud and clear was the doctor's concern for her. A single tear escaped down her cheek as she gazed into his blue eyes. She didn't bother wiping it away, and she didn't care if anyone saw it. You have kind eyes, she thought, but managed only to say, "What about my tiger? Are you hearing him?"

Dr. Stu looked up to where Fiona was pointing, to where her tiger was now snuggled up in a corner. Without hesitation, he said, "And you, Tiger, there. You behave yourself and slowly vanish, then don't bother her again, got it?" He assured Fiona that things would be back to normal in a few hours, although she might be feeling wiped out for a while. He added, "You might want to get some sleep and a little protein, when you can stomach it.

He turned his attentions back to Zach, who was already faring much better, though he hadn't quite landed. It was three more hours before Dr. Stu let the friends leave the hospital and return home, under their own power. He wanted to keep them long enough to feel confident they could make it home. He knew, if he called anyone's parents, these kids were going to be in a world of hurt. They looked like good kids, all of them, and he just hoped they'd get off the drug ride and stay clean.

Leaving the emergency room entrance into the still-bright light of day, Fiona noticed that the tiger had indeed vanished, along with most of the pretty dots that had floated so beautifully around the light fixtures. Fiona's head was clearing. "I think that doctor really cared about us, don't you?" she asked her friends as they walked along the sidewalk. But everyone was quiet, caught up in their own turmoil as they came back down from their long, strange trip. Fiona continued her thought process, but in silence. Maybe some people from that generation, even strangers, are worth listening to, worth trusting, she thought. The idea hit her so hard, she decided, right then and there, she needed to change her thinking about others. All because of one kind practitioner whom she likely would never see again.

Fiona's Rule #2 (Modified)—Trust Wisely.

Until today, Fiona had been a "try anything once" kind of girl— just like my Pop, she told herself—but now, her inner wisdom was whispering about rethinking that strategy. Maybe the doctor had a point. Maybe there were times she could learn from the sidelines, borrowing the wisdom of others as well. Maybe there were times when once was more than enough, when nonce was better than once. I wonder what Pop would say. Can't tell Mother. Heavens forfend! Pop won't judge. And anyway, he's a genius. Pop knows just about everything about everything. Mother's not like that.

Thinking of Pop in this way made her miss him. She missed how his face would light up with that broad smile whenever she came in the room, and how he'd ask, "How's it going, Fabulous Fee?" She missed his big, warm hugs that conveyed all his love. She even missed his terrible jokes and the thunderous laugh that followed, just a little too loud and a little too long. Frankly, she even missed his easy way with swear words. Mother used some profanity in her books, calling it "authentic character development," but not in life, and Fiona doubted she'd welcome it from an authentic daughter. She brushed the thought away and considered instead the questions she wanted to ask him. What would he think? Had she made a good choice? It had felt authentic. What about her friends? She wondered if he'd tell her to move on, as the good doc had, and try to find some different friends to match her new, more sober reality. All perhaps except Mary, who was a forever friend.

The next time Fiona and Pop talked, she brought up her little "trip to Neverland"—Never-Again-Land, as she liked to think of it—over the phone. He thought a while, and then simply said "Such a shame you had a bad experience, Fee. Frisco seems like a groovy place for an acid trip. But do take care of your magnificent mind."

"Nobody from here says 'Frisco,' Pop. It's San Francisco!" Fiona snapped back. She wasn't sure what she'd expected her father to say, and she really didn't know what she'd wanted from him. But that wasn't it. Would she have been satisfied if he'd joked about the dangers of playing amateur chemist with her brain, or made some cool chemistry experiment analogy about brains and acids and maybe being off base? Probably not. Likewise, if he'd said, "Do as I say, not as I do," or, "Bad idea, Fiona, take it from me, I know," she'd have dismissed him as a cliché.

She'd heard from Quinn that he'd gotten a lecture about his brain being like a race car, and he was driving it like a dump truck. Sooner or later, there would be a wreck, or a reckoning. Quinn's parents were no more sober than Pop. Maybe she'd been wanting Pop to get creative, like them. Or maybe, just maybe, now that Pop was in a 12-step program, what she really wanted was for Pop to apologize for all the drugs in her young life. Nobody should be as comfortable around them as she was.

Pop's words of caution may have been lost in the message about the groovy locale, but those of the good doctor continued to ring out, loud and clear. His clear, kind but direct message kept cutting through her cloudy thoughts, clouded perhaps by the sort of second-hand smoke that lingers from mystic meadows. She was considering them, in her heart. In the next few phone calls, Pop didn't raise the issue of drug use again, and neither did Fiona.

~oOOOOo~

Fiona headed downstairs, in answer to her mother's query, "Fiona, would you like to join us this evening?" It was the first time Mother had ever invited her to one of her regular dinners at the exclusive Narsai's restaurant, where she and her writer friends liked to "talk shop" while sipping something from a stem and eating exotic-looking things on small plates. Of course, she was thrilled. Unless there was some catch. "You bet!" she replied, running up-stairs again to change into her interpretation of sophisticated. She knew, in her mother's eyes, it meant a dress. She was back in a flash, wearing her knit dress over knee-high boots, with her hair pulled back, and nothing more than mascara enhancing her young face. Mother nodded approvingly, and together, they headed to Narsai's, in the neighboring town of Kensington, a secluded yet high-end spot where people went to be noticed in a quiet "don't notice me" way.

Mother was a big deal, and Fiona knew it. So did the maître d', who smiled a little too brightly and seated them quickly, just a little too graciously. Mother seemed not to notice. Fiona imagined she was pretending. Mother was good at that.

Mother's friends arrived shortly after, and tucked in to the round table reserved for them. Each greeted Fiona, but she caught them glance at Mother as if to say, "Really? You brought your child?" Mother seemed not to notice.

As soon as the appetizers arrived, Mother, who was writing under a tight deadline as usual, pronounced that she needed their help with a plot device. So, her friends began dreaming up intriguing ways she could kill off the victim in her new novel. Mother set the stage for them with the "strategic equation," the usual structure for her novels. Fiona already knew this meant threat equals target plus actors plus intent.

"I want an elegant plot," Mother said to her friends, eschewing their suggestions. "It must be simple, but not too simple." She turned to her reporter friend. "C'mon, Lee; don't fail me now. What've you got for me?"

As promised, Lee had paid a visit to a bar recognized as a local cop hangout in the city, right near the Chronicle Building at 5th and Mission. It was an open secret that a round of drinks could earn a sleuth all kinds of information about what was going down around town. Although he was in search of ideas only for Peggy's novel, not the usual crime tips he often collected for the *Chron*, he came up empty. Next, he'd tried the 24-hour donut shop at 15th and Mission. Still, nothing. Nada. Zippo. Zilch. Peggy would have to settle for recent headlines for plot fodder. In this regard, San Francisco usually did not disappoint.

"How about a business mogul's daughter is kidnapped and held for ransom, like the Hearst case in '74?"

"No," said Mother. "It's been done. And it's fraught with too many angles. Legal, for one."

"What about a monster like the Zodiac killer, with multiple murders remaining unsolved?"

"Too close for comfort," Mother said.

The conversation turned to assassinations and attempts: Kennedy in '63, King in '68, Ford in '75. Fiona, who'd been politely listening in silence, began to wonder why she'd come and whether all their brainstorming sessions were so dark.

Liam, who was enamored with Ireland, reminded Peggy that she'd yet to touch on the violence in Northern Ireland in any of her best-selling murder mysteries. "If you go there, you've got murder for days, Peggy."

"Let me guess; you're thinking I should name the protagonist Liam?"

"I'm just saying...You could work in something about the smuggling of arms."

Mother picked up the dessert menu. "You've all been enormously helpful," she said, with an eye roll. "Thank you for helping me see what I don't want to do."

The conversation shifted as everyone ordered an aperitif, plus a cheese plate to share. Before taking a sip of her Armagnac, Mother offered it to Fiona to try. Instantly, she coughed. "Omigosh, that's horrible," she choked out. "It tastes like cough syrup."

Liam laughed, as Fiona made a face. "Not quite a shamrock shake, huh Fiona?"

"Not quite Irish coffee, either." Fiona basked in their sudden laughter, feeling like she had a place at the table, after all.

"Sounds to me like your best source for a plotline, Peggy, is your daughter," said Lee. "You can serve your victim a little aperitif, if you know what I mean."

Fiona recognized that when her mother smiled but didn't speak, she had no interest in the discussion. Still, Fiona felt pleased with her participation and made a mental note to use the idea herself, some day."

~oOOoOOo~

Peggy didn't have enough material to develop an idea for her novel, and she knew it. Sitting at her writing desk in what Fiona called her "creative cottage," Peggy scoured the morning papers for clues and came upon an article about an ongoing criminal investigation in Alameda. She decided to investigate. She grabbed a notebook and went into the main house to find her keys. She called up the stairs to Fiona that she'd be out for a while. With more Victorians per capita than San Francisco, and a lagoon for the bodies, Peggy thought it would be the perfect setting for her next crime novel.

She had just parked outside Ole's Waffle Shop, and was considering ducking in for one of their famous 1927 original-recipe waffles, when Peggy saw something she would have been better off not witnessing, something Shakespeare would have called, "murder, most foul," down the street. She watched in horror as a swarthy, disreputable-looking fellow leaned into a vintage Bentley, and fired three bullets into the occupant at point blank range. Because of the fine silencer on his gun, not a sound was heard.

Her hands shaking, she started the engine of her Mercedes and slowly eased it down the street to the police station, where she reported what she'd witnessed. The police took down her information and asked if she'd be willing to testify. She wasn't sure.

Peggy loved writing murder mysteries, but she had no interest in starring in one. She had her privacy, a teen at home, a life. The idea of testifying to what she'd seen made her nervous. Worse than that, she'd been spotted. The perp, a hardened criminal with ties to organized crime, went by the initials JB. He had not only noticed her car; he'd looked up her license plate and had traced it to her. He knew her phone number, where she lived, and with whom.

The threats that came with each call seemed idle at first, but they became more frequent, and each one decidedly creepier than the last. One night, well after dark, JB called and threatened "A Bentley fate for you and your daughter, on Yom Kippur, to atone for daring to tangle with the great JB."

"This makes no sense," Peggy whispered, still holding onto the receiver moments after the call came in. "I am not the evildoer who needs to atone here. And anyway, a Jewish holiday? I'm not even Jewish." She hung up and sat for a moment, tapping her pen against her writing tablet. She wasn't comfortable backing down from bullies.

Fiona had overheard. "Hanna was Jewish," she offered, suddenly missing her dead stepmother. Still, Mother was right, it really made no sense. This JB was probably just toying with them, playing mind games.

~oO0O0Oo~

With Peggy's permission, the FBI put a wiretap on her home

phone to record the calls that came in. In response to the credible threat, an FBI agent suggested she lie low for a while. "Who knew that writing murder mysteries could endanger the author's life?" she muttered. "This is one reason I'm not a reporter. I'm too old for this sort of thing."

Peggy began packing a suitcase and told Fiona to do the same. Having called a friend from her office phone, she'd decided to "lie low" at her friend's cabin in the woods near Lake Tahoe until the court date.

She looked up to see Fiona, lingering in the doorway. "All packed?"

"Mother, if I go with you to Tahoe, I'll miss a lot of school. What if I stay with Bill while you're gone. You know, that guy from the Enneagram group? He's a responsible adult, and I bet he wouldn't mind. Besides, he's off the radar." Fiona had checked, and it was fine with him, though he didn't think Peggy would agree to such a plan.

Peggy stared out the window for a moment, considering the idea. Then, she surprised Fiona by agreeing. Fiona was thrilled. She went upstairs to pack, and as she was packing, she surprised herself by feeling ambivalent about the idea. It's good that Mother trusts my judgment and thinks I can fend for myself, Fiona thought. But wouldn't she want to stick to me like glue, if danger is near? It was weird to feel delighted and disappointed at the same time. At least Mother's not a smother-mother, like I'm in danger of being if I ever dare bringing kids into this insane world.

~oOO0O0o~

Staying at Bill's was surprisingly easy. The conversations they shared reminded her of evenings with Pop. He listened to what she had to say, and responded in ways that made her feel smart. When she left his house for school, she noticed that she lost a sense of security, and found herself on guard every moment until she returned to his home. Somehow, she felt okay there, even though he was often out at night, playing gigs.

As Fiona lay in her makeshift bed in his den, she wondered if she was starting to like-like him again, or if she was just grateful and feeling safe in his company. She decided it would not be cool to test it out, and let herself slip into sleep instead.

The heightened threat level subsided after Mother's court appearance a few weeks later, when she bravely testified to what she'd seen. JB negotiated a plea bargain, and was safely behind bars. Fiona and her mother returned to the Berkeley bungalow and to their routines. Everything was back to normal, wasn't it?

Wolf wasn't so sure. He hadn't heard about the traumatic experience until after it was over, and now he was livid. "Are you trying to get our daughter killed, Peggy?" he raged across the phone. Thinking back to the car accident she'd had with the infant Fiona, he realized he'd entered tenuous territory, but he didn't care. "Wasn't it enough that you almost pulled it off once before?"

"Don't you dare, Wolf," she said, evenly. Peggy knew, if he thought about it for even a moment, that he, too, had a treacherous tale in his past. Still he raged, so she held the receiver away from her ear to tolerate the volume. Peggy wasn't thinking about Fiona, up in her bedroom, and how she'd just given her an audience to parts of the tirade. Fiona was indeed listening in, trying to piece together the fragments of her parents' abbreviated argument. When Mother's voice got that low, and Pop's got that loud, both their faces got really red. She could almost hear their skin deepening into crimson.

"What if you and Fiona had needed to go into witness protection?" he spat out, "I might never have seen her again, Peggy! That's absolutely freakin' unacceptable!" Peggy rolled her eyes and took a deep breath. "Witness protection. Have you been reading my novels, Wolf?" she purred back, "I'm flattered, really." Her honeyed voice seemed to do the trick. Soon they were laughing, as Peggy conveyed the real scene, as if they'd both stepped into the pages of one of her books.

~oOO0O0o~

Fiona was sure of a few things about her mother. She was bright and beautiful. She was sophisticated and social—among people she believed had something to offer in return. She was demanding and, occasionally a little dark, especially in her murder mysteries. As a writer, particularly of her genre, Mother was always thinking, always researching, always sleuthing. What Fiona didn't know about her was that Mother had no boundaries. Particularly when it came to Fiona. Good sleuths got their information any way they could.

At the suggestion of Mother's most recent guru, and at the insistence of Mother, Fiona began seeing a therapist—not because she was upset, but because Mother and her guru couldn't imagine why not. After all, they reasoned, she surely had "mother issues" after the loss of her stepmother. The "therapist" happened to be a student of Mother's guru and, as such, was a friend of Mother's. Unscrupulous, unlicensed, and largely untrained, this young woman either did not know, or did not care, about the importance of informing clients of what will, and will not, be shared so as to maintain trust.

Fiona was blindsided, taken unaware by a pipeline that ran from her therapist directly to her mother. Peggy's intrusion into her daughter's sessions was, in a way, a worse invasion than if she'd just snuck into her room and read her diary. With a diary, there's no expectation of a helping hand, and no ripple effect of harm to other relationships of trust with helping professionals. Perhaps Fiona should have been wiser to her mother's tactics, since she was well aware of the way she worked sources for her stories. But Mother was so inscrutable, Fiona never quite knew what was on her mind.

Although Fiona didn't know the extent of the breach, she suspected the connection, and she kept her guard up. This left her in a tight spot, not knowing how to approach sessions she didn't feel she needed anyway, while not doing herself harm. She thought better of speaking about her parents, but she knew she had to talk about something, to look cooperative. She found herself talking about smoking pot. After all, Pop and every one of his peers smoked pot, so it wasn't a big deal, was it? She was crushing her schoolwork. Peggy, though, thought of pot as a gateway drug. Reefer madness. The start of something dreadful. After a couple of weeks of sessions, Peggy had heard enough to get on the phone with her best friend, Herb, right away.

"You know, Peggy, we're lucky," Herb said, "The kind of problems we have can be solved by throwing money at them. Not everyone has such luck." He wasn't wrong, and she knew it. "True, true," she responded, wistfully, "but a trip back East isn't exactly in the budget right now." Taking the hint, Herb quickly came up with the airfare and arranged to meet their flight. They would stay with him for a while. Just as he had helped with Karen, he also knew the institutions where Fiona could be placed, if that turned out to be necessary.

On a routine Wednesday-night dinner out at Walker's Pie Shop, Fiona and her mother faced some unpleasant truths about each other. The pie shop was a retro-style diner that featured American comfort foods, but was famous for its house-made pies. Fiona loved to go there for the food, and she welcomed the dedicated time with her mother—except for those evenings when it felt like she was under interrogation. Fiona had taken to preparing a list of subjects to discuss, in hopes of distracting Mother from her more pressing or controversial topics.

During dinner, their conversation progressed like a carefully choreographed dance. Fiona knew the steps. "So, Fiona, what's new?" Mother asked, without looking up from her menu. She was going to order her usual salad, so Fiona wondered why she bothered to study the menu.

"I got an A on my French quiz," Fiona volunteered.

"Super." Mother wanted more. "Anything else new at school? How's Mary?" The introductory questions and answers never changed.

"She's fine. She says hello. She invited me to sleep over on Saturday, if that's okay." Fiona knew it would be, since her absence opened up more time for Mother to write her book.

"Sounds okay. Can you write it on the fridge, so I don't forget?" Fiona nodded, aware that her mother hadn't really heard her.

"How's your book coming? Did you decide on a plot?" Fiona felt as if she were an actor in a play about a conversation between two strangers looking for something to say. She wasn't far off.

"Working on that." Again, Mother did not look up.

"You could go political with this one." Fiona couldn't resist the urge to offer suggestions. "Anything with activists is really hot among young people right now…"

"I need to appeal to a wide audience, Fiona," answered Mother.

Fiona wouldn't give up, pouncing on any opportunity to show Mother how smart she was. "Okay, so how about if you use Locard's Exchange Principle on two really weird, unrelated things, like maybe a cloistered nun and, um, a bat?"

Mother finally looked up. Mother was impressed that Fiona knew about forensic scientist Edmond Locard, the "Sherlock Holmes of France," who held that the perpetrator of a crime will bring something to the crime scene and leave with something from it, both of which can be used as forensic evidence. "Baseball or mammal?" she asked.

Mother then shifted the conversation.

"How's your love life, Fiona?"

"Still waiting for Prince Charming, I guess." Fiona fidgeted with her napkin, tearing the thin paper into bits. "For now, Fioner's a loner." Fiona smiled, hoping for a rhyme in return.

Mother had no more patience for the dance. "That sounds a little rehearsed. Here's one for you: I may have been born at night, but not last night, Fiona. Really, you have no poker face. I can see when you're weaving a story. All mothers can. And anyway, you should be glad I'm interested."

Fiona nodded, as if she accepted her mother's words, though she did not. Besides, her dating—or lack of it—was not a topic she felt like sharing. Not the little innocent crush she felt toward one of her teachers, not the cute guy at the dojo, and definitely not the kid who'd been passing her sweet, funny notes in class. Mother was right, now would have been a great time for a poker face.

Mother doesn't know me at all, despite what she says, Fiona thought, while watching her mother pick at her salad. Does anyone really know anyone? What parent seriously expects their kids to spill their guts? A little whisper emerged in her head, Tell her something real. Take a leap of faith and tell her about the acid trip. Fiona brushed it aside like a fly. No way. Really bad idea, she thought. A disaster, waiting to happen.

If she did try to break down the wall that had grown up between them, what would happen in the clear light of day shining through the space? Again, Fiona brushed aside the fly bedeviling her brain. But Mother already knew.

"Well, if you have nothing of substance to share," she said to Fiona, "I do." Mother set down her fork. "It has come to my attention that you have been playing with fire. And by fire, I mean drugs. Strong and dangerous drugs. Addictive drugs."

Fiona's first bite of berry pie caught in her throat, and she knew she was through with dessert. Had Mother heard about the mushrooms, the acid, or maybe the hash brownies? Or, was this about the therapist, and the grass?

"You and I are taking a little trip to New York, where my friend Herb knows some folks who can help us get to the bottom of this."

"I don't know what you're talking about, Mother. I don't do drugs," Fiona said, lying through her teeth. "This is ridiculous."

"Don't talk to me like that, young lady. You are to speak to me with respect."

"Why?" Fiona asked, defiant.

Mother slapped Fiona across the cheek, hard. All eyes turned to their table, and conversation stopped. Fiona's face grew beet red. It wasn't just from the sting of the slap, or from embarrassment, either. She cared less about the other diners than what a bitch her mother was. She was also a little startled that she'd talked back. It was a first, something she'd never dared do before. It was prompted by the sting of having her confidences betrayed. Mother's slap only made it real.

Peggy hadn't imagined such a perfect opportunity for a "wake-up slap" would present itself so quickly, but here it was. "You made me do that," Peggy heard herself saying, parroting words she'd found scripted in one of her many New Age self-help books. "It's your fault that I slapped you. Why do you make me suffer so?"

Slowly, as it became obvious in Fiona's mind what had happened, she realized what a mistake she'd made, in even agreeing to sit down with one of Mother's latest guru's cronies. Fiona, you dumb ass! screamed the voice inside her mind. You Stupid Idiot Dumb Ass! The voice continued, harsh and unrelenting. "You are so STUPID." Even as that voice screamed at her, she realized she'd overstepped her bounds by back-talking and needed to backpedal, fast. What she said—or, didn't say—next mattered. A lot. Talking back again now would be even dumber than talking to that so-called therapist in the first place. She said nothing. Mother paid the check, and they left the restaurant, without engaging in any further conversation.

~oOOOOOo~

It's not like I shot up heroin or did crack and got hooked, Fiona huffed, packing her suitcase for the New York trip, and preparing her arguments. Doesn't she think I've seen a thing or two, growing up? Anyway, Mother's wrong. I do respect authority, when it's earned, not demanded. I don't respect people who resort to violence. Pop had taught her the importance of nonviolence, and she had no idea of the irony in that. She could almost hear his voice chiming in, "Take care now. Just because you are paranoid doesn't mean the enemy isn't real. Never trust anyone over 30." Was Mother the enemy? She was ancient. She was over 40! Then again, so was Pop.

There was no point in arguing with Mother. She'd already booked the flights. Throughout the cross-country flight, Fiona felt the intensity of Mother's spyglass, stealthily examining her every breath. So, this is how that ant felt under Pop's magnifying glass in India, poor thing, Fiona thought, as she recalled the ant's spontaneous combustion. If Mother keeps it up, I wonder if I'll surprise her and just burst into flames.

Fiona's chess nemesis from Fire Island all those years ago had a home in Woodstock. The plan was to have Herb observe Fiona for any signs of drug-withdrawal symptoms: physical, mental, or emotional. Fiona couldn't bear the thought of one more person dissecting her well-being. But, she didn't say a word.

She'd save all that for Herb.

After all, she now knew speaking to any friend of her mother's would be like singing into a microphone, with her mother as the audience. Anything she said to him would get right back to Mother. She planned to choose her words carefully.

Before she set foot in Herb's office, Fiona set her intentions. While combing her hair in the luxurious guest bathroom of his house, she rehearsed her plan in the mirror. *Okay, I need to convince Herb that Mother is dead wrong about me. Whatever her excuse-for-a-therapist friend told her about my having smoked pot growing up, or whatever, I'm not some drug addict, and I don't need a freakin' intervention.*

Fiona stared into the blue eyes looking back at her and considered what she remembered about Herb. She would put on her best performance—the role of the model citizen—no matter what. This was all about survival in a situation where trust wouldn't save her. *You don't speak truth to people of power when they're just looking for an excuse to chop your head off,* she thought. Fiona fastened a barrette into her hair and took one more step toward perfecting her reasoning. *Let's all live in the moment. I'm not doing drugs,* she thought. *Not at this very moment, anyway.*

On reflection, it didn't feel like much of an ethical dilemma. With honesty pitted against survival, she chose survival. *This is the best you can do, Fiona, so go with it,* she told herself. *The less you say, the closer you'll be to getting things back on track with Mother.* She couldn't wait until the day when she wasn't under anyone's thumb—anyone's authority, expectations, assumptions. Would there be such a day?

Regardless, mum's the word. She snapped off the light in the bathroom.

~o0O0O0o~

The next time she and Herb were alone, Fiona raised the subject of marijuana. "You know I don't smoke pot, Herb. I hate the smell of it, and I resent having to inhale someone else's high." This, for starters, was the gospel truth. She'd rather get high or not get high on her own terms than suck up someone else's exhaust.

"Besides, if the Surgeon General says cigarette smoking is bad for your lungs, doesn't it stand to reason that dragging pot smoke into your lungs would be, too? Smoke is smoke, whatever dried foliage you're smoking. Don't you think so, Herb?"

Herb considered Fiona's logic and agreed with her, but he wasn't sold on her position. Not yet. He asked her what she thought about drugs and God. "I don't know much about God. You mean, like doing drugs as a path to higher consciousness? I've heard of people trying altered states for that, but I haven't heard of it working, have you, Herb?"

"You don't think drugs can speed-dial your way to God?"

"You know what I think, Herb?" She wanted to say he was full of himself, and that she knew he was baiting her. Instead, she offered, "I think it's like my viola playing. Turning on the radio won't get me further. It's an illusion. Only practice matters. Well, drugs are like turning on the radio instead of playing a tune. One's a copy, one's real. There's no comparison. Don't you think we should be going for authenticity, Herb?"

Herb looked at Fiona intently. Was she for real, or was she snowing him under?

At her official visit with Herb, he asked her what she liked to do in her spare time. She decided to take a literary track and make another point about how she wasn't into drugs. "I finished two books on the plane, *Light a Single Candle*, about a girl who goes blind, and *Perelandra*. When I ran out of things to read, Mother lent me a book about a guy who stuck cactus spines in a lizard's eyes and mouth to go on a vision quest. And you know what, Herb?"

"What?"

"I hated it. I hated it, Herb."

"Why? What did you hate about it, Fiona?"

"I hated all of it. The whole dang power trip. It was mean. But, like they say, there's always a reckoning. I think, in the long run, there are consequences to deal with."

"Such as?"

"Well, I don't know." Fiona, who just wanted to say benign things to help make her case with Mother, thought a moment before responding. She looked around Herb's office, realizing that although he seemed like a broad thinker, his office bore all the trappings of power, with his big leather chair behind an imposing wooden desk, his collection of original paintings decorating the walls, and that exceptional carved ebony chess set on a wooden side table, inlaid with the chessboard pattern. Still, Herb seemed like a fair and reasonable thinker. "It seemed like an act of selfishness, and that's no path to God, or at least I don't think it is. So, I don't think the author was very enlightened. I steer clear of people who hurt other beings for their own gain," she said. "I don't even like to read about them. How about you, Herb, what do you like to read?"

Before delving into his own reading list, Herb told Fiona he was glad she was smarter than to believe drugs could be a shortcut to God. "No shortcuts, right Fee?"

Don't I know it, she thought, nodding her head.

The conversation went well from there, she thought. The rest of the week, when she wasn't meeting with Herb to help him see who she really was and, mostly, to make her case, through him, to Mother, Fiona spent time by herself, as usual, looking at the trees around the house, or reading. Her plan worked. She managed to convince Herb, who then convinced Mother, that she wasn't an addict and that she had a pretty good head on her shoulders. Particularly for a teenager.

"You're doing a good job, Peggy," Herb told her. If flattery was all it took, Fiona thought, they could have solved this problem a lot sooner.

Fiona felt a little like she'd beaten Herb in a sort of chess game of her own, but she also had a newfound appreciation of him, as a kind, helpful person—not the jerk she'd thought he might be when he'd beat her so mercilessly at chess on Fire Island, so many years ago.

Before they returned home, Herb asked Fiona if she might like to see the Broadway show *For Colored Girls Who Have Considered Suicide When the Rainbow Is Enuf*, by Ntozake Shange, an African-American feminist poet and playwright.

It sounded super to Fiona, who hadn't heard of her or been to a Broadway play. Fiona took in the theater, and leafed through her copy of the Playbill before the house lights went down. "Hey, Herb, can I ask you something?" The Playbill had sparked an idea, and she realized she valued his opinion. After all, he'd paid attention enough to her to know she'd appreciate such a play. "Do you think social justice law would make sense for me? I'd like to make a difference, you know?" Just as he whispered that he didn't doubt she'd leave her mark, the lights went down, and the show began.

It was a powerful experience, a harsh, poetic depiction of the dark and bleak, yet hopeful experience of black women in America—not only of poverty and oppression, but of God and love, as well. Another side, rarely told, of the American experience. Fiona was mesmerized throughout, and left the theater completely smitten. Seven female characters represented by colors of the rainbow! she marveled.

"That was a great play. You would have loved it, Mother. She's some writer. You know, it might be possible to sneak some of those issues into your mysteries. Or maybe you could write a play someday, like she did. It was just such an important play!" Fiona gushed to Mother, who looked cross, as if Fiona had compared Shange's skill to her own, and found her lacking. Geez, Fiona thought. Can't say anything around here.

The night Fiona and her mother returned to Berkeley, there was a small earthquake. Fiona slept through it, yet when she awoke, she found that Mother hadn't slept much. "Good morning, Mother. How are you?"

Mother said she'd be fine, but earthquakes unsettled her. She was quiet all day, which made Fiona nervous. To try to build a connection with her mother, Fiona took to saying, "Hi!" or "Hey!" every time she entered a room where Mother was poring over property listings. Already exasperated with Fiona from what she had realized was an expensive and useless trip to New York, Mother finally snapped, "You do realize you've said that 10 times already."

Fiona headed out into the backyard to park herself in a lawn chair and wait out Mother's storm. She liked to stay outside as much as possible anyway, whenever there'd been a tremor. Earthquakes aside, Fiona had fallen in love with California. If she could just navigate her relationship with Mother, whom she didn't know or understand well enough to trust, and whose love and affection felt fleeting, she could build a future in California. This place, she'd decided, held possibilities for people like her. She was, after all, a California Girl. And she was determined to prove it.

~oOOOOOo~

The sky was still dark blue when Mother, carrying a cup of hot coffee, knocked on Fiona's bedroom door. "Up you get, Fiona. Early morning field trip." Fiona pulled on some jeans and a tee, backwards, which she was directed to correct by Mother's glance. Mother also nixed the open-toed sandals she'd slipped on in favor of some sneakers. "Where are we going, Mother? Asilomar? A work weekend?"

They were good guesses. She'd been dragged to them before, and had usually gone along gamely with Mother's unexpected, crack-of-dawn forays. Soon, they were buckled into the car and headed east on the freeway. The signs were pointing to Sacramento, but Fiona couldn't imagine why they'd go there.

"Sacramento, Mother?" Fiona asked.

"Grass Valley. We're meeting a Realtor in Grass Valley at 10 o'clock this morning. There's a nice piece of property there, about 45 acres. Really lovely. And land is so cheap out there, we can buy the whole thing for less than I'll get for this bungalow." Fiona fell silent. Having endured a rural existence once in her life, she wasn't thrilled at the prospect of having another go at it, particularly with Mother. Without additional information forthcoming, Fiona was left to her own imagination.

Maybe Mother doesn't think there are any drugs there, Fiona thought. Good luck with that. Yes, that was a motivation. Another one was Mother's desire to follow yet another guru, someone they called "The Wise One." Several of his devotees (and her friends) were moving to Yuba County in the Sierra Foothills because he promised to wake up people who were sleepwalking through their lives. This "Wise One" was said to be an angel who could communicate with other angels, including Benjamin Franklin.

Mother attempted small talk as they headed toward the property, commenting on the bubbling stream, the sparkly mica—or fool's gold—which might be fun for Fiona to collect for crafting. Fiona wasn't buying it. And she didn't even know why, yet.

Fiona peered out the open window, the wind in her hair as they rolled into town to meet the Realtor. The closer they got, the more her nose began to tickle. "Aaaaatchooooooo!" She started to sneeze. She sneezed when being introduced to the Realtor, she sneezed all the way up to and while visiting the property. She didn't stop sneezing the entire time she was there. She sneezed halfway home, as well. No amount of Sudafed or Coca Cola would help. By the time they arrived back in Berkeley, her nose was raw and almost bleeding, and her eyes were bright red. Mother suggested she head upstairs and take a shower, and Fiona didn't wait for a second invitation. She went to her room, with Starlight close on her heels, and set down her bag. "I sure am glad I'm not allergic to you, Starlight, and that you're not allergic to me."

Later, towel-drying her hair, Fiona overheard Mother on the phone to the real estate agent, telling her she wouldn't be pursuing the property. Fiona's allergy attack had put an end to the Grass Valley concept.

For the first time, Fiona was grateful for her allergies. However, thwarting a grand plan to move to Grass Valley hadn't helped her already-difficult relationship with Mother. For the next few weeks, Fiona and Peggy generally avoided each other's company, as if they were allergic to each other. They hadn't ever been fully comfortable with each other, even at the best of times; now, a year into their life together, living under the same roof was becoming exhausting for them both.

Fiona, though, was excelling at school, and showing signs of promise as a writer. Peggy had begun mulling over the question of college tuition—and how to pay for it. The answer came by way of her New York literary agent: three-book deal. But it had to be done in a year. That would mean a herculean effort. How could Peggy expect to get something like that done, while watching over her daughter and keeping her away from drugs?

"I can't fail again," she muttered to herself, wincing at the memory of all her conflicts with her older daughter, who'd finally fled in the night, before she'd even finished high school, "I just can't."

The idea of a foreign exchange program came to Peggy in the middle of another sleepless night. Fiona would be safe, watched over by a loving and capable (and thoroughly vetted) host family while she studied abroad, and Peggy would be free to slave over her typewriter in Berkeley, earning enough to put her prodigy through college.

Fiona was intrigued by the idea. She knew they both could use a break, and she understood, since Mother wasn't going anywhere, that it meant she was the one who would be leaving. She also imagined it meant she had, once again, failed to please her mother.

8. AWAY, AGAIN!

Peggy worked quickly. Putting some distance between Fiona and her drugged-out friends was her primary focus. It was important, too, Peggy told herself, so that she could succeed at meeting the extraordinary demands of her new book deal. She told Fiona only that it was a learning opportunity she wouldn't want to miss. Fiona, gamely, went along with the program.

Not long after she and Fiona began researching programs and countries together, Fiona had her renewed passport in hand and was counting the days until she left the country for a year abroad as an exchange student in Argentina. Fiona had been studying Spanish since she'd been in California, and she felt comfortable enough with the language to get by. She realized that though she understood some academic Spanish, she hadn't learned any slang, and she was certain native speakers would articulate much faster than she could. But, in time, she would catch on.

It took Wolf a little longer to catch on to Peggy's plans. Fiona hadn't told him. Nor had Peggy. Fiona knew he'd think up a reason to be mad, and she worried he might start lobbying for her to return to him. She wasn't wrong. He felt he was the superior parent. It was one of the reasons he'd fought so hard for Fiona, and found Fiona's adoration of her mother troubling. He loved strong women, but his idea of a perfect woman had been Hanna, who had decided to stay home and raise her girls. Peggy was not Hanna. Peggy was career-driven. Where had that gotten her with her older daughter?

Nowhere pretty. By contrast, Wolf felt confident he knew how to raise a bright child.

Peggy didn't solicit Wolf's input into the study-abroad scheme because, in her eyes, his opinion wasn't worth two cents. He didn't strike her as responsible, nor was she sure he would care if Fiona were doing drugs. Hell, Peggy thought, he might even encourage it. They shared none of the details of their private lives with each other. Still, she knew she needed Wolf's signature, alongside her own, on the paperwork for the foreign-exchange program. This necessitated one of their fiery conversations.

Peggy breathed a silent sigh of relief when Gram answered the phone. To her credit, her former mother-in-law listened patiently to Peggy's carefully crafted presentation of her idea to send Fiona abroad for a year. But, she didn't buy it, finally saying, "Listen, Peggy, dear. Fiona's been through a lot of transitions in her life. Wouldn't it be better to let her put down some roots at your home? And isn't she a little young for a full year alone in a chaotic foreign country? I really don't think this is a wise idea. If you think about it for a moment, Peggy, don't you agree?"

Wolf had overheard enough of the conversation to understand what Peggy had up her sleeve. He started in on his ex-wife, by way of his mother, in that screechy voice Peggy found so irritating, the one that signaled he was getting unreasonably emotional. "What the hell is wrong with her? Can't she get it through her head that Fiona just wants to spend time with her? How can she just ship her off somewhere because she's, what, inconvenient? If Peggy doesn't want her, she can send her back here on the next plane, where she belongs!"

Having heard enough, Gram decided to take herself out of the middle of the outburst. She handed the phone to her son and left the room. She believed that he, of all people, didn't care if Fiona went to Timbuktu; he simply sat on the trigger, ready to fire off his long-suffering angst that Fiona had left him.

Peggy waited until Wolf took a breath and then poured on the butter, followed by a little syrup. It wouldn't be the first time she'd seduced this man and gotten what she wanted from him. She'd done it then, she could do it now. Slowly, expertly, she convinced Wolf, not with her plan, but with her smooth, hypnotic voice that was capable of convincing nearly anyone of anything—especially men, whom she could wrap around her finger. Particularly Wolf, even after all these years. In less than 15 minutes, practically a record for Peggy, she had Wolf right where she wanted him, calm and willing to sign on the dotted line. She called Fiona down from her room and handed her the phone to speak with her father.

"Hey Fee," said Pop. "I hear you've got quite an adventure planned. So, you want to go to Argentina for a bit? That's a big step for a girl your age, but I talked it over with your mother, and we're copacetic. I'm down with it, if you are."

Peggy had her ways of convincing Wolf, and she knew he had his ways of building confidence in Fiona. Their child was on her way to spend the year in Argentina. Just as her mother had planned.

Fiona packed clothing, a couple of favorite books, and a few photos, including one with Pop, Hanna, Holly and Violet, another with Mother, and another with her friends, outside The Med. She decided not to bring her viola, but she hoped to rent an instrument while she was in Buenos Aires, and maybe take some lessons there. To that end, she packed the new book of scales and studies Mr. Ż. had given her as a parting gift.

Fiona felt very grown up as she embarked on her adventure to Buenos Aires, her first solo international trip. The worst part would be leaving her friends for a time. But the time will fly by, she told herself. It always does. Fiona hoped they'd wait for her, and continue their friendship as if nothing had happened, when she got back.

It was a beautiful fall day in Berkeley, which meant the start of spring in Argentina, so Fiona was anticipating mild weather and a warm welcome. Fiona said goodbye to Starlight and Mary as she was putting her suitcases into the car, and waved out the back window until Mother turned the corner.

Fiona almost turned to offer one last wave to Mother as she disappeared down the jetway, but she imagined Mother would already be gone. She was too afraid to turn to wave, only to find nobody there.

Fiona settled into her cramped coach seat for the long trip, grateful she was petite. She knew she wouldn't mind the long flight, during which she planned to read and sleep and maybe write a little in her journal. She was excited to make a stop in Rio de Janeiro on the way to Buenos Aires. Mother had saved money by avoiding a direct flight. Although she'd only see the inside of the airport, it could mean one more country stamp in her passport among her life's journeys. Under "countries I have visited" in her journal, Fiona had logged the countries in Asia she'd visited with Pop; she was hoping to add at least three countries in South America, maybe more, during the year. Just today, she would be able to add two: Brazil and Argentina.

As the flight neared her first stop, Galeão Airport in Rio, Fiona looked down at the commanding Cristo Redentor, or Christ the Redeemer, statue. She was thrilled to take in the beautiful Corcovado mountaintop sculpture, so clearly visible from the plane. South America was beautiful. The plane touched down relatively smoothly, and Fiona was impressed when the passengers applauded the safe landing. People should do that in the United States, she thought.

Fiona collected her things, deplaned, and made her way through the airport to her connecting gate. Just two short hours later, she was in the air again, watching the beautiful Cristo statue receding in the distance on her way to her final destination. Fiona knew she was tired, but she was too excited to sleep. Instead, she looked out the window for most of the three-hour flight. There was applause, again, as the plane landed and taxied up to the gate in Buenos Aires. Her adventure was beginning.

After heading out of the plane and down the stairs, Fiona collected her suitcase from baggage claim by herself, proceeded through customs, and headed out to the curb to look for her host parents. She assumed they would be holding a sign with her name on it. The warm, moist, slightly musky air felt somehow welcoming, and Fiona instantly felt all those hours of travel were going to be worth it. This would be the experience of a lifetime, and she planned to make the most of it.

Just then, two American businessmen who'd been on the plane

with her, perhaps feeling paternal, offered to share a cab with her from the airport. She told them she had a ride, and thanked them. One of them said, "You need to be careful in this city, okay?" Mother had told Fiona that Buenos Aires was crime-ridden, but she couldn't appreciate the level of danger, compared to her experience of American cities. Twenty percent of the country's people lived in the villas miserias, the slums. And the country was in the middle of a "dirty war" against its own people, reportedly torturing and killing tens of thousands of its own citizens as dissidents. Had Fiona known this, she might have been too frightened to come. If Mother knew this, she didn't mention it. Maybe she wanted to protect Fiona, to keep her from being afraid. But wouldn't that have meant keeping her daughter home, safe?

Presently, a car pulled up to the curb, and Fiona's Argentinian parents, Hector and Armida Silva, stepped out to greet her and load her luggage into the back. The car ride to their home took longer than Fiona would have liked, and seemed more so because the conversation was minimal. Eventually, they arrived at a little apartment in Recoleta, an upscale section of the city. Their home was pleasant and airy, with a light-filled kitchen and living room, five bedrooms, and two bathrooms. It had hot running water, though the climate was so warm, nobody seemed to need or want anything but cold water.

The Silva family had three daughters, Luciana, Mariana, and Julia, all students around Fiona's age, who seemed focused on food, parties, shopping, and music, music and more music. Fiona thought she'd arrived in heaven. The girls were instantly friends, as they welcomed her and showed her where she'd be sleeping, a lovely guest bedroom just off the living room. She tucked most of her spending money and her passport into the back of her suitcase for safekeeping, not realizing she should have kept her passport with her, at all times when outside her host home. She'd left the gold necklace Gram had given her, and had brought only her Timex wristwatch, her unicorn pendant—a gift from Pop when she was younger, which she rarely took off—and an inexpensive silver ring with a star and moon motif, a gift from Mary, with her to Argentina.

The sisters were heading out to attend a New Age lecture called,

"A Course in Miracles," a study in spiritual transformation based on the book by psychologists Helen Schucman and William Thetford. They invited Fiona to join them. She'd barely slept on the flight and could feel her fatigue slipping over her like satin sheets, but she went, eager to show her hosts she was grateful for their hospitality. It was still light enough to survey the regal European architecture as the girls walked, arm-in-arm, along the warm, cobbled streets to their destination. "¿Que te pasa, Fiona?" asked Luciana, "What's the matter, Fiona," as she tripped into her, having caught her shoe in a cobblestone. It took two streetlight cycles and all the courage Fiona could muster just to make it across the massively wide Avenida 9 de Julio with the girls, on the way to the lecture hall.

As her jetlag set in, Fiona knew she'd made a mistake in tagging along with the sisters. As soon as they took their seats, she found she simply couldn't keep her eyes open. She needed sleep, and it was coming at a most inconvenient time. Her new friends apologized for bringing her along on her first night, and suggested she take a cab home.

It was a decision that nearly cost Fiona her life.

When the cab came to rescue the dead-tired Fiona, her new sister-friends peered in at the cabbie and glanced at the ID on the sun visor of his car to make sure they matched. They took down his cab license number, and gave him directions to their apartment. Fiona climbed inside and slunk into the seat, relieved. She closed her eyes and began to doze.

Two blocks away, out of the sight range of Fiona's friends, the cab driver pulled over, saying his taxi had broken down. He hailed another cabbie—who would turn out to be his partner in crime—and made a good show of explaining the address where Fiona was to be taken. Fiona didn't wonder at how quickly that second cabbie had arrived, nor did she catch the wink and nod that were exchanged as the second cabbie took down the Silvas' address.

Soon, Fiona was speeding along again, looking out the window from the back seat of the second cab. There were no local witnesses nearby to verify this second cabbie, as Fiona's friends had done with the first. The first cabbie could easily hide behind his car trouble, pleading ignorance to whatever might happen next.

The cab ride was taking a long time. Longer than Fiona expected. The taxi began to ascend a hilly street, and Fiona grew alarmed. Hadn't the road to the lecture been flat? The scenery somehow looked even more unfamiliar than it had before.

As tired as she was, Fiona found her thoughts turning to her mother's murderous plots. Bad cabbie—that's a pretty cliché storyline, she thought. Yet the hair rising on the back of her neck told her this one would become only a story if it hit tomorrow's headlines somewhere. Something sinister really was happening, and no one would ever know about it.

Petrified in her seat, Fiona's creative mind left on a train of thought she didn't want to ride. She let it go and tried to focus on what to do. She didn't want to be kidnapped, or worse. Mother's books had taught her that a woman has a better chance at survival if she can get out of the car. Or not get in it in the first place, but it was too late for that. She had to collect her wits about her, get out of the car, and run. Where? It didn't matter. Just go!

Her hand instinctively felt for the door handle. There was no interior latch. Why was this happening? Her friends clearly were aware of potential dangers, hence their due diligence. They had checked out the original cab. This was not supposed to be happening. She inched her way over to the other side of the cab, hoping that door would open when she tried it.

Fiona's overwhelming fatigue had been replaced by overpowering fear, wrapped in regret. Where in the book of Fiona was this written?

Despite her racing heart, she didn't fully understand the situation she was in. She did sense, however, that something was very wrong, and she knew she was totally out of her element.

Mostly, she was terrified. Was she going to be killed for her money? Fiona wasn't ready to die. She was just starting to live. And, although she didn't know what it was, exactly, she held a strong conviction that she still needed to accomplish something in her life. Her thoughts darted through her mind as feverishly as the blood was coursing through her veins, causing her heart to pound. She did the only thing she could think of, which was to harness all her thoughts and feelings and send them up in the simplest of prayers, "Save me, Jesus, please!"

Maybe it was the time she had spent with the nuns during her few months in catechism. Perhaps it was the beautiful Christ statue she'd seen on both her descent and ascent through Rio de Janeiro earlier that same day. How long ago that seemed, now. For whatever reason, Fiona's mind had turned to prayer, and she was directing her prayer to Jesus. Maybe it was Mary's influence, so devout was her friend back home in her love of the Son of God. Fiona prayed hard to Him to save her because saving was exactly what she needed.

Mary, she knew, would have prayed for her, had she known what was happening. Still, since she'd told Fiona she'd be praying for her during her year in Argentina, maybe, just maybe, Mary was praying for her now, at this very moment.

The second cabbie drove erratically up a remote and very dark hill. His driving tossed Fiona from side to side. She couldn't stay steady long enough to maneuver to the far side of the back seat to try the other door handle to see if she could escape.

At a hairpin turn, the cabbie had to slow down. Fiona realized he had no intention of stopping until he reached his destination, wherever that was. She had to act now. But when she tried to open the second door to get out, the driver turned around quickly and slammed her hand, hard, using the butt of a gun. He then kept on driving. Quietly, she tried for the door again, and found it wouldn't open.

Maybe she could reason with him. When she tried to talk, he turned around again, and hit her across the face, saying, "¡Cállate, mujer!!" meaning, "Shut up, woman!" He told her he'd kill her if she didn't stop talking, "¡Si no te callas, puta, te mataré!" She knew just enough of the language beyond her textbook Spanish to understand he'd called her a whore.

Waving his gun into the back seat, he told her to give him all her joyería y dinero as a present. A love gift, Fiona thought. Bizarre.

Seriously? But she didn't say a word.

The street darkened and narrowed as they made their ascent. Fiona remembered learning the word for jewelry in that dialog she and Mary had presented during Spanish class. She looked down at her unicorn pendant from Pop and the simple ring from Mary. She hated to let them go, for sentimental reasons, and she could have kicked herself for bringing them. She was glad she'd left her watch back in her suitcase, and her precious necklace back home. She handed over her jewelry, along with her wallet. She hoped that was all he wanted, and now that he had some money and jewelry, he'd let her go.

And then, the car stopped.

Fiona had a moment to try to get out of the car when the cab driver opened the door. But, before she could get to her feet, he had shoved her further into the back seat of his cab and had joined her there. Fiona's head slammed into the torn vinyl. The scent of years of built-up grime filed her nostrils. He pressed the gun to her temple.

Fiona began trying to reason with him again, timidly. He yelled and then beat her before collapsing upon her. His weight and her fall slammed the air out of her, but now, as his rough, clammy hand closed around her small neck, she began to suffocate. Choking to the point of being unable to think, she prayed to pass out. When he saw she was weakened, he released his grip from around her neck and began to tear at her clothing.

This was not how her body was supposed to experience a man. Not yet and not this way. Everything she'd read in romance novels in her room and in Becca's *Cosmopolitan* magazines, had promised hot, sexy, satisfying, good. This was not good. This was ugly and horrifying. And this was not fiction. It was rape, and it was real. And it was happening. To her.

This was predatory. Violent. Evil. More so than anything she'd ever experienced, except perhaps that night she couldn't remember at Mystic Meadow. As the cabbie held her down with his weight and destroyed what remained of her innocence, something shifted for Fiona. She felt as if she were no longer the frightened child, being violated in the back of a cab in the hills above Buenos Aires, but a higher form of herself, elevated, as if she'd been lifted up and out of her body, where her vile rapist couldn't reach her. And she knew, with all her conviction, that she was either dying or being removed from the terror. Either way, she knew she was being saved. Maybe it was because, even through all that horror, she never stopped praying. She never entirely lost hope. Not entirely.

From the moment Fiona began praying, she found her broken Spanish becoming more fluent, enabling her to communicate more clearly. Something in her head and her heart told her to try, again, to talk to this man, to seek the shred of humanity that might be lurking in his soul. Maybe, just maybe, she could survive.

"No soy una mujer," she whispered, the words raspy in her damaged throat. "Soy una chica, solamente una chica." I am not a woman. I am only a girl. He didn't hit her. She went on, speaking of being an American, far from her mamá y papá. She said she didn't know her way around, and asked if he could help her find her way back to her host family. With a courage she'd summoned through prayer, Fiona forced herself to keep talking to this man, who had rolled off her but still held her at gunpoint. She sat up. Speaking, one person to another, she tried to find and appeal to his humanity. "¿Tiene hijas?" Do you have daughters?

He hesitated for a moment, and Fiona saw that she'd struck a chord. Then, he hit her across the face with his gun, called her a whore, and threatened, once again, to kill her if she didn't shut up.

She had everything—and nothing—to lose by trying. She didn't shut up. All the while, she kept praying.

When the man got out of the car, Fiona thought, for a split second, maybe he was abandoning her. Then he yanked her out of the car and flung her onto the ground. Fiona's head hit the earth, hard, and she could feel damp blood oozing through her hair. He shoved her again, and as she fell forward, she heard the cocking of his pistol. Then, he told her to kneel.

Fiona was alone, on her knees, with a gun to her head and traces of trauma throbbing throughout her body, on a dark, dirty hill, far from any other living soul who might care about the fate of a lone, teenaged traveler. She thought of Pop, the one person who would truly, deeply care, and a sob caught in her throat. She was all out of words. What do I do? she asked nobody in particular, in silence. Keep praying, was the message she heard in return.

There, on a desolate hill, with no witnesses, in a country where this perpetrator surely felt safe from prosecution, Fiona imagined she was about to become one of the unsolved murder statistics for which Buenos Aires was famous. Still, she kept praying.

Help me, Jesus. Don't let my life end like this. I think I've got more things—important things, even—left to do down here on earth, don't I? Jesus—omigod—Jesus, if you're out there, please help me.

Even as Fiona's waking nightmare was unfolding, during the drive up that bleak hill and through all that had transpired in the dark, something else was happening. Prayers were being heard. There was no army of angels, no Aurora Borealis lighting the heavens; the shift was much subtler than that. It was something in the quality of the air. Something holy and pure. A slight wind kicked up and swept over Fiona, soothing her. Fiona could feel her body relax, even in the path of a gun. She wasn't afraid anymore.

Fiona didn't know it, but the cabbie felt the same presence. Of course, he did. Jesus is "Emmanuel," meaning "God with us." Not God with one of us. All of us. It was the same bloody hill on which the cabbie and his compatriots had done so many wretched deeds. Yet now His presence was changing it, making it hallowed ground. As the slight breeze rustled the leaves, the cabbie looked at the gun in his hand as if he didn't quite understand why he was holding it.

He took a startled step back and lowered his aim from the back of Fiona's head. He shook his head, as if to clear it. Then, without warning, he stowed his gun in his glove compartment and told Fiona to get up and back into his cab. Fiona saw no other option. As she climbed into the back seat, she no longer felt any fear. The energy, so frenetic and fierce earlier, was still.

The cabbie drove the car down the hill of horrors to a busy street, and hailed another cab, a stranger to the first two criminals. This hadn't been part of the plan. The cabbie took a risk that the third taxi driver of the night might be able to identify him. After ordering Fiona to get into the new cab, Fiona's assailant handed the driver the Silvas' address and cab fare, and sped off into the night.

Fiona couldn't fathom what had just happened. Before she could think it through, she was whisked away from her tormentor and down yet another dark street. Stunned into silence, Fiona sat shocked, in the back, until the mystery of the moment lost its grip, and it dawned on her she was in yet another taxi. The moment of calm had passed, and she lost touch with the presence she'd felt earlier. Becoming hysterical, she began screaming at the cab driver, "Don't kill me! Don't kill me! Please, don't kill me!" in English.

The cab driver looked at the disheveled girl in the back of his cab, screaming her guts out at him, her tears cutting tracks in the dirt on her red, swollen face. With no idea how to reassure or calm her, he stayed silent.

When the cab pulled up in front of the Silvas' home, Fiona, all cried out now, was also silent. But she couldn't stop shaking. The driver left the car and went to knock on the door, summoning her host parents. They ran to the car, and Hector reached in and lifted Fiona out of the back seat, all the while speaking to the cabbie in a fierce, rapid-fire Spanish she couldn't follow. The cabbie explained where he'd picked up his fare and under what conditions, but he had no other information.

Armida called their doctor, a family friend who lived nearby. He came right away. He treated the abrasions on Fiona's face, put a plaster on the gash in her hairline, gave her something to calm her down, and administered a shot of penicillin. She understood there was nothing more to do on behalf of her health, or justice. Armida tucked her into bed. Fiona could hear the three sisters spilling into the home, brimming with stories from their lecture on "A Course in Miracles." Quickly the conversation turned into what sounded like an epic argument with their parents. The most Fiona could make out was her own name, but she slipped into a sound sleep well before the family was finished fighting.

The next morning, Armida suggested that Fiona phone home. She was surprised when Karen answered the phone. She was visiting Mother for the week. Karen could sense that something was wrong with her little sister, who was being cryptic at best, through a wash of unexpected tears. Karen didn't press Fiona to explain and, instead, handed the phone to Mother. Sobered by Mother's terse greeting, Fiona simply told her she'd had trouble with a cab, and let it go at that. As they were hanging up, she heard Mother say to Karen, "She's just lonely. She'll figure it out."

Fiona needed to talk to someone, so she called her stalwart friend, Mary. She knew international calls were expensive, and she kept it brief, hinting at what had happened. Mary pieced together the picture and sat in silence and in shock on the other end of the line. Fiona longed to be more explicit if only to get it out of her system. But she couldn't bring herself to say it. Not in English. She had heard the doctor explain it in Spanish, and she could say that. But not in English. Not yet. Maybe not ever. She created a kind of distance from the event for herself by framing it in another language. She found herself caught between needing the closeness of her friend, and as much distance as possible from what she had endured. The problem was that Mary was so far away, while the trauma was right here, pressing down on her throat.

Fiona had no doubt she'd been saved from being murdered, and she was quite clear about who had saved her. But everybody knows Jesus died 2,000 years ago, and Pop had clearly told her, "What's dead stays dead. Period." Okay, Pop, Fiona thought. But, what's a girl to do when received wisdom doesn't square with lived experience? And why didn't Jesus just make the whole taxi thing not happen at all? Gram's words of wisdom rang out. "It is not ours to understand everything in this life, Fee. Not until the great by and by." Okay, Gram, Fiona thought. Not understanding is something I can definitely do.

At night, in her dreams, Fiona revisited the statue of Jesus known as the Corcovado, and climbed the 365 steps to the top, where the sky was full of clouds, and offered her grateful thanks in unspoken words that Jesus somehow understood. Jesus had stopped the hand of a dark soul, a rapist and potential murderer, and had transformed Fiona's situation so radically, it left little room for doubt in her mind. Divine intervention had turned a would-be murderer from his intended course—to dispose of her body where she'd never be found—to deliver her, instead, to safety. As she stood on the stairs of her dream, her heart overflowed with gratitude. The next morning, *Godspell* came on the television. How perfect, Fiona thought, to hear Jesus in Spanish on TV. She could hardly pull herself away when her host parents called to her to come have coffee with them. There was something they wanted to discuss.

The Silvas made it clear there was no hope the police would bother to pursue justice in that sprawling, crime-ridden city. No police report would be filed because there was no point to it. What they didn't mention was that there was another option.

Fiona was invited by an old friend of the Silva family, Mr. Máximo López, to join him for lunch at the oldest yacht club in Latin America, the Yacht Club Argentino on Rio de la Plata. Hector and Armida insisted she accept. Once they determined she had nothing suitable to wear, she was encouraged to shop in the family's closets. Julia took charge of the hunt, delighted to have a way to help her new friend. When Julia declared success, Fiona could hardly recognize herself in the mirror. She looked cool, colorful, cosmopolitan, pretty.

The lunch service in the yacht club dining room was surely the most elegant Fiona had ever attended, and she was relieved to have practiced using a fork the "right way." Left hand, tines down, no switching hands. This was not the basic rustling-paper-napkins joint she was used to frequenting. The tables were covered in white linen and set with matching napkins that bore the embroidered crest of the club. The flatware looked and felt like real silver, and the dishes seemed to be porcelain. Fiona wanted to flip one over just to be sure, but she didn't dare. In great contrast, the walls were faced with a rich, dark wood, and the chairs were covered in burnt-red leather. Fiona was aware Argentina was known for its large cattle ranches, and she wondered how many had given their all for these armchairs. The whole place spoke of Old World elegance. Frankly, Fiona felt more comfortable in a more casual atmosphere. But fancy was fine, too. Fiona was still so fragile after her attack and so far from anyone or anything familiar, any outing was going to be awkward.

The service at the yacht club was superb; the wait staff was attentive but did not rush the meal. Fiona let her host order for her, and she feasted on Argentinian specialties, from carne asada with a zesty chimichurri sauce, to empanadas de carne y queso and milanesa de berenjenas a la parmesana. All this food was paired with a dark Malbec wine, which Fiona politely declined. After a dessert of flan, drizzled with dulce de leche sauce, she felt pleasantly full.

Wow, Fiona thought. There really was no other word for the luncheon. She had been quiet during the meal, studying her surroundings and soaking up the experience and language, which she lacked the confidence to speak without inhibition. As she peered out the window at the glistening harbor, she felt time stand still, this time, in a good way, perhaps out of respect for the beauty of the moment.

"Fiona, I'm sorry about what happened," said her host, breaking through her reverie. "I'm sure someone has explained how our system works here, all the pragmatic truths about how things are handled. Or not. I'm sorry you had to learn about the dark side of our beautiful city in that way. It is not how we want to welcome our guests."

"Gracias, Sr. López," she said, dismayed that her very private ordeal seemed to have become widespread news among the community. She was beginning to understand why she had been invited to lunch.

Does everyone know my business? she wondered. Is everyone in the upper circles of this community discussing what happened? Fiona sank a little lower in her oversized chair, her face, flushing. The room started to feel stifling and Fiona felt as if she were suffocating. Her stomach began to feel a bit queasy—maybe from all the rich food, or maybe from the physical and emotional trauma that, apparently, she was wearing like a sign across her forehead. She shuddered, slipping a little farther down into her chair, imagining all eyes were fixed on her, as the room began to close in on her.

"You know, Fiona," continued Mr. Lopez, "there is another option. This can be taken care of. Permanently."

Fiona didn't know what to say to what she thought she'd just heard. Was he suggesting...? She felt uncomfortable—awkward, unpleasant, scary. She said nothing. But she gave him a quizzical look, meaning she didn't quite understand. She wasn't entirely sure she'd understood the man's inference.

He explained to her that, sometimes when people look for justice and the legal system fails them, they turn to help from La Mano Blanca, which can track down and "take care" of problem people... permanently. "Someone who's considered a part of the family, as you are Fiona," he winked, "needn't even concern themselves with any of the costs. All they'd need to do is express an interest in that sort of a result. Do you follow?"

That was a lot to take in.

The lunch ended with rich black coffee. Fiona's host returned her to the apartment and gave her a warm, paternal hug. Releasing his embrace, he looked into Fiona's eyes and said, "Think about what I've said."

"Thanks, I really appreciate it, but honestly, no. I really couldn't." Fiona didn't want to be left turning that over in her head.

"Well, let me know if you change your mind. The offer is there." Fiona knew she wouldn't take him up on it, but she couldn't think of much else for the rest of the day.

Back at the Silvas' house, Fiona asked her host father if he'd please tell her more about La Mano Blanca. He told her they hailed from Guatemala and had expanded into other countries. Such groups—right-wing, anti-communist death squads that could be hired to effect justice or revenge—really do exist, he continued, and they can go where the police dare not enter. These vigilantes were even willing to venture into the city's lawless slums, when necessary, to get a job done. And "everybody knew" that nobody went there, if you valued your life.

There was a lot of "getting done" in Argentina, Fiona later learned. But it was mostly at the hands of the military dictatorship. People—mostly suspected dissidents—went missing all the time. At weekly mothers' marches at the Plaza de Mayo, across from the

President's Casa Rosada residence, women bore public witness to their loss, demanding their sons be returned to them. The regime ignored them, which fanned the flames of their passion for justice.

When Fiona tried to ask questions about these demonstrators, Julia called them Las Locas (madwomen), and gave her a concerned look that suggested she should stop asking questions. Well, that's unsatisfying, Fiona thought. She was so used to getting long, professorial answers to her questions, she hardly knew what to do with them, now that they were clearly unwelcome. She shook her head, as if to shake off all the questions that had gathered, shivering at the thought of those mothers on the Plaza. Maybe curiosity really can kill cats. Maybe feigned ignorance sometimes affords a queer kind of security.

Fiona's thoughts traveled stateside. She thought about how overtly people indulged their passions and protests there. Back home, you could march against something without disappearing, couldn't you? She had done it. Pop had done it. Lots of people had. Nobody she knew had ever gone missing. Sure, the tear gas wasn't any fun, and the dogs and the horses had been scary, but she hadn't disappeared. Wait, she thought, is that always true? I should ask Pop. He'll know. Anyway, back home, victims get justice, don't they? But, what justice could there really be for something like this? Satisfaction, then.

Then, Fiona remembered the offer from the yacht club. Satisfaction. She could get some. Even as the idea of vengeance repulsed her, Fiona felt oddly grateful that others had found her such a drastic option to enable her to seek retribution for the crimes against her. She gathered that her host family and their many friends were people of power and presence, if they were so well connected. Yet, Fiona wanted the events to die with the day, not live on. And she didn't want blood on her conscience. He was responsible for kidnapping her, beating her, tormenting her, violating her. She didn't want him to also be responsible for destroying her self-image. He did not hold the power to turn her into a murderer. And with that thought, Fiona had a startling realization. He had no more power over her, at all.

Fiona felt homesick when she considered the barbarism of the world, but it was a different kind of homesick than she'd ever felt. It was a wistful kind of homesickness that aches for a better world than this, or perhaps mourns the death of her belief in the basic goodness of the world. Would that ever be resurrected? She didn't think anyone there would understand this feeling, so she held her peace. Instead, she asked her new friends for help with her Spanish, learning a whole new vocabulary as she wrote about the entire ordeal, including horrible words she otherwise would not have had reason or desire to know. Words no girl—or boy—should ever need to know. Words one does not find listed in visitor guides. How ironic that the visitors were the very people who might need them. Mariana, helping her translate her thoughts said, "Look, it's just life. Everybody's been through it. Just get over it and move on. And be careful what you remember and whom you tell."

How hardened were the perspectives of these young women, who seemed to live in a culture of abuse, lurking around every corner. Fiona was getting a lesson in lawlessness and the language that went with it.

She had no idea how to puzzle her way to a comfortable answer for what had happened to her. Perhaps more important, how was she going to move forward? Night after night, her mind pondered the possibility of what to do with a pregnancy. She was consumed with considering her options: raising a baby of rape, giving away her child to some stranger, or submitting to an abortion and maybe dying. None of her options had a happy ending. She couldn't stop thinking about Mary's Aunt Evelyn, Bea's sister, who had died from a botched illegal abortion. Oh, poor Bea, coming home from school like that, finding her older sister dead, in a pool of blood. Fiona had heard that the article headline had simply read, "Teen Found Dead." So, folks assumed suicide. I don't want people reading something like that about me, she thought. And then the other thoughts continued: I wonder when, exactly, does a fetus become a person? And just because abortion was now legal back home didn't mean it was legal in Argentina. Fiona could find no easy solution.

The constant worry came to an end a week after Fiona's brutal attack when she was awakened at 6 am by terrible cramps. For the first time, she welcomed the pain; it felt like another miracle. With each cramp came a sigh of relief. It was, as Gram had agreed to call it, "moon time." Fiona gloried in her discomfort. She was over the moon. From now on, she said, I'll try to remember this relief and celebrate a little, as I face my PMS every month. Hooray! Thank you, God!

~oOO0O0o~

Even as her mood lifted, Fiona still felt like staying indoors. Her host family wanted to cheer her up. They plied her with delicious local foods. They talked of taking her to tango shows, and even a big concert, starring Luis Alberto Spinetta, considered the "father of Argentinian rock." They suggested a day trip to La Boca, a town built mostly by Italian immigrants who had painted their houses with leftover ship paint. She begged off every invitation. Julia gave Fiona a carved statue of St. Francis. Mariana explained the concept of secondary virginity, telling her, "You're a spiritual virgin," meaning that nobody can take this precious gift if it isn't given freely. It was oddly comforting. Yet for Fiona, at least for now, there was no erasing what had happened with what felt like a mere play on words. The doctor had told her she'd feel better with the tincture of time. She hoped so. Guess there are no shortcuts to anything, she thought to herself.

Fiona understood that everyone was just trying to help, that they wanted to guide their guest in moving forward from the tragedy. But all she wanted to do was curl up in a ball and never venture outside again.

"That just won't do," they all insisted. It was decided that Fiona would accompany the family to their seaside cottage a few hours south of town in Santa Teresita for the weekend. Because no one would be home to stay with her, protect her, keep her safe—not even the maid—Fiona had no choice but to go with them. But even there, she spent the weekend inside the cottage, with the TV on. The family kept the set tuned to the state-owned television station, Canal 7, but when Fiona had the house to herself she turned the channel to watch telenovelas, trying to follow the story lines of the Latin soap operas everyone loved. Mother would have forced her to get out and participate with the family. Pop would have left her alone. Gram would have watched with her. At least I'm improving my Spanish, she told herself, sipping a lemonade the family had left for her before traipsing down to the beach.

The sisters managed to coax Fiona out to a special party for locals, known as a porteño. Again, she didn't want to go. And again, she wasn't permitted to say no. The family had paid her way. The room was crowded and colorful, the energy high and bright, and the music was loud, with a beat that made hips sway and people dance before being asked. The mix included American disco and Latin rhythms from all over. When the Brazilian song "Lança Perfume" by Rita Lee came on, Julia leaned over and asked, "Know what this is about? It's about poppers. She's saying release the perfume; get it?" Fiona didn't get it. She wasn't sure what poppers were, until Julia's friend Miguel pulled one out of his satchel, and offered it to her. After she turned him down, he broke the glass vial and sniffed it, releasing a little scented amyl nitrate. "Wooo-eeee," he exclaimed, before heading out to the dance floor. Same everywhere I guess, Fiona thought. Just a variation on the theme of how to take the edge off. Just then, one of the revelers started freaking out in the middle of the dance floor, calling out, "No soy un egoísta," meaning "I'm not an egotist," over and over, while hogging center stage. Such melodrama!

The Silvas decided Fiona was emerging from her protective shell too slowly, and needed some hometown healing. They decided a *santería* service, held in a *casa de la adoración* in the Afro-Argentine community in the San Telmo district, was in order. Fiona was game. She asked Julia if the name meant saints were involved. "Sí," said Julia, "as well as *orishas*, spirit helpers." That sounded safe to Fiona, who followed Julia to her bedroom to find something white to wear. Everyone, she'd said, wore white, down to their skivvies, or the healing wouldn't work as well. So, dressed, head to toe in white, Fiona and her host sisters headed for San Telmo.

With a soft light emanating from white candles faintly glowing on saintly statues, Fiona thought the casa de adoración had a vaguely Catholic aesthetic, which made sense to her in this largely Catholic country. But, as she soon learned, the practice was grounded in *Candomblé*, which was a blend of traditional West African beliefs that had been brought with the slaves through the port city of Salvador, Brazil, before spreading to Argentina, Uruguay, Paraguay, and Venezuela.

Inside, the white-dressed participants were taking part in rhythmic chanting and singing and instrumental music, which continued for nearly an hour before several people fell into a trance. Only then were guests invited into healing rituals. As a healer put her hands over Fiona's head, she felt a strong, magnetic pull, as if she'd been placed into an electrifying light show. Her energy lifted in the safe and soothing environment surrounded by spiritual music and open hearts. Fiona was fascinated by the laying on of hands—anointed hands—she'd just experienced.

On the ride home, Fiona asked Julia to tell her a little about what her family believed. "Well," Julia said, "there's a spirit world around us, filled with pure spirits, light ones, and also dark ones, with one big God and his helper orishas. Each of us has a destiny to fulfill, and what we do will come back to us." It was a lot to ponder.

Back at the house with the Silvas, Julia put on an Elton John record, thinking it would help Fiona feel better. But as soon as Fiona heard, "Philadelphia Freedom," it brought on a fresh wave of tears. That evening, unbeknownst to Fiona, Armida picked up the phone and dialed Fiona's mother. She'd been hesitant to violate Fiona's privacy but now felt that Fiona needed her own flesh-and-blood mother, and not a stand-in.

Fiona found herself packing her bags again. She had expected to spend a year in Buenos Aires. Going back "home" to Mother filled Fiona with a panoply of feelings, none of them good. Someone had spilled the beans. I'm going to wring Mary's neck, thought Fiona. She was furious as she thought of her friend, the only person she'd told—only intimated, really—about her ordeal in Argentina.

Home. Fiona had never been sure what that word even meant.

~oOOoOOo~

Fiona could only imagine how livid Mother would be at having to incorporate her daughter back into her life after a mere two-week absence. She had anticipated a year of time to herself. Mother will be beside herself, Fiona thought, as she snapped her suitcase shut.

Fiona was caught off-guard by how difficult it was to say goodbye to the Silvas. Thanks to her ordeal, they had come to signify a great deal to her in a very short period of time. She was moved by their strong, lingering hugs and the tears in their eyes—and she already anticipated the longing she would feel absent their kindness and tenderness. She would miss this family she had lived with for such a short time. In a way, she already did.

"Lo siento, mija," Armida said quietly. "I'm sorry, my child."

"It was going to be so good," said Julia, her eyes brimming with tears. "It was supposed to be really good."

"I know," Fiona said, kindly. "And much of it was. Don't forget that." Fiona knew she'd miss Julia the most.

"No te olvides de nosotros," whispered Julia. "Don't forget us."

"Nunca," said Fiona. "Never."

~oO0O0Oo~

Returning to Rio de Janeiro for her layover, Fiona flew over Mt. Corcovado once again, gazing down upon the "Christo Redentor" statue with fresh eyes. She had felt a strong connection with the statue, when she'd first set eyes on it; it seemed to tell her that God was real, and that Jesus' arms were open so wide they could welcome the entire cosmos. Now, she didn't have to wonder, because she knew. And here he was, again, so beautiful and true. He's everywhere. Fiona marveled. Even with me. That's just outstanding.

Fiona peered out the window of the airplane, trying to catch a glimpse of the Southern Cross constellation in the sky as soon as darkness set in, but she was out of luck. The flight, and Fiona's extra layover in New York—a two-stop flight was the best they could do on short notice—left her exhausted. Fiona headed toward baggage claim, and waited impatiently until her bag finally emerged. It was heavy, and she struggled up to the customs line. Before she'd left, the Silvas had asked her if she'd please carry a few items along with her; something for Mother, and more for friends of theirs in California, and she had agreed. When she got to the front of the line, she dutifully opened her bag. The woman peered inside and asked her what these things were. A wave of panic washed over Fiona as she realized she didn't know. She'd simply trusted. She could have carried just about anything into the country. "Gifts from my host family in Argentina," she said, weakly. "I haven't opened them yet."

Fiona's thoughts turned to one of Mother's mystery novels, where women were sometimes used as "drug mules," carrying illegal cargo for mafia types, and sometimes met with unkind ends. At best, they ended up in the slammer. In one of them, wasn't the mule murdered? She wished she'd at least been smart enough to look at the packages she'd been given.

The officer finished searching Fiona's bag and, having found nothing of interest or great value, stamped her passport, and signed off on her customs form. Through the barrage of self-directed insults and accusations screaming inside Fiona's head, she hardly heard the officer tell her she was cleared to go. Never again will I be so stupid, she thought. I'm sure I said that last time, too. Fiona smiled meekly at the officer as she slung her bag over her shoulder and stepped onto the escalator, heading toward the next leg of her flight. Five more hours. She slept almost the entire way across the country.

The joy and relief Fiona sensed as the plane approached SFO was invigorating. Seeing the wonderful landmarks of the Bay Area filled her with gratitude. She was happy to be alive, to have traveled safely, and even, she realized, to be coming home. As she took in the city lights framing the Bay, Fiona started to hum under her breath, "If you're goin' to San Francisco…" She'd get some flowers for her hair first thing tomorrow, because she knew, at that moment, that California—not the East Coast, not India, and certainly not Argentina, was home.

Peggy was right on time at the front of the international exit, waiting to collect her child. Fiona didn't know what to expect and felt a bit afraid to face her. But, here she was, warm and smiling. After giving Fiona a longer hug than usual, her mother picked up her bags and carried them to the car. The hug and the smile had been a welcome relief, and the help with her bags had been an even bigger surprise. They made small talk as they walked to the car, where Peggy stowed the luggage in the back before getting in. After such a long flight, the 40-minute drive into Berkeley seemed interminably long. Once back on the ground, Fiona was so ready to be home.

Looking through the window of Mother's Mercedes, Fiona felt a deep sense of security at how familiar everything looked, especially as the car swung into the driveway. She climbed out of the car and, while Mother pulled her bags from the trunk, she stood there, feeling at home on her native soil. It annoyed her that, as hard as she tried to change her inner radio, she still couldn't get "Philadelphia Freedom" out of her head. It had been stuck there, in a loop, since her Argentinian sisters had played it for her. How do I get this out of my head? California is my true home. I am back home. I should be thinking San Francisco thoughts. But not even the Beach Boys could drown it out. Wait, I have it! Radio jingles! she thought. Maybe they're the answer. "My bologna has a first name…"

Although she was exhausted, Fiona picked up her own bags and carried them in through the front door. Once inside Mother's house, Fiona found she wasn't ready to go to sleep. She was so happy to be there; she just wanted some time to take it all in. The first thing she did as she came through the door was kneel down and gather an exuberant Starlight into her arms. The poodle was so excited to see her person, she could hardly control herself, and peed a little. Silly pup! As Fiona stroked Starlight's soft curls, an ocean of grief met with the wave of relief she felt to be home. Mother quietly picked up her daughter's heavy bags and escorted puppy and teen upstairs to their room.

9. SHE'S BACK

By the time Fiona awoke on her first day back in California, it was already late morning. It was a Saturday, and Fiona had the weekend to get over the jet lag before having to return to school. She was planning on taking it slowly.

She sat up and gazed out her window for a moment, orienting herself, before getting up to unpack and take a warm shower. Mother had come into the kitchen for a bite to eat and put the kettle on for tea.

When Fiona came down for breakfast, she took a seat in front of the plate of English muffins and jelly Mother had set out. Mother poured them both a cup of tea, and then she, too, sat down. Looking into Fiona's blue eyes, Mother gently told her she already knew what had happened. Fiona began to cry. "Mary promised she wouldn't say…"

"It wasn't Mary," said Mother. "Armida called, and we talked."

Fiona pondered that conversation for a moment, mother to mother. Then she steeled herself for a lecture. She expected an onslaught of questions about where she had been, what she'd been doing, what she was wearing, and what she was thinking, taking a taxi in Argentina by herself. Bracing herself for all the subtle and not-so-subtle blaming she anticipated, Fiona had her guard up. And yet, all she could do was cry.

Fiona knew a person could do everything right and, still, bad things could happen. She wished Mother knew that. She was already devastated that she had failed miserably—on the first night of her exchange, no less—and had been sent home in disgrace.

But, the blame and the shame never came. Instead, Mother did something unexpected and surprising. She reached for Fiona and sat her on her lap, as she hadn't done since Fiona was very little, and pulled her in close. Then she started in with a long and silly litany in a bit of a sing-song voice. "You know what I'd do to that monster? I'd rip out his entrails and feed them to the squirrels. I'd bash in his head, scoop out his brains and mash 'em in the blender before serving them to the raccoons. I'd tear his ears off and make him eat them. I'd pull his toenails out, one by one...and I'd let him know I was just getting started."

Mother, who was so creative in the way she wrote about how people were murdered in her psycho-thrillers, had no compunction about getting gruesome. Especially when using psychology to soothe her daughter. The more graphic Mother got, the more Fiona laughed. Mother seemed to be enjoying herself, as well. Then Mother thought for a moment before saying, "You know, Fiona, the next novel I write will include a cabbie who gets it in the end. Just wait and see what I dream up for him."

Fiona couldn't wait. Somehow, to have her mother work it out in writing, and then see it happen in her descriptive narrative, would feel a little like the retribution her Argentinian friends had talked about. Except not. Not really. Maybe that's why people enjoy a good movie or well-written novel, she thought, to step into an alternative reality where people do what you can't or won't do, in your own life, for whatever reason.

She decided now wasn't the moment to tell Mother how she really could have had that cabbie's life snuffed out. Fiona didn't want to do anything to destroy the moment. It was the sort of experience she had hoped and longed for since she was a young child, a moment of emotional honesty and intimacy with her mom.

"Did you tell your father?" Mother asked, as she got up to brew more tea.

"No," Fiona answered, watching her mother for a reaction. "I thought about it, but I decided he might freak out."

"You're probably right," said Mother, as she set the kettle to boil. "What about your grandmother? The girls?"

"Gram would be okay, I think, but she'd tell Pop. And the girls'd probably have nightmares." Fiona wanted to tell her father, wanted to feel his self-righteous indignation, enjoy all the swearing she imagined he'd unleash about the cabbie, but she'd decided that was just being self-centered. It was too big a price for her father to pay, just so she could have some comfort for herself. She wasn't so sure he'd believe her about how she evaded death, and the last thing she wanted was to choose between an argument and a half-truth.

"You know, Fiona," said Mother, sitting down again, "your father probably should be told, and it's better coming from you than me, I think. You don't need to call him today, but you might want to think about it. In the meantime, you can talk to me whenever you feel like it.

"They say a person needs to tell their story 100 times before it gets out of their system. You're not going to forget what happened, but you will get to a point when you're ready to let it go, and maybe use it as a writer later, or as a psychologist, or in some other way. If you're not scratched, you can't be polished. The attack was something that happened to you, Fiona; it is not who you are. Don't dwell on it; polish it away and shine brighter. Don't let it define you. Hmmm?"

Fiona reached out and tentatively placed her hand upon her mother's, just long enough to feel the warmth she was sensing in her words. Then she withdrew it before her mother could, so she could let the moment linger in her mind. This was the part of the whole ordeal she wanted to remember. Forever.

She didn't think she'd tell Pop.

~o0O0O0o~

Fiona slept until noon on Sunday. When she woke, she called Karen. "Fiona, I'm so glad you're alive, and I'm glad you shared your story with me. Please don't take this the wrong way, but be careful about sharing it with people. It's not because of what happened—if people don't like it they can lump it—but about how you got away alive. People say 'Jesus Saves' all the time, but they don't mean it the way you do, and some don't even believe it.

"What you call 'Jesus saving you,' others will call 'magical thinking.' That's sometimes dangerous. People could say it's impossible, and that you're crazy if you stick to your story. I know you want to share, you want to see how people react. It's kind of like verbal vomit. You want to get the toxin out. The thing is, you need to be careful. There's a real danger, Fiona. You could be locked up. Institutionalized.

"Did you know I was locked up once? I was. For trying to commit suicide. I found out you have to be careful what you say in a place like that, or you can wind up trapped in there. I guess what I'm saying is, be careful whom you trust in this world."

Tell me something I don't know, thought Fiona, but what she managed to say out loud was simply, "Thanks, Sis, I'll try to remember that."

The next day, while getting ready to return to school, Fiona was greeted by a torrential rainstorm. The storm meant she'd have to take the bus to school. Mother was in the kitchen, having coffee with a college friend named Jacques. After a quick cup of tea and a hard-boiled egg, Fiona secured her hood and slung her backpack over her shoulders, as she braced herself for the walk to the bus.

She was just closing the door behind her when Jacques came running down the hall, one shoe on and the other in hand, yelling, "Wait, Fiona; wait!" He was offering her a ride, something he hadn't done before. Fiona, not long back from Argentina, was uncomfortable with the offer from a man she didn't know well, but Mother's reassuring wink told her it was fine to agree to the help. If there ever a day when she needed it, this was it. The simple act of kindness cost him about 10 minutes, but it saved Fiona half an hour and a drenched head. It changed the feeling of her entire day. It was one small kindness that meant a lot.

Fiona sat in Mary's bedroom one afternoon, chatting about

nothing, while Mary played a mélange of her favorite artists she thought would be appropriate for the mood of the moment—Carole King, Jackson Browne, and James Taylor. Fiona took in the details of Mary's feminine room—her white wicker headboard and ruffled bedspread, her big-eyed Christine Rosamond posters—and the evidence of her faith: the simple carved cross by the door, a little statue of Mother Mary, and a Holy Bible on her nightstand. Fiona had begun to wonder about getting baptized, but she didn't want to go through official channels. She knew Mary would be the one to confide in about it. Mary was not only happy to talk; she was willing to officiate. After school the next day, the two friends walked down behind Mother's house to the stream that flowed along the edge of her property.

"Fiona, do you wish to be baptized?" Mary asked, as they made their way into the water.

"Yes." They had waded in up to their ankles and were both shivering. Mary imagined that their shivering was caused by the combined presence of Spirit and the ice-cold water.

"Fiona," said Mary, as she bent to fill her cupped hand with water. "I baptize you in the name of the Father," (splash) "the Son," (splash) "and the Holy Spirit" (splash). She seemed like she was enjoying getting Fiona as wet as possible, as she splashed a handful of water onto Fiona's head with each word.

Once out of the icy water and back on the grassy bank of the stream, the girls basked in the warmth of the bright, sunny day and Fiona's new status. Mary presented her friend with her own little pocket Bible, saying, "Here is your Bible. B.I.B.L.E. stands for Basic Instructions Before Leaving Earth. Take a hint and don't start at page one. It's actually a bunch of books. So, start with Luke. You'll like the social justice teachings in there."

B.I.B.L.E. Thought Fiona. Cute. I hadn't heard that one. As the friends sat by the stream, warming their bodies and sharing the sacred moment, Mary quietly considered everything that had brought them to this moment. "You know, Fee, it's really something that Jesus came in and touched your life. It's just huge. I don't think when that happens, a person is ever really the same. Not like I'd wish what happened on anyone; ; I just mean, well, you know what I mean."

"Not on your best friend, you mean?" Fiona laughed. "Watch out, I'll go get some of that water and douse you."

"It's like chemistry. Something interacts, and you're changed. Even the taxi man, I bet. Can't you just picture him, unable to kill and rob and cheat and steal and plunder anymore, disgusted by his own reflection, and his former friends all looking at him like he's from Mars. No way back. Can't you just see it?"

"You know, I like that picture. I like it a lot, Mare." Fiona couldn't help but laugh out loud. "He'd almost wish he'd been snuffed out, crushed like a bug by some great white fist, and never lived to see the day, wouldn't he? So, it's a fate worse than death, then? A little weird course in miracles of his very own? Well, why not? And then I could see him staggering off to some soup kitchen, to spend his last days feeding the hungry. Anything's possible. I wouldn't bet on it, though."

Mary sat up on the grass. "Never say never. That's one thing I'm learning." She said, giving her friend a warm hug. Fiona got the sense that she'd been waiting for this moment for a very long time.

~oOOoOOo~

Fiona didn't find it easy settling back into life at Berkeley High. She'd liked the idea of being far from her parents, in Argentina. She had been dreaming of a life where she controlled her destiny for some time now, and she was looking forward to the day she could strike out on her own. She could see herself in a white lab coat, with a stethoscope around her neck, as Dr. Fiona, chief neurosurgeon. Or with wings on her lapel, as Captain Fiona, senior pilot. Maybe Dr. Fiona, veterinarian. Or Fiona, editor-in-chief for the *San Francisco Examiner*. Perhaps even Fiona, principal viola for the San Francisco Symphony. Whatever she became, Fiona wanted it now. Just wait, she'd think to herself, just wait! It's going to be amazing.

One afternoon, as Fiona rehearsed those thoughts, she had a moment of clarity. It was as if a window had opened. Why not graduate early and go to college now? The next day she was in Mr. Iggy Salinsky's office. He was the school's college counselor, and Fiona was hoping for some direction and advice on how to accomplish her beautiful vision.

"You want to do what?" It was as if Mr. Salinsky hadn't quite heard her. Except, he had. "Why would you want to do that? You only have one more year left of high school to enjoy. It's one of the happiest times in life, when you have less responsibility than you ever will, again."

"Well, maybe for some. But high school is not the happiest time for everyone," Fiona responded. "In my case, I'm unwilling to believe this is as good as it gets."

Mr. Salinsky seemed personally insulted. Fiona was only considering leaving a year early, and surely her wealth of life experience should count for something. Rather than helping her brainstorm how to accomplish her goal, he brought up the roadblocks. "You haven't met the graduation requirements for Berkeley High, Fiona, and it wouldn't be feasible for you to graduate in the time remaining."

Fiona wasn't willing to give up so easily. "I realize that, Mr. Salinsky. So, let's get down to the actual college entry requirements. I'd like to test out of high school. I'd like to take the equivalency test. And, since I'm going to pass it, I'd like your help applying to colleges, now. That's what you do, right?"

At what he considered impertinence, Mr. Salinsky grew colder and more formal with Fiona. "Listen, Fiona, I urge you to reconsider this plan of yours. It isn't in your best interest. I don't know how best to say this to you, so I'll just give it to you straight. Everybody your age thinks they're special."

His words stung, but she wasn't about to show him that. What do you know? she thought. You don't know anything about me or what's in my best interest. But, hey, thanks for the vote of confidence. Fiona stood up silently, slinging her backpack over her shoulder. "Well, thanks for the time," she said, making her exit.

Fiona walked down the corridor more indignant than dejected, which served to fuel her fire. Her conversation with her college counselor could have stifled her dreams and, more importantly, her urgent plan. But, instead, it provided further confirmation that she didn't belong there. If she truly wanted out, she was going to have to find her own exit. His one quick comment had renewed her resolve not to be squashed by life but, instead, to go out and grab it by the horns, wrestle it to the ground, and then saddle up.

"Everyone my age thinks they're special?" Was he kidding? This, coming from a counselor who probably finds nothing even close to special in any of us. "Of course, we're all special, Mr. Salinsky," she murmured. You say that like it's a bad thing. If only we didn't have people like you stomping on our sense of self like one of those Apple Bonkers from *Yellow Submarine*, we might not forget it. As Fiona's inner radio began playing John Lennon's "Instant Karma," it was all she could do to keep from singing along when he asked, "Who do you think you are, a superstar? Well, right you are!" After all, we all do shine on, don't we? she thought, even if some people are too buried in mud to show it. Isn't the world soul-crushing enough without someone like him, and his toxic "You're nothing special, so don't bother trying" messages? Isn't he supposed to have our backs? she wondered. With freaks like him, who needs enemies?

The rest of the day, Fiona looked around campus at every single student, thinking about how they, too, probably had people stomping on their self-esteem. Sure, different people responded differently. She could suddenly see it. And as she did, she felt a solidarity with every other student in the school for the first time, ever. She smiled at everyone she passed, thinking, life can be a prison when you're under someone's thumb. Better plan a jailbreak or you might just shrivel up and die.

Still feeling the weight of Mr. Salinsky's words, given extra heft thanks to his position of power in her life, Fiona vowed she would never, ever step on someone else's dream, no matter how idiotic or impossible it sounded. Life is full of dream-killers, she thought. Count me out. That's a big part of my oldie-but-goldie, *Golden Rule #1: Love God, Love People*. In the meantime, watch out world, I'm busting out! With that, Fiona shoved her books into her backpack and went home to start paving the path to her future.

~oOoOOOo~

Sitting on her bed, with study materials strewn about her, Fiona thought about the life she would lead once she had a college educa-tion—which she assumed included bachelor's, master's, and doctor-ate degrees—and the wherewithal to apply it. After I've made my mark on the world, she thought, I'll go back to high school as a guest speaker for teens and encourage them to go for the brass ring and never let the bastards get them down! Fiona didn't think about the compassionate flexibility her PE teacher had demonstrated when he let her replace gym class with an off-campus Aikido class. She didn't think about the support and encouragement she'd received in orchestra. She forgot, for a moment, how impressed her math teacher was with her "fine mind." Fiona had her eye on the prize, and that was getting the hell out of Dodge.

In truth, her resolve had nothing to do with mazes and prizes. It was deeper, more fundamental. It was about finding a way to feel safe, secure, and at home in this world. It had been a long time since she'd felt safe with either of her parents, or at home in any of the places she'd lived. And her response, when she felt endangered, was to realize she must try harder—as if that were breaking news. Here, again, was the same old epiphany, repackaged. I will be excellent in all things, so I will be prepared for whatever befalls me. I will collect all the merit badges of life. With a little luck, I'll collect them all, starting with my college degree. Right now. Best get started, and move fast!

"With a little luck." That phrase had become Fiona's personal motto, and the song had become her anthem the first time she'd heard it. Paul McCartney's lyrics reminded her to turn her back on the inclement weather, just like a willow tree might do. She smiled, thinking how beautiful willows were, and how they bend and never break. Yep, we can work it out. With some luck. And maybe some elbow grease? She wasn't sure there was a "we" in this for her, but she sang along with McCartney anyway, "There's no end to what we can do, together."

When Fiona told her mother about her plan, Peggy took a deep breath and considered the added complexity to her difficult financial timetable, mentally adding in the cost of tutors Fiona might need to ace the achievement tests in subjects she hadn't yet studied deeply in high school. Peggy was thinking ahead. She didn't let on that the financial surprise of sending Fiona to college a year early might be an unexpected burden. Instead, she simply agreed, if that was what Fiona wanted to do, it was fine by her. Fiona took this as an indication that her mother wanted her out of the house that much earlier. It was a little more complicated than that.

Fiona sat down and wrote Gram and Pop, detailing her plan, and asking them for advice. By advice, she really meant approval and support. It came in the form of an early Christmas check for $25 from Gram, accompanied by a short note that suggested she relax a bit, because "sometimes we have to sit back and let things happen." Fiona understood her grandmother's perspective and appreciated her concern, but there really was no time for relaxing and waiting. Not now. Maybe not ever.

Fiona looked closely at the letter. In the envelope was a second check. It was from Pop. One hundred and ten dollars, with a short note typed up in memo form, in mock formality. It simply said, "To: Bank of Fiona Sprechelbach, RE: $100 loan. The attached payment with interest should bring my account to good standing. Thanks so much – Wolf S." Well, blow me over with a feather, Fiona thought. He must be at "Step Nine: Make Direct Amends" in his 12-step program, Fiona thought. How about that? Fiona thought to herself, shaking her head in near disbelief. Tomorrow that's going right into my savings account.

The money came in handy when Fiona started buying study guides for her equivalency exam. Pop's actual response to her letter came a few weeks later. While it got off to a slow start, ultimately, it was filled with just the sort of information she needed about test-taking, colleges and their entrance requirements. Feeling really supported by her East Coast family, Fiona got the sense she wasn't alone in this after all. They had the confidence she could do this, so why shouldn't she?

For her part, Mother quickly arranged for three of her own students to provide tutoring to Fiona, so she could ace the achievement tests and improve her odds of college admission. Happy for the help, Fiona shifted her intentions from escaping Mother to making her proud. She started cutting classes at school to work with her tutors instead. Even in that, Mother supported her, writing notes to say Fiona had been sick or at the dentist when, in her absences, she'd been studying for her tests.

"Mother, another royalty check came through," Fiona called out to the cottage. "And hey, can I have another excuse please?"

"Sure, hon. What should I say this time?"

"I don't know. How about, 'Fiona has this weird bug that keeps coming back.'"

"A math tutor bug named Mike? That won't go over too well, I don't think. Don't worry, I've got an idea."

Mother came up with a multitude of wonderful excuses. In planning the escape, they were perfect partners in crime. When Fiona wasn't on the phone, in her room studying, or practicing the viola, she sometimes picked up her Bible. She'd thought she might quickly read it, cover to cover, from Genesis straight through to Revelation, and then digest the whole thing. She read the words, but without any background knowledge it left her unsatisfied, confused, and a little bit angry. She picked up the phone and called Mary.

"You did it that way?" said Mary. "Didn't you remember my advice down by the stream, to start with the Gospel of Luke? It's really a whole bunch of books, not just one. You did hear that part, right? And anyway…"

"Listen, now I've read the Bible, cover to cover," Fiona interrupted, growing defensive, "And what I want to know is, do you actually believe this stuff?" She half expected her friend to say no. When Mary stayed silent, Fiona pressed on. "Creation in six days? Or, how can God come and walk with us, anyway? Where's the logic in that?"

"Wow, Fiona. Where do I start? When the beginning was beginning, the universe was formless and void. And, in the beginning was the Word. I can get into that. I mean, it's not head, it's heart. It's total poetry. Don't you see it? God dwelling among us, feeling what we feel, is pretty awesome. And God's time isn't our time. Don't get me wrong, I don't get all of it, but the Gospels I just love, which is why

I said to start with Luke. You could have started with Matthew just as easily.

"About that other stuff, maybe you should go talk to a priest or a minister or something, and they can shed some light. Anyway, why all this? Weren't you the one who had the experience with Jesus?"

"Yes, I absolutely did, but…"

"But, what?"

"It doesn't make logical sense, Mare," Fiona said.

"How can you know Jesus saved you and then reject that Jesus is actually a presence? How is that being logical? You didn't look for logic that night."

"Trust me; very little about that night made sense to me."

Fiona was about explain the laws of physics and biology to Mary, and Mary knew it. Mary could tell when Fiona was about to get teacherly. "Fiona, give yourself a break. You're always analyzing everything to death. Jesus loves you and helped you. So, what? Why not just let it be what it is, let it go, and move on?"

Because she couldn't. Mother's fascination with New Age spirituality notwithstanding, Fiona had been raised by very logical people who had taught her to question everything. The illogic of what she'd read, of what Mary was saying to her, drove Fiona crazy, and she said so. "We are both coming from the context of what we've been taught by our parents," Fiona said. "Mine taught me to challenge what I see and hear, and yours taught you to have blind faith."

"There's nothing blind about it," Mary huffed, "and maybe it's you who're blind to the obvious." Then, sensing Fiona's frustration, Mary offered an idea. "How about you take up these questions with God? You don't have to believe in anything for God to believe in you. Just go with that."

"Go with God?" Fiona smiled.

"Basically, yes."

The friends shifted their conversation to the notion of suffering, a topic that intrigued Fiona. "So, here's the thing, Mare. If God is great, and God is all powerful, and we're all God's children and all that, then why all the suffering? And while I'm at it, why did I get helped and not someone else? I'm no more special than the next duck. What's up with that? And there's another thing, about Jesus dying the way he did. What parent would actually go for that?"

"Fiona, you're making my head spin. I can go ask Father Murphy. He's a Jesuit and a deep thinker. In the meantime, how about giving my idea a try?"

"Which idea?"

"To go with God."

On Sunday afternoon, Mary called Fiona with an answer from Father Murphy about the world and suffering. "He said you posed great questions, and he wanted me to ask you one in return: 'Does God always get what God wants?'"

"Oh, right. A riddle. That's just great," Fiona sighed.

~o0O0O0o~

The following weekend, Bea took the girls to Half Moon Bay to ride horses. They made their way on horseback down steep cliffs to the beach, to ride through the spray at the shoreline. Fiona, sitting astride a sturdy mount named Walter, felt safe and happy, galloping along the beach with abandon. Although Walter took direction well, on some level, he was in charge. He was the only one making decisions about his footfalls. Fiona had faith Walter would carry her and not falter.

"Did you trust your horse, Fiona?" Bea interrupted the girls' animated chatter about their day, as they wandered back to the car to head home.

"Sure did. Walter was great."

"Have you always been so confident on a horse?"

Fiona thought for a moment. She couldn't remember. "Maybe not when I was a beginner, when I was just learning to ride."

"And yet, you were still willing to get in the saddle. What do you think made you do that?"

"I don't know. I guess I wanted to be a rider, like my older sister and my mother and stuff."

"Fiona, when you want to be a person of great confidence in something, what do you do?" asked Bea, unlocking the car door.

"Okay, I get it. I know where you're going with this. You're going to say that you practice. Then you're going to tell me when I decide to seek faith, the rest comes with time in the saddle. Am I catching your drift? Only, my brain doesn't work that way."

Fiona thought for a moment. "I'm not sure how my brain works, actually, or why I prayed as a last-minute Hail Mary in Argentina. But I see your point. After all, God made horses, and I do have faith in them. So, that's a start, anyway. Right?"

"Yes," said Bea. "It's a good one."

~oO0O0Oo~

Fiona had seen a parade of gurus, swamis, teachers, and self-designated enlightened ones come and go like infatuations, and she didn't like to see her otherwise intelligent Mother falling under the sway of what she imagined would be yet another charismatic clown. Mother's latest curiosity was the New Age teacher "The Cass," and when his oversized presence lumbered into Fiona's life, there was little she could do about it, other than try to be Cass-o-wary, herself.

Fiona had heard the name before. Wasn't he the same guy Brennan had told her about, the guy his brother had skippered for, the inventor of The CASST Process? Peggy and The Cass had hit it off extraordinarily well, and The Cass had begun spending quite a lot of time at the house. He gave Fiona the creeps, so she called all her friends to find out more. Word on the street was that he was selling an anger-centric path to personal freedom, framed in the vocabulary of tough love. Accessing your anger was loving, he said, because it was truth. Truth was love. By unleashing your truth, you could create your own reality and live up to your potential. Unleashing your potential was what the world needed. You could have what you wanted and be free, and CASST was the One True Path to your soul's desire. Anything else was, as he put it, "merde." People in life who held you back were "merde." Walking this path apparently involved confronting important people in your life and telling them why their love was toxic.

I don't know, Fiona thought, it feels like the wrong vibe. Don't most spiritual paths involve the cultivation of compassion and lovingkindness? I get it that truth is love and living your potential isn't bad either, but it feels a little, I don't know, a little something. Besides, her thoughts continued, if you end up free of all attachments except for him, isn't that kind of convenient for him? I guess once you fall down that rabbit hole, you see the upside-down logic, and it makes perfect sense.

Cassowary Cass was what he called his New Age alter ego. His real name was Harold Kargo, and he hailed from the South Side of Chicago. For some reason Fiona couldn't understand, Mother was attracted to his brusque superiority, which was really a kind of cruelty. Fiona noticed it wasn't long before Mother began adopting his manner. That afternoon, as Fiona sat in her room, she heard her mother's voice, loud, and clear, from the cottage. Her voice could carry when it was angry, and clearly, Mother was furious.

The Cass had Peggy right where he wanted her, exhausted and vulnerable. "You do want to breathe freely, don't you, Peggy?" he cooed, soothingly. "Take a baby step toward freedom. First, you throw away your old letters. That helps cut ties with the toxic past. Release them, and unleash your future potential."

The next morning, Peggy went to work. The letters from her parents and her sister weren't so hard to release. Into the bin with them! She and her daughter Karen had never really corresponded. Nothing to toss. Articles about her acclaim? It hurt a bit to toss them, but she did. What about Fiona's letters and gifts? Maybe Fiona would like to keep them!

"Fiona, come here," said Mother, summoning her into the master bedroom.

"What's up, Mother?

"See this box of stuff? I'm doing some spring cleaning, and I'm not keeping anything from the past. I don't know if you want any of these things. Cass recommends we declutter our lives from the past, but you can take a look and make up your own mind."

With that, Mother handed off a box, once treasured, containing every letter and handmade gift Fiona had ever given her. Fiona felt her lungs constrict, forcing the air out of her chest, as if she'd been punched in the stomach and winded. Of all the times in life she'd experienced distance or rejection, nothing had felt quite this acute. Box in hand, she backed away silently, and into her room again. Peggy returned to her session with The Cass.

Before Cassowary Cass entered her life, Peggy and her family had gotten along fine, or at least as well as families do. With The Cass' encouragement, Peggy began to revisit her personal history and, as she rewrote her life story from her new perspective as a victim, her resentments multiplied. Her marriage to her high school sweetheart now felt like a shotgun wedding, with her father's finger on the trigger. He wanted a boy, anyway, and wanted me out, Peggy now decided, with zero evidence. He surely didn't cultivate my intelligence, she thought.

Peggy's sister, Ce, was remembered for the special attention she got, not the babysitting help or the many times she answered Peggy's desperate calls for help. Her parents' support untangling her relationship with Wolf became unwelcome meddling. The events remained unchanged—they were the same pearls, but hung on a string black with anger, so they took on a darker, almost sinister hue. Peggy chose to tarnish the shimmer of a life well lived—a woman who'd been lifted to heights in her career, supported by her loving family—until it was no longer visible to her naked eye.

As Peggy vented her vitriol, Fiona tried her best to tune it out. She chose the Rolling Stones mix tape, and played it just loud enough to muffle the words coming from downstairs. It seemed to do the trick. Their songs, "19th Nervous Breakdown," "Paint It Black," and "Mother's Little Helper," seemed to fit the mood perfectly. It's said that "like cures like," so perhaps it was by matching the strange reality in which she lived and over which she had no control, to the very darkness in the songs that lifted her up and soothed her soul. Or maybe it was just the backbeat, beating back the blackness.

It was November 18, 1978, and Fiona was reading the newspaper at the kitchen counter, in shocked silence. Mother walked in, looking somber. "So, you've heard." Fiona nodded. "My reporter friend lost a buddy in the mess, a cameraman, who never even made it off the airstrip," she said, her eyes on the newspaper. It was just five days before Thanksgiving. *The San Francisco Chronicle* was reporting that cult leader Jim Jones had convinced more than 900 "Peoples Temple" followers in Guyana—teenagers, adults, and families with young children—to drink Flavor-Aid, laced with cyanide. Jones' Peoples Temple had been operating in San Francisco, supposedly offering social services for the old and the poor, but had fled to Guyana after tax questions were raised. Congressman Leo Ryan was visiting Guyana to try to understand Jones' mission and determine whether people were being held against their will, as had been reported. Hours before what was later called a "mass suicide," Congressman Ryan had been shot and killed.

Fiona just looked at her mother, taking in the depth of sadness. She could find nothing appropriate to say. She knew a thing or two about freaky bad communes, but this was up and over the top. She tried to read Mother's crafted poker face, looking for clues as to what she was thinking. She really had no idea how Mother and her colleagues would react to the massacre, but she had a feeling it wouldn't be good. She wondered if Mother's friends would follow their leaders that blindly. It seemed to her that they already did, sometimes. With a shiver, she forced her mind away from the subject, and onto her homework. Her grandparents Noni and Papi, were arriving for a short Thanksgiving stay in just a few hours. That was something to look forward to.

Peggy picked up her parents at the airport, fed them meals, and held her peace for the first day of the visit. On the second evening, after everyone had headed to bed, The Cass arrived at Mother's cottage, to continue Advanced CASST. She'd been granted private, after-hours "special" sessions to help her access and catalyze her anger, so she could synergize her intense inner strength. The fact that he lacked a license as a clinical therapist, or any training in panic situations, didn't give either of them a moment's pause. Fiona could hear the raised voices from her room in the main house.

"GAARGH!" Mother screamed, lunging with both fists, "I'm so

angry, I could…GAARGH!"

"That's right, beat the snot out of that pillow. Puke it all out. Take out that anger. Go back to high school. Women had no way out in the '50s. Your parents punished one moment of love, forcing a marriage that didn't last, ruining your life. How could they do that to you? You had so much potential!"

"They never <wham!> gave me <wham!> a choice!" Mother punctuated her words with punches, as The Cass egged her on.

Fiona cringed. She felt the need to walk on eggshells when he was around, for fear their "tough love" would be turned on her. Telling herself she shouldn't listen, she shut her window and turned the lock, then turned on her portable Sony television set and tuned it to Channel 9. Fiona didn't hear any more of the session, but it was far from over.

The Cass kept revisiting the old grievances, pouring kerosene on the fire. "Life hit you. Hit life back! Tell me more! What is it about those rat bastards that really gets your goat?"

"They colluded with Wolf! He stole <wham!> my daughter <wham!> and they agreed! They even got me to think it was the right thing."

"So, you married a wolf? A predator? He huffed and puffed and blew your life down, right? That blows, Peggy. Hit back. Hit back harder! Hit 'em where it hurts. Like you mean it. Kill that pillow."

"My little daughter. The one I wanted. <wham!> She hides everything from me. <wham!> She'd talk to Herb about her drugs and not me. <wham!> There's this un-spannable chasm. It's just hopeless." At that, Mother's anger turned to bitter tears, and she lost the strength to beat the pillow anymore.

Sensing she was wrung out, The Cass ended the session with a challenge. "No law says you need to keep toxic people in your life. Remember what the Buddhists say: 'True compassion isn't weak, it's strong.' It says, 'I won't let you hurt me; it's not good for your karma.' Stop letting other people hurt you. Every time you think of them, they're opening old wounds. And the law of karma says they should get theirs.

Listen, Peggy, what would that writer of yours, Sir Arthur Quiller-Couch do? When he said, 'Kill your darlings,' he meant get rid of what's not helping the plot along, no matter how dear. And doesn't that apply equally to your life story? Who's the author here, Peggy? Where's the fire in your belly? You've got one life to live, so don't buy into guilt trips. You don't owe anybody anything. Cut 'em loose, and you'll be a free woman. I say do it now. Tonight. Before you lose clarity of purpose. Freedom. It's the last step in Advanced CASST. It's yours to claim. The Holy Grail. But only you can claim it."

The Cass saw himself out via the path at the side of the house, unescorted, and Peggy headed to bed, where she tossed and turned for hours, The Cass' words echoing in her ears. Finally, around two o'clock in the morning, she decided he was right, and now was the time to act. She burst out of bed, threw on a running suit, and headed into the main house, where she roused her parents from their slumber. Startled awake by her mother's screaming, Fiona heard the whole thing from her bed.

"Wake up!" Peggy screamed.

"What's wrong, dear?" Noni asked, yawning. "It's the middle of the night. Is something wrong? Is there an emergency?"

"Listen, I hate you. Got it? Good. Now…Get out! Leave. Now! This visit is over. It's time for you to go. Now. I've called a taxi, which is on its way, so…Get—Your—Things—And Get Out!" Mother spit out her words like venom.

Papi couldn't quite believe it. "You've got to be joking, Peggy. You can't be serious. What's the problem, here? It's not even light out." But Mother wasn't joking. She was dead serious.

"I've never been more serious," she said. "I can't guarantee your safety if you stay. I'm telling you to leave, so if you value your life, you'll listen to me and get out. Now."

Fiona tried to fathom what was happening. Hadn't everyone been getting along fine at dinner? Had she misunderstood something about family dynamics? Had she missed something crucial? She knew the blame lay, somehow, with The Cass. Fiona didn't like him, or his perspective. He was a leader. Or, rather, a misleader. He was doing what cult leaders do. He was cutting ties, obscuring facts.

My life's a freakin' roller coaster, Fiona thought. I'm not sure if I'm caught in a nut house or a prison. This Cassowary Cat, this catbird dude, I don't like him. He's bad news. My mother couldn't be so heartless, could she? So, this must be his doing. She has always preached treating elders with respect, and she also talks about forgiveness as this awesome spiritual path. Where does this fit?

Where does this fit? It doesn't. Fiona felt so distant from the woman she had for so long desperately admired and wanted to understand. Fiona didn't even know how to refer to her anymore. Where did the word Mother even fit for someone who was throwing her own mother out into the street? Once distancing, "Mother" now felt too endearing. She could call her by her first name, as she'd unconsciously started to do with Hanna after her abandonment in India, but that might call attention to the estrangement. Better to just say nothing. When necessary, she'd refer to Peggy as "my mother."

As more yelling distracted Fiona from her musings, she wondered what might happen if she ran out and yelled, "Stop!" She wanted to give her grandparents a goodbye hug, but she didn't dare. Maybe she'd be sent away in the same taxi. She stayed in her room. There was no telling what might happen if she even cracked open her door to take a peek, let alone say goodbye. So, Fiona merely listened at her bedroom door, conflicted, and wishing she had the nerve...

The cab drove off, and the melodrama ended. Fiona was almost surprised her mother didn't toss out some "Don't let the door hit you on the way out" cliché. The scene she'd just witnessed could have been lifted from one of the telenovelas Fiona had enjoyed in Argentina. But now, an uncomfortable quiet descended on the house, like a sheet draped over a birdcage. Peggy had no trouble getting right to sleep, but Fiona did. In the wake of her mother's torrential, raging outburst, Fiona was left confused and deeply sad.

Fiona's mind accompanied her grandparents on their journey back to their beautiful home, with the window seat in the kitchen, where Noni had plied her with blueberries and from which she could watch Papi strolling with his pipe in the garden. She remembered the time Noni had taken her to see *The Nutcracker*, by way of Saks Fifth Avenue, where she bought her the ballerina jewelry box she still used every day. Fiona remembered the smell of the garden after a gentle rain. How could Mother think that such loveliness was toxic? Hadn't they talked about how that smell signaled Streptomyces, the soil bacteria that can cure TB? It was a healing home, only toxic to pathogens. So, why was Mother ignoring the obvious? More importantly, would Fiona never see it or her grandparents again? That thought hit her coldly, in the pit of her stomach. She felt ill.

Fiona sat up with a start. Why had her mother invited them in the first place, if she hated them? Surely, she'd known how she felt before her parents came out, didn't she? Her feelings hadn't just changed on a whim, had they? If they had, Fiona'd better be careful. Had she really brought them to Berkeley just so she could turn around and banish them? That was too awful to ponder for long. She went over and over her grandparents' visit, replaying the details in search of clues, partly for understanding, partly so she wouldn't make the same mistake, herself. What if her mother's rage extended to other family members? What if The Cass had convinced her this was her golden moment to make a clean break all around? She shuddered as she shook off a passing thought: I could be next.

~o0O0O0o~

Just a few hours later, in the early morning light, Fiona spied her mother in the backyard, deadheading her roses with a vengeance. Some of the blossoms falling prey to her shears were still vital. As she watched, she felt a chill run up her spine. She thought it best to leave her mother alone. She picked up the phone and called Mary. Maybe she would be able to shed some light. "Hey, Mare, how's it going?" Fiona dove straight in to her dilemma. "So, what's your take on dealing with toxic relatives?"

"I'm not sure I follow. What are you getting at, Fiona?"

"Well, let's say you hated someone in your family. You'd just had it, and you decided you never wanted to see them again, for some reason. What would you do?"

"Um…depends who, I guess. Something going on?"

Fiona explained how her grandparents had left in a hurry, after an argument with her mother. She didn't share how bad it had been. The phone fell silent for what felt like ages. "Wow. I think I met them, didn't I? Didn't these people put her through college and grad school and stuff?"

"Sure, and they helped raise my older sister, too. I think my grandmother also used her connections as an editor to help my mother out when she first started writing." The Cass didn't care. That was all beside the point. The point was freedom from a "poisoned past."

"I don't like it," Mary agreed. "It seems to me it'd be kinder to make up excuses why you're too busy to visit, and send Hallmark cards and fruitcake. It still sends that nice, poisonous 'I shun thee' message you're going for. By nice, I mean it the way Shakespeare meant it. I suppose it all comes down to whether you think nonviolence and respect for other beings are useful spiritual practices."

"You know, you're right, Mary. What a joke. And you know what's even funnier?" Fiona asked, remembering the time her mother had slapped her across the face for questioning her authority. "She told me to respect my elders. That's a laugh riot, don't you think?" But Fiona wasn't laughing, and neither was Mary. "Want to walk to school together tomorrow, Fee?" Mary asked, gamely. She already knew the answer.

Fiona slipped out the back door to the lawn chair, one of her favorite spots. It was where she had parked herself on her first day at Mother's more two years ago, when she'd had no idea what to do with herself. Leaning against the woven vinyl slats of the chair, Fiona closed her eyes and felt the sun, warm upon her face. She thought about her mother—who she thought she was, and how she'd come to understand her—and compared that version with her more recent behavior patterns.

Closing her eyes and listening to the sound of her mother, busily trimming away at the rosebush, Fiona had a sinking thought. Knowing how enmeshed her mother had gotten with The Cass on her quest for liberation and enlightenment, she understood this was much more than a tiff. Maybe she's dreamed up a new metaphor, Fiona thought, maybe she's living out her own analogy: life as rosebush, self as gardener. If so, she'd see herself as reasonable in trimming away everything that is seen to have lost its luster or bloom, for the good of the plant. If that was what was going on in her mind, Fiona realized, then maybe last night made some sense. Everyone's actions are always justified in their own eyes, right?

Noni and Papi had lost their bloom in Peggy's eyes, so it would be logical, in her mind, to trim them away. Toss them into the compost. Fiona hadn't started to blossom, so the big question in Fiona's mind was whether Peggy could see the potential, and wait. Her mother had a growing need for freedom from attachments, as though severing connections would help her grow closer to enlightenment. But if a rosebush chops off its own roots and branches in this quest, what then?

Fiona couldn't bring her thoughts to a conclusion without asking herself a key question—one she wasn't willing to examine. Was Fiona, herself, about to be deadheaded as well? And, did the fact that her mother was paying the bills make up for the crazy factor? Fiona did the only thing she knew how to do when she couldn't bear what was playing out in her mind; she changed the channel. She tried the Metta prayer she had learned just last year: a repetitive Buddhist prayer where she wished herself, her friends, her family and others, as well as her enemies—all things—well. It should have put her at ease.

It didn't work.

Fiona's thoughts kept flooding in and swirling around in her mind like a storm at sea. She decided to abandon the lawn chair and go upstairs, where she would turn on the TV, pick up a guitar or her viola, or maybe open a book—anything to distract herself from her thoughts. Maybe she'd even reorganize her closet...again. Nothing like a little brainless cleaning to refocus her head.

Instead, Fiona found herself drawn to the box of letters she'd retrieved from her mother. She picked it up and began pawing through the pieces of her life, once so carefully collected and saved.

She read one, then another. Somewhere inside, her inner DJ was at work, and as she lay back against her bed, she found herself listening to the silly but poignant song by Country Joe McDonald, "I Feel Like I'm Fixin' to Die."

"And it's 1, 2, 3, what're we fighting for? Don't ask me; I don't give a damn. Next stop is Vietnam."

She felt tired, down to her bones. *What am I fighting for, and whose side am I on? And do I really give a damn? It would sure be a lot less painful if I didn't.* Fiona thought about her hopeful and heroic cousin, her mother's inexplicable behavior, her grandparents' traumatic exit, and her own time in Argentina. It all just made her so sad. A sob threatened to erupt from her heart. She smothered her head in her pillow so nobody would notice her cries if they came, and she turned up the radio in her head. When Country Joe came around to the part about how it "ain't no use to wonder why...we all gonna die," she found she was laughing and crying at the same time. Quietly.

After a few minutes of Country Joe, Fiona caught her breath and splashed a little water from her drinking glass onto her face. *I wouldn't want anyone to think I'm having one of those "woe-is-me-teenage-angst" moments,* Fiona deadpanned to herself. *Heavens forfend!*

Fiona tucked all the items back into the box, which she then left on her bed. She went to the bathroom, washed her face properly, and went back downstairs and into the yard to return to the lawn chair. She sat there, dazed, watching a black squirrel bouncing up and down on a thin branch as he wrestled with a plum on the tree on which he perched, contentedly, king of Fiona's backyard. "Watch out, squirrel," Fiona whispered. "Just don't get on anybody's bad side around here."

The following Friday, Fiona decided to do her homework over at Mary's house and maybe sleep over. They walked together toward Mary's house and made light conversation. Neither one of them mentioned the previous weekend's events. As the two friends turned the corner. Nearing Mary's front door, Fiona suddenly felt very strange. She was so dizzy she thought she might faint. It was an odd sensation, as though her legs might give out from under her at any moment. If she kept going, she knew, she was in danger of falling over. With a gentle grab of Mary's arm, Fiona stopped to sit down under a neighbor's tree, and Mary joined her.

Eventually, the lightheaded feeling passed. "Just too much pressure at school, I guess," Fiona said, brushing herself off. Sure, she thought. That must be it. Not Argentina. Not her mother. School.

"Sure, Fee. Whatever you say. And de Nile ain't just a river, either."

"I'm not in denial!" Fiona huffed. But Mary wasn't wrong. Fiona was still trying to regain her footing after the horror of her first night in Argentina, and she was working to make sense of her mother's abusive and dismissive behavior toward her grandparents and, frankly, with her. If she'd been honest with herself, she'd admit that school didn't present much of a challenge, even on her accelerated timetable. It was something else. Something deeper. Something unsettling that she couldn't quite put her finger on.

"Don't even. I probably forgot to eat lunch is all. Or maybe this tree was just calling me to sit under it. You know, like the Buddha." Fiona chuckled faintly. "Hey, Mare, do you think I have what it takes to be a monk? You know, alone on a mountain, simply ringing chimes and chanting, turning a prayer wheel on behalf of all humanity, like Quan Yin, but far away from the world's machinations. Sounds kind of peaceful. Hey, are there even female monks?"

"Wow, Fiona," said Mary. "You still dizzy?"

"I'm serious, Mare. What do you really think?"

"I don't know. What got you going down that path anyway? So, like climbing Kilimanjaro? I hear the altitude and effort can make anyone feel enlightened. But it sounds exhausting. I do know a cloistered nun, though, and she lives on solid ground. Her main job is praying for other people, so it's kind of like your prayer wheel concept. Want to meet her?"

"Totally! What's her name?"

"I don't remember," said Mary, "Sister Mary something or other.

Remember, she's cloistered, it'll be through a door or a screen or something. My mom knows all about it. I'll ask her."

Of course, her name is Sister Mary Something, thought Fiona. Aren't they all?

Bea arranged for Fiona to visit the cloister, across the San Mateo Bridge in Menlo Park, and then drove her there on the appointed weekend day. Mary and Bea would stay outside, admiring the rose garden, as Sister Mary could receive only a limited number of visitors, only infrequently, and then only through a wide window that was locked until opened by the chief nun or prioress, who arranged the visit.

The window was so very wide, Fiona thought the nun could escape if she really wanted to, and that the barrier was meant to be symbolic. Any nun could leave at any time, for good. If she wanted. The door opened, and a caretaker entered, with tea and cookies. And then, Fiona was alone again, for what seemed like forever.

"Hello, dear," said Sister Mary, when she finally walked in to her side of the visiting room, assisted by a caretaker. Fiona could see she was very, very old, and she thought about how nuns could rest assured they'd be cared for in their elder years. How comforting, she thought.

"Hello, Sister Mary," Fiona replied.

"I hear you're interested in the contemplative life. Would you like to hear a little about it? About how we come to live this life, and what it means to us?"

"Yes, very much. Thank you."

As Fiona took a bite of a cookie, Sister Mary told Fiona how she'd felt a call from God as a young girl, and she'd entered the convent and hadn't looked back. She said she prayed nine times a day, according to the hours. She also shared how she enjoyed taking photographs, illuminating or decorating manuscripts in gold, and singing. Fiona hadn't thought about nuns having any passionate pursuits, other than praying. She thought about how worldly and wise Sister Mary seemed, for someone locked up in a convent. She reminded Fiona of the nuns in the little town of Pleasance where she'd gone to her catechism classes.

Sister Mary occasionally broke into song as she spoke and, even at her advanced age, she had an enchanting and transporting voice. In the middle of a song, she stopped and blessed Fiona, telling her how "the light of God will break forth as the morning" for her. It felt like a blessing. Her voice dropped to a near whisper as she added a personal benediction, telling Fiona that The Word, who spoke all creation into being and was nearer than our very breath, delighted in conversation with us. When she called, and then really listened, God would answer, and that when God called, she should also answer, "Here I am." Fiona loved hearing how listening to whispers in her heart would help her find her best way forward. She felt the deep wisdom in the elderly nun's words, and knew it would prove valuable, if she could only hold onto it. If only I weren't so absent-minded, like Pop, Fiona thought. If only I had perfect, total recall, I could keep this perfect moment, perfectly in mind.

As Fiona turned to leave, Sister Mary asked Fiona if she would like a hug. Fiona agreed, and leaned over to the big window. Again, the moment hovered for Fiona, and she felt as if Sister Mary could see right through her, to all her secret hopes and dreams—longings, really. She stepped toward the window and to Sister Mary and leaned in to the window, and was gently received into a warm hug. Sister Mary was stronger than she expected. It was almost a bear hug, like Pop liked to give, and it left Fiona feeling elated, floating, and filled with contentment. It was surprising, like being embraced by a secret saint. It was sublime, better than any buzz she'd experienced from drugs. And her mind was entirely quiet, which was, for Fiona, an extraordinary experience.

On their way home from the convent, Mary sat in the back of Bea's car with Fiona, watching her as she stared out the window, lost in thought. Once or twice, she even closed her eyes, and Mary wondered if she wasn't feeling well. Or maybe she was overwhelmed by her visit with the nun. Or maybe, just maybe, she was praying. Whatever it was, Mary decided it was a good time to let her be.

So, this is what being high on God is like, Fiona thought, as the feeling finally passed. I must tell Herb about this.

Bea decided to drive the girls back home across the Dumbarton Bridge, just for fun. It was the only bridge Fiona hadn't yet crossed in the area. They all crossed their fingers that a boat would go by when they arrived, and traffic would stop for a spell while a span of the bridge rotated sideways to let it pass. They were out of luck. "Maybe we should have prayed instead of just crossing our fingers," Fiona said, with a chuckle.

"Or asked Sister Mary to pray for us before we left," added Mary. "Hey, she seemed kinda worldly for someone so cloistered."

"Well, they are and they aren't," Bea chimed in. "They live apart but keep informed, so they can pray for the community. And they're part of a long history, like grafts on a big, old vine. Interesting thought, being a new cutting on such an old vine, don't you think?"

Fiona got a mental image of herself clinging onto something that's growing slowly upward, providing a great vantage, but keeping her grounded. She liked it.

Although traffic continued, unimpeded across the bridge, Bea slowed down, so she could point out a few of the native birds. She identified a tern, a mallard, and a snowy plover. "We need to wait for another tern," Fiona joked. "Because one good tern deserves another," said Mary. Her mother rolled her eyes, but her smile said she was amused.

~o0O0O0o~

Fiona thanked her friends and waved goodbye at the curb. When she walked in, she noticed the phone was ringing. She answered it. It was Uncle Jim. He asked Fiona how her social studies report had gone. "That was a long time ago, Uncle Jim, but it went okay, I guess. I mean, your story really helped my report, and my teacher thought it was great and everything. I'm just not sure my classmates thought so."

"Maybe it was all a little over their heads, Fee. You're brighter than the average bear, you know." Fiona smiled at his little reference to the Yogi Bear cartoon. She liked it that Uncle Jim thought highly of her enough to tell her so.

Uncle Jim told Fiona he'd joined a band in Nashville, and would be staying out there, with a mate from the Air Force. He said he was heading out in a week. Fiona wrote down his number and took notes on what he'd said, for her mother. Uncle Jim apologized that his motorcycle wasn't up for a ride across the bridge to come visit her before he left, but he promised to send her a postcard once he got to Nashville.

Before Uncle Jim hung up, he said, "You know, Fiona, we're family. You can always come visit me and stay any time you need to. There's always room on the couch. If you want a little sightseeing visit, or if you get stuck, just come. Besides, there's a lot of cool music happening in Nashville, Fee." Fiona loved his idea and intended to take him up on his offer, just as soon as she could. Knowing her mother, it might be sooner than later.

Fiona decided not to tell her mother about her little dizzy spell. It could have been anything. Maybe she'd been overwhelmed, or maybe she'd just needed a snack. She refused to think back on the week, on her grandparents, and how stunned, how frightened, how sad they must have felt at being kicked to the curb in the middle of the night. But she continued to mull it over. A chill textured her skin with goosebumps as she wondered what she would do if her mother startled her from her sleep with an order to get out. With that, Fiona decided to pack a suitcase.

It wasn't hard to gather her things or decide what to bring with her if she were sent away. All her life, she'd kept a suitcase at the ready—for unexpected travel from one parent to another, or for another sudden move. Even in California, she had never fully unpacked. She'd kept her trusty suitcase in the back of the closet, filled with a little money, a simple change of clothes, and some toiletries. Just in case. Besides, she really didn't have that much stuff. Not that she'd take with her, anyway. She looked around the room at the things she'd accumulated since she'd arrived. She wouldn't be able to take her books, her model horses, her guitar, or her record player on the fly, but she could grab her viola for busking, a few pieces of jewelry, her memory box of letters, a few photos, and that lovely little teacup for tea roses. Wait, Fiona thought. Why the teacup? It'd just make me sad. No, I think I'll leave the teacup behind.

Fiona added a few more clothes to her suitcase, some allergy pills, a few aspirin, and a few tampons. The only thing she'd truly lament not taking with her would be Starlight. So maybe she would. Maybe she'd grab the little poodle as she went out the door, and not look back. Plenty of homeless people had dogs for companionship. She would, too. Why not?

Fiona snapped shut the clasps on her suitcase and returned it to her closet, remembering how many times she'd packed it and unpacked it over the years, living with Pop. She thought of how many nights she'd spent imagining what it might be like to move to California to be with her mother. In her dreams, it had been so wonderful. In real life, it had been a bit of a nightmare. She thought for a moment, and then went to her desk, looked up Uncle Jim's phone number, scribbled it on a page from her notepad, and tucked it into her suitcase. Just in case.

Fiona thought about the rules she'd created to help herself get through life. Looks like I'm invoking Rule #5—Be Prepared. In this case, it means keeping a "bug-out bag" at the ready in case of any untrustworthy event, like getting kicked out. It's a logical interpretation, just another way of being a good Girl Scout.

Fiona peered at her reflection in the Victorian table mirror on her dresser as she recited the Girl Scout Promise, and realized something had changed, deep inside herself, since her scouting days. It wasn't just about being a good Girl Scout anymore. Now, it was life and death. From now on, she would live her life with her bag packed and one foot out the door. She would never trust the invitation, the welcome, the commitment, or the love offered her by anyone, ever again. Except from a dog. Moreover, if ever Fiona sensed a welcome wearing thin, she would try to leave preemptively, to spare herself a scene and protect her heart.

This will come in handy for my Christmas trip to Philly, Fiona thought, as she looked at her bugout bag with satisfaction. It was good practice to have one, she told herself, for anyone living in earthquake territory. She would be ready for any sort of earthquake, including a total rupture in the foundation on which she and her mother stood so shakily. Much like anticipating when the next big quake might strike, Fiona could never be sure when the fissure would arise that could threaten to swallow her up. She needed to be vigilant, because there was no doubt in Fiona's mind that the West Coast was home. If her grip on the bungalow in Berkeley was tenuous, she knew wherever she landed next, it would be here, in California.

Later that night, while sitting on her bed with Starlight and writing in her journal, Fiona thought about the relative peace that might be found hiding out in a convent. "No!" Fiona said out loud, startling her dog. "I'm already on contemplation overload. I bet I think much too much for that sort of a life!" She closed her journal and turned her attention to snuggling with her favorite furry friend. "Oh, Starlight," Fiona cooed. "I wish you could meet Gram's Afghan hounds. Christmas will be here soon. I'll say hello to them for you."

Fiona wondered if she should have waited to wrap all her presents until after she had arrived. She had carefully folded the colorful Christmas wrap around each gift, even more carefully chosen for each family member, affixed the tape, and then, using spools of curling ribbon, had tied a pretty bow on each. Now, as she tried to pack them into her suitcase for her customary holiday visit home, she lamented that they might be a little squashed or the bows, quite flat, by the time she landed in Philadelphia.

I hope they like their presents, she thought, as she strategically placed each gift in the bottom of her suitcase, wedged one against the other, their bows protected by the heavy tights that would replace the nylon pantyhose she wore in California's milder climate. Fiona had put a lot of care into coming up with good gifts for everyone. For Holly and Violet, she had chosen some groovy Pet Rocks, secured in their homes of cardboard, complete with air holes and instructions for their care and feeding. I wish I'd thought of that, Fiona thought. Making a million dollars off of rocks by selling the sizzle. It's kind of like the emperor's new clothes—being paid for nothing. Still, she thought they made cool gifts for her little sisters, who would love their pet rocks. Fiona wondered what they'd name them.

For Pop, Fiona had picked up a Rubik's Cube and a can of smoked oysters, which she knew he liked. She had also woven a braided keychain that ended in an alligator clip she'd found for him at Radio Shack. For Gram, she chose a good book and a bright red drinking bird in a fabulous blue top hat. She even got a couple of organic bones for the dogs. Wondering if she'd forgotten anyone or if she might meet someone for whom she wished she had a gift, Fiona tucked in two small boxes of See's candy, just in case. If no one materialized, she could share them with her family.

Safely tucked away in the back of her closet was another pet rock Fiona had saved as a gift to herself. She'd taken to buying herself a little something every year, just so there'd never be nothing under the tree for her. Just to avoid the potential for disappointment. This year, though, she wouldn't be disappointed. Mary had a lovely gift awaiting her, to replace a silver ring that had been stolen in Argentina. Fiona had never mentioned the theft, thinking, why worry her? Gifts don't come with theft protection. Lucky for Fiona, sometimes good friends do.

When Fiona arrived in a chilly Philly, Pop was there at the gate to greet her, sweeping her off her feet with an enormous bear hug. When they arrived at the front door of Gram's house, Fiona just stood there for a moment, her bags at her feet, taking in the sight and the reality that she was there; she had come home. If only Gram's house were in California, she thought. Then I'd have everything that says "home" in one place.

Once inside, after a flurry of excited hugs from her sisters, Fiona stood before her father and looked up. Pop reached out his hand, took hers, and twirled her around once, taking in the child he hadn't seen in two years. No longer a child, really, he thought. Then he drew her into a warm hug. Fiona felt the familiar scratch of Pop's sweater and the scent of tobacco on him as she lingered in his embrace. Yes, this too, was home.

Fiona was touched by how beautifully Holly and Violet had decorated her room to welcome her. As she looked at the paper-ring garlands strung across the walls in red and green, the handmade cards propped on her desk, and the real flower about to open in a small vase on her night stand, Fiona's heart swelled at how thoughtful it all was, how special she felt. This, she thought, is some crazy kind of welcome. A welcome that won't wear thin. I can really unpack, here, if I want to, and make myself at home.

Fiona also realized how much she had missed the rest of her family while living with her mother. She imagined packing Holly and Violet in her suitcase and taking them back with her to California. If only Philadelphia and Berkeley were biking distance from one another, she could see her little sisters every day, after school. Imagine.

~oO0O0Oo~

The road was icy, but it was still light out, and Pop suggested Fiona might like to try her hand at driving in the snow. Both nervous and excited by the idea, and climbed behind the wheel of Pop's enormous Buick at once. It took almost as long to bring the seat forward and adjust the mirrors as it did to inch her way around the block and park the car back in the driveway. After she turned the key and listened to the engine shut down, she turned to face her father and beamed. She'd done it—a driving experience with her dad, in addition to coming home to visit. It was all Fiona needed this Christmas.

"Hey, want to go to the t-shirt store tomorrow, Fee?" Violet had all kinds of ideas about how to spend time with her sister. Her little sister's enthusiasm and efforts to win the attention and affection of her older sister kind of reminded Fiona of her own connection to Karen. "Maybe you'd like to see what they've gotten in at the antiques store. Or maybe we can go ice skating. Would you rather go roller skating? Remember, the rink's not far from here."

"Let's do it all!" Fiona gave her little sister a big hug, just like she would have liked from Karen. The three sisters started with roller skating. They rented their shoe skates, and Fiona was relieved to find that hers looked fairly new and didn't smell. She was glad she'd thought to pack her bright-pink skating leotard with its attached skirt; although she'd imagined spinning around in it on the ice. Maybe they'd do that, too.

Gram, who'd stayed home to prepare dinner, had commented on how grown up Fiona looked, as she and her sisters headed out to the rink. Fiona figured it was Gram's way of referencing her recent growth spurt, but when she examined herself in the mirror, she decided she did look a little more grown-up. Her face was narrower and, with her hair up in a bun for skating, she thought it did give her a more sophisticated, *Breakfast at Tiffany's* aesthetic. All she needed was a strand of pearls, much like the one Mother wore on special occasions and which she so admired. Okay, and maybe a little black dress. But the bun with the bangs was spot on.

The girls glided round and round the worn wooden rink, with Fiona showing her sisters how to cross step their way around to the beat of the music—a well-loved playlist of "Golden Oldies" being played by a live organist. They sipped their sodas at the end of their session, as was their tradition. It should have felt like old times, except that something felt different. Fiona realized she was now a visitor in her former home.

As the days went by, a strange sense of panic seeped in, though Fiona couldn't quite pinpoint it. She was unaware of the many causes of her anxiety because she'd never looked closely at her relationship with her parents. If she had known to look, she'd have seen it, plain as day: a topsy-turvy life with her father; the many ways he'd let her down, time and again; the ambivalent welcome her mother had offered, and the mixed messages she continued to send. Dependent on her parents, Fiona couldn't afford a close examination. She couldn't afford to look, to acknowledge, to see. The unexplored and unwelcome emotions were buried. The deeper Fiona pushed them down, the stronger the anxiety that arose in their place.

Fiona soon started expecting—waiting—for the phone to ring, with a kind of reverse invitation from her mother, "Fiona, I've decided you should just stay in Philly, and I'll send you your things in a box." Night after night, Fiona tossed in her bed, unable to quiet her mind long enough to soothe herself into sleep. As the days wore on, her panic grew to an overwhelming obsession about getting back to California as soon as possible, to stake her claim to her adopted home state.

One morning after a particularly bad night's sleep, Fiona announced her decision to leave early and return to California—and to the mother she was so sure was about to forget her.

"I don't know if your father will forgive you, Fiona, but I never will." Fiona felt the sting of Gram's words. "Aren't we good enough for you? Have you gotten so fancy out there in California that you can't bear to spend time with us out here in Podunk, Pennsylvania? Do you really miss your mother that much? I don't get it, Fiona. I just don't get it."

Neither did Fiona. She didn't miss her mother's actual company. She didn't miss her formality and the detached manner that went with it. Didn't miss her critical eye or her volatile temper, her New Age friends, or her old-school rules. Most of all, she didn't miss her own discomfort and insecurity in her mother's presence. "I miss California," was all she could manage to say.

Gram's comments hurt Fiona to her core. Her face felt hot, and she couldn't stem the tears as she sat there in Gram's kitchen, realizing she didn't quite fit anywhere anymore. She turned her back on Gram, certain she wasn't going to let her grandmother see her tears, if she could help it. She wouldn't give her the satisfaction of knowing how hard her words had hit. It was part of Fiona's new plan: keep your cards close to your vest. Never let 'em see you cry.

Fiona watched her grandmother as she busied herself in the kitchen. She couldn't expect Gram to understand her motives, when she could hardly understand them, herself. The same was true of Pop and her sisters. If she tried to explain any of her thought process to any of them, they'd just press her into staying. Really, it was already hard enough to breathe, without additional outside pressure. She wasn't trying to hurt anyone. Certainly not the people she loved most. She already had a sense of the kind of pain she'd caused them all by moving to California. Fiona thought back to her flight to Philly. The stewardess had told her to put on her own oxygen mask before helping anyone else. Does that go for me, too, or am I just supposed to make everyone else happy?

Fiona's thoughts did a sudden 180 as she watched Gram dry her hands on her old floral apron. Too bad Gram—heck everyone—had never thought about moving out west. She'd have loved it, and she could have encouraged Pop to find a job out there, as well. Hadn't he lectured at the School of Engineering at UC Berkeley, before Fiona was born? Forget that, thought Fiona, as she headed upstairs to pack her bags for the early morning flight. That's just a pipe dream. No way anything like that would ever happen. Instead, the fracture would just continue, and everyone would just keep being upset and lonely. One great big, unhappy family, like just about everybody else she knew.

It was still dark outside when Fiona was roused the next morning by her trusty alarm clock. Always darkest before dawn, she thought, dragging her suitcase down the stairs and hugging her little sisters, who were still partially asleep. Chin up, old girl, she told herself. Stiff upper lip. No waffling.

Pop put Fiona's bags in the back of his car, and everyone said their goodbyes at the curb. He looked terribly sad as he drove her to the airport. She just felt terrible. Even so, she was anxious to be on the plane, heading to San Francisco. She knew she was heading home, but it felt bittersweet.

~o0O0O0o~

Gram forgot all about never forgiving Fiona for her early departure from Philadelphia. Over time, their weekly phone calls resumed their regular cadence, except that Pop's voice seemed imbued with a little more sadness when he said hello.

Fiona was happy her relationship with Gram had thawed. Back in sunny Berkeley, life felt pretty frigid. Her mother, who had been so warm and compassionate in welcoming her back from Argentina, had cooled to a frosty, distant tolerance. Fiona invented all sorts of reasons to spend time out of the house, to keep a safe distance from the colorless and cold loneliness that waited for her within its four walls, to keep its icicles from piercing her heart, and freezing it forever.

When she was out with her friends, Fiona easily remembered why she liked living in California. Unpleasant angst and experiences aside, it was good to be a teenager in the '70s. The energy of the era and the sense of possibility filled her with a spirit of joy. Most of the time, Fiona was happy. Most of the time, she wasn't home. And she imagined her mother, sequestered in her writing studio out back, was not aware of it. She was wrong. Peggy may have rarely inquired about her comings and goings anymore, but she noticed, and she felt the distance keenly.

Yes, most of the time, Fiona whistled her way through the week. At the very least, her music, her daydreams, her plans, and, of course, Starlight, kept her happy and believing she was okay. Everybody was okay. As long as she was California dreamin', it was all good, right?

If all went according to plan, this was to be Fiona's last semester in high school. She took the relatively new California High School Proficiency Exam, and found it surprisingly easy. She committed herself to studying anew, for the SAT and achievement tests she'd have ace to secure her admission to college.

Fiona took out the paperwork from the manila envelope on her desk, unfinished, and started in on it. She had toured only one college—Mills College—and loved it, so she'd decided that was where she wanted to go. She had to make this application count. As she filled it out, using her best penmanship, she made sure to note that, by the time decisions were to be made, she would have received, and forwarded, the results of all her exams. She wrestled with the words for hours, on lined paper, before writing on the application itself. Slipping it into its envelope for mailing, along with arts supplements she hoped would boost her chances, she knew she had done the best she could with it. She affixed the stamps and walked to the nearest mailbox drop it in the mail.

Fiona took practice tests for the SAT and the English Composition, Literature, and Mathematics achievement tests on most days after school—when she wasn't cutting school to study for the tests, that is. Those days, she studied all day for the tests—usually in the local library, away from her mother's steely presence. With all that studying, she knew she shouldn't have been worried. She was ready. So, why was she climbing the walls? She had no clue. She picked up the phone and called Mary.

"Why are you doing this to yourself?" Mary asked, having patiently listened to Fiona's fear and frustration pour out through the receiver. "Of course, you'll pass." Mary told her that, for someone so smart, it was crazy how she could be so clueless, so often. This was one of those times. Sitting at her desk, with study guides strewn all about, Fiona found herself worrying that she might not pass at all.

"I love you Mare, but I don't think you see the situation. What if I don't? I really haven't thought of an appropriate Plan B. So, you see, I MUST pass this test, Mare! And you already know the reason. I HAVE TO get out of here! I just know college is where I need to be."

"Whoa, easy Hoss," Mary said, in her best spaghetti western accent. "Hey, trust me here; you'll do fine. If you would just slow down a minute, you'd realize you know you will, you're just working yourself up."

"Nay to you, too," Fiona whinnied, not catching Mary's reference to a character on an old TV show called *Bonanza*, "And hay is for horses."

"*Hoss,* not horse, silly. You're absolutely, impossibly clueless, Fiona," Mary said, laughing, "which is exactly why you're going to ace this test."

The two friends spent another two hours, laughing and talking on the phone. Fiona turned in early, which didn't come naturally, but she knew sleep was really important. With Starlight sharing her pillow, she slipped off easily.

Fiona showed up at the SAT testing center a little early, with a zippered pocket filled with sharpened pencils, on that bright, brisk morning in May. She sat down, arranged a few of her pencils on her desk and, when the clock struck 8:00am, she began reading the test questions thoughtfully, quickly choosing her answers from the multiple choices before filling in the circles on the page. When she completed the exam before anyone else in the room, she wondered if she'd aced it or spaced it. She'd just have to wait and see.

The following Monday, a reporter for the high school newspaper interviewed Fiona about her choice to leave high school early. She told the reporter she'd applied to Mills and was looking forward to attending the nationally renowned liberal arts and sciences college for women, nestled in the foothills of Oakland. She added how she'd taken and passed all the required tests. As the words left her lips, she realized she didn't yet have confirmation that what she was saying was true. The following Friday, the newspaper came out, bearing the headline, "Teen Anxious for Early Exit!"

"Anxious?" Fiona laughed. "You bet! How about, 'Teen Dead Set on Getting the Hell Out of Dodge'!" she said out loud, adding, "It's college or bust."

"Why are you so driven, Fee?" asked Mary, when Fiona recounted the story to her. "I get that you want to get out of here and go to college, and you are. I believe you'll make that happen. But if you keep running all the time, you'll never catch your breath. If you stop…"

"And smell the roses?" Fiona interrupted.

"Actually, I was going to say look around, you could find more peace and freedom. Freedom is inside us. You'll never be free if you're always running. Freedom is for the pilgrim who finds meaning in the journey. You're more like a prisoner on the run. Why run so hard? It's so exhausting, Fee. Didn't Ram Dass say, 'Be here, now'? Maybe he should have said, 'Be free, now'! Take a rest. Like your mom says, take a breath. Be like a billy goat, and stop and eat some roses. Chase your tail like Starlight. Scream out 'I am a shining star!' You might be happier that way. You might even let yourself feel excited at the adventure."

Fiona hung up the phone at the end of their conversation and thought maybe she needed to sit with Mary's advice for a moment. She actually liked what her friend had said. Especially the part about the billy goat, or being a shining star. Maybe Mary was right. She'd been running so breathlessly, headlong into her future, she hadn't taken a moment to take it all in, get excited. Then again, maybe Mary was wrong. Mary wasn't the one getting out early, was she? I'll rest when I'm dead, she told herself, and I'll save the excitement for when I get where I'm going. Meanwhile, I'll write Vi and Holly and send them a copy of the article.

Violet wrote back almost immediately, expressing her support, and requiring her to write, just as soon as she knew the test results. Fiona promised herself she'd do just that.

When Fiona received the good news she had been waiting to hear—that she'd passed her exams with flying colors—she tossed the thumbed-over CHSPE and SAT study guidebooks in the trash, reveling in the satisfying thuds they made as they nearly toppled the can. Then, she called Violet. When Pop heard the news, he grabbed the receiver and gushed, "So many standard deviations above the mean, Fee, that's no mean feat! Ha Haaa Aaaaaa." His booming laugh let her know how much she'd made him proud.

So, she was out. The question remained: Was she in?

Week after week, Fiona checked the mail daily for an answer to her solitary college application. To make up for her missing year, she'd included poetry and drawings, and even tapes of viola performances. She'd included letters of recommendation from her dojo and her viola teacher, plus an essay touching on her parents' accomplishments and how her maternal grandfather was friends with Alan Turing. She wasn't above name dropping, when needed. She had wanted the admissions office to see her potential.

They did.

Fiona was accepted for the Fall 1979 semester. She read over the closing words in the acceptance letter, "We look forward to seeing you on campus and to counting you among our women of Mills." Well, Fiona was looking forward equally as much to being counted! The letter made Fiona's spirits soar. Before, she'd only hoped. Holding the ticket to freedom in her hands made it real. When she showed the letter to her mother, she could see a wave of unmistakable pride wash across her face. Her mother was beaming. How about that!

This was a good thing, right? As smug as she felt, Fiona felt a sudden twinge of self-doubt. Was she ready? Fiona laughed. She had spent her whole life adjusting, often on a moment's notice. From here on out, it would be on her terms. And, in just a few short years, with her degree in hand, she'd land a great job that made her rich and famous. She'd have a home of her own in Sausalito, watch the sun rise over the Bay, and take the ferry to her office in San Francisco.

Life was going to be beautiful. And safe and secure, all on her terms.

Strolling down the sidewalk after school the next day, her mind still mapping out her future in Sausalito, Fiona saw one of her friends from math class. She turned to tell her the good news, taking no notice of the tree in her path. "I did it!" she said. Slam! Fiona hit the tree so hard, she ricocheted onto the sidewalk. Sitting there, rubbing the goose egg already forming on her forehead, she remembered a childhood toboggan accident with Pop. Afraid to hop on the long, narrow sled and coast down the slippery slope, she had, nevertheless, climbed on in front of Pop to give it a go. As they neared the end of the run, Fiona yelled, "I did it!" just before they slammed into a tree. "Did what?" Pop had responded, wryly. That was his moment to teach her about declaring success too soon. Well, tree or no tree, Fiona had done it. She'd gotten herself out of high school and into college. Early. Just like Pop!

As she wandered home, Fiona pondered that tree. Smacking her upside the head like that, it had the effect of bringing her back down to earth. As with the toboggan incident, maybe, in this case, she hadn't quite "done it," yet, either. After all, she didn't have that diploma in her hands...yet! Maybe the time wasn't right, just yet, for celebration.

~o0O0O0o~

Once inside the house, Fiona discovered her mother wasn't home. Or maybe she was out in her studio, writing. Either way, Fiona was on her own. Restless in her continued excitement, she searched for something to do. Having noticed her mother's plum tree out back, its branches laden with ripe fruit, she thought perhaps she'd try her hand at making plum jam. She'd already learned to stew prunes, so why not jam?

I hope I don't get myself in a jam! Fiona laughed out loud in the absence of audience, as she grabbed a bag and went out back to pick plums. Wait, I already got out of a jam or two, she thought. As in, out of high school, which is just plum awful, and into college, plum perfect. Plum, plum...I put in my thumb, and pulled out a plum. Oh, what a fab girl am I! She continued pulling plums from the tree, thinking in sing-song, basking in the silliness, a teenager reciting nursery rhymes about college.

Back in the kitchen, Fiona pulled out her mother's copy of *The Joy of Cooking*. The recipe for plum jam called for pectin, but there wasn't any. "I'll just use sugar. How hard can it be?"

The sweet smell of ripe plums was heady. She emptied her bag into a colander and rinsed off the plums before she picked one from the pile and took a big, slow, juicy bite, savoring the sweet treat and wondering if she should skip the jam and just eat them all, fresh.

She needed something to do, and she was in the mood to celebrate. She wanted something tangible to show for her efforts, something that tasted as sweet as the victory she felt, on the inside. She picked up the colander, dumped the plums into a pot, and added a little water, three cups of sugar and a sprinkle of cinnamon before setting it on the stove, to simmer. Then, she went upstairs, to find Starlight, turning on her TV so the ads could serve as gentle reminders for her to stir the pot every ten minutes or so. She knew she could be absent-minded, like Pop, and she didn't want the firefighters breaking down the door on her account.

A few hours later, the plums had reduced to a thick, dark soup. Fiona hoped, as it cooled, it might thicken a little more to work as the perfect spread for morning toast. But she doubted it really would. Plum soup, anyone?

Her mother came in from her writing studio and noticed the sweet smell in the air. She lifted the lid on the large pot. "Are you trying to make jam, Fiona?"

"Trying," she said.

"But we didn't have any pectin, hon. Trying could become achieving if you had all the right ingredients. You handicap yourself when you're not prepared." Her mother dipped a spoon into the sticky broth and brought it up to her mouth. "The good news is that it tastes really good. All you need to do is mix a little corn starch with water until it's fully dissolved, and then slowly stir it into your jam. Keep it simmering on low until it reaches the consistency you want. And corn starch, we happen to have."

Fiona was reminded, once again, that her mother pretty much knew everything about everything. Yet she knew a few things, herself, too. Sitting in her room, having set the kitchen aright after her "jam session," Fiona was messing around on her guitar when she thought of how it really wouldn't be bad at all, to be a writer.

10. TASTE OF FREEDOM

Her parents agreed. Fiona would continue to live at home and commute to Mills. It would save money, since she'd chosen a not-inexpensive private college. Somehow, four more years at home wasn't quite what Fiona had envisioned for this next phase of life that was to be on her terms.

"Listen, Fiona," said her mother, "I have a plan. What about the side studio?"

"You mean the garage?" Fiona replied, intrigued. She hadn't considered it before. Peggy's concession to Fiona's newly minted status as a college student was to offer her the option of moving into the attached garage, which she had modified years earlier to serve as a rental suite. It had a kitchenette—refrigerator and sink—with access to the kitchen and bathroom in the main house via the sliding glass door in the backyard. Peggy had rented out the space to students for quite some time, and had decided that now, the best student for the space would be Fiona.

"Right. The converted garage," Peggy continued. "My renter is moving out at the end of the semester, anyway. How about instead of finding another renter for it, I rent out your room, instead? That way, you can live out back. It'll be almost like having your own home. Of course, you don't have to do that if you don't want to. You also could keep things the way they are."

What if I get scared out there? Fiona wondered. Maybe I should have applied to Cal. It would have cost a lot less, and I might have been able to live in the dorms. Out loud, though, she heard herself say, "Sounds like a good plan."

~oOOOOOo~

High school ended with a whimper. On the last day, Fiona packed up her books, and said her goodbyes. Everyone took the occasion to write in each other's yearbooks. Most of her classmates would be seeing each other again in the fall. Looking around, Fiona wondered if she would see most of the people who were busily signing each other's yearbooks, ever again. One of them wrote, "Keep in touch!!!" She used three exclamation points. Fiona thought, does that mean she meant it? Then again, who kept in touch from any of the dozens of schools I've been in up until now? She read and re-read the inscriptions from Zach, Quinn, and Becca. She had felt so close to them just the summer before, but Fiona realized that high school friendships were a lot like the river otter dance she remembered watching at Mystic Meadow: they come together and break apart with the shifting currents.

Biking home, Fiona felt as if a great door were slamming shut behind her. Well, that's behind me anyway, she thought. As she turned the corner, she spied something large and pink in the driveway.

What Fiona had glimpsed from up the street, she soon learned, was a big ribbon around an even bigger bug. Could this be for me? she thought. She hardly dared hope. But when she saw her mother sitting on the front stoop dangling the key, she knew this gift had her name on it. Peggy had surprised Fiona with a gently used VW Bug in a darling shade of pink for her high school un-graduation, in anticipation of her daily drive to Oakland.

"A Volkswagen bug? It's perfect! My own Love Bug! Ohmigaaaw-wwwwd, wowwwww! Thank you! This is so freakin' amazing! Did I mention thank you?" she gushed, jumping up and down and—in a rare display of affection these days—she hugged her mother exuberantly.

Fiona had been in love with the Volkswagen Beetle ever since she'd seen the 1968 Disney movie *The Love Bug*. The gas-sipping car was a smart choice. Gas prices had skyrocketed; people were spending hours in gas lines and rationing was in effect. Folks could only fill their tanks on odd- or even-numbered days, depending on their license plate numbers. Peggy also bumped up her allowance so she could fill the tank for a week or more if she limited her driving to coming and going from campus. Twenty dollars felt like a fortune. She was rich, she had wheels, and she was living in her own California pad. Life was awesome.

Fiona surveyed her love bug. I need to drive better, she thought. Much better. No dings for this pretty baby. In her mind's eye, she pictured images from *Red Asphalt*, the gory film she'd watched through fingers splayed across her face, in her driver's ed class. For the entire day afterwards, she hadn't been sure she ever wanted to drive. Now, that's all she could think about. She wanted to drive expertly, and keep her car this beautiful, forever. Peggy told her she'd heard there was a way you could make a bug "fart" by double-clutching it. That sounded amusing. Fiona decided to find out how it was done, and practice until she had it down pat!

Fiona noticed the other key on the key ring she'd been handed. A key to the studio. This, Fiona thought, is about the grooviest, most extraordinary day anyone has ever had. Ever.

~oOo0O0o~

Is it still dark? Fiona had been waking up hourly to check the clock. Her plan was to wake up super-early and beat the commuter traffic rush to Mills for the first day of Orientation. It was finally 5:00am, late enough to hit the road. She got to Mills before anything was even close to open, parked her car, and cracked open an Ursula LeGuin novel. It's too cold to wander the campus, and they'll be touring us later, she reminded herself. Eventually, the tea shop opened, as did the bookstore, and she wandered through both, before heading toward Toyon Meadow.

During the Orientation Week welcoming address, Fiona was reminded how special it was to be joining the Mills community. Established in 1852, just two years after California was granted statehood, Mills was once a young ladies' seminary. "Parents just like yours—farmers, merchants, and miners who'd struck gold—wanted their daughters educated back in 1852, and found Mills a safe and appropriate place to send them. Take your cue from the many kindred spirits who came before you—bright and curious students committed to learning. The very meadow where you are standing was once a Native American village of the Ohlone people. It takes its name from a plant they used in healing ceremonies. Consider it well: You are on hallowed, healing grounds. Breathe it all in deeply during your time with us."

As she toured the campus, Fiona was reminded how Mills had really come into its own under the leadership of Oberlin College graduate Mary Atkins, a founding mother from a conservatory of music back East. "Welcome, Mills Woman! You have arrived!"

Fiona made her way over to registration and waited in line. She had selected her class schedule with care, with thought to her commute, and the hopes of sleeping in. She was looking forward to a Monday-Wednesday-Friday class schedule. It almost worked out exactly as planned, except the English class she wanted was full, and she had to choose another. Same day, but super early. *If I can't sleep in, at least I can keep up with* General Hospital, she mused. Her favorite soap opera ran daily, but Tuesdays and Thursdays would be enough to know everything that went on in Luc and Laura's glacially slow romance. Even if studies got heavy, she figured once a month would be enough to catch the general gist.

"YOU! YAY!" Fiona shrieked, delighted in recognizing her old friend Shakti from the ashram, when she saw her across the meadow grounds. "Fiona? Outstanding! How long has it been!" Shakti was two years ahead of Fiona, but it didn't matter one whit to either of them. The junior and the freshman spent the rest of the day catching up. And with the knowledge that she had at least one friend on campus, Fiona felt reassured she'd made a good choice.

~oOOOOo~

On a free Tuesday morning, Fiona headed up to Peet's Coffee on Walnut Square, to study. Walking toward the coffee shop, her backpack laden with books and her mind preoccupied by the Dragonwell tea she'd seen in the window, Fiona didn't at first notice the police car as it pulled alongside her and signaled her to stop walking.

When the cop finally caught her attention, Fiona was alarmed. Had she been jaywalking? Not that she could remember. What, then? It turned out the officer thought she was a high-school-aged truant, hanging around a coffee shop, headed for trouble of some kind. He was right about everything except the truant and trouble parts. He'd guessed her age correctly but had been surprised when she produced her Mills College ID card. "Good for you," he said, as he drove off, leaving Fiona feeling supremely independent, and a wee bit smug. She walked into Peet's to buy herself a tin of tea for her garage abode.

Fiona's need for freedom ran deep, making it hard for her to see the obvious: People were covering the costs, supporting her "free and easy" college existence. Like a kid riding down the sidewalk for the first time without training wheels, she didn't notice who might be behind her, holding her up, stopping her from falling. Not looking back at them allowed her to imagine she'd mastered the ride.

Nobody was holding Fiona back anymore, she felt, and nobody was standing in her way. She was peddling all on her own. She had no clear idea where she was going, but she was definitely on the move, excited about the open road. If only it would rain, she thought, I could dance and sing, and splash through the puddles, like Gene Kelly. She watched absent-mindedly as pigeons eagerly snatched at bread crumbs tossed to them by a child at a nearby table outdoors. On the outside, she was smiling quietly at the mother and her son. Inside, she was supremely excited, confident she was going to make a big splash in life.

The next afternoon, Boris Żywny raised his hand to pause her playing and said, "Fiona, you are playing the notes correctly, but you must play with more freedom!"

"Yes, Mr. Ż," Fiona replied, laughing. "I am playing with more and more freedom every day, actually."

~oOO0O0o~

A few weeks into her freshman year, Fiona realized she missed the performances she'd enjoyed in high school. Lessons and guitar jam sessions with her new girlfriends just weren't enough. She decided to try out for a local community orchestra.

Fiona had been compensating for sub-par sight-reading skills by listening well and remembering the tune. That way, she could perform familiar music much faster than she could read unfamiliar music. That tactic didn't work well at the community orchestra level, where musicians tackled more complex works more quickly than she could ever have imagined possible. After the third rehearsal, Fiona got the call: Don't come back. She'd been cut before she'd had a chance to get started.

Fiona was devastated. Except for gym class, she had never before failed like this. She had always excelled. She was used to being a pro, and it was how she saw herself.

She put down the receiver after the call, tears coursing down her face. All the put-downs and demands from Mr. Ż. came flooding back into her consciousness. He had a way of imploring her to work harder by criticizing her harshly. She started hearing his words, berating her, once again. "Tone, tone, tone. What kind of viola is that, anyway? A mono-tony? A no-toney? Baloney! Wake up, Fiona, and play that thing like it's a bloody Stradivari."

As the critical voices crowded in, Fiona began losing her confidence. So, this is failing, she thought. It sucks. I'm terrible at failing. And, apparently, at playing the viola. All those years Mr. Ż. said the reason he pushed me was that he saw a glimmer of greatness. Maybe he was just pushing to push.

She got the sinking feeling she was just like all those kids whose best days were behind them, who had left their talents behind them, in high school, like the captain of the football team who couldn't get a draft pick to save his soul. Well, I've got something in common with those has-been jocks now, she smiled, ruefully.

Eventually, her tears dried up, and Fiona felt a hot headache, a sick feeling in her stomach, and exhausted. She examined her viola, running her fingers across the smooth wood surface, lifting her nose to one of the beautiful and symmetrical f-holes to smell the fabulous wood, and contemplating how much more dark, earthy, and mellow they were than violins. Well, I'm anything but mellow, Fiona admitted to herself, so maybe viola was never my instrument to begin with. With that, she packed up her sheet music and viola, shoved it all into the back of her closet, and closed the door.

Suddenly, her left hand ached, all the way from her shoulder down to her index finger. It was the old pain from playing too much, which she interpreted in tandem with the new pain of quitting. Fiona thought of the drill Uncle Jim had taught her about how to feel better without meds. She went down the hall and got some ice for a "contrast bath." Soon, she was dipping her hand in one bowl—almost too hot to handle—and opening and closing her hand to the count of thirty before plunging it into the other—almost too cold. As bad as she felt about herself, she enjoyed punishing "the hand that played her. Or betrayed her."

When both bowls of water had lost their sting, Fiona dried off her hands and drove to Mills, where she headed out to the campus pond. There, she found she could relax, sprawled out on the bench above the grass, out of danger of being crawled over by anything creepy-crawly, and watch the dragonflies. She looked up at the willow, its leaves gently rustling in an almost imperceptible wind. She closed her eyes and breathed in, letting herself relax on the exhale, and dozed off.

When Fiona was back home later that day, she called Mary to tell her she was putting down her viola. Mary said, "Well, maybe it's for the best, Fee. The viola's not really a practical pursuit. And you never liked your teacher; what was his name? 'Boris Badenov,' right? Good riddance to rubbish, I say!"

Fiona smiled at her friend's reference to the antagonistic character of Boris from the *Rocky and Bullwinkle* cartoon. "Żywny. Boris Żywny." She realized Mary knew his name but called him the cartoon character whenever Fiona had felt particularly hurt by his putdowns. But Mr. Ż. wasn't the problem; she was. Maybe Mary was right. Maybe it really was for the better. Not all dreams could blossom. Time to move on. To what?

From the moment Fiona banished her viola to the back of the closet, everything seemed to spiral downward. In biology lab, after carefully preparing a glass slide, she set it under the microscope upside down, lowered the lens too far, and cracked the slide. In her music theory class, her attempt at compensating for slow sight-reading by using "figured bass" math exercises, sounded great in her head, but what she'd written often sounded sour, out loud. Fiona had a pianist friend who would play her creations for her, so she could hear what she'd written and correct herself. She wished she didn't need that level of support, but she did. Fiona was used to being good at whatever she tried. She was used to feeling special in school—it was one place where she'd thought she knew how to succeed. Somehow, she'd lost her grip, and everything seemed to be slipping through her fingers.

One night, while Fiona was chatting on the phone with Pop, he said, "Remember that old joke, Fiona, the one that says the difference between theory and practice is that in theory, they're the same, but in practice, they're different." That was one joke Fiona and her father really loved. They lived in their heads, in beautiful theoretical frames, and got in trouble when they came out into the real world to play. Maybe that's why they kept on telling each other this same joke, time and again. Right now, it wasn't funny. It was hitting too close to home.

Going to college early had seemed like such a great idea. In theory.

~oOOOOOo~

Fiona's early optimism about college continued to take a hit. She found herself slogging through the semester, struggling in both music theory and biology, and hanging on in her other two classes. She knew she needed to get it in gear, and fast.

If I can't even get through English Lit, then my stint at Mills is going to collapse, just like the Beatles, Fiona worried, donning the black armband she'd taken to wearing since John Lennon died. She wondered if she'd soon be mourning her short-lived college career, as well. I'll never forget him, Fiona mused. I'll light a candle every December 8th for John. Life's so sad. She thought about how his mother had taught him happiness was the key to life, so at school when they asked him what he wanted to be when he grew up, he said, 'Happy.' It's great how he talked back, telling them they didn't understand life, when they told him he didn't understand the assignment. That's so John. And now, he's gone. I could just cry.

To calm herself, Fiona often did what she had seen Pop do when he was puzzling out big sonar problems: She listened to Bach for the lovely sense of beauty, order, and balance his music conveyed. For the same reason, Fiona avoided the sort of moody jazz and blues that Pop liked best when he was very stoned. It hurt her head, and it reminded her of the bad old days she'd rather forget.

When music didn't work, Fiona turned to her letter box. Letters from Fiona's sisters always brought her back down to earth. They made her feel at once more lonely and less alone, by reminding her of the people she loved, and the distance between them. That distance evoked songs like "Golden Slumbers," by the Beatles, and Carole King's "So Far Away," which asks, "Doesn't anybody stay in one place anymore?" Fiona was the one who'd left, she knew, but, now, it felt like there was no way back. Still, her sisters had a way of writing real, in-the-moment stuff that helped her feel connected. Which is why she stored them so carefully, along with every letter she'd ever gotten from anyone she loved, in her keepsake shoebox. This sense of connection, along with help from her touchstone songs, helped Fiona find her rhythm by the end of her chaotic first two years of college.

~o0O0O0o~

Fiona ended her sophomore year on a high note, scholastically. She had hit her stride. And so, she began bargaining for different living arrangements. At first, she'd felt special, moving out of the house and into her own space, as Peggy's newest tenant. But having to go through the backyard into the house to go to the bathroom got old fast, especially during the rainy season. Running from one house to the other, trying not to get soaked in the process, reminded Fiona of the summer they had lived in their friends' barn when they'd been on the hunt for the Mystic Meadow. By the end of her second year as a boarder, she was tiring of her living quarters, which were neither indoors and cozy, nor remote enough to feel truly free. After some intense lobbying, Fiona had convinced her parents to let her live on campus the next fall.

Fiona was filled with eager anticipation as she prepared to move into the dorms. She had made it through two years of living in that drafty old garage, and her mother could rent it out again, she reasoned. Everyone would be happy. Fiona was so used to seeing her mother's poker face that she'd stopped looking for emotion. She didn't notice Peggy's sad eyes, as she packed up her things in the back of her bug, and headed out the door.

Fiona whistled a happy tune as she wandered into the Mediterranean-style Mary Morse residence hall. She walked into her dorm carrying two boxes of books, with a duffle bag slung over her shoulder, and still had many more items in the car.

"Need help?" a warm voice called out from behind. Fiona turned to meet the face behind the voice. From that moment, Tracy and Fiona became fast friends, along with Tracy's roommate, Terri, and Lynn, down the hall. Terri was from the Midwest, while Lynn hailed from Atlanta. Fiona was fascinated to learn that Lynn had been a piano accompanist to the choirs at black churches across the South, including Ebenezer Baptist Church, Martin Luther King, Jr.'s pastoral home. Now this, thought Fiona, feels like home.

On Monday through Thursday evenings were formal sit-down dinners at the dorm, the college's nod to "finishing school," Fiona imagined. She enjoyed dressing up for dinner, liked using cloth napkins and, thanks to her mother, knew how to use the right fork. She was especially fond of the Thursday-night menu, beef with broccoli, and looked forward to the evening all week. Hanna was right; learning is yummy, she thought.

Terri sat at the end of the table, delighting everyone with her napkin-folding ability. Fiona wondered what to expect, today. Maybe a sailboat, a fleur de lys fan she'd fit into her water goblet, or a French fold? On today's menu, a bird of paradise. As usual, Terri was happy to explain how she did it. Fiona decided to try her hand at it, and it worked, sort of. Napkin folding reminded her of the creative play Hanna engaged Fiona and her sisters in at the table when they were little. The thought made Fiona miss her late stepmother, but the momentary pang faded quickly. She was too happy being a full-blown college student to wallow in past. The sense that she was really on her own—except for the part about her parents paying for it all—made her feel as if her heart were made of butterflies.

After dinner, the four friends headed down to the living room, where an old grand piano lay sleeping, waiting for someone charming to kiss the keys and awaken it again. Listening to Tracy play distracted Fiona from any concerns she had. In the moment, all was well. "Hold up a second!" Fiona called out, already halfway to her room. She emerged again a few minutes later, guitar in hand, ready to join in on the jam. Tracy had a gig on Saturday at the alumni house, and she wanted to practice a few of the numbers. "Promise you'll sneak 'Rock Lobster' in with the schmaltz, Tracy. Promise?" Tracy promised, gamely.

"Let's have a party," Lynn called out. It had been a particularly heavy week of schoolwork. "Fiona, I double-dog dare you to stir up some Tequila Sunrises, like you said your sister taught you to make." Fiona did know how, theoretically. But she wasn't quite sure it was the best idea on a school night. Before she could object, Lynn said, "I'm buying. But only if it's California OJ...none of that Florida stuff. I'm supporting the boycott." Off they went to the corner store to purchase the orange juice, tequila, grenadine, and ice. The orange juice was frozen, but it was local...sort of. The friends felt good about buying local OJ, in solidarity with the boycott that arose in response to the anti-gay activism of Citrus Commission spokesperson Anita Bryant. Fiona figured the guy behind the counter knew exactly what they were planning to make as he rang up their items. But, he didn't say a word. He clearly wasn't new on the job.

Back in the dorm, they borrowed a blender from a friend down the hall, who had a reputation for having one of everything anyone might need. In exchange, they promised to bring her a beverage. Fiona resolved to make her big sister proud, in absentia, by creating stunningly beautiful works of art. She tried her best at putting on the airs of bartending, picturing each step as Karen had demonstrated. She made each drink with such care that the girls got a little antsy, waiting. But the drinks tasted great, and each glass was laced with beautiful sunrise-colored striations. Fiona, who'd tasted each drink as she made it, was already tipsy by the time they began toasting.

"I'm hungry," Terri said. "Let's go out and get something." Fiona was the one with the car, but she was in no condition to drive. She handed her keys over to Lynn, who seemed sober enough, and everyone piled into her VW Bug. Fiona loved these spontaneous adventures with her friends, but her stomach didn't like the fast food-alcohol combo at all. She spent the rest of the night retching in the bathroom, a little embarrassed that she couldn't handle her liquor, but feeling too sick to really care.

Feeling depleted and done in, Fiona sank into the chair by the window and looked out to see the most exquisite sunrise—truly a tequila sunrise. She smiled. She'd lived to see the sunrise. Feeling a little buzzed but surprisingly well and chipper, Fiona joined her friends for breakfast. She filled her plate with eggs and toast, but she found she couldn't eat them. Back in her room, she decided she shouldn't treat her body like that too often. Not with tequila, anyway.

~oOO0O0o~

It was a beautiful fall day, and Fiona was contemplating the finish line. It was time to focus. She had declared communications as her major, and now she had two years to get it done. Her idea of a career in an orchestra was sitting in the back of the closet, with her viola. Pop had wanted her to be a budding young scientist, but she now imagined herself a writer.

Fiona had no interest in writing murder mysteries, like her mother, but she enjoyed science fiction and imagined she'd be good at writing in that genre if she tried her hand at it. And it would be okay to write about people, so long as she didn't have to kill them off in the process. To that end, her mother suggested she blend her interests by taking a class or two on psychology, so she could learn a little about what motivates people. By having a better understanding of people, she would be able to write more nuanced stories. That advice made sense and pleased Pop, who was hoping her sci-fi interest would lead her back the sciences. For her part, Fiona was expecting it to be interesting and helpful, particularly if her science-fiction stories ever ventured into the arena of psychological thrillers.

Fiona hadn't given up on science entirely. Maybe she would become a medical researcher, epidemiologist or psychiatrist, and moonlight as a writer of great works of fiction. She already had determined that all her works would have a plotline carrying a message of hope. With her future career in mind, Fiona signed up for what looked to be an interesting class, through which she could offer peer counseling, hearing people's real stories, while also helping them.

The idea was a good one. The problem was, no one showed up for peer counseling. *What, is everyone emotionally perfect right now, and nobody has any stress?* Fiona thought. *I highly doubt that. I mean, here I am, the counselor, and I am feeling like I could use a little peer counseling, myself. What right do I have, trying to be a peer counselor? What sort of wisdom do I have to share, anyway?* There she sat, in her cubicle, day after day, waiting for someone to walk through the door.

One afternoon, a student came by, and Fiona straightened up, her heart pounding a little at the opportunity to help someone. "Hi, I'm Fiona," she said. "How can I help you?" False alarm. "I'm handing out flyers for the jam session happening in the park tomorrow night," the student said, sliding a colorful page across the desk. "You should come. It'll be like a mini 'Day on the Green.'"

Fiona had missed the legendary first Day on the Green concert in 1973, but after arriving in California in 1976, she'd tried to attend as many as she could. As she fingered the edge of the flyer, she grew aware of the large white wall-clock ticking an annoying reminder that time was her only companion. She passed the afternoon by doodling, catching up on homework, and dreaming up little jokes. *"Hey, what's the sound of one counselor clapping? Hey, if a counselor falls in the woods, would anyone hear her?"* Fiona could almost hear her old friend Zach, *"If anything happens in the forest, who the hell cares?"*

The truth was, she cared. She'd wanted to help people. What's worse, the solitude was hard to handle. It felt like rejection. Like failure. *My mother would just say something about hard experience building character. Well, what with community orchestra and peer counseling, I'm becoming quite a character.* Fiona looked up at the clock, realized she'd overstayed by ten minutes, packed up her books, and headed out to the pond by the music building. She still had almost an hour before her next class, and nothing that needed doing.

Between classes, Fiona spent a lot of time by the pond, watching the fluffy white cumulus clouds roll by in a vivid blue sky, as she stretched out on the bench, twiddling blades of grass between her fingers—she was a daydreamer like Pop. Sometimes she followed the dragonflies. Usually, the experience by the pond seemed soothing and lifted her spirits. Today, not even the frog that created an audible splash as it jumped into the water could generate a smile. She had begun to wonder whether her horrible high school counselor, Mr. Salinsky, had been right. His words, "Get over yourself," and "everybody thinks they're special," rang in her ears, over and over, as if he'd somehow cursed her future. Had he? No!

You can't curse someone else's future without their permission.

That thought was enough to make her rise up. Fiona headed back to the dorms with renewed purpose. Back in her room she pulled out her sisters' most recent letters. Still in the nightstand drawer by her bed, they hadn't yet made it into her keepsake box. As usual, they were a great source of comfort and strength. She felt her resolve returning.

~o0O0O0o~

Fiona continued to show up for her weekly peer counseling practicum, even though no other students ever did. She had to write a term paper about her experience as a peer counselor. That's going to be a super short essay, she thought. I wonder if my professor would like an essay on the psychological dynamics of sitting and waiting, in silence, for something that will never happen. Very Zen.

She stopped by her professor's office, without waiting for office hours. She had no desire to fail the course, and no idea what to do about the term paper. To her surprise, she wasn't the first student who'd experienced this situation. The professor promptly assigned an alternate research paper: the development of anorexia nervosa and bulimia in teens. Fiona was indeed very thin—she preferred it when people said "petite," so she hoped it wasn't a jab about her weight.

Right on! Fiona thought. One thing I really know in spades is how to write papers. I'm going to ace this because writing's my bag! This is fantastic! And I may be thin, but I am not too thin!

With an "I'm too cool and definitely not too thin" swish, she headed resolutely to the library across campus and checked out every book she could find on the subject, and carted them to her dorm room.

~oOOoOOo~

It was a cool, gray Monday morning, the kind Fiona liked best, socked in before the fog cleared. Even with the beautiful fog, Fiona was feeling a little down, though she wasn't sure exactly why. She'd completed her anorexia paper early, as she loved doing, but even the thought of relaxing at the end of the term while everyone else around her was going crazy wasn't enough to lift her mood. She was sitting in her dorm room, savoring a cup of tea she'd brewed, and reading *The Campanil*, the student newspaper, hoping to catch up on campus news before heading to class. But two of her hallmates stopped in with more compelling gossip than she'd found in the paper. Judy, from down the hall, had been assaulted at a party the night before.

The buzz in the dorm was that her punch at the party had been heavily spiked. Judy hadn't remembered much of her evening, but she could tell well enough what had happened when she came to, disheveled and bruised.

"How stupid," said one of the girls.

"She should have known better," said the other. "Everyone knows you don't turn your back on your drink."

"Are you holding Judy responsible?" Fiona asked, setting down her tea. "So, you're saying it's her fault? Like, she dressed up and didn't guard her drink like a watchdog, and so now she brought it on herself? As in, she deserved it? And what, the guy was just being a guy? Seriously?"

The news and her friends' reactions had triggered something deep and desperate inside Fiona, rocketing her back to her own violent attack in Argentina. She felt awful for this girl, Judy, whom she didn't know well but certainly had seen in the halls and dining commons. She felt a kind of kinship, knowing what it was like to be judged, accused, even, for something bad you've suffered.

"Geez, Fiona. Take a chill pill." Her neighbors let themselves out of her room.

Later that morning, Fiona found herself taking the long way down the hall, to the far stairs, just to pass by Judy's room. She wasn't sure why, exactly, but she felt drawn to her.

The door to Judy's room was slightly ajar, so Fiona knocked, faintly. "Hmm?" a weak voice answered.

"Hey," Fiona offered. "I just thought I'd stop in, maybe see how you're doing. Do you maybe, you know, want to talk about anything?"

Judy, who was sitting on the floor by her bed, her hair tangled and shrouding her face, shook her head, no. "News travels fast," she whispered. Fiona sat down on the floor next to her anyway, and said nothing for what felt like a good five minutes. Judy didn't push her away.

The minutes passed slowly. Through the simple fact of her presence, Fiona tried to convey, "I get it. Really, I do. I've been where you are, in my own way." True, Fiona thought. Different, maybe worse, but the same, too. It made no sense to compare pain, she sensed. Anyway, in the moment, Judy's pain was just as real.

After a time, Judy began talking, so quietly Fiona had to strain to hear her. She listened to Judy, as whispers became sobs. In a torrent of words and tears, Judy let all the details tumble out. Fiona remained silent with a concerned look on her face. Judy had decided she wasn't going to report what had happened. What was the point, right? Fiona placed her hand on Judy's. "I'll support you, whatever you decide," Fiona said. "But, by reporting it, you might help keep this from happening to someone else. For now, you might want to get checked out at a clinic, don't you think? Just to make sure you're okay? I can go with you, if you want."

Judy looked up briefly, then averted her eyes by pretending to examine her watch. Clearly, she was considering it. Then, she really did notice the time. With a start, she realized she was late to class. She stood up, snatched her backpack and, with a quick, "Well, aren't you a surprising friend?" rushed out the door. "I'll think about it. Catch you later," she called down the hall.

What's this? Fiona thought. Me, a surprising friend? Is that a good thing or a bad thing? It would be bad if it meant that people would find it surprising whenever she behaved in a way that was compassionate or kind. But maybe she'd meant the whole "friend in need, is a friend, indeed" thing. She didn't have to be close to someone to offer a hand in friendship.

Fiona really hoped Judy would reach out to her, maybe if she did decide to go to the clinic and needed company. As she made her way to her own class, she mulled over how much she liked the idea of being a surprising friend. Someone who shows up when needed. She even decided it would make a great epitaph: "Here lies Fiona Sprechelbach, who was, above all else, a surprising friend." That made her laugh inside.

Later that day, Fiona found a card slipped under her door. It was hand-drawn, showing two stick figures lying on the ground. Above the image was the phrase, "Friend: (noun) Someone who'll lift you up and, when it's impossible, will get down on the floor with you and just listen." Below, it was signed, "Thanks, Judy." This went right to Fiona's heart and on into her keepsake box, to join her collection of special cards and letters. She didn't need to pull out those letters for reassurance or a special lift today. Not in this moment. Judy had seen to that.

How funny, Fiona thought. I was trying to cheer up Judy, and it turns out she's the one doing that, for me. And maybe I'm not so bad at peer counseling, either.

Fiona got the sense that the act of lifting someone up and out of a ditch when you're in the ditch yourself, can bring you both up and out. Pop would say it defies the laws of physics, that it can't be done. Simply impossible. Sometimes when there's nothing left that's possible, the impossible is the only thing left to do.

~oOOoOOo~

Fiona awoke with the sun, stretched, looked at the steadfast oak outside her window, and had an epiphany of sorts. Why not try, try again? she thought. She was thinking of joining another orchestra. You love the viola, so why abandon it and banish it to the back of the closet? Those strings were meant to sing! Fiona fairly danced out of bed, and skipped over to retrieve the instrument she'd grown to love so much in high school. She opened the case and ran her fingers across the smooth, shiny surface. "Welcome back," she whispered.

With that, Fiona started asking around to find a kind, accepting, and capable conductor in the Bay Area. She found the answer from a student on the second floor of her dorm, who not only held a place in the string section but also occupied first chair in the orchestra that had dismissed Fiona so harshly. Mr. Ray Karey of the Oceanside Orchestra was her man. That orchestra didn't even require auditions. Fiona decided to give it a go, even though it meant quite a trek to rehearsals in Half Moon Bay. At least the drive was beautiful, motoring across the San Mateo Bridge directly onto Highway 92, until it almost ran straight into the ocean.

Fiona called Mr. Ż., to tell him she was going to try again. To her great surprise, he not only encouraged her to go; he volunteered to accompany her and sit beside her in the string section, until she got comfortable. Further, he offered to pick her up at her dorm and drive her to Half Moon Bay, so he could help her mentally prepare on the way. Either he misses sitting in orchestra, Fiona thought, or he really doesn't think I can make it on my own. Just maybe, though, he believed in her. She decided the motivation didn't matter, and she'd be foolish not to take his help.

On the drive to Half Moon Bay the next Wednesday, Fiona was filled with self-doubt. "Mr. Żywny," she said, "What if they kick me out of the orchestra as soon as you stop coming with me? I'm not like you. I'm not God's gift to the string section. I wouldn't be able to play like you do, no matter how many hours I practiced. I mean, you've got perfect pitch. Perfect everything, actually."

Mr. Ż. thought for a moment as he drove. "First, Fiona, this isn't about me. It's about you and your music. You're right; you could never be a perfect me. Only I can. So, you need to focus on being the perfect you. Don't worry about being anything but your best self. There's always going to be someone who's better at something or worse at something than you are. A high school violist may not be as good a player as I am, but does dwelling on that help? I've got many years on them, so if I'm not better, something's wrong. I don't compare myself to anyone except myself. Neither should you. You're going to be fine. Perfect pitch, shmerfect pitch. You don't need it."

Fiona didn't agree. "But perfect pitch is so cool," she said. "It's legit. It says you were born to be a musician. I think it's cool. Pop has it, and I think Hanna may have, too. I sure wish I did."

"It's cool? So, that's what this is about? You want to be cool? And here I thought you wanted to be a musician. You kids all want to be cool, to have another way to show off. You want to use perfect pitch as a parlor trick. If all you want to do is show off, I can give you a parlor trick to achieve the same result."

Fiona knew she should confirm that what she wanted most was to be a fine musician. But right now, she wanted access to any and every trick that would secure her a seat in that orchestra. Mr. Ż. had trained her classically; now she was ready to slip a few tricks up her sleeve. "Seriously? Can you teach me in the car, before we get there?"

Mr. Ż. relented, having known he'd have to deliver, the moment he brought it up. "Well, first, you need to have good relative pitch, which you do. You couldn't play the viola in tune without it."

Fiona was about to object that she didn't always play perfectly in tune. He saw the words forming on her face before she said them. "You do fine, Fiona. Trust me. People make mistakes, but, generally, you have a good ear. And, if you want to play more in tune, continue to practice, meticulously, and you'll get the muscle memory. Want me to prove you have good relative pitch? Sing me a seventh from this note. Laaaaa."

Mr. Ż. sang a note, and Fiona followed, singing a seventh above.

"See? Good job."

"I cheated," she said. "I just sang the third note of the song, 'Somewhere Over the Rainbow.' It's a seventh up from the first note."

Mr. Ż. didn't consider that cheating. It was a demonstration of knowledge and understanding. "That's fine. It still indicates relative pitch. Nothing wrong with that. The more you do it, the faster you'll be. Soon, you won't have to search for a song."

Fiona was now convinced she had relative pitch, but she also knew she'd had that before, when the first orchestra had dismissed her. What was going to make the difference this time? Mr. Ż., as if he'd read her mind, continued with his advice. "Now, Fiona, you need somewhere to start, perhaps using tonal or melodic memory. Some people bring up a song in their head, knowing where it's going to start, as you did. Still, tonal memory can be a few cents from perfect. Same thing for vocal range; it can vary. You need something constant, like electrical humming that's all around you, at 60 Hz, just a few cents below a B but not flat. You just raise it up in your mind to what seems like a B. All you need to do is add relative pitch to that, and you're golden."

Fiona understood what Mr. Ż. was talking about, but she didn't like the trick, particularly because she knew he didn't need it, himself. "I get it, Mr. Ż., but it's not what you have to do, and I don't want to, either. When you walk into a room and hear a phone ring, you just know it's 50 cents off C sharp. I've seen you do it. Man, I wish I had that gift, like you do."

"Once again, we're not talking about me, Fiona. I'm trying to give you the tools to be successful. Take it or leave it." Growing frustrated with Fiona's obstinance, Mr. Ż. was talking faster. "Work with who you are and what you have. Believe me, perfect pitch is not all it's cracked up to be. It hurts my ears when people are even a little off. It's hard, when all the electricity buzzing around me is slightly out of tune. Can you imagine that? Today, in this little orchestra, you'll hear my playing centered on the music, not pulled by the pitch of the others. But, I'll be making a choice. If the conductor tunes us a few cents off, I'll go with that. I try not to be inflexible, except when it really matters. I don't have a solo today, if you know what I mean. I need to blend in with my colleagues."

"Isn't everyone in the orchestra trying to do that?" Fiona asked.

"Yes, or they should be. And the great musicians achieve it. I tune out any dissonance except when I need to listen to my students to correct them. That's my day job. In concert, I go with the flow, but I tune out anything that hurts my ears, and I keep playing. Life's like that, isn't it, Fiona? Sometimes it can hurt when we listen too closely.

It also can be painful to be the only one in tune with what's highest and best or what's right, when everyone around you is behaving off key. Often, they don't even know they are. When that happens, if you stay true to pitch, you're the only one who sounds wrong. Do you know what I mean? So, you think about the situation, and you make choices. Sometimes, you end up leaving one orchestra for another." And, sometimes, he thought, one country for another. But that was another story for another time.

Fiona could tell that Mr. Ż. had departed his orchestra prep speech and was going on about something else, some life lesson she was supposed to get, but she wasn't sure if it was more about him than her. She had a feeling she needed to slip Mr. Ż.'s words into her inner treasure box, and pull them out later, when they made more sense. Still, Fiona hadn't considered that there might be a downside to being so attuned to perfect pitch. Fiona now realized he was sitting with the orchestra because he cared about her, and for no other reason. Fiona sat with her realization, in silence, for a moment, letting the conversation ebb as he, too, slipped into his own thoughts. They spent a bit of quiet time, driving across the San Mateo Bridge, with Fiona occasionally pointing out sights—the salt flat, an egret, a heron.

Mr. Ż. decided they needed to rehearse. "Now let's warm up with vocals," he said.

"How does that help us?" she said.

"Your viola is your voice in the orchestra, so let's warm up your actual voice. Sing in tune, get the flow of the music. Trust me; it helps. Do you remember when I taught you to sing arpeggios while saying, 'I can' and 'I will'?" Fiona remembered. And she could and she would. "Yes, I remember." And so, they did. Eventually, they got to laughing, singing, "We caaaAaaan, and we wiiiIiiill."

~oOoOOOOo~

Fiona and Mr. Ż. arrived at the high school where the orchestra rehearsed. After being welcomed, handed sheet music, and escorted to their seats, they took out their instruments, rosined up their bows, and settled in to await the conductor's baton. Curious, Fiona wanted to look around the room, study faces, get her bearings, but Mr. Ż. suggested she look over her music.

This time, with Mr. Ż. seated by her side, Fiona felt at ease. Just a few measures into the first song, she began to play the emotion of the music. Once, when she momentarily lost her place in the piece, Mr. Ż. whispered the bar number under his breath. He whispered other hints as well, such as "upbow" or "more vibrato." Mostly, she surprised herself by how well she kept up. Then, she made a glaring mistake. She played a B♮ where she should have played a B♭. Mr. Ż. gave her a sideways glance and raised an eyebrow but said nothing. Although they'd all sounded sour, she'd only noticed her own fatal flaw. The conductor stopped the orchestra and said, genially, "I meant the other B flat," and everybody laughed. Mr. Ż. whispered, "That's the musician's version of the military joke about 'the other left foot.'" She had to laugh. Fiona got the feeling she'd be okay at Oceanside. She was getting off on the right foot…the other left foot.

At the first break for tea and cookies, all eyes were on the viola section, and not because of Fiona. Boris Żywny's reputation was well known. Fiona had never understood the depth of his ability and had little sense of his notoriety. She knew his music was breathtaking and his teaching was exceptional, albeit a bit harsh at times. Most all, she had learned that he had her back. Sharing a stand with him meant she didn't get lost. He didn't let her. It was like dancing on air with Fred Astaire.

The concertmaster approached Fiona and Boris, and welcomed them with open arms. Mr. Ż. emphasized that he wouldn't be making the concert; he was just sitting in for a few sessions because he enjoyed the orchestra. The concertmaster said she'd be thrilled to have him sit in, any time, even for one of their concerts. Mr. Ż. smiled and said he was flattered. He accompanied Fiona to two more rehearsals, to ensure she'd be fine. Meanwhile, she spent a couple of focused hours a day woodshedding—diving in to the material with her whole heart. She had found her musical home.

The concertmaster sent an open invitation to a play-and sing-along performance of Handel's *Messiah*, to be held at a large private home in Atherton, a tiny, toney town on the Peninsula. Her first paid gig. Fiona was excited; it was a new opportunity. She got an advance copy of the music, to prepare. Many of the other players did not need to practice, but she felt she did. She was looking forward to it, right up until the point where she was rosining up her bow at the rehearsal. That's when she noticed the conductor wielding the baton was the very same one who'd kicked her out of his orchestra.

Her heart started beating hard as she considered her options. The door was only a few feet away. She could still bolt. She could pretend she had food poisoning. Or, she could stay. Her friends were staying. One of them, who was sharing her music stand, was an outstanding player. What were the odds she'd be kicked out again?

Fiona summoned her best self, and whispered a prayer for a little help. Then she took up her bow, and set to work. She played superbly, going beyond the notes to play the reverence and the meaning of the music. Even the parts where the music was so beautiful it made tears well up, and she found it hard to see the sheet music, came exquisitely through her bow. It happened during, "I know that my redeemer liveth," and, "He shall feed his flock like a shepherd." Not just because it was so beautiful, so enchanting to play, but also because she was playing about being held in God's arms, like a lamb. That was just too beautiful not to shed tears.

At the break, the conductor approached Fiona and invited her to join his orchestra. She was thunderstruck by a simple realization. He had no idea who she was.

"You really don't remember me, do you?" Fiona said.

"No." He raised an eyebrow. "I'm sorry, have we met?"

"I was in your orchestra briefly, last spring. Until you kicked me out."

"Oh, I'm sorry. I hope I wasn't too harsh."

Fiona just stared at him for a moment, taking it in. She thought of all the things she could say. She thought of telling him how it had wounded her so deeply that she'd almost quit playing entirely. She thought of telling him it was like he'd kicked her in the teeth, or in the soul. But as it sunk in that he had absolutely no memory of her, she realized he must have done this with dozens of musicians. Maybe hundreds. Finally, she said simply, "It's good to know you enjoy my playing now, since you've invited me back, but I'm happy where I am, thanks." She proceeded to make sure he knew how wonderful her current conductor was, and how happy she was to be a member in good standing of the Oceanside Orchestra. He seemed to get the message and excused himself, escaping to the refreshments table.

Driving back to her dorm, Fiona pondered how one person could have such a devastating effect on another, and yet not even remember them later. But she also knew, from her current conductor's examples of kindness and encouragement, that it was quite possible to have a very different effect on others while still running something as expressive as an orchestra. Yes, she thought, those are two completely different takes on the same task. She'd seen Ray Karey advise a player that they weren't quite ready yet, and to come back in a few months, sending them home with scales and studies. He didn't let "just anyone" in to his orchestra either. But when he let them go, he let them down gently, without dashing their hopes and dreams. And, Fiona somehow knew, he didn't forget them, or anyone else who'd played for him.

It just blows my mind, she thought to herself, driving home from the gig, cash in hand, how you can just devastate someone, leave their self-esteem totally shredded, and not even give them another thought. He didn't even recognize me. It's like I never even existed for him, thank you very much. Well, what's good for the goose is good for the gander. He's vanished. Lifted from my page like unwanted letters corrected by my inner Correcting Selectric typewriter. There may be a little imprint where the ink once was, but basically, he's gone. Gone, and good riddance, I say. I bet he and my high school counselor would get along great. They should look each other up.

People should learn how to take care with other people's dreams, thought Fiona. Dreams are fragile things. That's almost important enough to make a rule about, if I'm still making them. Am I? I guess it doesn't really matter. It's covered by the Golden Rule. But maybe I should consider a rule about holding on to your dreams, though, and not letting the world steal you blind.

The sky had been spitting all day, in one of those very predictable "April showers" sort of ways that bodes well for the gardens. The air smelled deliciously of wet eucalyptus. Fiona felt right as rain, watching the rivulets course down her dorm room window while she sipped hot chocolate and studied psychology. One more year to go! All was well with the world...until her mother let loose her thunderstorm. She was selling her home, and moving with a group of other like-minded souls, to New Zealand. What Fiona didn't know was that, beyond the cloudburst, there would be a hail storm to follow.

"New Zealand? Why so far away?" Fiona asked into the telephone, in shocked disbelief.

"Listen, Fiona," Peggy intoned. "It's important to leave here before California falls into the ocean in 1985. There's a big quake coming by then, and what's going to happen is that it all collapses. It's going to be a big wipe-out. California is just not going to be the same anymore. Many people are going to die and I, for one, don't plan on being one of them. The good news is that a group of us have gotten together and pooled our resources, and there's some land in New Zealand that looks amazing."

"But, wait, New Zealand has earthquakes, too, doesn't it?"

"Yes, it does, but New Zealand isn't going to crumble into the sea like California."

"How do you know that?"

Peggy didn't answer, but it didn't matter, because Fiona already knew who'd put the idea in her head. It was Cassowary Cass. It just had to be. Peggy invented stories for a living, but hadn't ever concocted anything as weird as this one. Her real life story. In her own strange way, Peggy was copying Wolf. She was going live in a commune, halfway across the world. After a long and uncomfortable silence, Peggy continued the conversation.

"So, Fiona, let's discuss what this move means, regarding Mills." Peggy was building up to the perfect storm.

"What do you mean, exactly?"

"I don't think you should stay at a California college, and I'm not willing to be a party to paying for you continuing to stay at one. Now, of course you're in no position to care for a dog right now, so I've already taken care of that."

Fiona sat in stunned silence. Did she really just give away my dog?

"I've found a good home for Starlight," Peggy continued, confirming Fiona's worst fears. "She's already on the East Coast with one of my former students, on a lovely farm. You can visit her there, if you ever get to Vermont." Yes, the deluge had arrived. As singer Albert Hammond might describe the rain in California, "It pours, man, it pours."

Fiona hung up the phone, numb. Good thing she can't take back this year's tuition, Fiona mused, or maybe I'd be packing my bags right now, like Noni and Papi. She made herself a cup of tea. She tried to think, but the thoughts wouldn't arrive.

I could call Pop, Fiona thought. But I know what he'd say. I can hear him now. He'd say, "New Zealand? Far out. Far away and far out, Fee." And then tell me to come home. He'd say that since my mother isn't in California, I have to come home now to Philadelphia where I belong. He'd crack a joke, but it was no joke. Not at all.

Fiona imagined that Pop would want her to finish up at U. Penn, where he was teaching. Once he thought Peggy wasn't keeping a watchful eye, California would be out of the question. But it was moving back to Philly that was out of the question, to Fiona. Not that U. Penn was such a bad idea. It just wasn't part of her plan.

Fiona gazed absently into the Victorian mirror on her stand. I'm a California girl now, she thought, and I intend to stay one. That's the plan. I won't bug Pop about any of this. I'll puzzle it out for myself.

Two hours later, Fiona stared down at the hot chocolate, now cold and uninviting, in her Mills College mug. Should I toss the mug across the room? Fiona wondered. Her practical nature won out over her impulse to indulge in a grand gesture nobody would see anyway. She poured her chocolate down the sink, washed the cup, set it back carefully in its proper place, put on her PJs, and headed to bed. Before tucking herself in, Fiona peered out the window into the darkness. The night had no Starlight. Neither did she, Fiona thought, as she ached over her little dog. If there were any stars behind those clouds, she couldn't see them. Fiona's heart hurt with a pain she could not name. Sleep came remarkably easy. She'd think tomorrow.

~o0O0O0o~

A cool, gray morning arrived too quickly. With her mind still reeling from the tsunami Peggy had unleashed, Fiona felt completely ill-equipped to handle her new quandary. It had released a host of old, traumatic insecurities from somewhere deep, down inside.

It wasn't the money. It was the leaving.

Fiona was too shocked to cry and too angry, too scared, too sad—most especially about the loss of her beloved Starlight—to do anything about it. This was so much worse than getting kicked out of orchestra for her inability to play. And it wasn't just that she might get kicked out of college for her inability to pay. It was that the sky was falling in some ineffable way. It was still up there, but it was definitely falling. And she was pretty sure it was landing on her.

Fiona was sitting on her bed, tracing the pattern on her bedspread with her finger, staring sightlessly, when it hit her. The orchestra fiasco had only been a dress rehearsal for this catastrophe. All her life she'd been listening to advice about what to do, how to handle a setback. She had persevered. And she had moved on—and up.

The next move was completely up to her. She could sit there, winded, like she had in gym class back in Detroit. Or she could rise up, and find the proverbial pet skunk. What was her Hogan in this situation? Was it dropping out and finding a job? Should she really think about going to Penn? At least she could have a pet, there. Could she somehow make it through Mills? How far from the finish line was she? She pulled out her course catalog and started doing the math.

As if she had been living with a premonition, Fiona had been collecting course credits at a strong pace each semester, plus additional units through summer classes at Cal Berkeley. It was as if, somehow, she knew she needed to get through college as quickly as she'd hauled herself through high school. Was it fast enough? If she killed herself trying, would she make it? Cats had nine lives. Did she?

Fiona calculated that, to cover even the basic college requirements for an English Lit major, she still had seven more courses to complete after this semester. That would have been fine, if she'd had a year to do it. Would it be fine in half that time? Even if the college could be convinced to let her try, Fiona wasn't sure she could handle all the units she still needed. Seven courses would create a pretty big mountain to climb. I'll bet no one's ever carried that heavy a load before, she thought. The risk of failure is just too great.

Failure? Fiona shivered. Heavens forfend. Dropping out beats getting kicked out or failing out. But, seriously, dropping out? Where's the integrity in that path? Mr. Ż. says, to play a piece through on viola, you need to find the best path. Sometimes, that means shifting fingerings from one position to another, and not just first position or third. Even that cursed second position can be the best way forward through a piece of music to the finish line. The first time I realized he was right, I had to laugh. But he's right, of course. Mr. Ż. is always right. So, what's my second position here?

What to do? What to do? What would Mr. Ż. do? As she went over her situation, Fiona's thoughts began to loop: Yes, she would stay in school. She would find a way. No, it would not work out. She would stay, but drop out. Or, she'd pack up and move back to Philly, tail between her legs. Maybe things could work out. Maybe not. Maybe her life plan was over. Maybe it wasn't. Maybe she needed a new plan.

Weighing her options with "on the one hand, and on the other," Fiona quickly ran out of hands. If only I were an octopus, Fiona mused, I could mull over eight options. On the other tentacle, maybe I'd be better off as one of those multi-headed multi-handed Hindu gods. More heads could puzzle out my problem better. Or hey, since I'm wishing for the impossible anyway, why not wish for the wisdom of Solomon? That way I'd know just what to do. But I don't. Fiona realized, dejected. Suddenly, she felt very small.

Fiona also felt dizzy and sick, as if she'd been punched in the stomach and was about to throw up. Maybe it was a migraine. Her mother had told her these were self-inflicted. Psychosomatic. Was that true? Had she punched herself in the eye, all these times? Had nobody else, as bullies do, pushed her hand close to her face, making the "self-inflicted" punches happen? Honestly, had she, and nobody else, thrown this punch? Or that first punch, so many years ago, when she'd experienced her very first migraine? Deep down, Fiona agreed with her mother that the pain she was in was somehow entirely her own fault, which didn't help her feel any better. All she knew for certain was that she was hurting, in every way she knew how to hurt. Punch drunk from exhaustion, she fell into a deep sleep.

~o0O0O0o~

Fiona awoke with a start before dawn. Overwhelmed with the sensation she would never puzzle her way through her situation or the feelings surrounding it successfully, Fiona decided she needed a break from everyone and everything. Maybe even a permanent break. Permanence. Quiet. No more pain. Maybe that was the solution to the riddle. Seems logical enough, she decided.

She looked out the window at the torrential rainstorm. No worries, she thought. I'll just bring an umbrella. In the time it took her to close the umbrella and open the car door, her face and hair were drenched. Turning the key in the ignition and idling the engine, she gave the car time to warm up, so the heater would finally work.

"I'm glad you're a small car," Fiona said, as she patted the dashboard. "I just wish you were a convertible." In her mind, she was picturing modern dancer Isadora Duncan, who'd famously died from tangling her dramatic scarf under the rear hubcap of her convertible. It seemed to offer a romantic demise, and so did all the steep hairpin-turns along the route to Mount Tamalpais. She pored through her boxes of tapes, and settled on Carole King's *Tapestry*. Some of those songs suit my mood just fine, she thought, pushing in the tape and hitting play, as she headed out toward the freeway. "So Far Away" came on, prompting a fresh round of tears and making it even more difficult to see in the blinding rain. But, the harder it got to drive, the more Fiona had to concentrate on keeping her car on the road, and the less time she had to focus on her plan for purposefully driving off the edge. Before she could remember to take drastic action, she found she had arrived at Mt. Tam.

She thought of hiking the trail. From the top, it would have offered an amazing perspective on life and the San Francisco Bay—if it weren't entirely socked in. Instead, she wandered over to an elderly oak and stood there, steadying herself against the wind and the rain, yelling at God. "Hey Jesus! Hey! Where are you! I figure you saved me for a reason, right? Some plan or something? So, what am I supposed to do now? Can you please clue me in here? A little help, maybe? Hey, are you listening? Hello? GAAAAAARRGH." And then, she stopped.

It felt good to lose control and yell her guts out in the wild weather. It had felt a lot better than her prolonged scream, long ago at Mystic Meadow. This time, she felt listened to. She felt heard. So, she stopped screaming.

"Okay, God, I'm ready to listen. Talk to me, show me the way."

Absolutely no voice came through the storm, at least nothing Fiona could interpret. But she felt better. Chilly, but better. And dripping wet. When she got back to her car, Fiona wrung her hair out; she could have filled a bucket. Her feet squished in her saturated sneakers. She felt silly for having driven all that way, seemingly for nothing. I could have curled up in the closet, warm and dry, and gotten the same inspiration, she thought. Bidden or unbidden, God is present, isn't that what Jung used to say? I didn't have to go searching; God was right there in my dorm room.

Driving back to the dorm, Fiona blasted the heat. Reaching into her collection of tapes while keeping one hand on the wheel, she reached down, fishing for what she hoped would be the Eagles' *Hotel California*. Because her collection was neatly alphabetized, she came close, with Emerson Lake & Palmer's *Trilogy*. Okay, she thought. Why not? Fast forwarding to the song "From the Beginning," she blasted the volume just as loud as the car's speakers would go without distortion. That wasn't as loud as she'd have liked, but it was loud enough that she couldn't hear the rain falling on the car, or her own voice singing along to the music.

The warm air and upbeat music filling the car were soothing, as if Fiona were in her own cocoon. As she pressed on in the rain, Fiona became mesmerized by the rhythmic switching of the windshield wipers, clearing her field of vision. She strained to see the road before her, and she thought about Jesus and God and storms and silence, and the idea of being washed by water.

Fiona hadn't come to seek solace. No, she had driven up the hill to rage at the rain on the mountain top. To pour her heart out—an idea she now thought was all wet—and ask Jesus, who'd promised to be forever present, where He'd disappeared to lately. Having spoken—okay raged—her peace, she was rewarded with a sweeping sense of peace that had nothing to do with her situation. Nothing had changed except she was reminded that God was with her, not against her, and in fact had never left. With God so close—closer than her very breath—it looked like she'd been the one to sideline the conversation. Fiona felt a little sheepish, for having been so blind to what now felt so obvious. She shivered and wondered if it was because she'd felt that presence in the rain or was about to catch pneumonia.

Fiona knew she had landed on her most important realization, one befitting at any age, one life rule you never grow out of needing.

Fiona's Rule #8—Never Give Up Hope.

~o0O0O0o~

Another sleepless night. Fiona rolled over and looked at the bedside clock, wide awake. The luminous dial and hands told her it was 2:30am. Again. Maybe it would help, Fiona thought, if I could get a good night's sleep. Inner peace and hope were still there—just buried under an avalanche of insomnia.

Fiona remembered how, after her misadventure in Argentina, the kindly doctor had given her a prescription for some valium that had helped her relax and get a good night's sleep. She decided, as soon as it was properly morning, she'd head to Health Services on campus to see if she could get a prescription.

She arrived half an hour before they opened. The nurse practitioner who saw her told Fiona she would first have to meet with a counselor before she could write Fiona any prescription. Well, those are the rules, Fiona thought, though she was exquisitely aware of how dismissive Pop was of the benefits of talk therapy. Before leaving, Fiona asked about the first available appointment. She was in luck; there was an opening with a counselor named Mr. Green the very next day.

The following afternoon, Fiona was sitting in the waiting room, reading the text from her psychology class to avoid making eye contact with any other student in the room. A clock radio, tuned to white noise, was creating an ambient buzz to muffle the conversations and enhance privacy. It's kind of like being a back-up singer in a band, Fiona thought. You can contribute your voice without feeling featured. Then, her name was called, and she made her way to the office marked "Y. B. Green, LCSW"

Inside his office, she found two comfortable upholstered chairs in a bright, sunny room. The window, glazed to avoid glare and exposure to passersby, was slightly open. She appreciated the fresh air. A box of tissues sat on a side table between the two chairs, and Fiona could see there were others, on Mr. Green's desk, atop a cabinet, and on the bookshelf. She thought about how much sadness must come out in this room. It made her feel sad, just thinking about it. She also noticed a clear decanter of water and two glasses on the table. She could sense the attention to privacy and comfort Mr. Green had put into the space, and felt soothed by it. Still, she wasn't planning on spilling her guts. She just wanted a prescription so she could sleep. What would that take, five minutes? She could spare that. Yet, when Mr. Green walked in, introduced himself, and settled into one of the easy chairs, motioning her to do the same, Fiona realized she was probably going to have to spend an hour. She sighed.

He heard it. "So, Fiona, what's going on?"

At first, she sat there, unsure of where to begin. But he seemed to really care, and so, hesitatingly at first, she told him why she was there. She needed sleep. "Good, self-care is good," he said. "Any idea what's causing the lack of sleep?"

"I don't know. I guess I'm feeling a little stressed out." After a slow start, she eventually shared that she kept wondering if she should drop out and move back to Philadelphia. Why? Because she felt like she was failing. Why? Because maybe she didn't even belong in college. Maybe she was wrong to think she could plow through college early. Then again, maybe if she could just get some more sleep, she could think more clearly. "So, there's the big answer to all your 'why' questions. I need a sleep aid. You sound like I must have sounded to my father with all my questions, at about four years old." At that, Mr. Green shifted gears.

"Let's talk about that—about you and your parents, I mean. How are things going, between you and them, Fiona?"

"What do you mean?" Fiona barked back, defensively. This was not an area she wanted to go into with a stranger. It was none of his business, and anyway, that wasn't the problem. "It's great. They're great. My father's a scientist and my mother's a mystery writer. They're great, like I said. That's not why I'm here. Haven't you heard me? I'm here for..."

"What I mean," Mr. Green continued, "is that, sometimes when you're down or anxious or confused, that can be a part of the equation, and it can be worth a look."

"Maybe sometimes, but not with me," Fiona interrupted, "My mother's famous and fabulous. And my dad's a total genius. I can tell him basically anything, and he doesn't judge. Like I said, I am not here about that. I'm here to get help sleeping."

"I see, and..."

"And nothing. I don't want to talk about them."

"Okay, I promise to never talk to you about your parents if you'll do me one favor. Can you take a long, deep breath for me?"

Gawwwwd, Fiona thought, rolling her eyes. Déjà vu all over again. "What's that, you say?"

"Take a moment and breathe," Mr. Green said in a soft voice. Fiona played along, and it actually helped. Once she had slowed down her breathing and her mind, he asked a simple but surprising question. "Fiona, you talk about thinking a lot, and wanting to think things through. Tell me, do you believe everything you think?"

"No. Yes. I mean…" The question caught Fiona off guard, and she had to think about it before finally coming up with an accurate answer. "I haven't really thought about it."

"Well," Mr. Green continued, "let's think about it, now. Not all thoughts are created equal. For example, do you agree that, when you practice viola, thinking, 'I'll never finish' isn't only unhelpful, it's untrue?" As Fiona nodded, he continued. "So, we see how our own thoughts can lie to us. Sometimes, we get into unhelpful thought habits, called Automatic Negative Thoughts—or ANTs—which can multiply and bring you down. But you can look at your thoughts. You can hold a magnifying glass up to them, and if they're ANTs, kill them dead."

Fiona had to laugh. Kill ants with a magnifying glass? I've actually done that. She got a mental picture of a bug with the words "failure" painted on its abdomen, bursting into flames, just like Pop's science experiment in India. Mr. Green smiled, seeing he was getting through.

"Ever thought of taking charge of your thought life, and making choices about where your mind goes?" Mr. Green continued. "That's called discernment."

"Nope. I believe thoughts are free." But she didn't. Not anymore. It was like a lightbulb had gone on, and she understood. She thought back to Pop's radar work, which was all about deciding which signal to pick up on, and which to ignore—which mattered and which could be filtered out. She'd realized thoughts are like that.

"You're free to act on them or not. Want to know how to spot a bad time to make a decision?" Mr. Green continued. "Here's a key: HALTS. Don't make important decisions when you're Hungry, Angry, Lonely, Tired, or Sad."

"These days, that's pretty much all the time," Fiona said. "What then? Anyway, that's why I'm here."

"Right, right. But can you see how now's not the best moment to decide to give up on school?"

"That's fair. But how am I going to get some sleep?" she asked, earnestly. "That's the whole reason I came here."

Mr. Green smiled. "Yes, it's clear that you're not getting enough sleep." Fiona nodded. "Good for you, for noticing, and seeking help. Don't worry, I have decided to request an authorization for a two-week supply of the prescription you asked for," he said. "But I want to see you, again, before I authorize a refill. Okay?"

"Okay, thanks," she answered, but she was stunned by an incredible thought she absolutely couldn't dismiss. Maybe Pop was wrong, and thoughts weren't entirely free. They were anything but. Didn't Mary say something once about taking thoughts prisoner? She'd have to ask her the next time they talked. No, her thoughts weren't free at all. Some of them came at quite a cost. Also, she was finding value in this counseling session, something Pop eschewed.

Fiona's first experience with Health Services had given her a lot to think about, a plan of action, and a prescription to help her sleep. Best of all, she realized she was not alone. Not in her feelings, and not on campus. Now, she had a friendly ear.

After filling her prescription, Fiona counted the pills. Only 14. What if Mr. Green is busy in two weeks? Fiona thought. What if I drop one? Maybe I shouldn't start right in, just in case. And so, for the next three days, she hoarded them, thinking about the Girl Scout motto: Be Prepared.

The fourth night, she began taking her sleep aid. It took some time after that for her mood to begin improving. Dark thoughts hounded her. She thought about the biggest sleep of all. Maybe I should just dive into that ocean of the unknown, she despaired. Would ending this life stop the pain she was feeling, or would it just change the scenery?

She didn't share her negative thinking with anyone, but her friends had noticed a change in her demeanor. She'd lost interest in them, the very people she'd spent every free moment with since she'd moved to campus. She seemed irritable, impatient, unavailable, and she was getting awfully thin. Sensing she was in trouble, and concerned she might be contemplating self-injury, but not knowing how to help, Fiona's friends approached the counseling center for guidance. It was the first time any of them had ever been there. Mr. Green was the available counselor; he invited them into his office, and they laid out their observations and concerns. "We're worried about a friend of ours. We're afraid she might…Well, we don't know what she might do, but something's very much the matter, and we're worried. We just want to know how to help her."

Mindful of client confidentiality, Mr. Green was blunt. "I appreciate your concerns, but I can't tell you anything about anyone who might be under my care."

The friends looked at each other and back at him. "But what if we tell you who she is? Her name is Fiona Sprechelbach. We know she's been coming here; she told us, herself," said Tracy.

Mr. Green continued to keep Fiona's confidence. "Whatever a student may or may not have told you wouldn't affect their right to confidentiality." His face betrayed no insight or emotion as they pleaded with him.

"Just help us help her. I mean, what if something happens?" Tracy continued. "I hardly think any of us wants a disaster on our conscience, in the interest of confidentiality."

Mr. Green thought for a while, then chose his words carefully. "Okay, listen. Let's say, hypothetically, I know a fellow student is under stress, and let's say I'm growing concerned. I wouldn't be dismissive of her words, ignore her behavior, or toss out platitudes. Instead, I'd remember that the best way to help her is by really listening without judging. Be a loving presence, and share your hopes for her. That's how I'd be a friend. Maybe I'd encourage healthy eating and sleeping habits. Now, here's a pamphlet on teen suicide. If you see the danger signs or if someone is talking about self-harm, take it seriously, and contact Health Services ASAP. Make sense?"

As he turned away, Fiona's friends knew the conversation had ended. It hadn't ended for Mr. Green, though. He knew to act on their concerns and contact his young client. Just in case. He had that alchemy of professional and personal responsibility that worked wonders. Though the school acted legally as a substitute parent, in loco parentis, he believed his job extended beyond even the parental role. He felt like an uncle, sometimes, to these students. So often, he wanted to tell them, "It'll work out," though he knew from sad experience that it often did not. He had to find a way to help Fiona while maintaining his professional distance.

Fiona's friends wandered out into the sunlight of their day, accepting that Mr. Green couldn't discuss Fiona with them, or tell them exactly what to do. None of them felt especially comfortable talking about mental health—it was something most people dealt with silently. They couldn't imagine themselves in Fiona's shoes, and it made them uncomfortable that someone in their circle needed help, so they started imagining ways in which Fiona was different from them. After all, if she was no different, and she could fall off the deep end like this, could one of them be next?

"Fiona's younger than us," said Lynn. "Maybe it would have been better for her if she'd stayed back and finished high school with her peers. And anyway, she's a bit of an odd duck."

"Just younger by a year. What's a year? I think Fiona gets a lot of pressure from her parents," replied Tracy. "She doesn't say much about them, but I just get that feeling from how she handles herself and how driven she is. You know? Maybe it's just the pressure. Maybe we can be encouragers."

Fiona's friends didn't really know how to help, but they resolved to try. Fiona began noticing Tracy and the others inviting her to eat with them more often, asking how she was sleeping, and what was new in her life. She wondered what was up with them, but she decided they were being big-sisterly. Regardless, she appreciated the attention.

Fiona was still struggling with what to do about her future at Mills. She made sure she was waiting at her academic advisor's door when office hours began. She wanted to be first—in and out—and get this thing over with. Her advisor was an armchair psychologist, she would later decide. He listened patiently to Fiona's story, laced with pain and pressure, disappointment and self-doubt, and plenty of hesitation, followed by her reasons for thinking maybe she should just drop out, go to a community college, move back East, or get a job.

The advisor thought for a moment about how to best approach Fiona's concerns, and then asked, "Do you think so little of us?"

Fiona, startled by his blunt question, answered, "No, actually. Weren't you listening? It's not about you. It's about me. Mills is great. I'm the one with the problem here."

Her advisor kept talking. "I'm glad you agree that Mills is great and that we know what we're doing here. We've been at it for more than 130 years. We'd be out of business if we didn't know how to spot a good student, don't you think?"

Fiona opened her mouth to speak, but her advisor continued.

"We chose you to come to Mills because we saw something you aren't seeing. You belong. You fit. You're a Mills woman. This mountain you think you're facing is just a little molehill. Let's figure out how to step over it.

"Are you in a rough spot with a class? If you have been tasting a few things you don't like, so what? You gave it a try, and it brought you closer to knowing what you like and don't like, what you want to do and don't want to do, through the process of elimination."

Fiona breathed in, preparing to respond that this wasn't the problem. Before she could correct him, he ploughed on.

"Writing tastes great to you, doesn't it Fiona?" She nodded. At least he gave her time to nod. "Help yourself to more classes that require writing. That peer counseling experience where nobody showed up to you for guidance must have smacked of isolation. That's not a tasty dish. But you must remember, you're not alone here. This means, you don't have to eat alone. Why didn't you reach out earlier? Well, here we are, and we hardly have time for a relaxing dining experience. You need a fast-food solution. A recipe for success."

Fiona finally found her counselor interesting, entertaining, even. She joined his game. "So, can you help me with the menu of classes?"

"Deal!" He smiled. "Here, can you tape this on your mirror for me?" Fiona accepted the piece of paper he handed her, and nodded. She stuffed it in her coat pocket and promptly forgot about it.

The following week, Fiona returned for a second meeting with Mr. Green at the counseling center. She'd been pleased, if a bit puzzled, to get a call from him in between visits. *I guess he checks up on all his new patients,* she thought. She was excited to tell him the good news from her advisor: she had a new plan. But before she could get to it, because Mr. Green was such a patient listener, Fiona shared a bit of what had happened in Argentina. Hesitant, with voice quavering, she asked, "Do you think I'm damaged goods? Am I some butterfly that, once mangled, can never fly again?"

Mr. Green smiled, warmly. "No, I don't think that, but you do. I don't think that one bit, and I wish you didn't, either. I encourage you to rethink that idea, and let it go. You know what I think? I think you're a treasure." Fiona smiled shyly, feeling her face flush.

The next day dawned, chilly and overcast. Fiona stuck her hands into her coat pocket for warmth and promptly found her academic advisor's forgotten handwritten note. On one side, it said, "Tape up this note." On the other, it said, simply, "Hello, gorgeous; you'll do great today!" As she fingered the creased paper, reading its words over and over, she knew her advisor would help her find her new path, leading her away from failure and toward her productive future.

When she got back to her dorm room, Fiona dutifully taped the tattered piece of paper to her dresser mirror, where she couldn't fail to read it every day. She promised herself she would do so. Out loud. "Hello, gorgeous; you'll do great today!" She saw it every time she looked in the mirror. And she saw herself as she said it. It reminded her how Pop had taped words all over objects in the house when she was little, to help her learn how to read. *Why not add more messages?* she thought. Pulling out a pen and the pad of paper she kept by her bed, Fiona began to write joy-filled, life-affirming notes and post them. "You rock!" said one. "Beam on, you beautiful beam," said another. There also were references to scripture. Just the numbers, so it'd be a bit of a game, to see if she remembered them.

Proverb 3:5. Psalm 55:22. Romans 8:28. Isaiah 58:8. James 1:22. Pop would approve of her affirmations, Fiona thought to herself as she looked around the room and contemplated the results of her efforts. Except the Bible stuff, of course.

For a final touch, Fiona went into her closet, retrieved the rolled-up poster of Desiderata by Max Ehrmann that Gram had sent her for her birthday, and plastered it over her poster of Hendrix. Now, everywhere she looked in her dorm room had messages of faith, hope, purpose, and validation.

Every morning, Fiona made it her habit to check her college post office box for a letter from family. She turned the key expectantly and, seeing nothing, went to close it up again. Just then, she spied a small envelope, in the back. I almost missed it, she thought, admiring the envelope. It was addressed to Ms. Fiona Sprechelbach, from the Oceanside Orchestra. Very official.

Hesitating, Fiona took the letter out of the envelope. A ripple of fear ran down her spine. As she unfolded it, she thought, Dear God, please don't let it be another expulsion. I don't need more bad news right now. Instead, it was good news: Mr. Ż. had decided to participate in her orchestra's "adopt a musician" program. She'd been adopted! This only meant that Mr. Ż. had made a small donation in her honor, nothing more. Still, Fiona felt thrilled beyond words. He was still in her corner. She could do this. She shifted herself into problem-solving mode.

With renewed resolve, Fiona headed off to the financial aid office to explore loan possibilities and financial support. Perhaps she'd take out a loan. Wanting to take on as little debt as humanly possible, Fiona decided to take out a loan that would cover just tuition, and for just one semester. If I find someplace else to live, double up on my course load to fit a year's worth of work into one semester, and manage to pass every class, I could do this. If…

Sitting across the desk from the campus loan officer, Fiona gasped. Her rough concept about the cost of Mills' tuition looked very different as real numbers on the piece of paper in front her. Her parents had been paying a mint for Mills, she thought. Was it worth it? It took a moment for the sticker shock to wear off. But then, she took a deep breath and signed the paperwork.

Fiona had always been a hard worker. Wasn't this just more of the same? Yes, she would be gambling on herself. But, whom else did she really trust anyway, to get things done? Walking across campus to the dorm, her mind turned to her older sister. Karen said I should trust my higher power. So, I will. Anyway, I remember reading something about all things working together for good. Fiona unlocked the door, surveyed the room she still called home, and thought, let's go get it done!

When it came time to consider the classes she'd need to arrange in time for registration, turned to Dr. Gerda Engel, a kind professor who was inclined to help students learn to skirt the quicksand of life. "You're not going to sink if you don't step into it," she was fond of saying. Fiona made an appointment, so she could explain her situation. "Dr. Engel, I've got a plan to pull this off," she said, "but I can't figure out how to fit all the classes I need to satisfy graduation requirements into my schedule, given the course offerings next semester. Do you see a way?"

"I'm glad you came to me," Dr. Engel answered, "because when you believe you're completely on your own, you run the risk of missing some very good options that may not be immediately apparent."

"That's why I am here, seeking your advice," Fiona agreed.

Dr. Engel smiled. "There's always a way. So, let's see what we can do together." Surveying the course schedule and seeing absolutely no options, Dr. Engel came up with one of her own. "An independent study program could satisfy a letters requirement and a language requirement, at the same time. So, let's create one. You read German, yes? So, let's focus on Thomas Mann, in German. You have fresh eyes, so I'm sure to enjoy your insights. We'll discover him, together."

Professor Engel leaned back in her desk chair. "I think you'll learn more from this process than from hearing me lecture you on his 1929 Nobel Prize in Literature. It's a simple and elegant solution. Mann would approve. After all, he once said, 'Order and simplification are first steps toward mastery.' What do you think, Fiona?"

"I think I'd love that," Fiona answered. Internally, she added, and

I think I love you.

Professor Engel possessed not just intelligence but also compassion, creativity, and clout. She got the independent study project, along with the rest of Fiona's nearly impossible course load, approved with one phone call.

Heading back to her dorm room, Fiona was elated about having what she felt was a workable plan. Surely this was her ticket to freedom and independence, a ticket that would shield her from the fallout of other peoples' freak-outs. What remained was a "simple" matter of food, shelter, books, and living expenses.

The house was about to be put on the market, so staying in the repurposed garage wasn't an option. Fiona found it somewhat ironic that her mother was moving away from California—earthquake central in her eyes—before it was cast off and swallowed up by the Pacific "any time now," while Fiona was trying so hard to stay there. Peggy was abandoning her home and her child in search of solid ground in equally earthquake-prone New Zealand. Stability was a tricky thing.

Fiona had learned not to spend too much time pining for something she couldn't count on. She made a mental list of friends who would welcome her in. Peggy's bungalow wasn't on it. Couch surfing could be fun, she reasoned, *I wonder how long I could keep it up?*

Fiona knew she would need money for gas and food—maybe just food if she found a couch near campus and didn't need to drive. In the meantime, she could sell the stuff she didn't really and truly need—some records, her beanbag chair, her lamp, rug, poster collection, and even her guitar. Not her viola. She could possibly collect some cash as a busker, performing in public places for gratuities. Still, she needed to do more than just that. She needed real income, too. She decided to post a sign on the dorm bulletin board, offering up her typing skills. She cut fringe at the bottom of the page, with her phone number, so students could tear off a tag and call her. *I'll bet I could get a buck a page,* she thought. *Maybe more, if I offer to correct their grammar. Heck, I could even teach them how to write a winning paper. But that's too much work. Better to just stick with brainless typing.*

Two weeks before the end of the semester, Fiona drove by her old Berkeley home, just to see what it looked like as it was getting ready to be put on the market. As she slowly drove down the street, she noticed immediately that the garden had been groomed. The house had a fresh coat of paint, and the old fence had been fixed. Same as it ever was, Fiona thought, considering all the times she'd moved from home to home, through life. And the song, "Once in a Lifetime" poured into her head, all at once, in a rush that almost made her dizzy. Well, she thought, that's for sure. This is not my beautiful house. And nope, it's not my beautiful life, either. Not anymore, it's not. If it ever was.

The rosebush had been trimmed. Fiona contemplated that the rosebush she'd loved since the day she'd arrived in California, billowing over the side of the house in an explosion of pink, the same color as her VW Bug. At least her mother hadn't cut it down. She hadn't pulled it up by its roots and put it in a root bag. That was something. Was she doing that to herself? Fiona wondered. Pulling herself up by the roots and replanting? That can't happen for me. You can't just tie me up in a "root bag" and think I'll bloom wherever I'm planted next. Sometimes, when you rip someone up by the roots like that, they can't catch hold somewhere else. The soil isn't right, or the climate's too harsh. Sometimes, a plant will just wither and die. I think I'm like that. I think I'd just die, if I were dragged away from California.

Fiona got an image of herself as a nonviable rosebush after one more transplant, her barren canes unable to blossom. With all her strength, she would fight to keep her roots firmly in the rich California soil. She was no hothouse flower; after everything she'd weathered in her life, she was more like that giant bush of tiny tea roses, bursting forth in a riot of color after every harsh frost. But only if she remained in California. Fiona sped up, and turned the corner. There was only one other place she'd spent time most every week since she'd come to California, and she was almost there: Mary's house.

Fiona gave Mary a long embrace, which was followed by a hug from Bea. Then, the two friends sat down in the living room to talk, while Bea made them some tea. The drive past the house had really gotten to Fiona in a way she hadn't expected. She was near tears.

"I want to hear all about how it's going at St. Mary's, Mare, but right now, I'm just such a wreck..." a sob caught in Fiona's throat.

"First things, first, Fee," said the friend who'd been Fiona's sounding board and source of comfort since she'd moved to California. "Let's help you get this story out, and then we'll figure out what to do about it."

Fiona started somewhere in the middle, and jumped around a lot, but Mary, and soon, her mother, got the gist of the situation. Mary reached a protective arm around her friend, and glanced at her mother, with a knowing look. Bea smiled and responded to the unspoken question with a barely imperceptible nod.

"Fiona, you are so close to that freedom you've been fighting for," said Mary. "You should be so proud of yourself. Just one more semester, and you'll be a college graduate. Here I am, trailing behind. And I'll tell you, while it's been great and all, and I'll fill you in later, the hardest part was how much I've missed you during school time."

"Really?" Fiona whispered, wiping her face with the back of her hand.

"So, whadya say we spend the summer getting caught up? Don't you think that's a good idea, Mom?"

"I certainly do," said Bea. Fiona looked from Mary to her mother, confused.

"My brother's not coming home from college this summer, Fee; he got this really cool job fishing in Alaska—you know, if you're into that sort of thing—so his room will be empty. That is, until you fill it."

"What?" Fiona could hardly reconcile what she was hearing.

"How about you live here with us for the summer? Oh, Fee, it's a total no-brainer. I mean, you could do your own thing and all, but you'd have a place to stay—for free—and you and I, well, it would be amazing. Right?"

Fiona's tears ran, unchecked, once again, only this time, in pure gratitude, appreciation, joy, and love. All she could do was nod.

"Then, it's all settled," said Bea. "Mary can help you move whatever you need from your dorm into the house and, as soon as you're ready, we'll welcome you home. And Fiona, both Mary and Michael will both be back in school next fall. If you'd rather live here during the fall semester than back in the dorms, you're welcome to do so. I would certainly enjoy the company. You don't have to decide, now."

"Seriously?" Fiona exclaimed, "That would be amazing. Thank you! Wow. I mean, um, thank you."

"Then it's all settled. Welcome to the family." said Bea, smiling warmly, "Welcome home!"

"Home. Welcome home," Fiona let the words settle over her like a security blanket. She got up and hugged Mary and her mother, once again, her eyes still glistening with tears but her smile, bright.

"Hey, Fee," said Mary. "Why don't you stay for dinner? You okay with meatloaf?"

"More than okay," Fiona said. "Totally okay."

~oOO0O0o~

"Home is where the heart is," read the sign in Fiona's new bedroom. Seriously? Fiona thought to herself. That's quaint. While her heart was filled with gratitude, it was also confused by feelings for her family, whom she still missed. I'm grateful, and Bea's a saint, but I'm just an interloper. It's possible that Bea is just be helping me because she feels sorry for me. Where's my heart anyway? I feel like I have bits of it all over the place. She turned the sign backwards. She didn't feel free to take it down since it wasn't her room, but she didn't want to look at it. Despite Bea's overflowing generosity, the words made her sad.

Fiona found a summer job at a gift shop on Solano Avenue in Albany. Every day, she went to work, helping customers select beautiful treasures to adorn their nests. Other than a few groceries for Bea, who'd refused any cash contribution, Fiona bought nothing for herself, saving her pennies, as always. Where's my nest, anyway? she wondered, as she dusted the glass-art paperweight hearts and flowers in the decorative display case. She knew that Bea was inviting her in, but she felt a little like a cuckoo's chick, taking advantage of a hen's egg. It helped that every day when Fiona returned to the house after work, she was greeted with a smile and a heartfelt "welcome home."

After two weeks of daily "welcome home!" greetings, Fiona found herself staring at the sign on the wall, which she still thought of as trite. Her heart had surely settled in the home where she was now living, with Mary and Bea, to whom she felt eternally grateful. So, she turned it right-side-round. She told herself it was because she didn't want to risk anyone seeing it flipped over and feeling bad, but it was more than that. Fiona was beginning to feel at rest, settled, and at home. After turning the sign over, she sat down on her bed to take in her surroundings, and ended up staring at the wall and the plaque, taking in the meaning of home.

Four hours earlier, one of the customers at the Solano shop had dropped a glass heart while admiring it. Mortified, she'd blamed the owner's dog for startling her. It had taken Fiona half an hour of hard work to completely remove the shards from the case. As she worked, taking care not to cut herself, she spied dozens of miniature rainbows emanating from some of the shards. Looking more closely at the glass paperweights, she noticed how some of them played with the light in lovely ways. This got her thinking about hearts and homes, and shards of glass. Here it was, nearly eleven at night, still thinking about those shards. She finally decided she'd better turn out the light and turn in for the night, but the image in her mind's eye persisted.

Oh, I get it! Fiona realized, nearly jumping out of her bed as she equated home and heart with the paperweight. I think you need to keep your heart together, wherever you are. You can't leave broken bits of your heart scattered all over the place, some in Pennsylvania, some in India or wherever. Light can shine through the broken bits, but rainbows—beautiful, unified prisms—are stronger. Maybe you have to be more like a prism, together and whole, to be capable of sending love at a distance without shattering. I still love my family deeply, but I think I've let them shatter me a little.

Is it even possible to un-shatter yourself? Fiona wondered.

Maybe not by yourself, but with help, I could make a mosaic. And if the mosaic is better than the original, then what's the point of placing blame? She asked herself.

Fiona was beginning to feel a new sense of calm, and suspected that not only was it possible, it actually was happening. Safe for the first time, Fiona had slowed down enough to look back at life and take stock. She thought about all the places she'd lived. They all sheltered people. They all had walls and plumbing and windows and doors. But that didn't make them home, for her. She'd never settled, never felt rooted to one place. Had she ever felt at home? No, she didn't think so. And at that moment she realized it was no wonder she was never comfortable anywhere. It was a wonder she was beginning to feel comfortable now.

Wonderful indeed. With Mary and her mother in her corner, Fiona was finding her stride, though she wasn't yet as "together" as Bea or Mary, her current role models. Through Bea's example, Fiona could learn to expand her definition of home and hearth, of the blending of friends and family. By that definition, she was no interloper.

Though her own mother was across an ocean, and the rest of her family nearly 3,000 miles away, a curious thing was happening: Fiona was growing calmer and more self-assured. She was changing, setting aside a restless ambivalence that had plagued her all her life: uncertainty about what home meant, and where she might find it. If all went well, the fall of 1982 would be Fiona's final semester at Mills. She took a deep breath, and successfully registered for a huge course overload. I can do this.

By summer's end, Fiona's inner growth-spurt had left her transformed. Gone was the restless girl, searching for a mother or a home, or acceptance as some way to be "good enough" to stay at someone else's home. She was a young woman poised to break through. Her new resolve, in many ways forced upon her, had brought upon her a time of change. I've heard there are little flowers that bloom only after forest fires, Fiona thought. Fire ephemerals. What a beautiful thing to imagine yourself to be.

This new sense of self—what was possible and what she could

440

achieve—was more than simple stubbornness of which she'd often been accused in her life. It was deeper. It was settled. She finally understood what her old music teacher, Mr. Ż., had told her, about "visualizing the after-party," a trick to dismiss fearful thoughts about performance, like naughty little children to be sent to their room. Focus, she told herself, keep your eyes on the prize.

"Fiona, are you worried about this performance?" he had once asked, before a recital. "Picture yourself having already accomplished your goal brilliantly, celebrating with the people you love." She had often used that technique in prepping for performances, picturing the camaraderie afterwards, with everyone patting each other on the back. She had a feeling it would work for college finish lines as well.

In her mind's eye, Fiona could see her college graduation "after-party" very clearly. It would be a full-heart graduation, not a shards-hope graduation. The people who loved her and whom she loved would all be there. Mary and Bea, Wolf, Peggy, Gram and all three of her sisters, and all of her friends, old and new. So would all the mentors who'd helped her over the years. Every last one of them.

Fiona visualized the genuine love and pride in everyone's eyes as she walked on stage to collect her diploma. She imagined the hugs of congratulations. She'd wear the pearl that Gram had given her long ago, maybe accompanied by another necklace, that captured her imagination. Hadn't Peggy promised her that strand she'd so often worn on special occasions? For as long as Fiona could remember, she'd admired it. A single strand, elegant, the perfect symbol of strength and femininity. Yes, she visualized herself wearing both necklaces. After all, this was her visualization, so she could create it however she wished.

She could see it all, as if it had already happened. Yes, it would be real. There was only the simple matter of seven classes to complete.

In her mind, Fiona began to form a picture of that little ant she'd once imagined, walking across the string of life. No! Fiona thought. Thoughts can lie. Liar ANT! I will scorch you dead with my inner magnifying glass. Here's a true thought. I'm not an ant, and I'm engraving my own song. Mr. RCA Victor, can you hear me roar?

Toward the end of a day whose sunny skies matched the optimism Fiona was feeling, her mood began to shift, even as the weather remained warm and the breeze, light. She was in her final semester and Fiona could almost taste the freedom that awaited her in just a few weeks when she finished. She somehow was handling the load—the heaviest academic load she'd ever imagined tackling and a record for the college—and was on track for making the Dean's List. At this rate, she'd be holding her degree before 1982 was over. With every day that passed, she felt a little freer, especially on days like this one, when the sun was shining.

As daylight shifted the hour into evening, she felt a strange yet familiar sense of foreboding return, walking with her friends as they wandered the path through campus to the to the cafeteria, after an evening class. Lynn had offered to treat Fiona to a meal there, and Fiona had, of course, gratefully accepted. Mary's mom was out of town for the week, and Fiona loved having a reason to spend time with her friends on campus.

"It's a Hunter Moon tonight, Fiona," said Lynn, as she held open the door for Tracy and Terri, and joined the others in line.

"A what?"

"A Hunter Moon," repeated Lynn, grabbing a dinner tray and handing it to Fiona. "It's a full moon in October."

"You took astronomy?" asked Tracy.

Lynn smiled. "Nah. I learned it from my grandpa. Stuff about Blood Moons and Hunter Moons. Tonight, it's like the moon is out hunting, and you need to take care it doesn't come after you and bite you.

"Cut it out, Lynn, you freak. That's creepy."

This stuff about the moon hunting people down didn't help Fiona, who was already living in a heightened state of alertness, as if a wolf or a tiger might pounce on her from any angle. A constant diet of nightly news had only fed her fears, focusing her mind on what it might mean to be graduating during the worst recession the country had experienced since before World War II. Why don't they get real and call what it is—another depression, Fiona thought. It's certainly depressing enough.

Fiona continued to periodically wrestle with sleep, leaving her what Lynn had called, "rest depressed." Everything, she'd said, looks gloomier on too little sleep. And her final exams loomed large. Fiona just couldn't let herself relax, knowing finals were just weeks away. And certainly, part of it was that today was the seven-year anniversary of Hanna's tragic death. This close to Halloween, there was something both sad and creepy about that. Although Fiona had tried to put it out of her mind and hadn't shared it with her friends, she couldn't shake the memories, and her somber mood wasn't lost on anyone.

To lift Fiona out of her funk, Lynn raised her arms and said, "Werewolves will be out in packs tonight. If we get bitten on the way home, 'we're wolves,' Rrrrrrrr!"

"Getting bitten by werewolves. That would suck," said Terri.

"Bite. That would bite." Despite her mood, Fiona couldn't resist the chance to land the joke.

"No duh," said Lynn. "What would suck would be to have anything happen to us, Hunter Moon or no Hunter Moon, so close to graduation. We've come too far to lose it now, especially Fiona, who's packing it in a semester early."

"Packing it in sounds like biting the dust," Fiona said. "Of course, since I'm determined to finish this semester, even if it kills me, you might be right."

"Very funny," said Terri. "You've got this, Fee. If you don't get hit by a bus or something...Oh, wait. You're the bus driver. We're the ones who need to watch out!"

"Oh, my gosh, you guys! We're pretending that getting to graduation is the hard part. But after that, we need to make something of it, get jobs, be productive and stuff. Let's face it; life's a bitch..." Lynn joked, waiting for the others to chime in with the expected response. "Then, you die!" The darker their ideas got, the lighter they felt, inside. What are friends for?

"Wait, there's more," Fiona declared, deciding to take a stand against the darkness. "We're together, right here, right now. We're not dead yet, and whatever doesn't kill us will make us stronger. So, let's make it great, starting now."

Everyone was game, but how? They couldn't exactly throw a tequila party on a Thursday night, particularly with finals looming. So, what was going to be great about going to someone's pad to study? The friends stood under the street lamp, thinking, but coming up with nothing.

"I know this great backroad path to St. Mary's College," Fiona said. "It's got switchbacks and mountain caverns, and it's a kick to drive. I bet my friend Mary will be up for something. You remember Mary. She's cool. She's got great ideas.

"Can we all fit in my car? I'll drive, if someone will pitch in a buck or two for gas."

Everyone agreed, and squeezed into Fiona's VW Bug, Moraga-bound. Half an hour later, they tumbled out in front of Mary's dorm. Soon, with Mary on board, they were back on the road. Where next? Denny's for one of those cherry shake concoctions? That was a nice cheap and cheerful option. "Wait," Mary said. "Fiona and I used to love this coffee shop in Berkeley." But it was too late. They'd already arrived at Denny's.

"The parking gods have smiled," said Lynn, spotting a prime parking place.

"No, they haven't. Mary helped. I was saying my usual, 'Hail Mary full of grace, please may we have a parking place,'" Fiona replied.

"That's nuts, Fee. Well, whatever works…until they pick us all up in butterfly nets, I guess," Lynn answered, and hinted at a song by Napolion XIV, singing, "They're coming to take me away, ha-haaa!"

As if on cue, the friends linked arms. As their steps synchronized, they started in with that song, their words matching their rhythmic stomp. As they sang about plastic weavers twiddling their thumbs and toes and nice young men in clean white coats, quite a few faces turned their way. Had they been in Berkeley, no one would have noticed.

The friends were soon seated comfortably, with slushy, sweet cherry shakes all around, and an order of fries, to share. Later, back in the car, Paul McCartney started singing on the tape player, and Lynn cranked it up and started singing with him, "With a little luck…"

Someone else asked for Stevie Wonder, so Lynn dropped in a tape of "Songs in the Key of Life." Soon, they were all singing along with Stevie, at the top of their voices, heads facing out the open windows, immune to the chill in the air. It was as if they had embarked on a shared mission to broadcast their sentiments about their last semester together, the friendship they trusted would endure, and this night, which had brought it all into sharp focus: "I am singing someday sweet love will reign throughout this world of ours, I am singing of love from my heart!"

"Oh, I wish this night would never have to end," Fiona whispered between songs, as much to herself as everyone in the car.

"It doesn't," said Lynn. "Take the exit here, Fiona."

"What?"

"Crank it, sister!" Fiona made a hard-left turn, just in time to take the freeway exit. "What're you doing? Where are we going?"

"Just follow your nose to the salt sea air, my friend!" Soon, they were headed toward the ocean. "Woo hooooo! It ain't over 'til it's over!"

Fiona was too intoxicated by the evening to worry about the textbooks waiting in her room or the cost of gas or how hard it might be to get up in the morning for class. She had a feeling she'd remember this night forever, without even trying. There was something magical about it.

Twenty minutes later, the friends piled out of the car, slipped off their shoes, and began making their way across the sand of Ocean Beach toward the water. All the sassy seagulls and bothersome beachgoers had left for the evening, save a couple of lovebirds walking arm in arm along the strand. The night was quiet, except for the crashing waves, crescendoing as they neared the shore and then dissipating into the sand. With nothing more than a single bonfire glowing in the distance, the entire world was theirs alone; for the moment.

"You know, you guys, this place has me thinking of Goethe, Fiona said, "You remember, Terri, don't you, from our German class?"

"Hmmmm…honestly? Not really."

"Well, anyway, it turns out Goethe wasn't just this mad, literary genius. He was totally into science as well. Who knew? He had this idea about color that's totally different. Okay, so, if we look at the universe, it looks blue, right? But that's what darkness looks like through air that's translucent, not completely transparent, with some ambient light. And this is the neat part. You know how red the sun is just before it sinks into the sea? The sun's light goes to red at the horizon, because there's more atmosphere between us and the source of light. If you leave out that green flash at the horizon, it's just like the song. You know the one, 'The morning sun is shining like a red rubber ball…' It's cool, right?"

"Fiona's back," said Mary, and they all laughed. Even Fiona.

"How can you think like that, girl, this late at night?"

It was such a clear night, they could see the beach completely, lit up by the milky moon, overflowing generously into the ocean. Each friend felt the magic. The sand, wet from the recent wave, sparkled beneath their feet, as they ran up and down the shore, holding hands, laughing, and stopping to dance in a circle, splashing in the briny seafoam as they went. The ripples of the water created an illusion of many moons, connected, bouncing along in syncopation with their laughter, a liquid string of glowing pearls.

Watching the moonlight dance with her along the water, Fiona was shifting, changing, just as effortlessly as the moon. She was becoming lighter, clearer, braver. Her eyes followed the moonshine. Trails of moonbeams wandered out to sea, their color growing ever deeper, until the rivulets darkened into wavy strands of coppery red, the color of Fiona's hair, before fading into the distance.

The future might have been as vast and unknowable as that ocean on which the moon's silver tresses were waving and dancing, but the present was undeniable. Right here, right now, in this very moment, everything was perfect.

Fiona was supremely, exquisitely happy.

FIONA'S RULES

1. Love God, Love People.
2. Trust Wisely.
3. Shine Out.
4. Be a Good Citizen.
5. Be Prepared.
6. Fear Not.
7. Practice Self-Care.
8. Never Give Up Hope.